THE LAST
DESPERADO

A NOVEL

REBECCA ROCKWELL

DENVER, COLORADO

The Last Desperado
A Novel
All Rights Reserved.
Copyright © 2014 Rebecca Rockwell
v2.0

Outskirts Press, Inc.
http://www.outskirtspress.com

ISBN: 978-1-4787-2544-2

Outskirts Press and the "OP" logo are trademarks belonging to Outskirts
Press, Inc.

PRINTED IN THE UNITED STATES OF AMERICA

ACKNOWLEDGEMENTS

I would like to thank all of the friends and family who encouraged me as I was writing this book, particularly my mother Jennifer and my father Jim, along with my dear friends Kith Presland, Tiffany Garrison, Gus Bro, and Tricia Daniel. I also want to acknowledge the support of all my co-workers at Santa Barbara Pet Hospital, particularly Hunter McCrea, Natalie Lutz, Gena Raichelle, Marly Goldberg and Julie Birmingham, whose support and encouragement meant so much when obstacles temporarily appeared. A very special thank you to Kate Salokorpi for lending her time and talent when taking my publicity photos. A big thank you to Sally Mobraaten, and thank you to Tracie Shepard and Cindy Kloe for the long-distance support. I want to acknowledge K.C. for speaking words that have always encouraged me to pursue my passion for Westerns, no matter what. And finally, a million thanks are due to my late grandmother, Virginia Rockwell, who was always more supportive of my writing than anyone else.

A NOTE ON
THE DUNN BROTHERS

Probably because they became the most confusing of all the many confusing things in my research for this novel, I feel compelled to write a brief note regarding the infamous Dunn brothers. Various written sources cite the bounty-hunting Dunn bunch as having consisted of brothers Bill, Charles ("Dal"), Bee, George, John, and Calvin; others insist that Bill Dunn was a cousin to the other five and that Bee was the leader, and still others say there were not two people named Bill and Bee, but rather one person that was at times alternately referred to as either "Bill Dunn" or "B. Dunn," leading to the "Bee" nickname—which I personally believe. An examination of the Dunn family's entry in the 1880 United States Federal Census reveals that there was only one brother by the name of William Dunn; therefore I have chosen to eliminate any separate character by the name of "Bee."

PROLOGUE

August 25ᵗʰ, 1896
Lawson, Oklahoma Territory

THE NIGHT THEY killed Bill Doolin was a warm one. Cicadas droned incessantly and the sweltering air seemed to press down on the posse of men stealthily positioned along either side of the dirt road that led to a farmhouse about a half-mile away. They fought the urge to mop their sweaty brows under the brims of their hats, and their palms grew damp around the stocks of their rifles and the butts of their revolvers as they waited, keeping silent, trying to calm their racing heartbeats. A couple of them were experienced lawmen and their leader was a legend, but right then those facts gave them little comfort, for the man they hunted's name loomed larger than any of theirs and this would be yet another of many attempts before it to bring him under the heel of the law.

The sky was clear, and the moonlight made eerie shadows chase one another over the road and the grasses that lined it. Crickets provided an inconsistent accompaniment to the cicadas' song, and somewhere in the distance coyotes were on the prowl, their yaps carried on the warm breeze.

Laying on his stomach in a patch of tall grass behind an outcropping of rocks, his double-barreled shotgun at the ready beside him, U.S. Deputy Marshal Heck Thomas felt rare impatience well up within him and fought against it. Impatience would do him no good tonight; it would only blow his cover, and he would *not*, he told himself resolutely, allow that to happen. Doolin had been on the run for far too long, his day of judgement elusive. Tonight it would end. Thomas refused to believe otherwise.

He knew, even as his resolve grew, that chances were good a life would be lost tonight, his or Doolin's. Doolin had been captured and jailed before, and Thomas was quite certain he would not be taken alive again. And if he escaped, it would only be because Heck Thomas had met his own end. Bill Doolin, he had learned over the years, did nothing unless he did it thoroughly.

Near him, newly-deputized Bill Dunn shifted his grip on his Winchester, and in the moonlight Thomas saw him set his jaw as he eased his first finger closer and closer to the trigger of the rifle. His eyes shone like those of a wild animal and, Thomas thought wryly, he might as well have been one. Dunn was on the hunt, all right—and Doolin was his prey. He and his bounty-hunting brothers had tipped Thomas off that Doolin was here, and in doing so had earned the right to help take him down. Thomas just hoped Dunn wouldn't let his eagerness get the better of him and blow their cover. If he did, the marshal thought, Thomas just might shoot *him* instead of Doolin.

The Dunn brothers were an interesting bunch; small-time cattle rustlers who'd recently discovered that collecting the bounties on the wanted outlaws they associated with paid more than rustling cattle—and got them cleared of the charges against them, besides. Thomas and his fellow lawmen didn't begrudge them the bounties they'd collected; they'd already taken down several key members of Doolin's notorious Wild Bunch, and the lawmen were grateful. Like the Dalton Gang before them, the Wild Bunch were a plague to Thomas and his cohorts, not to mention the railroad companies and citizens they held up, and the disposal of any of them, whatever the manner or means, was a relief.

The soft snort of a horse and the muffled *clop* of hooves on packed dirt suddenly drew Thomas's attention away from Dunn, and he tensed, looking toward the sound.

A man was walking a saddled horse down the road, leading it by the reins and moving with a gait hindered by a slight limp. He was a tall man, long and lean and fully-bearded, and the moonlight was bright enough for Thomas to see his features clearly—along with the Winchester he held in his hands, at the ready. A few soft notes came, carried on the breeze, and Heck realized the man was whistling, very faintly, under his breath.

For a moment, Thomas just watched in amazement, unable to believe what he saw. Bill Doolin was a cunning man, well-skilled at his chosen craft of crime, smart as a whip and always two steps ahead of the law. Why, then, was he walking right toward their posse on foot, when he could have gone off in any number of other directions to avoid the road?

The answer to that question was one Heck Thomas did not know, nor, he realized, did he care. He took a breath and called loudly, "Bill Doolin!"

"Halt, Bill! You're surrounded!" Deputy Cannon shouted from the other side of the road, as Thomas had instructed him to do.

What happened next happened fast. Doolin tensed and turned toward Thomas and Bill Dunn, raised his rifle, aimed, fired—and missed. Dunn fired back, and Thomas saw Doolin's rifle fly out of his hands as the bullet struck it. His horse shied at the noise and the smell of gunpowder, throwing up its head and jerking the reins from Doolin's hands. Thoroughly spooked, it cantered away, moving off into the underbrush.

Doolin's hand went to his hip and he drew his revolver from his holster with impressive speed. Before he could take aim, however, Heck Thomas had sighted and fired, the kick from the old shotgun nearly knocking him backwards. Smoke poured from the double barrels, and as it thinned, wafting upward into the moonlight, Thomas saw Doolin laying motionless on the roadside.

For a few seconds, there was silence. The cicadas stopped droning, the crickets' chirping ceased. The men all held their breath, waiting for any sign of movement from the outlaw.

There was none, and Thomas let out a breath he didn't know he'd been holding. He lowered the shotgun and stood up stiffly, his aging body aching from having laid prone in the grass for over an hour straight, and motioned to the others to do the same.

One by one, the posse-members rose up from their hiding-places, all of them keeping their weapons at the ready, in case Doolin was only playing dead and was ready to rise up and make an escape, or a fight.

Thomas was the first one to reach the outlaw's body, and it was clear that there would be no last stand for Doolin. The shotgun blast had hit him squarely in the chest and cut his torso to pieces, peppering him with holes, and blood gleamed on his shirt and the grass beneath him. His blue eyes were open, staring vacantly into the night sky.

"Jesus Christ almighty," Deputy Cannon breathed. "You got him good, Heck."

Thomas nodded, never taking his eyes off the body, then cleared his throat and looked up at the other men. "Go get the wagon, and we'll get him to the undertaker's in Guthrie. Someone's got to go tell his wife, so she can claim the body once we're done with it." His voice was brisk.

George Dunn and Charles Noble, one of the other town informants that had earned a place in the posse, turned to do Thomas's bidding, while some of the other men stood protectively around the body and Thomas. Bill Dunn watched from a few feet away as one of his brothers went out to retrieve Doolin's horse, which by now had calmed and was cropping grass as if nothing were amiss.

Thomas paid no mind to any of them. Instead he stared down at what remained of the man he'd been tracking for so long. The so-called King of the Oklahoma Outlaws was finally dead, his gang's reign of terror over at last, and Thomas found himself wondering how a simple cowhand could have taken such a prominent place among the many outlaws of those days, and in such a short amount of time. It was, Thomas thought, a question only Doolin himself could answer, and now that answer would never come. Thomas shook his head and raised his eyes from the dead man at his feet, watching as Charles Noble and George Dunn came up the road with the straw-filled wagon and the mules that would bear Bill Doolin on his last ride to the undertaker's.

ONE

"BILL, DON'T GO out there, *please.*"

Edith's voice was unusually loud and had a strange tremor to it that I'd never heard there before. I'd been reaching for my hat where it hung on the steer horns fastened to the wall near the back door, but at the sound of her voice I stopped what I was doing, turning to face her.

My wife was standing in the doorway of the parlor, watching me, and she had a pleading look in those soft brown eyes of hers. She'd taken the pins out of her thick black hair and it flowed down to her waist in a cloud, gently waved from the braid she'd had it in all day. Chewing on her lower lip like she was, with her hair all loose and her big eyes sad and watery like she was going to cry, she looked like a little girl instead of a grown woman.

"Edith, honey, I told you, I got to go," I said, trying to sound gentle. Lord knew I didn't want to leave her and our boy tonight, but the hair on the back of my neck was standing on end and I felt like a hunted animal about to be trapped and caged. I'd heard rumors today that a posse was out, and if I stayed where I was, there'd be trouble. Not just for me, I'd tried to explain to her earlier, but for her, too, and for our son, and her folks, who owned this farm and lived in this house.

"What if they're out there, Bill?" she challenged me. "What if they're waiting for you?"

I fingered the bullets in my gun belt, then the butt of my revolver. Just the thought of meeting up with a posse made my trigger-finger itch, but I fought against it. I dropped my hand, left my hat where it was, and went over to her, putting my hands on her shoulders and pulling her to me. "Then I'll get away from them," I replied, lowering my face to the top of her head and kissing the white parting of her hair.

I heard her swallow, like she was gulping back a big sob, and I steeled myself. I knew that if she cried I'd weaken, let her convince me to stay just one more night, and I knew I couldn't chance it.

In truth, I never needed much convincing when it came to anything to do with Edith. I was plumb off my nut for her; had been from the first time I'd laid eyes on her, and it was only my seeming inability to go too long without seeing her that made me keep on taking as many chances as I was. I knew I had to get her and our boy out of there soon; the price on my head was too big now, and there were too many people out for my blood. They'd already taken out so many of my friends as it was—Bitter Creek and Charley, Tulsa Jack, and so many others. And, of course, they'd taken out Will, too, and Bob and Grat and Bill Power and Dick Broadwell before that. I fought down a sudden wave of anger, thinking about how many lives those bastard lawdogs owed payment on. Their debt was growing with every man they cut down, and I knew I'd be the best prize of all. I wouldn't be surprised if Heck Thomas had plans to hang my head on his parlor wall, like a hunting trophy.

I forced myself to return my attention to Edith, who, much to my relief, was not crying. She was a strong woman and didn't cry at the drop of a hat, the way some of them did, though the Lord above knew I'd given her plenty of reasons to over the three years we'd been married. I stepped back aways and held her at arm's length, leaning my head down a little to force her to look at me. "I got to go, Edith," I repeated softly. "There ain't nothing for it. You know that."

She took a deep breath. "Will you stay out of trouble, this time? Can you at least promise me that?"

Don't hold anyone up, Bill, was what she meant.

— 3 —

Don't take any trains, stages, or stores. Do like you've promised me and start going straight. I raised an eyebrow at her. "I'll try my very hardest, sweetheart." Even to me, my words sounded like a lie, but she took the high road and chose to overlook it.

"What about Jay?" she asked me. "Will you see him before you go?"

I nodded, then let her take my hand and lead me into the little room where our son slept. I had to tiptoe; I'd already put on my spurs and they jingled as I walked.

Edith and I moved to the little bedstead and looked down at the little boy we'd made together. It was hot out and he'd thrown off his quilt; the moonlight coming through the window played over the chubby little limbs protruding awkwardly from his nightshirt, and his mop of blond curls. He was sucking his thumb as he slept and when Edith moved a hand to stop him I whispered "let him be, Edith. Don't wake him up. He's got plenty of time to get out of the habit yet."

I felt my chest grow tight and my throat started to feel a little choked. My boy was nearly three now and I'd only been around him a few months at a time since he was born. He knew me, and loved me, but I felt like I'd missed a lot already. Edith wrote me letters about him when we felt it was safe, every time I was gone, but it wasn't enough. I felt a renewed determination to get him and Edith out of the country so we could start a new life as a proper family. I had to let the Wild Bunch go, as I'd promised her I would, so many times.

I leaned down and let my hand skim ever-so-lightly over his little head, then turned and headed back to the front room. She followed me and I felt her watching as I put my hat on and took my rifle from the corner. Pretty soon there wasn't anything else for me to do and I turned at looked at her.

She came over to me and I kissed her, and she put her arms around my neck. I heard her make that little gulping noise again and I let her go quick, reaching for the doorknob. "I'll see the both of you tomorrow, Edith, when you meet up with me like we've planned," I told her. "I promise."

"Be careful, Bill," I heard her say, in a little tiny voice I could barely hear. I nodded but I didn't look at her; I couldn't or I'd lose my nerve to go. Then I stepped out onto the porch and shut the door behind me, leaving that, that.

The hot night closed in around me as I quietly stepped off the porch and made my way to the barn, my Winchester tucked up under my arm. That hunted feeling came back to me and I scanned the moonlit landscape quickly, looking for anyone or anything out of place. I didn't see anything, so I slipped inside the barn, feeling around in the dark and wishing I had a lantern but knowing better than to light one.

My horse was already saddled; I'd asked Edith's father to tack him up when he'd gone out to do the barn chores before supper. I heard him nicker at me from the stall closest to the door, and once my eyes adjusted to the darkness I reached up and took him by his reins, close under the bit. I undid the rope that closed off the stall and led him out of it, then eased the barn door open.

I paused for a moment before I went out, thinking once again of all those men whose deaths I'd felt I had to avenge, all those friends I'd lost, and Will Dalton's memory kept coming to me more than anyone else's. Before he'd died, we'd led the Bunch together, him looking to keep alive the memory of his brothers Bob and Grat, who'd died in Coffeyville, and both of us wanting revenge for what had been done to his brother Emmett, who'd lived through the Coffeyville disaster but had been shot up and then thrown into prison for life. In my mind's eye I saw Will's twinkling blue eyes, heard his great rolling laugh, and I missed him. I missed Bitter Creek, too—the greatest friend I'd ever had—and I missed Emmett. I'd left the Dalton Gang just a short while before Bob had hatched the Coffeyville plan. At the time I'd thought I was damned lucky that I missed being in on that job, but now I felt like I should have stayed; maybe if I'd been with them, things would've gone differently.

Then I thought about how I'd promised Edith, so many times, that I was done with the gang and I was ready to go straight and get shed of the whole outlaw life, and I knew I had to keep that promise, once and for all.

I led my horse out of the barn and set off down the road that led off the property, leading him by the reins so I could keep him from breaking into a run; I didn't want Edith to hear the sound of me riding away. I knew it would make her cry, if she wasn't already.

I forced myself to think of something else so I wouldn't lose my resolve to leave, and my mind turned to my days as a cowhand, back before I'd taken up robbing trains and banks for my living. I'd enjoyed most of my years on the ranches I'd worked— loved the work, in fact—and I'd already decided that when I got Edith and Jay down to Mexico or South America, whichever we ended up in, I'd start up a cattle ranch of my own. A man could make a good living there raising cattle, so I'd heard; wasn't like here, where the cattle trade was dying out.

I'd only told Edith bits and pieces of my life before I'd met her, and how I occupied my time when I was away from her, wanting to spare her as much as possible; truth be told I'd glossed over a hell of a lot. She knew what I was; there wasn't any way in hell I could hide it all from her, and why she still agreed to marry me, God only knew. I'd stopped pondering on it a long time ago; best I could figure, she saw something in me worth putting up with all of my faults and the way I spent my spare time. Whatever the reason, I was a lucky man when it came to her and Jay. Maybe when we got settled on our own place and all this was past, I could tell her the whole of it, how things *really* went down, and in the telling I could put the Wild Bunch behind me for good and close the door on that part of my life, like I'd been wanting to do for awhile.

I started whistling, very softly, under my breath, feeling a little less blue, and feeling like maybe I really *could* do it this time, just like I'd promised.

TWO

AFTER MY PA died I had to help my Ma keep our farm going; without me and Pa both, she would've lost it and had nowhere to go. When I was sure she and my sister were settled and had a good foreman to help out with the hardest work, I left to make whatever way in the world I could scratch out for myself. I'd grown up poor and hadn't had hardly anything in the way of schooling, but I made myself useful in whatever way I could, honed my skills with a gun and with tools, and soon I ended up working cows.

I got more than I bargained for out of it; besides a trade I loved, I got a little bit of the education I'd never had the opportunity for. The first ranch-owner I worked for, a man by the name of Oscar Halsall, took such a shine to me that he taught me to read and write, and simple arithmetic besides. I thanked him for it by working hard, earning his trust and being loyal, and in time he made me the foreman of the ranch he owned on the Cimarron River. From there I drifted to other ranches throughout the country, getting good and experienced in my trade, and at life in general. I always thought that if I ever met a young cowboy just starting out that I took a liking to, I would take him under my wing and look out for him, just like Halsall had done for me. Emmett Dalton would turn out to be that cowboy, and, looking back on it, it was Emmett's decision to leave the ranch we both worked on that sort of set the stage for what we'd both turn out to be, in the end.

The morning that Emmett left was a cold one in January of 1889, and I could see my breath around my head as I rode the fences of the pastures at the Courtney Ranch, checking over the stock. I remember I was rounding the corner of the far pasture when I heard a sharp whistle and someone call my name.

"Doolin!"

I looked over and saw Dick Broadwell, a fellow cowhand, hailing me with his hat from over near one of the holding pens, and I headed over, my horse picking its way through the melting slush and sticky mud.

"Your boy Emmett's leaving, Bill," Dick said to me, once I'd reached him. "He settled up with Courtney. Looks like he won't be coming back.

I thought I'd tell you, since I know how you been looking out for him. He's in the barn, tacking up."

I quickly dismounted, feeling disappointed. Emmett was one of the youngest hands on the ranch, but he'd earned my respect. I considered him a good friend and I'd miss him, if what Dick said was true.

I tossed the reins to Dick. "Will you finish up for me? I just had that last bunch to look at." I waved a hand toward the last pasture.

"Be glad to." Dick put a foot in the stirrup and mounted up, then trotted away through the muddy stockyard. I marched toward the barn, pausing to stamp the mud from my boots and spurs before I headed inside.

Down at the far end, I saw Blackjack, Emmett's big black stud, tied to a hitching-ring, and I leaned against one of the barn pillars, watching him tack up. He didn't notice me there; as usual, Emmett was intent on the task at hand and was paying no attention to anything else that was going on around him.

He tossed the saddle on and cinched it, his smooth, boyish face set in an expression of concentration. Emmett was just barely seventeen, but he'd proven himself a capable cowboy in the mere year he'd been working on the ranch, and I liked him enormously. He was a tall, slender fellow with a head of thick dark hair and expressive gray eyes; I always teased him and said he'd be quite the thing with the ladies, once he put his mind to going after them. He had a kind heart and a quiet way about him, and I liked to think of him as the little brother I'd never had, teaching him the ways of the ranch and a few other things besides, like how to drink whiskey without coughing and how to play poker good enough to win. He tended to be a bit too serious at times and I'd made it my life's mission to loosen him up a little. Now, it seemed, I wouldn't get the chance to finish what I'd started.

He'd finished tacking up and looked about ready to be on his way, so I opened my mouth and said, loudly, "Now, just where in the hell do you think you're goin' off to?"

I startled him; he jumped about a foot in the air and spooked his horse. I saw his hand move toward the gun he had on his hip and I laughed, holding my hands up. "Easy, Em, don't shoot me, now!"

He looked irritated as he dropped his hand and busied himself with calming his horse. "Damn it, Bill, why'd you sneak up on me like that?" he asked me, stroking the stud's muzzle.

"'Cause I couldn't resist it," I told him, still grinning wide at him. "I don't know if you know this about yourself, Emmett, but when you get intent on something, you don't pay much mind to anything else, and that makes you easy to sneak up on. You ought to work on that." I jerked my thumb at Blackjack. "You going to answer my question?"

"I'm going to visit Bob and Grat in Wichita," he told me. "I settled up with Courtney this morning."

Emmett had nine brothers, most of which were spread all over God's green earth, and another lay under it. A few of them were lawmen, including the two he was going to see. Em had told me they were deputy U.S. marshals, like their older brother Frank had been before he'd been killed in a shoot-out a few years ago.

Emmett talked a lot about his brothers, Bob most of all. From the way he talked, Bob Dalton was just about the greatest thing that ever put on a tin star and could do no wrong. I'd form my own opinion on that subject later on, but that morning all I felt was disappointment, because Emmett's words meant that he really was leaving for good.

"You ain't coming back here, then?" I asked, frowning a little.

"Ain't planning on it," he replied. He suddenly brightened, his youth breaking through that seriousness of his, and his eyes gleamed with sudden inspiration. He looked like an excited kid. "Why don't you come with me, Bill? You can't tell me you're not getting tired of this place, same as me. You'd like Bob. I'm gonna try to get on with him as a guard; maybe you can, too."

I smiled at him. "Thank you kindly for the invitation, Em, but I think I'm gonna stay on here for a bit. I ain't got the constitution for working with lawmen. Sometimes I think I'll be damned lucky to stay on the right side of 'em, to tell you the God's honest truth." I let my voice go dry when I said it. I watched him tie his bedroll behind his cantle and spoke again, getting serious myself now. "You think you can persuade Bob to take you on, what with you being so young, and untried?"

He frowned at me, and I knew I'd hit a sore spot. It'd been hard for him, coming here so young when so many of the rest of us had been doing this since he was in short pants. He never liked anyone to mention his age, and most of the time I didn't, but I was worried about him, when all was said and done. He'd gone right from his Pa's farm to Courtney's ranch, and though the year with me and the others had toughened him up some, he still had no idea what might be in store for him.

"I ain't really all that young, Bill," he muttered, checking over his saddlebags. "I'll be eighteen soon. Bob's only two years older than me, and he's a deputy, ain't he? Besides, you all thought I was too young to work cows, in the beginning, and I convinced you I had the sand, didn't I?"

I straightened up from my slouch against the pillar and came toward him a bit, hooking my thumbs onto my gun belt. "You convinced us just fine after awhile, Em, but being a lawman's a sight different from working cows. I ain't saying you don't got the sand, 'cause you got a hell of a lot of pluck in you for just bein' seventeen, but you're still between hay and grass, when it comes down to it. I'm just warning you. Shooting a man ain't the same as hunting."

He didn't look me in the eye just then, instead he sort of fiddled with the ties on his bedroll, even though they were done up proper already. "Have you ever shot anyone, Bill?" he asked me, all of the sudden, and I knew then that he was just as worried as I was.

I took a deep breath, unwilling to go into the story of the first time I'd ever shot another man, back when I'd had to defend the home farm from a couple of horse-thieves bent on stealing our plowing team. I'd been just about his age when that happened. I'd never told him about it and didn't intend to now. "I have, once or twice," I finally said, "and that's all I'm gonna say about it. I hope you don't ever have to."

He was quiet for a few seconds, then shrugged

his shoulders and pulled his big buffalo overcoat off the nail he'd hung it on while he tacked up. "I guess we'll see," he said, slipping into it. Its bulk made him look bigger. I knew he'd have need of its warmth, once the temperature dropped during the night. He wouldn't make it to Wichita in one day. "Will you tell Dick and Charlie and the rest of the boys I said goodbye?" he asked as he pulled his hat down a little more snugly on his head, and I nodded.

He sort of heaved a little sigh then and came over to me, sticking out his hand. "So long, then, Bill," he said to me, and I could tell he wanted to say a lot more but couldn't. The Daltons, I would learn, weren't good at saying good-bye; it seemed to be a family trait.

I shook his hand and gave it a firm squeeze as I did so. "You take care of yourself, Em, you hear? And if the law don't work out, you be sure to look me and the others up. I imagine we'll be around these parts for a good long while, seeing as how we ain't got the ambition to do anything else." I let my eyes twinkle at him and laughed carelessly to lift his spirits. It worked, 'cause he flashed me a grin as he turned back to his horse. I watched as he put his foot in the stirrup and swung into the saddle, urging Blackjack out of the barn. Just before he put him into a lope he turned back and looked at me, and I waved at him, watching him go. Pretty soon he and the horse were just dark specks on the prairie.

I heard shod hooves on stone and saw Dick leading my mare into the barn. "Did Em get on his way, then?" he asked me.

I nodded absently, still watching, then turned to face Dick and took my horse from him, making ready to untack her and rub her down.

"Hope he finds whatever it is he's looking for," Dick remarked to me. "I met Bob Dalton once in Vinita 'bout two years back. He's a wildcat if I ever met one. I ain't never met Grat, but if half the things I've heard about him are true, Emmett better watch himself."

I felt my brows come together. "Grat's his *brother,* Dick," I pointed out, rolling my eyes a little.

Dick shrugged. "From what I heard, that don't matter none. When Grat Dalton gets in a temper, sharing blood with him don't win you any favors. Of course, I reckon Emmett knows that already."

I cocked an eyebrow at Dick. "You gonna tell me how the rest of them steers were?" I didn't like all this talk about Emmett getting into trouble. I really had grown to think of him like family, and I'd become somewhat protective of him.

"Fine and dandy, Doolin," Dick said breezily, and moved off to attend to the branding we were behind on.

The trouble with Emmett leaving, I came to find in the year and a half that followed, was that I had too much time on my hands without him there. I'd sort of made him my project, and without him to look out for and teach things to I found myself getting bored. The monotony of ranch life, the riding the acres, the branding, the roping, the cutting and all of the other things we had to do started to get to me in a way it never had before. When spring came me and some of the other boys loaded up some of the herd into stock-cars to be shipped, instead of taking them to fresh grazing, like we'd done in years past. Most of the range was fenced off now and none of the big drives, like the ones I'd gone on in the early eighties, existed anymore. The executioner of our old cowboy way of life—the life I'd always loved—was the God-damned railroad.

Most all of the other boys shared my hatred of the Iron Horse. A lot of us had come off farms, and the if the railroad decided it wanted to lay a track down on a farmer's land, it simply shoved the farmer off and did it. Many a farming family had been ruined that way. Then when we tried to get somewhere in the cattle trade, the railroad took away the need for the drives we'd made our living at. The big cow-towns like Dodge City, Abilene and Newton turned into sleepy little holes, and most of the fun they'd offered dried up. The saloons closed, the red light districts broke up and the best girls moved on. It was enough to make a lot of us find other ways to occupy our time—and they weren't hobbies the law much approved of.

Some of the boys would drift on and off the ranches, myself included, but we always came back, for we knew the work and, as I'd said to Emmett on that January day, we lacked the ambition to change our occupation to anything else.

In midsummer of 1890, Dick left for a time, say-ing he was through with cows. It didn't last, though, and he came back from a dalliance over in Newton bearing the first news I'd heard of Emmett since he'd left. Dick had been in a saloon in Newton with some other cowhands he knew from a neighboring ranch when, out of nowhere, Emmett had come in with Bob and Grat.

They'd gotten into a poker game, and the Daltons had said the three of them were out of the lawdog game for good. One of the other deputies in the Territory had pegged Bob and Emmett for whiskey-peddling—a false charge, they'd said—and they'd been arrested. Around that time Grat had lost his commission, too—something to do with his temper—and though Emmett had gotten off for lack of evidence against him, and Bob had gotten out on bail, they'd all decided to give up their tin stars for good.

The news had stunned me. How had fresh-faced young Em gone from guarding prisoners to becoming one for a time? What the hell had happened?

Dick knew nothing more beyond the vague information he'd gotten from them at the poker table, and he'd lost track of them after the game had broken up. He figured they'd left Newton the next morning, and where they'd gone, he didn't know. I stopped fretting about it after a time; after all, Emmett was with his brothers, and even though things hadn't worked out like he'd planned, they *were* his family, when it came down to it, and I figured they'd look out for him as best they could.

When the summer of '91 came, I got even more restless, and Bill Power, Tulsa Jack Blake and I changed ranches, moving on to the Bar X Bar on the first of July. The third day we were there, Tulsa Jack got into a scrape with another cowhand, and it ended up being a good thing, because I got a hell of a couple friends out of the whole affair.

"Doolin, you'd better come out here, quick! Tulsa Jack's getting into it with Charley Pierce, and if Charley's got a gun on him, Jack's as good as dead."

I looked up from the brand I'd been heating up, an answer on the tip of my tongue, but Bill Power was already gone. When I straightened up and looked out the window of the shed I was in, I saw him running toward two bodies grappling with one another near the water pump.

I cursed and threw the red-hot brand into the water bucket; it let out a hiss and steam rose up, threatening to scald out my eyeballs right out of my head. I ducked out the way, quick, then ran outside, heading for the fight. We'd only been there a few days but I'd heard a lot of unsavory tales about Charley Pierce, who'd developed a bit of a reputation for being surly and hard to get along with. He and Tulsa Jack took an instant dislike to one another, and I'd known this would happen, eventually. Even if they didn't kill each other, they were both liable to get kicked off the ranch. Neither option was one I wanted to see happen. Tulsa Jack was a handy fellow to have around; he always seemed to be up for a good time, and also always seemed to know where to find one.

"For Christ's sake, Jack, knock it off!" I shouted, once I reached them. They ignored me, just kept cussing and throwing wild punches at one another as they wrestled around in the dirt. By now it wasn't just me and Bill Power watching; a bunch of other hands had gathered around besides. Some of them started cheering on Charley, since Tulsa Jack was the newcomer and they figured he had to prove himself. Besides that, none of them wanted to answer to Charley after the fight was over; if he thought they'd wanted to see him beat he'd make 'em pay for it.

Suddenly, out of nowhere, another man came flying right into the middle of them. I never did figure out where he came from. He was tall and strong-looking, and when his hat flew off in the ruckus I saw a flash of bright coppery hair before the cloud of dust they were kicking up made it hard to see any of them. He latched onto Charley, somehow, and pried him off Jack. I jumped in right then and grabbed Jack, hooking my arm around his neck and twisting one of his arms behind his back so he couldn't move. He fought against me but I didn't cuss at him, just held him back.

The man with the auburn hair suddenly tossed Charley face-first into one of the straw-stacks near-by, then started laughing, a great, booming laugh. "Charley, you ornery old cuss, what the hell do you think you're doing, abusing the new hands? You ain't got enough to do around here as it is?"

Charley got up and spit out straw, and his whole

body went rigid. Everyone backed up a bit, waiting. As I held onto Jack I glanced at Charley's waist, looking for a gun belt. He wasn't wearing one, but that didn't mean he didn't have a derringer in his boot, or a knife somewhere on him.

The auburn-haired cowboy didn't look the least bit concerned. His laughter slowed to chuckles but he kept that wide grin on his face; I could see it under his sweeping mustache. He was bronzed from the sun like all of us, but with his copper hair and devilish brown eyes, and his teeth showing out white like that, he reminded me of a fox on the hunt.

"Where the *hell* you been, Creek?" Charley spat, violently brushing bits of straw out of his curly black hair. His beady little black eyes were narrowed to slits and his face was good and red.

"I been making some arrangements for us to have some fun, is where I been," the man Charley called Creek said airily. "Apparently I should've taken you along; seems you tend get yourself into trouble when I ain't around."

Charley's fists balled, but he didn't rush at the other man. Instead, he turned and stalked off to the bunkhouse. Tulsa Jack, who had been standing still, suddenly twisted in my grip. "Let me go, Bill." His voice was dark.

"You gonna be good if I do?" I asked him, in a

tone of voice I knew he wouldn't like. I liked Jack, but if he kept this up with Charley he'd get all of us in trouble, and I could do without that just now.

"I ain't gonna go after him," Jack growled. "Turn loose of me."

I twisted his arm just a little more to make my point, then let him go. He straightened his vest, picked up his trampled hat from the dirt, and stomped off in the opposite direction from where Charley had gone.

All the other hands had scattered by then, none of them wanting to run into Charley or Tulsa Jack for a time. I was left standing there alone with the newcomer, and he turned to me with that same easy grin and stuck out a hand. "You must be Bill Doolin," he said, surprising me.

"How do you figure that?" I asked him, shaking his hand as I did so. He had a strong grip.

He laughed. "You got a reputation around these spreads," he told me. "The men all like you, say you're a fair foreman and know how to have some fun besides. Glad to meet you, finally. I'm George Newcomb, but they call me Bitter Creek."

I raised an eyebrow at him. A lot of the men had handles like that, they all meant something to each of them, but I'd never heard one like this before. "And why would that be?"

His grin got even more devilish. "Tell you what,

Doolin, you and your boys from Courtney's place join me and mine tomorrow up in Coffeyville, and you'll find out. We're gonna have a proper Fourth of July around here, for once." He tipped his hat jauntily at me and started to head off, leaving me wondering.

Before he'd gone too far he turned back. "Don't you worry none about Charley," he called, walking backwards for a few paces. "I know him like he was my own brother. He's all talk. He don't mean a damn thing by it, and I can tell you for sure, one we get 'em together tomorrow, he and your boy Jack'll be best of friends." He put his hat back on and covered up that flashy hair, then turned his back to me and went off whistling like a lark. I couldn't place the tune.

THREE

AS IT WOULD turn out, I'd learn a hell of a lot more than where Bitter Creek got his nickname that next day. In fact, that day marked a milestone for me, a sort of turning point in my life. Looking back on it later I couldn't say I regretted anything that happened there; if I'd had it to do all over again, I would've done the same.

Intrigued both by Bitter Creek's promise of fun, and his promise that he could get Tulsa Jack and Charley to see eye-to-eye, I gathered up Bill Power and Jack and headed out for Coffeyville. Bitter Creek, Charley and some of the other Bar X Bar hands had left before us, but we weren't too worried. If they had the type of fun in mind that we were guessing they did, it wouldn't matter when we got there. Along the way we ran into Dick Broadwell, and he came along with us.

We were feeling pretty fine by the time we got to

Coffeyville, glad to have a day off from the ranch and ready to enjoy ourselves for a bit. We found Bitter Creek and Charley and a few of the other hands in a little grassy area on the outskirts of town, with plenty of trees to tie the horses and make shade from the heat. They'd sawed some barrels in half and gotten ahold of some ice, and there was plenty of cold beer in the barrels. Where in the hell they'd gotten it I wasn't sure; we were in a dry county, but we all decided to overlook that little issue.

We set to drinking and shooting the breeze, and just like Creek had predicted, everyone got along just fine; I always have found it a funny thing how drink can either make men fight with each other or make them get along. Lucky for us, it did the latter that day. I started trading miseries of the dying cattle trade with Creek, who'd been working cows since he was a boy, and I sort of lost track of time, and of how much beer I'd had. Once I looked over at some of the others and was shocked all to hell to see Charley Pierce and Tulsa Jack actually laughing together, their feud apparently forgotten. I looked back at Creek in surprise, and I must've had a dumb look on my face, 'cause he winked at me and started with that big laugh of his.

"What'd I tell you, Doolin?" he asked. I shook my head and didn't say anything. I didn't care why they were getting along today; I wasn't going to press my luck any. Peace among my friends and Creek's friends meant the whole bunch of us would have a lot easier time at life in general.

I figure about the time things started to go south was when some of us started turning our attention to our guns. Drinking and wasting time are fine; they ain't the worst things a man can do, but when guns come into the mix, you got trouble.

Bitter Creek started talking to me about shooting, and Dick Broadwell heard him and told him I was the next best thing to a trick gunhand in Buffalo Bill's traveling show. I was a good shot, I'd never deny that, but I wasn't one to brag about it, at least not at that time. Charley—surprisingly good-natured now—joined us and said he bet Creek could top me. Charley, I would come to find, really was like a brother to Creek and the two of them rarely went anywhere without the other. Creek had a personality like a stick of dynamite—light his fuse and you'd pay for it eventually—but he loved a good joke and a good laugh and he didn't like to be in a bad mood. His jolly take on life tempered Charley's mean streak, and I always liked Charley a lot better with Creek than without him.

Tulsa Jack took some of the empty beer bottles and lined them up on boulders and tree stumps here and there. He was pretty drunk by that time, so it took him about three or four tries just to get them to stay up there proper. When he was finally done Charley dared me and Creek to a shooting match, to see how many bottles we could each hit in a row. All the other hands gathered around to watch, and a few of them even took bets.

Creek told me to go first. I let one side of my mouth go up in a smile and casually drew my gun; before Charley could even say 'go' I'd popped off three shots and gotten a bottle with each one. The beer didn't alter my aim any, but it *did* make me show off far more than I normally would have. I took out the rest of the bottles quick, and for the last two I shot from the hip. Then I twirled the gun back into my holster, all fancy-like, and raised an eyebrow at Creek, waiting.

I heard some whoops from my friends, and Dick pounded me on the back. Charley looked impressed.

Bitter Creek stared at me for a minute, then started laughing. "Well, seems I got a tough act to follow, don't it?" he asked no one in particular. His eyeballs were getting red from the beer but they were just as twinkly as ever. "Charley, set up some more bottles. Jack's too drunk to do it again." Charley, who was just as drunk as Tulsa Jack, moved unevenly forward to do as Creek said, and while he did it, Bitter Creek started singing, in a booming liquored baritone that wasn't anywhere near the proper key:

I'm a wild wolf from Bitter Creek
And it's my night to howl!
I'm a bucking cayuse from—

A loud voice cut Creek off in mid-verse just as all us new hands were learning where he'd come by that handle. "All right, that'll be enough now, boys!"

The bunch of us all turned and saw three men on horseback coming up to our little party. They were all stiff and serious-looking. The leader was in his shirt-sleeves against the heat and I saw sweat rolling down his temples from under his hat brim as he rode up to us. He had a Winchester in his saddle scabbard, and a fancy-Dan watch chain and a tin star glinting out from his vest. I'd seen him a few times before when I'd come up to Coffeyville for one thing or another; I could tell he thought he was a big-shot.

"Looks like you boys have been doing some drinking," he said in a high-and-mighty tone of voice I didn't much care for; neither did the others.

"What's it to you? We ain't hurting anyone," Charley retorted, puffing out his chest and strutting around like a Banty rooster. I fought the urge to laugh; Charley was much shorter than me and Creek, but there he was, coming out in front of us like some kind of guard dog with his hackles up and his teeth bared.

"I'm afraid it's a great deal to me and my deputies, here," the leader said, still using that tone like we were a bunch of unruly children, "because this is a dry county. You aren't allowed to be drinking at all, much less as much as you've been doing. Come on, now, and give up your guns."

My brows came together and I felt myself begin to get a bit hot under the collar. "Wait just a damn minute, there ain't a no-gun law in Coffeyville."

"No, there isn't, but you boys are drunk, and I'm not going to let you keep your irons on you like that. I'll give them back when you sober up some."

Bitter Creek's eyes narrowed and so did Charley's, and I was good and mad now. "How's about you let us keep our rightful property, and we'll be on our way, seeing as how our good time's been ruined," I shot back at him.

He didn't answer me, just shook his head and signaled to his deputies, and the three of them got down out of their saddles and started pouring out the little bit of beer we had left.

I drew my gun, more to make a point at that moment than anything else, and Creek and Charley drew theirs, too, following my lead. I'd never been in trouble with the law up until then; I'd always been too busy with my chosen trade, but my chosen trade was dying out and I'd started to figure that I'd need to find some other way to make my living, pretty soon. The beer didn't help matters none.

One small-town lawdog and his deputies weren't any match for the bunch of us, but they were too stupid to know that, evidently. The deputies looked nervous but they kept on watering the ground with Creek's hard-won beer.

"Pour out one more bottle, friend, and you ain't gonna like the result," Bitter Creek growled at the nearest deputy, thumbing back the hammer on his gun.

The sheriff or marshal or whatever he was jerked his pistol then, clearly intending to put a bullet in Creek, so I put one in him, first.

My shot went through his shoulder, just like I'd intended it to, and the impact caused him to drop his gun. One of his deputies tried to draw on me, but Creek got him square in the groin before either one of us could blink, proving to me what a good shot he was. Dick and Charley both fired off rounds, too, but the beer altered their aim and their bullets hit off the rocks near the last deputy. He jumped onto his horse and lit on out of there, heading toward town and leaving his friends moaning in agony in the grass.

"Put your damn guns away before you kill each other," I snapped at the others, and to my satisfaction, they all obeyed me, even Charley. Bitter Creek was smiling at me and I saw respect in his gaze as he holstered his revolver.

"Come on, let's get the hell out of here before they come out with a lynch mob," I said, and I jumped onto my horse, no longer feeling all the beer I'd drank. Everyone got up on their horses and put their reins to rumps, none of us paying any mind to the two wounded men we'd left behind. In our minds, they'd asked for it.

We rode out aways into the Territory and stopped to water the horses at a stream. While they drank, Bitter Creek asked me what I thought we should do next.

"They'll have the law out for us, that much I'm sure of," I said. "I been to Coffeyville a lot and there'll be folks that'll identify me. Won't take too much brains to figure out where to look for the rest of you after that."

"We can't go back to the ranch," Tulsa Jack said in an agitated voice. He was keyed up and jumpy and couldn't stand still for more than two seconds. "I ain't gonna be strung up for being an accessory to no murder!"

"They ain't dead, Jack," I pointed out, rolling my eyes.

"They might be, after a bit," Jack replied stubbornly, but he wouldn't look me in the eye. "And even if they ain't, I still ain't sticking around that damned ranch."

"If any of those lawdogs try to get me on anything, I'll make sure I'm the last one they ever go after," one of the other hands growled, and spat on the ground to punctuate his words. He was one of the men we'd met when we came to the Bar X Bar. He had even redder hair than Bitter Creek and the disposition of a rattlesnake; I'd only been around him four days but I'd already decided I'd never met a crosser or more ornery son of a bitch in my life. He had a chip on his shoulder the size of Texas, which is where he hailed from. In truth, I wished he'd go back there; otherwise I had no doubt in my mind that he'd kill more men than the four he already bragged about having killed, and without any good reason. His name was George Weightman, but they called him Red Buck, because of his hair. He'd just finished almost three years in prison for horse theft, but he had a lot worse than nag-rustling to his credit.

"You all do what you like," I said coolly. "I ain't going back to that ranch, either."

In truth we probably could've gone back for the

night; they likely wouldn't come out looking for us until the next day, but I was a cautious man, always had been, and I saw no reason to chance it. I had everything important right there with me—the money in my saddlebags, the gun in my holster, and the horse under my saddle. I had two hands and good health, so I knew I could find work, once my money ran out, until I figured out what I was going to do with myself from then on.

Everyone agreed that we'd all look out for our own selves, but if we were ever questioned about what had happened back there, we wouldn't name names and get anyone in hot water. Most of the Bar X Bar hands headed off in different directions then, including Red Buck. Tulsa Jack and Bill Power rode off together, saying they were going to Newton. They asked me to come but I shook my head and waved them off. Pretty soon there was just Bitter Creek, Charley, Dick and me left.

Bitter Creek had been kind of quiet since we'd stopped to water the horses, but all of the sudden he threw back his head and laughed. "Well, I told you boys we'd have some fun today, didn't I? Only I didn't figure on us having quite this much of it!"

Dick grinned at him. "You *do* know how to stir things up, Creek, I'll give you that." He moved over and grabbed his horse's reins, quick; it had finished drinking and had decided to try to take a bite out of Charley's mare.

Creek slapped at a mosquito on his arm, then looked at me. "Charley and I'll go out to see a few friends of ours near Kingfisher, then head out to my claim, I suppose. You want to come along, Bill?"

I reached for my own horse. "I think I'm going to rough it a bit out here for awhile before I go back to anyplace that's got the law attached to it," I said. "I may look you up later on, though, if you're around."

He nodded. "You ever need us for anything, Doolin, you just say the word. Me and Charley are always up for anything. You can look us up at my claim at Cowboy Flats on the Cimarron." Charley nodded at Creek's words and went to tighten up the cinch on his saddle. Then he and Creek mounted up and gave us careless waves before cantering off in a cloud of dust.

FOUR

DICK AND I camped out for a few nights, eating small game, though there was getting to be less and less of that around these days as the Territory was settled up and pickings were pretty slim. More and more folks were taking claims now, those that didn't decide to push on further West, and the game was all being hunted up or scared off. After a few days Dick got to missing the taste of whiskey and the wares offered by the girls in the red-light districts and went to join Bill Power, but I went into Indian lands.

I headed into Vinita for provisions and to get my horse re-shod, and I got a newspaper there to see if there was anything about our little party on the Fourth. I never got to see if there was or not, because another article caught my eye and made me forget why I'd gotten the paper in the first place.

The headline read "Notorious Train Robber Gratton Dalton Convicted In California," and it told about how the Dalton brothers had attempted to rob a train in Alila, California, earlier that year. It said they'd only been able to capture Grat and William Dalton, and how the other two suspects, Bob and Emmett, had evaded the law and were on the run. Furthermore, it said that the Bob and Emmett had since robbed the Santa Fe train at Wharton in Indian Territory, back in May, with the aid of two other men. One of those men, the article said, was thought to be a cowhand known as George Newcomb, alias "Bitter Creek."

I swear to the Lord above, I was struck completely dumb by that article. Not only had my old friend Emmett become a full-fledged train robber by the looks of it, my new friend Bitter Creek was one, too—and knew the Daltons to boot. Their names hadn't come up during our little ruckus up in Coffeyville, so he didn't know that I knew Emmett.

I took the paper and my provisions, and instead of going back out on the trail, I took a room at a hotel and read the article again, still trying to get my head around it all.

There were a lot of men that made names for themselves by holding up trains in those days. I guess Jesse James had sort of started the trend just after the war ended and kept it up into the seventies, when he and his brother Frank had the James Gang in its full glory. It had since become a way for men like us to get back at the railroad and settle the score some for all of that damned land-grabbing they did, and the unwelcome changes they'd brought to the cattle trade. It was also easy money, when all was said and done. The satisfaction that came with it was an added benefit. Let the railroad suffer a few losses. It was only fair, in my mind, after everything it had done.

It was a funny thing, I would find, how a man could come to turn from one side of what the law figured was right, to the other. I would come to know many who'd just happened to fall into the lifestyle without really meaning to; even some who lived that way when they really didn't want to; they just got in deeper and deeper until there wasn't any way they could pull themselves out. There were still others that simply craved the notoriety and the chance to have their names spelled out in the newspapers alongside words like 'deadly' and 'notorious,' and whatever way they came by that end was just fine with them. Me, I just wanted to take the railroad down a few notches, plain and simple—at least it started out that way.

The day I got to Bitter Creek's claim, I arrived just as the sun was going down. I found the place easy after asking a few people in the area; I was finding that Creek sort of stuck out among folks.

I rode my tired horse at a walk toward the tiny claim shanty I could see in the dimming light. There was smoke coming from the stove-pipe and I could see a small stable and corral built off to the side. None of the section, as far as I could tell, had been cleared for crops.

I approached cautiously; I didn't want to get mistaken for some lawdog out to hunt up Creek and get shot for my trouble. I didn't need to worry, though, because the door to the shanty came open and Bitter Creek came marching out to welcome me with a big grin and a careless laugh. "Well, look who's come to call!" he said, as Charley came out behind him. "Hello, Bill!"

"Hello, Creek," I said, getting down off my horse and giving him a tired half-smile. I nodded to Charley. "Charley."

"I was hoping you'd look us up, though I didn't figure on you coming so soon," Creek said. "You look like you been riding hell-bent for leather. Let's get your horse put up and get you some grub."

The one-room claim shanty was nearly empty inside, the only furnishings were the tiny old stove, the table with the lamp on it, a few worn chairs and a couple of boxes. Creek and Charley's saddles were piled in one corner with their saddle blankets, and their horses' bridles hung on a nail above them. The place was slim on comforts, for a fact, but being bachelors, they didn't need much more than a place to take shelter in.

We ate supper together and I told him about the article in the paper that I'd seen. He gave me his hunting-fox grin, like he was proud of himself, and he looked surprised when I told him about how I knew Emmett Dalton.

"I never put two and two together, Bill," he told me. "I've known Bob and Grat for a time, and I met Emmett back in Newton last year, before they went out to California. You ought to come with us, our next time out. Charley here plans to." He handed me a bottle of red-eye he'd pulled out of a dry-goods box next to the stove.

"Think I will," I said casually, taking a drink of whiskey. I hadn't had any in awhile and it tasted good, so I took another tug. "You got a job in mind?"

Creek stretched his arms out above his head and leaned his chair back against the wall, propping his boots up on the table and sticking a toothpick in his mouth. He could do that because there weren't any womenfolk around. "Ain't up to me, Bill. That's Bob

Dalton's call. He's the brains of this gang. He'll pick the train he wants, then he'll look us up. He plans these jobs to the letter and he don't take any bullshit from any man comes with him. Sometimes I forget he's as young as he is; you wouldn't know it by how he pulls these larks off." He leaned forward and took the bottle from me, then handed it off to Charley after taking an impressive swallow.

"How's Emmett?" I asked him, changing the subject a bit.

"He's a quiet kid, but he does his part and doesn't go weak between the ears when it's time to take care of business. He always goes along with whatever Bob comes up with. I never saw anyone so loyal to his brother as Emmett is."

I nodded thoughtfully. "You know where I could find them?" I asked.

"Nope," Charley said, speaking for the first time in a long while. He'd been concentrating on the whiskey pretty hard while Creek and I talked and it was almost gone. "Bob Dalton finds you, you don't find him. Word is they got hideouts all over the Territory, and Bob keeps 'em moving a lot. The great Heck Thomas is all over the place like a damn bloodhound, trying to get 'em, so they don't stay in one place too long."

There was a lot of sarcasm in Charley's voice

when he mentioned Heck Thomas; everyone in these parts, whether they were on the wrong side of the law or the right one, knew who *he* was—a deputy U.S. marshal who, along with his compadres Bill Tilghman and Chris Madsen, had made it his great mission in life to take down every outlaw, be it small time cattle-rustler, horse-thief or train robber, in this part of the country. They were called the "Three Guardsmen" and were hell-bent on getting the whole of Indian and Oklahoma Territories crime-free. All I could say was, they had a hell of a big job ahead of them.

"The Daltons've got a dugout around here we used the last time out, but I couldn't really tell you where it is," Creek told me. "We got there at night, following Bob and Emmett, and left before the sun came up, and I'd had a little too much whiskey by the time we left besides, so I ain't too sure where it is. Bob wants it that way, anyway. He's a cautious sort. He don't trust too many, when it comes right down to it. I figure he'll tell us how to get to it when he thinks the time is right."

"Well," I told them, casually plucking the whiskey bottle out of Charley's hand before he dropped it, and downing another tug, "whenever they go out, you can count me in."

Bitter Creek chuckled and looked at Charley. "I

do believe this will make things even more interesting than they already are." That big sly grin of his shone out in the lamplight, and his eyes started twinkling as Charley gave him a knowing look across the table.

I couldn't know then, of course, how much of an understatement Creek's words would end up to be.

FIVE

AS CREEK HAD told me, we were waiting on Bob Dalton. Days passed without any word from him, and I started taking a look around the country, getting myself more familiar with the area until I knew it so well it was like I'd lived there all my life. I figured once we went out on a train job, I'd better know where the best places were to hide out, in case Creek's claim was compromised somehow.

Days turned into weeks, and Creek, Charley and I started to wonder if something had happened to the Daltons. Some of the papers were claiming Bob had been killed in a gunfight, but for some reason we couldn't explain, we didn't believe it. I'd become close to Creek and Charley over those weeks, and we spent our time playing cards at the little saloons in the area, practicing our marksmanship, scouting out new hiding places—and waiting on Bob.

One evening I went to a lonely little saloon in

Morrison by myself, leaving Bitter Creek and Charley to sleep off their impressive hangovers. I was sitting at a corner table with a bottle of whiskey when the door opened, and two newcomers sauntered inside.

I sized them up, a habit borne of the Fourth of July incident, for which I was still looking out for the law to come calling. They were both tall and slender, with gun belts around their waists and hats pulled down low around their brows. One of them was carrying a Winchester and walked with a deliberate stride and steps that seemed heavier than they should've been for a man of his build. That one had a fine-featured face covered with blond stubble. The other was dark-haired and dogged the first man's heels. I almost knocked over my bottle when I got a better look at the dark-haired one—it was Emmett Dalton.

At that very moment, he turned and saw me, and his gray eyes lit up with surprise and gladness at the same time. "Why, Bill!" he said, and came over to me. The other man stopped and watched, glancing at me suspiciously, then followed, sizing me up as he did so.

"Well, now, ain't *you* a sight for sore eyes!" I said to Emmett, grinning at him wide, relieved to see him. He looked older and harder-edged somehow, with stubble on his face and a sort of hunted look in his eyes. I stood up. "Come on outside, now, and tell me how you've been." I moved for the door and heard their spurs chiming in unison as they followed me.

Once we got outside I turned to him in the moonlight. "By the Lord Almighty, Emmett, you've gone and turned into a man of some fame since I last saw you!" I reached over and slapped him on the back. "Told you the law wouldn't agree with you none." I felt my grin get wider.

He gave me a sort of wry half-smile. "I suppose that's the truth, when you get down to it," he replied. He gestured to the other man. "Bill, this is my brother, Bob. Bob, this is Bill Doolin, an old friend of mine. He took me under his wing when I worked at the ranch. Looked out for me and taught me a lot— depending on which way you want to look at it."

I'd already guessed the other man was Bob Dalton; even though their hair and eye color was different, they looked a lot alike in their faces and it was easy to see they were brothers. But Emmett had some warmth in his gaze; you could tell he was a good man just by looking him in the eyes. Bob, to me, was different. His eyes were blue but they weren't warm; they were sort of cold and calculating. I could almost see wheels turning in his head when he looked at me. He had an air about him that sang out his position as boss of the outfit, and I could tell he was damned comfortable in that position.

I'd always had a gift for sizing folks up; I could tell a lot about a man's character pretty quick after I'd met him. Bob had something about him that gave me pause, like something wasn't quite right in his head; I could see it right off. I sensed trouble ahead, but I was still determined that if he took another train, I'd be with him and Emmett. I was eager to try my hand at it and see if I could even the score some with the railroad for damn near robbing me of the only occupation I'd ever really felt good at.

I shook his hand with my usual firm grip and told him I was glad to meet the brains of the Dalton Gang. I told him and Emmett how I'd read about them, and I surely was glad to have run into them.

"If you need a man on your next venture, Bob, I put myself forward," I said. "I've practically been put out of work by the God-damned railroad, and I got relations that have been put off their land by it, too. I got no love for them thieving express companies, nor for law in these God-forsaken Territories, and I'll stand with the shooter, if that's what's called for." I spoke bluntly, getting right to the point; I figured that was the best way of convincing Bob to take me on, from what Creek had told me.

Bob sort of stared me down for a minute, and then said evenly, "well, Emmett here's talked about you in the past, says you're handy with a gun and as brave as they come, so I suppose I'll take you on as a favor to him, see how things go."

I nodded and gave him a smile. "All right then. I'm staying at a claim just south of here—Bitter Creek Newcomb's, to be exact. Come see me when the time comes."

Emmett raised an eyebrow. "You know Bitter Creek?"

"Quite well. Charley Pierce, too." I smiled at him, more warmly than I had at Bob. "I sure am glad to see you again, Em. I knew you'd go on to bigger and better things, once you got off that ranch." I put a hand on his shoulder, then headed toward my horse, who I'd tied at the hitching rail at the back of the saloon, whistling softly under my breath.

As I left I heard Emmett say cheerfully, "Come on, Bob, let's go play some poker."

⸺◉⸺

"Bill, Charley, wake up!"

Bitter Creek's voice was tense in the darkness, and I heard, rather than saw, him kick at Charley's leg with the toe of his boot. Charley sort of groaned and turned over in his bedroll, resuming his snoring. He'd had a hell of a lot to drink that night.

I heard the scratch of a match, and a tiny flame lit the darkness. It danced on the end of the match as Creek carried it over to light the lamp. He touched it to the wick, then cursed under his breath and made a sudden violent motion with his hand; the match must've burned him. I heard the matchstick bounce off into a corner somewhere and I hoped it wouldn't set the place on fire.

Creek lowered the wick so the lamp was just barely giving off light, then glanced out the window. He had his vest on but not buttoned, and his galluses were hanging down off his waist.

I yawned and sat up in my bedroll. Creek's claim shanty didn't have any bedsteads in it so we just bunked down on the floor every night. "Creek, what is it?" I asked.

He looked at me. "There's a couple of horses coming. Looks like they're heading this way." He kept his voice real quiet as he spoke.

I tensed, wide awake now, and reached for my gun, which I never let get very far away from me these days. I got up and dressed, quick, then picked up my gun again and moved over toward the window next to Bitter Creek. On the way over I kicked

Charley again, a lot harder than Creek had. "Charley, damn it, wake up!"

He started awake and sat up quick, then winced, rubbing his head with the palm of one hand. He looked a little green to me in the feeble lamplight. "What the hell's the matter, Doolin?" he mumbled.

"Someone's coming," I hissed at him, and he woke himself up a bit then, reaching for his revolver and getting unsteadily to his feet. He came over to the window, too, and we all three saw the dim, indistinct outlines of two horses trotting through the tall wild grasses, coming toward the shanty. Creek motioned for Charley to stay with me at the window, then he moved stealthily to the door, crouching to one side of it, his gun pointed at the ceiling, at the ready.

The cloud-cover outside cleared a little bit then, and the moonlight got bright enough for me to see the riders a little clearer when they came closer. Something about them looked familiar to me; seemed to me I'd seen them before somewhere. Then they got even closer and I recognized them. "It's all right, Creek, it's the Daltons." Just as I said it a sharp, two-note whistle sounded from outside; I would learn that that was Bob Dalton's signal to others in his gang.

Creek relaxed and put his gun away, and Charley and I did the same. Outside, the Daltons took their horses around to the sod stable. Creek moved toward the lamp and turned it up, giving us a little more light. He pulled his galluses up over his shoulders, then ran a hand over his face and through his thick auburn hair, making it stand on end a little.

Charley got himself dressed while we waited, and in a few minutes the door opened and Bob and Emmett came inside.

It was the second of September, and we'd been waiting a long time to hear from them. We'd kept ourselves busy with one thing or the other, but we were all anxious to get the job set, mainly because the bunch of us were starting to run out of money and we weren't going to take a chance at trying to get hired on again at one of the ranches.

"Hey there, Bob and Em," Creek said cheerfully.

"Creek. Charley. Hello, Bill," Bob replied. His eyes shone out in the firelight and I could tell he was a little lit up. I was glad about that; it seemed to make him friendlier. I echoed his greeting, then said hello to Emmett, who did not look like he'd been sharing Bob's good time. That didn't surprise me; he never had been much of a drinker.

"Sorry to wake you boys up, but I've decided on our next venture, and I thought I'd invite you three along," Bob said breezily, once Creek had shut and locked the door.

Creek scratched at his stubbled chin. "What've you got in mind, Bob?"

"The Katy train, at Leliaetta, this time," Bob replied. "We'll take her on the fifteenth. She should have a pretty big haul, so I want a bigger group of us, this time out. I'm thinking two more. You boys know anyone we can trust?"

I spoke up. "I do. Fellas by the name of Dick Broadwell and Bill Power. You remember them, Emmett," I said, glancing at him. He nodded, looking surprised when I said their names, but he kept quiet. Emmett kept quiet a lot around Bob, I was to learn. I would come to find out that he had a lot of objections to certain things we were doing, but if he voiced them, Bob shot them down, so he'd just started saying nothing. He idolized Bob—why, I never did figure out—so he couldn't bring himself to tell him no.

Bob nodded. "I know Broadwell, and I've heard Power's name before. You know Power, don't you, Creek?"

Creek nodded. "Bill here introduced me to him, for a fact." He waved a hand toward me.

Bob nodded again. "All right, then. Rustle them up and get them here tomorrow, if you can. Then tomorrow night, Em and I will meet up with you here and go over the plan."

"Sure thing, Bob. You want to bunk down here for the night?" Creek asked.

Bob surveyed the almost bare shanty, with our bedrolls and our guns laid out here and there, along with a few empty liquor bottles and the tin plates we'd eaten off of earlier that all three of us had neglected to wash, and one of his eyebrows went up. A smile played with the corners of his mouth. "Thank you kindly for the offer, Creek, but we'll be on our way. I don't want the bunch of us in one place right now, just in case."

His words made sense, but something in the way he said it irked the hell out of me. He and Emmett were bachelors, too, so I didn't imagine wherever they were holed up looked much different, but Bob acted like the shanty was beneath them. I wasn't sorry to see the back of him when they left, but I supposed I'd give him a few more chances, for Emmett's sake.

———)(●)(———

Bill Power had filed on a claim not too far from Bitter Creek's, and Dick was with him, as he usually was. We rode over and got them just after sunset, then went back to the shanty and waited up for the Daltons. Charley wanted to break out the last bottle of whiskey we had, but Creek and I stopped him. Everyone needed to be good and sober when Bob went over the plan; if anyone messed up, they'd pay for it by way of Bob's gun.

"We'll save it for after the job, Charley," Creek said with a grin, taking the whiskey bottle from him and putting it away. "To celebrate with."

We sort of sat around then, smoking down the cigarettes Dick had rolled and handed out, and just waited. No one in our present bunch had ever held up a train before, except for Bitter Creek, who told us a little bit about what to expect.

"The main thing is, do what Bob tells you to do," he said. "He's got this whole game down like clock-work, and it won't do anyone any good to stray from whatever it is he plans. Personally, I don't much care to be shot up, so I follow his lead."

"Is there much gunplay in it, Creek?" Bill Power asked eagerly.

"Some. You got to fire some shots, just warning ones, to keep everyone in line. But we don't shoot any men unless they're shooting at us—which they were too yellow to do, the time I was out." He laughed. "I'm telling you, boys, this'll be the easiest damn money you ever made in your life. The railroad don't train its men for the likes of what Bob Dalton plans. You'll see."

As if on cue, like in some theater show, Bob's two-note whistle sounded from outside, and we saw the horses coming. Everyone sort of sat up a little straighter when he and Emmett came inside.

Bob was sober this time, and that "boss wolf" look was back on his face. He was on guard a bit, since there was a newcomer in the bunch. Bob knew Dick pretty well but he'd never met Bill Power before that night, and I could tell he had to size him up a bit, the way he'd done to me the first night I met him, before he'd trust him too well.

Emmett hung back a little, and his greetings to Dick and Bill Power, who he'd known at the old Courtney place, were kind of subdued. He looked troubled in the lamplight and I wished I could talk to him proper, but I somehow knew he wouldn't say anything in front of Bob—at least, not anything Bob didn't want to hear. I could tell he wasn't too fond of holding up trains, and I guessed why—he'd told me back at the ranch once how his Ma had tried real hard to raise her boys up with good morals, and how he sometimes suspected that maybe he was one of the only ones they'd stuck to besides his murdered brother Frank and his oldest brother Ben, so I figured his conscience was probably hurting him pretty bad by now. Besides that, he was too young to share the hatred of the railroad that me and most of the others had. Bob was, too, when it came down to it; he was ten years younger than me and he'd never worked cattle—never had his living whittled down to almost nothing with every piece of track they laid across the range. He was in it for the money, the thrill and the fame, and he wasn't shy about saying so, either.

He had us gather around the table, where he laid out a schedule for the Katy train. "We're gonna take the number three at Leliaetta on the fifteenth," he said without pleasantries. "We'll flag her down at eight o'clock. Emmett, Creek and me will take the express car like usual." He glanced at Creek, and Creek nodded soberly. He didn't bother to glance at Emmett; he knew he didn't need to. "The rest of you," Bob said, looking around at all of us, "will concentrate on keeping the company men and the passengers in line. I want two alongside the train right where the express car joins the passenger cars, at the ready, in case anyone tries to get off and try anything stupid. Em and Creek, you know what to do. Then when I give the signal—" here, he let out a piercing whistle that could've woke up the dead "—you all *get out of there*, quick as you can, and get back to the horses, which Power will stay with. We'll hitch 'em just beyond the platform."

His voice was firm, he wasn't giving Bill Power a choice in the matter. Power was the newcomer and the one had to earn Bob's trust, so he'd get the most menial job. Bill didn't seem to care, though, and knowing him like I did, I figured he was just happy to be asked along. He was a restless sort of man, always looking for something new to try his hand at and always looking to get rich, and he didn't care none how he got there.

Bob spoke again. "Every man gets to his horse, and then we all head back to the dugout we got near there to divvy up."

"But Bob, how will we know where—"

"You'll follow us," Bob interrupted Dick, gesturing to himself and Emmett. "I ain't showing anyone the way there until after the job. If you want your cut, you'll make sure you keep up with us." His eyes glittered warningly in the lamplight, and none of us protested.

Throughout the whole of this, there wasn't a single shred of doubt in Bob's voice. He had it laid out to the letter, all right, and the way he said it, it was easy to believe that things would go off exactly like he'd planned. Underneath his confidence was a clear warning—if we didn't stick to his plan, we'd be damned sorry we'd ever been asked to come along.

"There's an outcropping of rocks and a big cottonwood tree about a mile from the Leliaetta platform," Bob told us. "We'll meet up there at seven on the fifteenth, four days from now. Bring your guns and something to hide your faces with. Everyone clear?"

We all nodded and said we were. I shot a look at Emmett and saw him heave a very quiet sigh. He was fingering the handle of one of his revolvers, running his fingernails over it as it sat in his holster. He saw me looking at him and stared back at me for a few seconds before he looked away, the muscles in his jaw going tight. I thought he looked uncomfortable.

"One more thing," Bob said firmly, drawing our attention again, and I looked away from Emmett. "None of you are to get lit up before we do this. If I see any man who ain't good and sober when we meet up, he ain't going along. I won't have any mistakes made. I don't care how tight you get yourselves afterward, but before, you keep away from the bottle. Understood?"

We all nodded again, and Bob looked satisfied. "Till seven on the fifteenth, then. Em and I'll be going now. Get yourselves ready for an easy haul, boys," he said with a grin, his eyes alight with the promise of another claim to fame. He and Emmett put on their hats, took their rifles from where they'd set them by the door, and left unceremoniously, collecting their still-saddled horses and riding off into the darkness.

I sat back in the chair I'd been sitting in, thinking things over. For some reason, I kept picturing the look in Emmett's eyes, just before he'd looked away from me.

SIX

WHEN WE ALL walked our horses up to the meeting-place at Leliaetta four nights later, the cicadas were going but everything else was still and almost eerie. We dismounted and checked over our guns while our horses all swished their tails and shook flies off their hides, stamping their front feet.

Everyone was excited and keyed up, ready to go. What we were about to pull didn't seem real to most of us, at least not until the Daltons came up. Bob looked just as cool as you please, like he was out for a nice ride on a summer evening. Emmett had no expression on his face.

He and Bob got off and tied their horses, and Bob went to speak to Bitter Creek, in amongst the small herd of horses we had tied to the lowest branches of the cottonwood. I took the opportunity to speak to Emmett alone.

"How're you doing, Em?" I asked him lightly,

cuffing him on the shoulder like I'd used to do back at the ranch, trying to gain back some of our old ease with one another; it seemed it had sort of disappeared now that Bob was in the picture.

He gave me a weak smile; I saw it in the dying light, and hooked his thumbs on his gun belt. "Fine, Bill. I'll admit, though, that this sort of throws me a little." He gestured to some of the others. "Seems strange to be getting ready to do this with all of you boys from the ranch."

"Bigger and better things, Em, remember?" I teased gently. "That goes for all of us, not just you. I guess you're an old hand at this business, now."

He started chewing on his lower lip when I said that, and then I heard him take a deep breath. "Guess I am, for a fact. Don't mean I have to like it, though."

I grinned at him, trying to lift his spirits. "Why, Em, ain't you having fun?"

He gave me a dark look as Bob called "time to go," at us. "Sure, Bill. So much fun, I ain't sure I can handle it all," he shot back, so quietly I almost couldn't hear him. He raised his black neckerchief up around his nose and mouth so that all that showed were his eyes, and I did the same. The last light disappeared and night closed in around us. We got up on our horses and rode slowly through the dark to the platform, just a darker black shape in the distance.

We tied our mounts up just like we'd planned, and Bill Power stayed with them, tense as a hunting panther as he listened to us move off in a big group toward the edge of the platform. Bob lit a lantern he'd been carrying and set it on the edge of the platform, so the engineer would see it and know someone wanted the train to stop. Then we waited. I heard Bob snap his watch-case shut, just as a faint rumble started up aways down the track. In the soft ring of light thrown off by the lantern I saw the loose rocks at the sides of the track start to tremble and slide a little, and a low whistle sounded. She was coming closer now, and Bob spoke sharply in the shadows. "At the ready, boys. Creek, wait for my signal."

Creek stepped forward a little and the rest of us moved back, crouching down out of range of the lantern's light and drawing our guns, reaching up to adjust our masks one last time. Charley's breathing sounded loud next to me, until the train got closer and drowned it out. The big light at the front of the engine suddenly cut through the blackness as the train rounded a little bend and headed for the platform.

"Easy…easy…*now,* Creek!" Bob said, and Bitter Creek took off his hat and started to flag her down.

Puffs of steam rolled out from either side of the train as it slowly rolled to a stop. Then Bob and Emmett emerged out of the shadows, moving though the steam with Bitter Creek, and boarded. They looked a little like spooks to me, with all that steam going up around them and lifting up the hems of their frock coats, making them flare out behind them.

"All right, now, no one try anything, and no one'll get hurt!" Bob bellowed out, and, as I'd been told to, I moved up behind them. I raised my gun and covered the conductor, who'd come boiling out of the next passenger car and then stopped short when he saw me, his face going as white as a sheet.

"Put your hands were I can see 'em, friend," I said pleasantly, "and I'd be much obliged if you'd stay right were you are while we go about our business." Behind me, Emmett turned in the other direction, covering the fireman. I heard Bob and Creek moving toward the express car, shouting orders as they went. Outside, I could see Dick and Charley on either side of the train, their rifles raised to their shoulders, covering the doors and windows.

A few of the passengers started screaming, and Dick and Charley fired warning shots into the air to shut them up. Emmett fired one, too, into the floor of the car, when he saw another company man coming toward us. "Ain't gonna warn you again," I heard him say, and it took me aback to hear it, because if I hadn't known he was standing there I wouldn't have believed it was his voice. The man froze. I could see the sweat popping out on his face in the light from the passenger car.

I kept focusing on the company men; they represented the railroad to me. They'd thrown in their lot with the very thing that pushed poor folks off their land and cut up the range so it became like pieces in a child's puzzle, and payment was due for that, in my mind. I didn't look at any of the passengers for any length of time, and none of the men in our group tried to hold any of them up. Our business was with the company, not with them, and as long as they stayed quiet and orderly and didn't try to get in our way, we would leave them be.

Nothing happened for a minute or two. My heart was thudding pretty hard in my chest, but my palms stayed dry under my gun. Then I heard that shrill whistle, and I knew they were done in the express car. I turned on my heel and sprang down off the train, my boots thudding onto the platform. I heard Charley and Dick coming, too, and Em and Bob and Creek. Our spurs chimed as we ran together in one big group, and when we reached the horses we vaulted up into our saddles—how we managed to get on proper, I wasn't sure, since we couldn't see our hands in front of our faces—and got going. Bitter Creek started laughing; his laughter boomed out around us. I saw the white tail of the paint horse Bob was riding streaming out ahead of me and followed it, kicking my horse into a full gallop. Emmett was riding alongside me and he was laid almost flat against his horse's neck, slapping at its rump with his reins to get as much stride out of it as possible. He had his neckerchief up around his face still, but even so I knew he wasn't smiling.

The seven of us galloped along blind through the darkness, pushing our horses hard and never slowing their stride for anything, praying they'd find their footing as they went. Finally, after we'd been going for some time, Bob and Emmett cut to the right and headed for a strand of trees and a creek bed. We plunged on through, water from the horses' hooves flying up around us as we put them up onto the far bank. Then Bob called out to us to slow up; we were going downhill a little into a low place on the prairie. In the moonlight I saw a door cut out into an embankment where the ground started to slope up again; it was a dugout. There was a sod stable there, too, and it was just barely big enough for all of our horses. As we put them up by the light of the lantern Emmett lit it started to sink in some, what we'd just done, and I couldn't believe how *easy* it had been. No one had gotten hurt, and we'd made another strike against the railroad. I couldn't help it, I grinned wide at Creek, and he grinned right back. "Damned easy, wasn't it?"

he asked me, low, as we scraped the lather off our horses' necks. He looked like he could go out and do it again that very night, a few times over.

"Sure was," I said.

We all went inside the dugout, where Bob had another lantern lit. He took up the flour sack that held the haul and started pulling cash out of it, dividing it up amongst all of us. I took mine without a shred of guilt, as did all the others, except Em. He took his share, but was slow about it and his face looked grim in the glow of the lantern. I hadn't noticed until now that he had dark circles under his eyes; the light threw shadows over his face and made them stand out clear. They made him look older, somehow, and tired.

Bitter Creek took my attention away from Emmett when he pulled the saved-back bottle of whiskey out of his saddlebag and started handing it around. Everyone took to drinking and talking at once then, remarking on the ease of the job and the size of the haul we'd taken, while Bob sat by the door with his rifle across his knees, watching us with a funny little smile on his face. I guessed we'd done well by him that night and showed him we could follow his orders.

I offered Emmett the bottle after I took a good drink from it, but he shook his head. He'd been real quiet since we got in and after a bit he got up and put his coat back on, and his hat. He took his saddlebags over his shoulder and headed for the door after giving me a quick nod.

Bob stopped him from going out. "Wait just a minute, Em, where you off to? The law might be out."

I saw Emmett look him square in the eye. "I'll be careful, Bob," I heard him say. "I need to clear my head."

Bob got a real suspicious look on his face then. "You ain't just going out for some air," he said. "What're you up to?"

Emmett sighed, then spoke, low. "I'm going to go see Mother, Bob. Just for a bit. It's been too long and God knows she's probably worried out of her skull by now."

Bob took him by the arm and pulled him outside so they could talk alone. After a few minutes, Bob came back in by himself, so I figured he must've let him go.

We stayed the night there, all of us good and liquored up, and it took some time for everyone to get up and get going the next day. The dugout was so dark that ten in the morning looked the same as ten at night, so I was a little astonished when I finally dragged myself outside and pulled my watch out of my vest pocket, squinting bleary-eyed at it in the bright sunshine. It read twelve-sixteen in the afternoon.

Bob never seemed to show his liquor like the rest of us, and he'd taken a careful look around before he let any of us leave, just in case we'd somehow led the law to us last night. When he was satisfied things were clear, he told us he'd come see us for the next job, once he decided on one. He said we'd all done well by him last night and we were all welcome the next time out, if we cared to come along. We all told him we did. Bill Power and Dick Broadwell left together, and once Creek and I had managed to get Charley put together enough to ride, we took our leave, too. I asked Bob if he'd like to join us for a bit, seeing as how he'd be on his own once we went, but he said he needed to stay and wait for Emmett. He had a troubled look on his face when he said it and I could tell he was worried that Em might get himself caught, coming or going, but he didn't say so.

"You boys be careful, now. Stay clear of the law," he told us, and we nodded solemnly, bidding him to do the same but knowing he'd have no trouble doing it. Bob Dalton had a sixth sense when it came to the law and he always knew how to evade it. We mounted up and headed out, our heads aching and our share of the haul burning holes in our pockets.

We traveled along slow for awhile, not in any particular hurry to get back to Creek's claim, which was still a hard two days' ride away. Once the whiskey wore off we started talking about spending some of our newfound wealth, and we decided to head into Ingalls to see about celebrating a little. Creek knew a good saloon there and figured we could get into a poker game.

We put our horses up at the livery, leaving them saddled, and then went to get a paper to see what they were saying. There was a big article on the Leliaetta job, and it credited it to the Dalton Gang. When we were done reading it over, we ventured into the saloon Creek favored for awhile, playing poker with a couple locals. After a bit we went to get some supper at one of the restaurants, keeping one eye out for anything funny while we did so. No one even gave us a second glance, so we started to relax some.

When we were coming out of the restaurant, I caught sight of a young woman coming out of a dressmaker's place aways up the gallery. She was dressed in dark blue calico sprinkled with little white flowers and trimmed with lace, and had thick black hair done up in braids that were coiled around and pinned into a big knot at the back of her head. When she turned toward me I paused a minute, because her face was so lovely I felt struck by it. She must've felt me looking at her, 'cause her huge brown eyes met mine for an instant, and then she looked away, quick. I thought I saw her cheeks go pink just before she did. She had an apron on over her dress and she took it off, bundling it up under her arm, and I saw her pull a thimble off her finger, so she must've been working in the shop. She smoothed her skirts down in a sort of prim way and walked away from us, a lot faster than I figure she needed to.

Bitter Creek had seen the whole thing and was looking sideways at me. "Oh, no," he said, shaking his head. "Don't you go getting any ideas, Bill."

I was craning my neck to look after the woman and it took me a few minutes to respond. "What are you talking about, Creek?" I said innocently.

"You know exactly what I'm talking about, Doolin," he said with a chuckle. "Leave that one alone. She ain't your type."

"How the hell do you know?" I retorted.

"Because of who her daddy is," Creek said, laughing a little harder now. Charley was grinning, too, like he was in on some secret.

"Lawdog?" I asked, arching an eyebrow at them.

"No, but maybe worse, considering," Creek

said. "Preacher. So in other words, you're just about the worst thing that little girl could encounter." He slapped me on the back, hard. "Forget it, Bill. Let's find you something to get your mind off her." His grin got even more wicked and he headed for the red light district, Charley at his heels.

I followed them, but only after I could no longer see the girl in blue anymore.

———◉———

As it turned out, the whorehouse did not help in taking my mind of that pretty young woman I'd seen, and I found myself heading toward the dressmaker's shop the next day, hoping I'd catch a glimpse of her again. After Bitter Creek had had a good amount of whiskey last night I'd been able to get him to tell me her name—Edith Ellsworth. He didn't know her personally but a few locals he was acquainted with had talked about how her Pa had been hoping to get a good church going in Ingalls but was finding it hard, since a lot of unsavory types like us liked to spend our money and time there. He supported his family by doing different kinds of work, like going for the mail and taking carpentry jobs. He had a farm in Lawson, too, but he'd had bad luck with crops, so she'd started working for wages last year to help them out, first at McMurtry's drug store, then at the dressmaker's. She was nineteen and unmarried.

I milled around near the dressmaker's for awhile, and I caught a glimpse of her inside through the windows. She was sitting in a chair in the corner sewing on something, and she never raised her head from her work, not even once. After awhile, folks who passed by started to give me looks I didn't like, so I decided to go find Creek and Charley. Besides, I thought to myself, I'd shot a man in Coffeyville, robbed a train, and was planning on robbing more of them—there wasn't any way in hell she'd want to associate with me. Creek was right, I knew, and all my fool mooning over her would do would be to get me caught.

We rode out of Ingalls a short time later, and I made myself put her out of my mind.

SEVEN

WE HAD A mild winter and even milder spring, when 1891 turned into 1892, and as the seasons came and went we laid low and waited for the day when we'd hear from Bob about our next time out. Turned out part of the delay was caused by Grat Dalton, that infamous bad-tempered brother of Em and Bob's I hadn't met yet.

Right after we pulled the job at Leliaetta, as it happened, Grat managed to bust his way out of jail in California. I knew from Emmett that Grat had been wrongfully convicted; he hadn't been with them at Alila when they'd tried their first train job. But even though there'd been several witnesses to put him in Fresno the night the job went off, the state had been out for Dalton blood and so they'd pegged him for it. It seemed to me, when I read about it, that they didn't give a damn which brother they put in the calaboose, so long as the last name was Dalton.

So Grat cooled his heels in a cell and stewed in his rage at being put away for something he didn't do, and then the Dalton brother that no one ever seemed to give much credit to for thinking things through managed to plan and pull off one hell of a jail-break. Once out, he got ahold of a horse and a gun and rode hell-bent for leather back to the Territory to join Bob and Em, making it there in such good time he might as well have sprouted wings and flown. I first heard about it from Bitter Creek, who'd been out to the dug-out to see Bob when Grat showed up out of nowhere, shocking the hell out of them. Em was gone to town that afternoon, and Charley and I were in Kingfisher, so it was just Creek and Bob at the dugout when Grat arrived, dirty and bedraggled and full of hatred for anything to do with the law. There would be eight of us out, come the next job.

We figured now that Grat was back it would be any time that Bob settled on something, but more weeks came and went and we had no word. Heck Thomas and his posse were on their trail like hunting hounds and so they had to keep moving all over the place to avoid capture, and Bob didn't have time to think of anything besides staying one step ahead of them. Creek and Charley and I laid low, abandoning the old shanty for a time and moving around a lot ourselves, just in case.

For some reason I kept thinking about the girl I'd seen in Ingalls, and it riled me up some because I hadn't spoken to her or even met her proper, so why couldn't I let it go? There were plenty of women around who didn't care a lick about what I'd been doing with myself, and what I planned on doing, but I knew this one *would* care. I needed to do like Creek said and forget her. Instead, I found myself saddling my horse one day and riding into Ingalls alone, hoping maybe I'd actually get to talk to her, this time. Maybe she'd say right off she didn't want anything to do with me, and I could get myself shed of the idea.

I put my horse up at the livery like usual, and, like usual, I took a good stock of the folks going about their business as I walked toward Main Street, just to make sure no one looked twice at me. We were lucky in those days; a lot of people living in the Territories, and in Ingalls in particular, were sympathetic to our vendetta against the railroad and as a result they covered for us, warned us when anyone with a tin star was on our trail, or even put the law off our tracks when they came around asking questions, but even so, we couldn't any of us be too careful. I saw nothing amiss and kept going, heading for the section of the street where Edith's dressmaker had her shop. I found it funny that I felt more nervous doing that than I had when I was about to hold up a train for the first time.

I sort of strolled casually by and glanced in the window when I did. Disappointment came over me because I saw no sign of Edith inside, and the chair she was sitting in doing her sewing that last time I'd been there was empty. The woman that owned the shop, Mrs. McAllister, was leaning over the big table she used for cutting out fabric, and she had some kind of shiny black cloth spread out over it. When she picked up her big scissors and went to cut it she looked up just as I was peering in, and she gave me a frown, like she knew I was up to no good, so I kept going, thinking about how big a fool I was to have come all this way for nothing.

I walked a little ways up the gallery, my hands in my pockets. The little bit of money I had left from the Leliaetta job was jingling in them, going along with the sound of my spurs as I walked, and I thought about heading for the saloon and getting into a card game to take my mind off my reason for coming.

Just as I walked past the general mercantile store, none other than Edith Ellsworth walked out of it. She was carrying a big armful of packages and heading for a wagon and mule hitched at the rail in front of the store. She was alone, looked like, with all those things to load up. After I came to from my surprise at seeing her there I took my chance and boldly hurried to her side.

"Looks like you could use a hand, Miss Ellsworth," I said politely, and she turned toward me in surprise. "Let me help you with those." Before she could say anything I'd reached for the two packages on top of her armful and put them in the wagon.

"Thank you," she said in a shy voice, letting me take the rest from her and load them into the wagon box. I touched a hand to my hat brim in response and hoped I didn't look too shabby from the trail. "How do you know my name?" she asked me, and it took me a minute to find my voice to answer her, because up close she was even prettier than I'd first thought.

"A few friends of mine come into town a lot and know who your Pa is," I told her. I gave her a smile. "I'm Bill Doolin."

"Edith Ellsworth," she said. Her cheeks went pink and she looked down a minute. She had the longest, thickest eyelashes I'd ever seen, and her hair looked like spun silk. I swallowed hard; my mouth felt suddenly dry. "I saw you in town awhile back," she told me, surprising me. Seemed she'd noticed me too, that day I'd noticed her.

"I saw you, too," I said, and wanted to kick myself. This conversation was becoming downright stupid, and I was pretty sure she'd end up taking me for a complete fool.

We kind of stood there for a few minutes, both of us unsure what to say. I had never been at a loss with a woman before, but then, I'd not talked to a young woman like her, from a good family, in a good long while. Lately it seemed the only women I'd been around were saloon girls and the ones that made their living in the cribs at the other end of town.

"You know that cowboy that comes into town a lot, the one with the red hair, don't you?" she suddenly asked me.

"You must mean Creek," I said to her, and she looked confused. "We call him Bitter Creek," I told her. "It's after a song he sings a lot. His real name's George."

"Oh," she said. "Some folks say he's trouble. He and his friends."

"He's harmless," I said, watching as she raised a slender little hand and tucked a stray lock of that thick hair behind her ear. She was wearing little jet earbobs and they swayed against the curve of her jaw.

She gave me a pointed look. "Are *you* harmless, Mr. Doolin?" The corners of her lips curved up a smile so quick I almost wasn't sure I'd seen it, but I definitely heard the shy tease in her voice.

"Relatively," I replied. I couldn't help it, I gave

her a grin. I'd already decided it wouldn't do no good to try to act like something I wasn't. I'd use my best manners—I still remembered them, when it came down to it—but I wasn't going to act like I was some saint. If I were to win over this girl with a bunch of lies, she'd up and leave when she learned the truth of it. I waited to see how she'd react.

To my relief, she smiled at me again and her eyes danced a little. "I guess I'll take you at your word," she said.

We stood there looking at each other for a minute, like we were sizing each other up. Then I cleared my throat quick and shifted my weight from one boot to the other. Before I could speak, she took a real deep breath and smoothed her palms against the skirt of her dress. She was wearing brown calico today, and it had tiny pink roses all over it. "Well, thank you for the help, Mr. Doolin," she said in an almost brisk voice, like she'd suddenly remembered that I wasn't the type of man her folks thought she should be associating with.

"It's Bill, Miss Ellsworth, and it was no trouble. Do you have a long way to go?"

"Oh, no. Our farm's not too far from town," she said. "My Pa normally goes for these supplies but he's laid up with a sprained ankle right now." She was taking good and fast, almost like she'd gotten nervous. She gave me another smile, but it was a real quick one, and then went around to the front of the wagon, untying the mule from the hitching rail.

I followed her, not wanting our conversation to end like this—or end at all, to tell the truth. "It was nice to meet you," I said warmly, and I meant it. She took the driving reins in hand and went to climb up into the seat, putting her foot on a rung of the wagon wheel. I moved to help her but she didn't need it; she was up and settled before I could even offer.

"It was nice to meet you, too," she said, looking down at me and smiling. Her eyes were dancing again and I felt better. I guessed that she'd heard whispers in town about me and Creek and Charley—our names were starting to be thrown around a lot with the Daltons'—but something made me think she didn't care as much about all that as her folks probably did.

"I'll see you again," I said, boldly. I knew I would; I would make it happen.

"Will you?" she asked, raising her eyebrows at me.

"Next time I'm in town. I'll look you up at the dressmaker's—unless you're afraid to be seen with me." I pushed my hat back a little on my head and stood there with one hand on my hip, looking up at her. I let a big grin come out on my face again and I knew my eyes were twinkling back at hers.

"Oh, no, I'm not afraid to be seen with you at all, Bill," she said, still smiling, and I liked the way my name sounded when she said it. "Maybe you and yours will be afraid to be seen with *me*, though. You said you know who my Pa is."

"Don't bother me none," I said. "I got nothing against the man upstairs."

She laughed aloud at that, it didn't seem like she could help it. Then she flicked the reins across the mule's back. The wagon started off, and I stood back, watching. Then I realized I was standing in the middle of the street with a big, dumb grin on my face, and I went quickly back onto the gallery, continuing on toward the saloon. I flipped a silver dollar up in the air as I entered through the swinging doors, whistling under my breath and looking around for a poker game to join. I was feeling pretty damned lucky, right about then.

EIGHT

WE NEVER WENT back to the old claim shanty again, as it turned out. Creek couldn't prove up on the land because he'd never even cleared it for crops, let alone planted anything, so he relinquished it in March. The three of us went to hole up with Bill Power and Dick Broadwell on Power's claim, and it was there that the Dalton boys finally hunted us up one night in late May.

I was sitting at the table with a pile of bullets and the lamp nearby; I was supposed to have been cleaning my guns but I was too busy thinking about Edith to finish anything I started doing. I'd been thinking a lot about her lately, mainly because I'd become determined to somehow court her proper, but I wasn't sure how to go about it, seeing as how that would involve her folks in the matter.

I'd seen her quite a few times since that day we'd met outside the general store; and I was good and smitten with her by then. Funny thing was, she was with me, too. I wasn't sure how I'd gotten so lucky, but I didn't waste time wondering on it, instead I just tried to enjoy it as best I could.

Just last week we'd walked together outside of town for a long while after she got done at the dressmakers', and we'd spent our time talking. She wanted to know more about me, and I told her I'd been a cowhand most of my life, and been the foreman on a couple of ranches. I said I'd left the cattle trade the year before last because the railroad was killing off the need for men like me in it. It was all the truth, but I glossed it over real good, of course, and I left out the Fourth of July party in Coffeyville, and the Daltons and the Katy train.

I tried to explain to her some about what I felt for the railroad, though, so she might have some idea of where I was coming from in case she read anything unsavory in the papers. Turned out I didn't need to, because her family shared my feelings—though not quite as strongly. She told me her Ma and Pa had had their land in Kansas grabbed by a railroad company. It had set them back a lot and they'd had to push on, coming out to the Oklahoma Territory during the land rush of '89. She told me they felt they could've done well in Kansas; their farm had good rich soil and showed a lot of promise for crops, and if it weren't for the railroad, they might be a lot better off than they were now.

I felt a lot of relief when she told me this; it made me feel like maybe she'd understand in some way if she ever found out about Leliaetta, or anything else we might do in the future. She had, I'd found, a way of being able to look at things from all sides, and she didn't let the opinions of her Ma and Pa or their like color her judgement. She made up her own mind about things, and that included me. I was damned grateful for that; if she'd been like most women of her upbringing, I wouldn't have had a snowflake's chance in hell with her.

Creek and Charley, and now Bill Power and Dick, knew about Edith and me, and once all their good-natured teasing died down, they became a little worried about the whole thing. Creek had told me so, straight out, just the night before last.

"You thought about what might happen if she finds out for sure what we've been doing? Or her folks? Hell, Bill, they could give us up to the damned Guardsmen and their posses, easy."

"She don't know where we're staying, Creek," I'd snapped back at him, getting testy about the whole thing. "And I think she *does* know what we are. She's got no love for the railroad. She won't say anything."

REBECCA ROCKWELL

"How do you *know* that?" he'd pressed.

"I just *know*." I'd leaned forward in the chair I was sitting in, looking him straight in the eyes. "You trust me, don't you, Creek?" I'd asked him.

He'd worked his jaw back and forth for a minute before he answered. "Yes, I trust you. I guess you've shown you know what you're doing." He'd heaved a heavy sigh. "I'm glad for you, Bill, but the gang—"

I cut him off. "This ain't got anything to do with the gang. So I'd be much obliged if you wouldn't say anything to Bob Dalton about this." My voice sounded hard, even to me, but I had to be firm. If Bob found out about Edith, he'd probably cut me out of the gang for fear she would turn on us.

He sighed again and crossed his arms over his chest, sitting back in his chair. "I won't say anything, and neither will Charley or the others. I just hope it works out like you want it to."

"It will," I'd told him, as he struck a match and lit the cigarette he'd rolled.

Now, two nights later, I was still studying on just *how* I was gonna make it work out like I wanted, when out of nowhere, I heard that shrill, two-note whistle we'd been waiting on for months.

"Creek," I said, sharp, "you hear that?"

He'd been counting his money at the other end of the table; when the whistle came he stood up and stuffed the thin stack of bills into his vest pocket, fast. "It's about damn time," he said under his breath. He looked over at the other three, who were all stretched out on the floor in their bedrolls. "Charley, Bill, Dick, wake the hell up!" he said loudly.

"What is it?" Dick asked groggily.

"The Daltons," I said tensely, and put away my guns. Outside, three horses moved past the dirty glass window, and I heard low, indistinct voices, along with the squeak of saddle-leather and the jingling of spurs as they all dismounted.

Charley, Bill Power and Dick shook themselves awake and pulled their galluses up over their shoulders, then came over to the table in their stocking feet.

The door opened and Bob and Emmett came inside, followed by a third man who must've been Grat.

I eyed him from where I sat. He was tall, like Bob and Em, but he wasn't as slender as they were and looked a good deal older than both of them. He had hair the same color as Bob's, but his eyes were a lot paler blue than Bob's were, and he wore a mustache, while his brothers were clean-shaven. And while Bob and Emmett were both handsome fellows and cut dashing figures, Grat had a much rougher edge on him, and he wore his fabled unpleasant disposition on his face. I could tell before he even said a single word that the things we'd heard about him were probably all true, and seeing him standing there next to Em gave me pause; it was hard to believe they shared the same blood.

"Evenin' boys," Bob said breezily. "Been awhile. You all been occupying yourselves well, I trust?"

We all nodded and greeted him, and then he gestured to Grat. "This is our brother Grat, boys. Broke himself out of jail in California and lived to tell about it, and he'll be joinin' us from now on." He introduced each one of us to Grat then, and he nodded at us all and give us a short, terse greeting. He clearly didn't like to talk much and when he did he spoke in a gravely, heavy voice that matched his expression. I felt for him though, when all was said and done— even though he didn't say so I knew jail had to have been pretty close to hell on earth, and I guessed I would have a pretty big chip on my shoulder, too, if I'd been in his position, locked up like that without any cause to be.

Bob pulled a chair up to the table. "We got ourselves another train to take, boys, and word is she's gonna have the biggest haul yet in her express car."

"How big?" Creek asked, raising one eyebrow.

"Seventy thousand, if my information's correct," Bob said calmly. He was talking in that low way he did sometimes, like he knew we'd all lean forward to hear his words and not miss anything he said.

"Holy Jesus!" Dick breathed, and the others echoed his reaction, looking at each other with excited grins. If that were true, we'd all be rich as kings after this.

"When and where?" I asked, speaking up for the first time.

"The Santa Fe train, at Red Rock, on the second of June."

Creek threw back his head and laughed. "Same train we took at Wharton! What a joke."

Bob gave him a sly, smug smile. "Thought you'd find that funny, Creek." His eyes shone out in the lamplight and I thought he looked pretty damned proud of himself for having concocted this latest scheme. Behind him, Emmett turned away from the table and busied himself with taking a long drink from the dipper in the water pail. It was clear his attitude toward our activities hadn't changed any since I'd last seen him. Grat, however, looked both amused and proud of Bob, standing to one side of him with this arms crossed over his chest. After a minute he lit a cigarillo and drew in a slow lungful of smoke. The lamplight illuminated the hollows in his cheeks and the heavy circles under his eyes, both of them relics, I imagined, of his escape and hard journey back.

I pondered him out of the corner of my eye for a minute, thinking on how it was sure looking like he let Bob lead him just like Emmett did, even though he was clearly so much older than Bob. Bob was smart, all right, and cunning, and just about the best shot I'd ever laid eyes on, but whatever that charisma was he had that made them follow him like a couple of leashed hound dogs was lost on me and I still thought him too full of himself and too power-hungry. I wouldn't cross him unless he gave me cause to; I'd defer to him as our leader—but that didn't mean I had to like it any.

Dick and Charley and Bill Power were all still stuck on the amount of the haul and were jabbering at each other like a bunch prairie chickens. Bob frowned at them and leaned back in his chair. "Damn it, get ahold of yourselves and listen up," he barked. "We got to follow this plan to the letter if this is gonna work."

They quieted and turned their attention back to Bob right quick, and I fought the urge to laugh. Creek was still standing at the head of the table, across from me, and I could tell he was amused, too, by the way his eyes were dancing in the glow from the lamp, but he kept his ever-present laughter in check for once and waited to see what Bob would say.

Grat shifted his weight, deliberately, and spoke

for the first time since his introduction to us. "Go ahead, Bob."

Bob knitted his long fingers together on the table-top and started talking. "When the train stops at Red Rock, Em and I will jump on into the engine and get them to stop her at the stockyards, where the rest of you'll be waiting. Then Em, Grat and I will attend to the express car while Creek and Bill"—he looked at me and I nodded—"will cover the front cars. Dick, you and Power will be on either side of her, covering the passengers. Then I give the signal like usual, and we'll be on our way, plain and simple."

"Any sign of Thomas, Tilghman or Madsen in the area?" I asked, wanting to know whatever Bob knew about whomever was on our trail.

He looked at me, one eyebrow arched, like he was surprised I was asking. "They been sniffing around some, but I ain't worried they're gonna get us, if that's what you're asking." His tone was dismissive. He wouldn't give me any specifics, like he thought I didn't deserve to know, and that lowered my opinion of him just a little bit more. I held myself in check, though; it wouldn't do me a damn bit of good to try his patience. And he *had* shown himself to be good at keeping the law off our trail so far. It took some doing, but I held my tongue.

Bob told us when and where to meet up, and then

we all shared some whiskey. Grat, I would discover, liked whiskey a whole hell of a lot and could drink any one of us far under the table if we let him. Trouble was, if we ever let him get that deep into a bottle it made him even more ornery than usual, and since none of us cared to tangle with him, we got to be pretty careful about how much liquor we had around at any given time.

As they drank, I glanced up and saw Emmett go outside. I wanted to talk to him alone, make sure he was getting along all right. I was still protective of him; it was a habit I'd gotten into at the ranch and I found it a hard one to get shed of. I waited a few minutes, and when Bob was occupied with the whiskey bottle and listening to one of Bitter Creek's wild yarns, I slipped outside, too.

"Em?" I whispered, looking around and squinting while my eyes adjusted to the darkness. The moon was partially hidden over by clouds and it wasn't too bright out. I found him standing by the water trough, letting his horse drink.

"You all right, Em?" I asked, keeping my voice light.

"Just fine, Bill," he said, but he didn't sound very sincere. I reached out and let my hand run over the horse's neck. It lifted its head from the trough, poking its wet muzzle at me, hoping for something to eat. Emmett chuckled softly in the darkness and reached into his britches pocket. "Here." He handed me something, and when I opened my hand I saw it was a lump of sugar.

I laughed softly and let the horse lip it up out of my palm. "You still carry sugar in your pockets for your horses, Em? I stopped doing that when I started wearing long pants," I teased good-naturedly.

"You never know when you might need to bribe a horse, Bill," he told me with mock-seriousness, and for the first time since he'd left the ranch he sounded like the Emmett I'd taken under my wing.

I laughed and kept patting the horse as it put its head back down and started cropping grass. Emmett let it, even though we both knew it was probably getting the bit all choked up with weeds.

"I hear you found yourself a girl in Ingalls," Emmett said suddenly, out of nowhere.

I almost dropped my jaw on the ground, I was so surprised. "How in the hell did you hear that?

I could almost hear the smile in his voice when he answered me. "Bob and Grat and I went into Ingalls a few days ago, and I was talking with John Murray," he said, naming the bartender at the Ransom & Murray, the saloon we all frequented. "He said you'd taken up with a preacher's daughter." He chuckled again. "Pretty bold, Bill." I could hear the tease in his voice.

I grinned wide at him, even though I knew it was really too dark for him to see it. "I can't help who her Pa is, can I?" Inside, I was a little nervous. Sounded like maybe Bob knew about me and Edith, which was the last thing I wanted to happen.

"No, I guess you can't. And if she'll have you, what does it matter? I'm happy for you, Bill." There was some new tone in his voice now, something that I couldn't put my finger on. Was it envy?

I stepped out of the way a bit as the horse swung its head closer to my boots, wanting to get at the grass I was standing in. "You haven't found yourself a girl yet, then, Em?" I asked lightly.

He was quiet for a minute and I was afraid I might have upset him. But then he spoke and his voice was real soft. "I did, actually. It was when we were out in California, staying with our brother Will. I had to break it off with her because of Alila." His voice got real matter-of-fact. He didn't say so, but I knew it had been Bob's doing, because of all of his plans for them, and the fact that they'd had to get the hell out of California or risk getting caught once they'd tried the Alilia job.

"I'm sorry, Emmett. Sounds like you cared for her pretty good."

"I did. But there ain't nothing for it. I shouldn't have gotten close to her in the first place, not with—"

He stopped talking abruptly and I knew it was because he didn't want to say anything about the gang, or anything disloyal to Bob. Before I could answer him he spoke again, quick. "Wasn't meant to be, I suppose," he said, and I saw him shrug his shoulders. "Hope you have better luck with yours. Sounds like a real sweet girl."

"She is," I said. "I ain't too sure how things are gonna work with us, but I'm bound and determined to figure it out."

He was quiet for a minute, and he reached out to take his horse up; we could tell from the way it was chewing that it couldn't fit anymore grass in its mouth around the bit. "What's her name, Bill?" he asked me, out of nowhere.

"Edith," I said. "Yours?"

He sighed. "Laura. Come on, we should probably get back inside. If Grat gets drunk Bob and I are gonna pay for it later." He clicked his tongue at the horse and led it over to where Bob's and Grat's were tied, muttering at it under his breath and yanking long tufts of grass out of its mouth.

I followed him after a bit, my hands in my pockets, thinking about how it was too bad Em had had to leave his girl behind in California because of something he really didn't want to be doing, when all was said and done.

NINE

THERE WAS A kind of electricity in the air between us on the night we met up for the Red Rock job, and I knew it was because of the size of the haul that would soon be filling the feed sack Bob had tucked up in his coat. We were tense, keyed up, our hearts going fast like we'd been running, even though all we were doing was getting ourselves positioned here and there around the station, ready to spring.

We all had our guns at the ready as usual, our faces well-covered with our neckerchiefs, our hats pulled way down. Most of the boys were a little more jumpy than usual tonight, but they were ready and the plan was good and clear in their minds.

For my part, I was focused on the task at hand. I never had any trouble staying on target during a job, never found myself thinking about anything but doing what I needed to do to get in and out clean and not get myself or anyone with me caught. So I didn't notice right away that Bob wasn't acting the way he usually did.

Normally just as focused as me, and as cool and calm as if he'd been holding up trains all of his twenty-three years instead of just the last one, that night Bob seemed unsettled and spooked, and it turned out to be because the hair on the back of his neck was standing on end and he had a feeling something was wrong.

He said so the minute the train rolled up, instead of giving the signal. In fact, when Charley started to move forward automatically as the train came, Bob reached out and checked him, roughly, throwing his arm out across Charley's chest and sort of shoving him back into the shadows. Behind them, Grat tensed up; I heard his boots scuff against the hard-packed dirt as he moved. The others all looked to Bob, too, and Charley looked too surprised to protest.

"Something don't look right to me."

Bob's voice was quiet, but it was as tense as a tether pulled taut and about to break. The train rolled to a slow stop, steam wafting up around it.

Charley came to from his surprise and shifted impatiently. "Ain't you gonna give the signal sometime this *year*, Bob? She's gonna leave before we get ourselves situated!" Even whispered, his voice sounded almost shrill and I could hear the panic in it. Charley wanted that haul bad, just like we all did, and our chances of taking it were getting slimmer and slimmer with each second that went by.

"Shut up, Charley, and stay where you are," Bob hissed, his voice hard. "That train ain't the one we want. Something's wrong with it." There was iron in his tone, like that was that.

My brows came together in disbelief. *Bob* had planned this, *Bob* had picked this train. And now he didn't want to go after it, with it sitting right there in front of us? I felt my fingers curl so hard around the grips of my revolver that they began to ache, and I felt anger come up in me and make my chest feel tight, like I couldn't breathe proper. I didn't let myself get good and mad too often; I'd seen blind anger cause too many men a whole lot of trouble they didn't figure on, but right then I was seething. I'd gotten the idea in my head that my share of the haul from this job would get me money enough that I could someday consider asking Edith to marry me—someday soon. The idea of the railroad that had wronged us both financing our new life together seemed rather fitting to me. But if we let it go, we'd likely never have a chance like it again, and the loss would be Bob's fault.

"What the hell are you talking about, Bob?" I hissed, knowing my anger was sounding out plain in my voice, even though I was near to whispering. "You know damn well she's got a bigger haul than anything we ever took in that express car! If we miss our chance—"

"Go ahead, Doolin!" Bob suddenly snapped, cutting me off. "You want that train so bad, there she is! Take her by yourself, if you want her. *I ain't going,* and neither is any man who's with me. See if I shed any damn tears if you get yourself shot up or thrown in some calaboose." I saw his fist clench around the handle of his gun, same as mine was doing, and his voice was coming out like a growl, now. Fighting words. I was near to seeing red.

It was Emmett who broke the tension, Emmett who made me see reason. His voice came out of the shadows at Bob's left shoulder, low and calm. "Easy, Bob. Put your horns away. You too, Bill. Bob's right, something's wrong with that train."

I looked at the train then, too irritated to have done so good and thorough before. And I saw what was bothering Bob—the passenger cars, which normally would have been aglow with the light of lanterns hanging along their ceilings, were dark. A shiver went up my spine and I realized Bob was right.

"She's too dark," Grat confirmed in his gruff voice.

The train let out another few big puffs of steam,

the wheels starting to roll forward, slow at first and then faster. "There she goes," Bitter Creek said softly, as we watched it pull out of the station. I sat back on my heels as the express car, with its seventy thousand dollars still secure in the safe, streaked past in the moonlight. The train's whistle sounded, wolves and coyotes answering from somewhere out in the prairie.

"Well, what'll we do now?" Dick asked. We didn't have to whisper any longer. I could tell he was disappointed, too, just like Creek and Charley and Bill Power. We all stood up, our guns dangling limply at our sides.

"We wait," Bob said. "We'll take the next one, when she comes."

I rolled my eyes freely in the dark, knowing he wouldn't see it. "What if there's no cash in the next one?" I snapped. Even though I knew Bob had likely been right to let the train go, it still irked me all to hell that a man ten years my junior figured he had me under his thumb good enough to dress me down that way in front of my friends.

"Then I suppose we'll consider it a practice run," he snapped right back, giving me a hard stare. He took a step past Emmett, who'd tried to move between us. "You don't like the way I do things, Doolin, just say so. You're free to quit, anytime." His tone was good and dark now, and I could tell he was just about ready to call me out. My finger moved toward the trigger of my revolver, like it had a mind of its own.

I didn't raise the gun, though. Mad as I was, I had no desire to get into a gunfight with Bob Dalton. I knew I was a good shot; far better than good, to tell the God's honest truth of it, but Bob was downright exceptional, and there was no way in hell I'd challenge him, especially not now, like this, in the dark of night in front of a train station we'd been set to hold up.

"Bob…" Emmett said nervously, from where he stood next to Grat. I felt the tension around us like something I could pick up with my bare hands. Out of the corner of my eye I saw Creek edge toward Bob in a vaguely threatening manner, the bullets in his gun belt catching the moonlight, and I felt a little better, knowing at least he was on my side. Creek was one of the most affable men I'd ever met; he liked all of us, but I knew he considered me and Charley closer friends than all the rest, and it was nice to see him show it when it counted.

I forced myself to back down then, and I let out a slow breath. I held one palm out, slowly put my gun in my holster, and then raised up the other palm, holding them out toward him. "Don't get riled up, Dalton," I said, making my voice good and calm.

It took some doing. "I'll stand behind you. I guess you've shown you know best."

Bob stared at me for a minute, that funny regal stare of his that was like a sign saying "I'm the boss!" Then he put his own gun away, giving me a slow nod. I read the message in it: *next time you ain't getting off so easy.* He turned away from me then, a pointed gesture, almost as if to say I wasn't worth dealing with any further, and turned his attention back to the track, waiting on the next train.

As we moved back into the shadows to crouch back down into our positions again, Creek walked past me and put a bracing hand on my shoulder before dropping it quick so Bob wouldn't notice.

When the next train came, we were ready.

———————— ((◉)) ————————

We got in and out of the next train clean, but no one who'd been in the express car was hopped up like usual after a successful job; they were almost grim as they came back onto the platform, and I knew right away there wouldn't be much to divvy up once we got back to the hideout. I sprang up into my saddle along with the rest of them, almost like we'd spent time practicing how to time our mounts perfect, and heeled my horse hard, getting him going into a dead run right off. I wanted to outrun this whole miserable night. Part of me considered not even joining up with the others and refusing my share of whatever we'd taken, but I knew that if I did, that would probably be the end of my career in the Dalton Gang, so I forced myself to follow the others.

We crowded into yet another dugout; the Daltons seemed to have a whole handful of them around the territories. Then Bob faced us all and spoke. "I'm afraid it don't look good, boys. We'll do some better next time." His words didn't soften the blow none when he took the money out of his pocket—there'd been no need for the sack.

"Fifty damned dollars," Creek said with a snort of disgust. "What's that, six-twenty-five apiece? That trip wasn't worth the wear it put on our nags' shoes."

Bob arched an eyebrow at him. "Better that than not a dime. You want your share or don't you?"

Creek laughed then, but it wasn't his usual brand of it. "What the hell, I helped, didn't I?"

Bob suddenly shocked of all of us by bursting into laughter himself—and it was good-natured laughter. "Aww, hell, I ain't got any quarters."

The remark broke the tension and our bad moods, and the rest of us started chuckling. Pretty soon we were all laughing, even Emmett, and even Grat, who hardly ever laughed, as far as I could tell.

I wiped the water out of my eyes and took what he handed me—six dollars. And I'd hoped for near to nine thousand. I shook my head and headed for the door, shouldering my saddlebags and tucking my rifle under my arm. Dick had a whiskey bottle but I left him and the others to it, bidding a carefully deferential goodbye to Bob as I passed him. I had to grit my teeth a bit when I did it, but I managed to sound sincere. He nodded to me and didn't mention our little scuffle—instead he just said "see you the next time out." I felt a little better then. I said goodbye to Emmett just before I went out. He looked worried, and he looked like he wanted to come after me, too, but he didn't.

I was heading cautiously over to the rickety corral where we'd tethered the horses—there was no stable at this hideout—when I heard footsteps behind me. "Bill, hold up a minute." It was Creek's voice. He and Charley were coming toward me. They had their saddlebags, too, and their Winchesters.

"If you're leavin', then so are we," Charley said firmly, and Creek nodded.

"You could stay if you wanted. Have some of that whiskey Dick brought," I said. I didn't want it to seem like I was trying to coax them into taking sides.

"Dick only ever gets ahold of cheap whiskey," Creek explained. I saw him grin wickedly at me. "Hell, if we three pool our six dollars, we can get us a bottle of *good* stuff for once!"

"Nothing ever gets you down, does it, Creek?" I asked, smiling as we all got into our saddles and started off though the tall grasses.

"Not at the present," he said. "But I might get sore if you two don't take me up on my fine idea."

"By all means, then, let's go hunt up the most fancy-Dan whiskey we can find," I said with a grin of my own. I was feeling a lot better about that time. I might not be rich like I'd planned, but at least I had good friends with me, and there were few things in life more important than that.

Just a few days later we all learned that as hard as it had been to let that train go, it had likely saved all our lives, for Heck Thomas and a few dozen other lawmen had been hidden inside it, all armed to the teeth, figuring we'd try to take the small fortune in the express car.

TEN

WHEN I RODE into Ingalls a week after Red Rock to meet up with Edith one Saturday afternoon, she was waiting for me under the big cottonwood tree just outside of town, where we usually met up. She had her Pa's mare under saddle that day and we planned to take a horseback ride together by the river. She was all excited when she saw me; her eyes were lit up and she had a rosy flush spread out over her cheeks.

I dismounted and took my hat off so I could kiss her proper, and I smiled at her wide. "Now, what's got you so excited?" I asked her, putting my hat back on.

"There's a midsummer social planned in town next Friday," she told me. "They're going to have a fiddle-player. There'll be dancing, and some of the ladies are making cakes. Ma and Pa and I are going. I thought maybe you could come—it'd be a chance for you to meet my folks."

I felt my grin fade just a little. I knew sooner or later I'd have to meet Edith's parents; she'd already told me they were getting pretty disapproving of her keeping company with a young man they hadn't met yet, but the idea of it made me damned nervous. I knew they had no love for the railroad, and it wasn't like I was going to introduce myself as 'Bill Doolin, train-robber and Dalton Gang member,' but the fact of it was that most folks around Ingalls knew exactly what I'd been doing with my time, and who me and the others had been riding with. I'd have to charm Edith's parents good if I wanted them to continue to allow Edith to see me, and hope that they were on the side of the all the folks in the area who were sympathetic to our doings. Edith was a grown woman, having just turned twenty a few weeks ago, but she lived under their roof still and until she was married, she had to obey them. I wouldn't ask her to run off with me, either; I didn't know what the future held and if we did marry one day like I planned we would, I'd need to know she had somewhere to go in case something happened to me. Her sister had already married and moved on, and had no other kinfolk this far west, so she had to stay on good terms with her Ma and Pa.

"If you think it ain't too risky, then I'd be glad to go," I told her.

"Will you bring your friends with you?" she asked

me, and I smiled at that. I couldn't picture Charley, Dick or Bill Power at a social, but Creek was another matter—he just might fancy such a thing.

"Maybe Creek will want to come," I said. I took a deep breath. "You sure about this, Edith? Maybe I should just meet your folks if I ever escort you home, sometime."

She shook her head. "I'd rather introduce you at the social, Bill. Trust me, it'll be better this way."

I figured she meant because at the social, her Pa couldn't take a gun to me to scare me away from his daughter, the way he could do at home, if he were so inclined. She wouldn't say it, though, of course. I heaved a sigh to myself as I got up onto my horse after helping her into her saddle. I figured I'd better enjoy myself as much as I could today, and any time I might see her before next Friday, because it was likely that after the social I'd be forbidden from doing so again.

⸺●⟨◉⟩●⸺

I'd been right when I thought that Creek might be up for the social; he agreed to come along without any hesitation. Though he was used to keeping company with less-than-reputable folks, he could turn on the charm and the manners when needed, same as me, and he was always up for a good time, no matter the source, or people involved. Aside from that I was also beginning to suspect he was a little envious of me for having taken up with Edith and was pondering the idea of finding a girl for himself other than the ones in the red light districts. I couldn't imagine Creek ever taking a wife and settling down—he was just too wild and devil-may-care for that—but the challenge of finding a girl that might consider such a thing was one he couldn't resist.

The social, Edith had told me, was supposed to start at six o'clock, and it was being held at the schoolhouse they'd built in Ingalls. They'd moved all the seats the students sat in out of the big room and put out a bunch of food on a long table near the blackboard. Someone had mixed up a big batch of lemonade, too, and all the families that came brought lanterns or lamps with tin reflectors to hang on nails driven into the walls, so the place was aglow with light. There was a fiddler there, just like Edith had said, and another man with a banjo, and everyone was merry and friendly. Creek and I were a little wary at first, since we'd recently seen the wanted notices the railroad company had out on us and the Daltons, but no one batted an eyelash when we came in.

We'd gussied ourselves up some, washed and

shaved and trimmed our mustaches, and slicked our hair back neat. We'd put on fresh shirts and vests, tied on neckties and shined up our worn boots as best we could. We left off our spurs and our gun belts— but we each had a pistol tucked up under our coats. There was no way in hell either of us were going anywhere without being heeled.

"There's your girl, Bill," Creek said to me, low, giving me a wink when he saw Edith across the room. I didn't answer him; I was too busy staring. She was dressed up, too, wearing a dress of lilac trimmed with cream lace, and her hair was done up different, all curlicued and knotted. Her corset was laced so tight her waist looked small enough to span with my two hands. She was the loveliest thing I think I'd ever seen and my mouth went dry.

"You shy, now?" Creek teased, rolling his eyes. "Go get her, Doolin! It ain't like the two of you ain't never met before."

I hesitated. Edith was standing with an older man and woman who I guessed were her folks. The man was tall and thickly-built, with a graying brown beard that was neatly trimmed, and deep-set dark eyes. The woman was small and plump, with the same thick black hair as Edith, only hers was starting to gray a little at the temples. Creek elbowed me in the ribs. "I'll cover you if her Pa decides to call you out," he whispered with his fox-like grin, then purposefully left me alone, going to get himself some lemonade. I figured the lemonade would be a treat for both of us, since we hadn't neither of us had anything but water and whiskey for a good long while.

I took a deep breath and made myself walk over to them. "Evenin', Miss Ellsworth," I said politely, remembering not to call her Edith; her parents might think it too familiar for their liking.

Edith turned and smiled warmly at me. "Good evening, Bill. I'd like to introduce you to my Ma and Pa. This is Mr. Doolin, whom I've been telling you about," she said, standing back just a little and watching the three of us anxiously.

Her Pa stepped forward first. "John Ellsworth," he said, and I was surprised when he held out a hand for me to shake. I did, firmly.

"A pleasure, Mr. Ellsworth."

"And this is my wife, Ida," he said, gesturing her forward. She arched an eyebrow at me, looking me over quick from head to toe like I was a horse one might buy, and I sensed a little coolness from her, but she held out her hand and let me kiss it.

"I surely am pleased to meet the both of you, and I'm sorry it's taken me this long to do so," I said smoothly.

"Yes, I suppose we should have met earlier,

considering how much time you've been spend-ing with our daughter, but there's no use regretting things we can't change, is there?" Mr. Ellsworth said, and there was kindness in his eyes. I was damned if I didn't like him, right off. I felt so relieved I thought my knees might go out from under me. The stern, forbidding preacher I'd been expecting was in truth a fair, kindly man who seemed bent on giving me a chance. I was determined to do my best to convince him I was good enough for his daughter.

Mrs. Ellsworth, however, seemed like she was going to be harder to win over. She wasn't down-right cold to me, but she wasn't friendly, like her husband. I cleared my throat. "Can I bring you two lovely ladies some lemonade?" I asked, giving her my most charming smile. To my relief, she smiled back at me. It was a pretty small smile, but it was there nonetheless.

"I see you have manners, at the very least," she said approvingly.

"Ida," Mr. Ellsworth groaned. Edith looked embarrassed.

I just smiled more widely at her. "I do my best, ma'am," I said. "Sometimes they're hard to remem-ber, for a fact, on account of I've been mostly keep-ing company with cows and cowboys, but I still got them in there, somewhere."

She actually laughed a little at that, and when I brought her and Edith the lemonade, she nodded to me and thanked me nice. I was so relieved now that I felt like singing aloud, the way Creek did when he got drunk. I didn't, of course. Instead, I asked Edith for a dance; the fiddler was playing a waltz and it was the only one I knew how to do; my Ma had taught me when I was a boy. I wasn't that good at it but if I could manage to stay off her toes, I'd consider it a success.

She gave me a big smile and put soft little her hand in mine, and as we were heading out amongst all the other couples she stood on tiptoe to speak softly to me. "That went well, didn't it?" Her eyes were sparkling.

"Better than I thought it would, if you want to know the truth," I admitted.

"I think they like you," she said, and put her hand on my shoulder for the waltz.

"Hope they don't change their minds once they get to know the real him," a voice said from behind us, and we turned to see Creek standing there, leaning against the wall. He was giving me a devilish grin, his arms crossed over his chest.

I rolled my eyes. "Edith, this charming fellow is George Newcomb."

He gave her a little bow. "Miss Ellsworth. Happy

to meet you proper, finally. You're of some fame around our circle, on account of the fact that Bill here don't ever shut up about you." He was teasing her, but I wasn't worried—Edith could hold her own in that department. She had wit as sharp as one of her sewing needles.

"Well, I would certainly hope so, Creek," she said good-naturedly, surprising him with her boldness, and her ease around him.

He let out his big laugh. "You got yourself a fine one, Doolin," he told me with a chuckle, and I winked at him as the waltz started up.

After we'd shared a dance and had some of the cake that was set out, I started to feel a lot more comfortable and enjoy myself. As much as I liked the freedom of my current lifestyle, I had to admit it was nice to be around civilized folks again, enjoying the music and the company like a normal person, instead of a longrider on the run. I talked a bit more with her folks—just small talk—and they stayed nice and friendly, even her Ma. Her Pa told me that he was going to be starting work as the postmaster in Lawson come the fall, and he was going to hope for better luck with his crops the next time around. We talked about ranching and the cattle trade, or what was left of it. He asked where I'd been living, and I told him Creek and I were baching on a claim on the

Cimarron, leaving out, of course, just where it was, and who else shared it with us.

Edith left us at one point to talk with some women she knew from town, and her Pa turned to me, speaking low. "I have to tell you, Mr. Doolin, that I'm aware of what's being said about you and the men you keep company with." His voice was serious and I felt my heart drop. He kept talking. "I don't condone unlawful behavior, but I do understand how a man can come to want revenge against the railroad. Our family has had our own share of problems with it." He looked me square in the eye. "I'm not going to ask you for details, so long as you don't bring the trouble down on Edith. All I ask is that my daughter is safe and that she's happy. Edith is a grown woman now and free to make her own choices. But she's also my child, and I *won't* have her hurt."

I leveled my gaze at him. "I don't intend for her to be, and that's the God's honest truth. She means a great deal to me, Mr. Ellsworth. You got my word I won't let her get hurt." I spoke firmly; I meant what I said, and he gave me a slow nod in return. I felt like we had us an understanding then.

There were some other men who'd come in that I started noticing while I was waiting for Edith to come back over to me. There were three of them, and they were clearly brothers; they all had the same dark hair and brown eyes set in round faces. Two of them looked around mine and Creek's ages. The other one was young, probably only around fifteen or so, if even that. I noticed them because they were dressed like me and Creek—cowboys trying to look like young men from good families, and I saw that at least two of them were heeled—I could see pistols tucked up under their vests. They had a young woman with them that I guessed was their sister, because she had the same color hair and eyes as they did. She was real pretty in the face—so much so that she stuck out in the crowd. Creek noticed that, too; I saw it from the way he was looking at her.

"Who're they?" I asked Edith quietly, when she came back over to me.

"Those are the Dunns," she told me. "Bill, John and Calvin, and their sister, Rose. They have a ranch near Council Creek, just outside of Ingalls. There are five boys that still live there; I don't see George and Dal here tonight."

I felt myself get a little wary. I'd heard tell of the Dunn brothers; they had a reputation for cattle-rustling and it was said they'd pulled a few small-time robberies, too. Creek had mentioned Bill Dunn once or twice to me, some time back.

As if on cue, Creek caught my eye from across the room; he was standing with them. He motioned me over, and I turned to Edith, excusing myself from her.

"Bill Doolin, meet Bill Dunn, and his brothers John and Calvin," Creek said to me, and I nodded to them in turn. "I've known them for awhile, ain't I, boys?" Creek said. The younger one, Calvin, was looking at me like I was some kind of big hero.

"They say you're one of the best shots there is," he said to me, all solemn-like.

I glanced at Creek. "I guess I can handle a gun all right," I said evenly. Before he could answer their sister came up, and Creek introduced me.

"And this is Rose, their sister, who I've just had the pleasure of meeting for the first time tonight, my-self." His voice took on a tone I'd never heard from him before and I gave him a look, but he didn't see it. He was looking at Rose. Up close, I could tell she was pretty young—maybe only sixteen or so—but she had a way about her that made her seem more grown up. She gave me a smile and shook my hand like a man instead of being all delicate like most young girls. She was bold, this one. Creek would tell me later that she'd been mostly raised up by her broth-ers, once their Pa died; her Ma had remarried and she didn't care much for her step-Pa, so she chose to live with her brothers instead. They'd taught her to shoot and rope, and she rode just as good as any of them—and not sidesaddle, either. It was plain to see she was taken with Creek; she couldn't take her eyes off him and shared every dance of the night with him, besides.

Creek told me a lot about the Dunns as we were riding back to the claim that night after the social was over. They would offer us a place to hole up, if it came to it, and they'd let us know if they saw any sign of Thomas or his lot. By the time we were putting up our horses, I could tell he was more interested in Rose than he'd let on to me, but I didn't tease him about it. I was too busy being thankful that Edith's parents had seemed to accept me.

ELEVEN

"REMEMBER WHAT I told you, boys."

Bob's voice was low; I could barely hear it as we crept, in as near to silence as we could manage, toward the train station at Adair one Thursday night, Bob in the lead. We fanned out a little as we got closer, just like Bob had told us to do, all eyes on him, waiting for his signal. We were in easy sight of the depot now, and Bob threw his arm out to one side, fingers spread out, making a halting motion with his hand. We all stopped dead and crouched down into the shadows, guns ready. In front of us, the station was quiet; the lanterns hung off the eaves in front throwing off soft rings of light that we were all careful to stay just out of reach of. The night operator was out on the platform, drawing up some water from a cistern set to one side of the little building. He looked relaxed and I didn't figure he had any idea we were out there.

Slowly, Bob turned and gave Dick a deliberate nod, and he stood up and headed for the man at the cistern, his gun at the ready. "Evenin'" I heard him say pleasantly.

"Evenin'" the man replied over his shoulder, straightening up with his pail of water. He saw Dick's gun then and dropped the pail; it hit the platform and water went everywhere. His hands shot up into the air. I heard the hammer on Dick's gun click as he thumbed it back.

"I ain't gonna hurt you, so long as you do what I tell you to. Understand?" Dick said firmly, and we all saw the man nod, his hands still raised.

"When she rolls in, flag her down, then sit down on that bench, *on your hands*. If I see you make one false move, it'll be the last one you ever make. Am I clear?"

"Yes," we heard him say tensely.

The train was coming now; we could hear the faint, low hum and feel its rumble in our chests. The whistle sounded and set the coyotes going like always.

The station manager stepped forward and took up the signal flag, and then he raised his arm and hailed the engineer, while Dick stood just out of sight in the shadows, his gun still leveled right at the man's back. When the train rolled to a stop, we all listened for Bob's command.

"*Go*," he ordered in a quiet voice, and we all moved forward. He and Grat boarded the engine then, Emmett and me on their heels. Creek, Dick, Bill Power and Charley all moved to cover the sides of the train. As I put my foot up onto the step I saw some men pile out of the smoking car—guards employed by the railroad—and advance toward Creek and Charley. They had rifles. I didn't let that deter me from my task, though; I knew Creek and the others could handle themselves, even though we hadn't figured on the guards being there. Shots started ringing out, and somewhere I heard yells and screams from some of the passengers.

"Send them to hell, boys!" Creek shouted, and more shots came in answer to the first. I heard someone cry out in pain as they were shot, and I hoped it wasn't one of ours.

Bob ignored the whole thing. He and Grat were standing at the place where the express car was connected to the engine, and Emmett was covering them. I had my gun on the engineer, but I glanced over my shoulder as Bob fired a few shots into the express car door, which had remained closed, even though the conductor, who they had at the end of their guns, had called for it to be opened.

Bob fired again. "I'm gonna keep shooting until you open it!" he called in a pleasant yet firm tone of voice.

"Hold your fire! Hold your fire!" I heard a hoarse voice call out from down by the smoking car. It didn't belong to anyone I recognized, so it must have been one of the company men. Bob wouldn't be happy, I thought, clenching my jaw. He never wanted anyone shot up during these little parties, but from what I'd overheard, it couldn't have been helped.

The door to the express car came slowly open, and I saw two palms come at Bob and Grat.

"Thank you kindly," Bob said sarcastically, and he and Grat and Emmett went inside. I moved forward, too, easing in with them but keeping the engineer and the conductor at bay.

"Attend to the safe, if you would," Bob ordered the messenger, and the man did as he was told, his fingers shaking as he dialed the combination. "Sounds like it's gettin' a bit messy out there," Bob said to the messenger, like he was shooting the breeze. The messenger stayed silent and moved quickly aside once the safe was open.

Bob scooped out stacks of bills, directing them into the sack he'd pulled from inside his coat sleeve. When he was done, he handed the sack to Grat. The messenger stood by, tense as a rabbit caught by a fox, averting his eyes from all of us. Sweat was coming off his temples in little streams.

"Go!" Bob snapped at us, and called "so long!"

to the messenger, grinning slyly. I let him and Em and Grat off first as we'd planned, still covering the messenger. When I'd heard three sets of boots hit the ground, I jumped off, too.

Bob whistled then, sharp, and we heard the sound of running steps. Creek, Broadwell, Charley and Power all came out of the darkness and into the light from the station lanterns, their eyes like those of wild animals above their masks, their guns still smoking. I heard more panicked screams from the train, and the moans of someone in pain.

We didn't say anything to one another, just jumped onto our horses, spurring them hard. We were heading straight through town and I felt my heart sink a little as I realized we were being chased. Guns started going off behind us, and without thinking I drew mine and turned in my saddle to return fire. I was damned if I was going to be shot off my horse after all this. Creek and Charley did the same, both of them unwilling to be taken out by some small-town vigilante, just like me.

Folks were coming out of stores and houses to see what was happening, but we ignored them, firing into the direction the bullets were coming from. A few of our shots went wild, and Charley, whose expression looked near crazy to me as his horse drew up next to mine, carelessly fired a few rounds toward the buildings we were passing, aiming at anything that moved in the light from the lanterns hung here and there above the galleries and on porches.

"Knock it the hell off, shithogs!" Bob screamed, his voice going shrill with rage. Hearing him sound like that brought the three of us back to ourselves again, and we all stopped shooting. The shots behind us stopped, too, and the only sound in our ears became that of the hooves of our horses. After a few seconds I heard screams from the porch of one of the buildings we'd passed and I knew someone had been hit in the ruckus—and it couldn't have been someone who was chasing us, either, not coming from a porch like that.

But, I thought, as I dug my spurs into my horse again, there was nothing any of us could do about it. All we could do now was get away. There would be hell to pay from Bob once we stopped, I knew, and as we galloped along, I tried to decide if I was going to take it or not.

<hr>

We were all of us in trouble with Bob, that much was clear. Nobody talked while we put up the horses, or while we piled into an abandoned claim shanty

Bob had found for us to hide out in. He was as tense as a coiled rattlesnake and his eyes looked like ice. He stood still against the wall while we all went inside, turning to face him while he stood by the door. Grat silently lit the lamp, and in its light we could see Bob's face going almost purple with rage.

The explosion, when it came, was near to a stick of dynamite going off. "What in the name of almighty God do you think you stupid sons of bitches were *doing* out there?" he raged. He was looking directly at me and Creek and Charley. "What the hell was going through your fool skulls?"

Charley winced, and, to my surprise, so did Creek—but I didn't. There wasn't any way in hell I was going to let that self-proclaimed God's gift to the train-robbing trade dress me down any further than he had that night at Red Rock. I didn't check myself this time, like I'd forced myself to do then. I'd about had my fill of Bob Dalton, and it was time he knew it.

"Lower your voice and cool your heels, Dalton," I said, and my voice came out cold and commanding. I saw Creek, Charley and Emmett all looking at me in surprise and a little unease, but I kept my eyes directly on Bob's. "You think you've pulled off every Goddamned lark you've ever tried, clean as a whistle and pretty as a picture?" It was Alila I meant, the robbery Bob had failed at, back in California. A company man had died there, and it very well could've been Bob who shot him. I knew he didn't like anyone to mention that little fiasco since it tarnished his record some, but I sure as hell would! "We got away, didn't we? We got the haul. So some idiots got themselves a little shot up. We didn't kill anybody."

"Did you even stop to *look,* Doolin?" he asked me, his hands clenching into fists. "Every damned one of them could die, for all you know! It was careless and damned sloppy, and I won't have it in my outfit, understand?"

I let my hand come to rest on the butt of my gun, just to let him know he wasn't intimidating me in the slightest. I let him hang a minute, my manner cool. I knew it was irritating the hell out of him that I wasn't drawing a line in the dirt and challenging him to a draw, but I wasn't stupid, like he seemed to think I was. "Well, son," I said evenly, reminding him that I was his elder, "I'm sorry you see it that way. Guess maybe we'll take our parts and be off, then. It ain't worth gettin' in a scrape over." You *ain't worth it, Bob,* was what I meant, and I could see he got the message. I knew by my words I was, in effect, withdrawing from the gang for good, but I didn't give a damn about that right then. A man could only take so much.

Bob glared at me, but then he set to divvying up. When he handed me my share, his whole body tense and his eyes avoiding mine, I looked at Bitter Creek and Charley, knowing this moment would determine what became of our friendship from here on out. "You boys going with me or staying here?" I asked them calmly, my meaning clear.

Creek looked at Emmett, and I knew it was because of Em that he was hesitating a bit. The both of us liked Em a lot, and since he was so much younger than us, we sort of thought of him as our responsibility, in a way. We didn't want to go off and leave him to whatever fate Bob and Grat had in mind for him. But he was a man now, twenty-one, and he'd have to make his choices just like we were making ours. Creek looked at me. "I'm going with you, Bill," he told me firmly, and came to my side.

Charley hesitated; he loved being part of the gang and wasn't keen to leave it for good. But it had probably been him that shot whoever that was on the porch in town, and I could tell he knew it. Besides that, if Creek was going, so was he. He and Creek stuck together, plain and simple. He came over to us, his fate decided. "Guess I'm going, too."

Bob raised his chin and crossed his arms over his chest, while Grat stood at his side like a burly, protective hound, saying nothing, his eyes cold, his jaw clenched. "Get a-goin', then," Bob said. It was a dismissal.

Bitter Creek and Charley moved past me, muttering their good-byes to the rest; Dick and Bill Power were staying, too and so the three of us would no longer hole up with them like we'd been doing. I didn't mourn the loss any. They'd been my friends, but they'd chosen their path and couldn't have it both ways. I lingered, my focus on Emmett, who, like usual, was wearing his feelings plain in his eyes. It made him look younger than his years and I could tell he didn't want me to go. That chirked me up some, knowing that a man like Emmett Dalton thought I was worth keeping around.

"You take care of yourself, now, Em," I told him with a smile, and I meant it. "You ever change your mind about this, you look me up." I put a hand on his shoulder and gave it a squeeze. Then I tucked my Winchester up under my arm and walked out.

———— ◦《◉》◦ ————

We rode aways in silence, and finally Charley spoke. "Well, where the hell are we supposed to go now?"

I rolled my eyes. "It ain't like Power's claim was

the only place we know to hole up in, Charley," I reminded him. "We'll figure it out. Hell, we got the money from the haul, don't we? We can get hotel rooms in Wagoner for the night."

Creek spoke up. "Bill, I think we should push on and stay out of Wagoner. If the law's out already, they could hunt us up there, since it's so close."

"You got a point, there, Creek," I conceded. "Where do you think we should head?"

He reined his horse up next to mine. "I think we should hole up at the Dunns' ranch," he said to me, low. "There's hiding-places all over the place on that spread of theirs. It's close enough to Lawson so you can see Edith, too," he reminded me.

"It'll take some days' ride, but it seems like the best place to go," I agreed, and we settled on it.

When we camped that night in a protected little hollow we found, all of us on edge in case the law was on our trail, we finally talked about what had happened. Creek told me, all solemn-like, that he was behind me in whatever I decided we should do from here on out, and Charley echoed that. I was the one who would lead them from now on, seemed like, now that we'd split from the Daltons.

I hadn't thought about what would happen next, and I'd never thought hard about leading my own gang, but now that Creek had put it in my head I found myself liking the idea. I knew I was well-liked by most of the men I'd ridden with, both now and back in my cowboy days, and I realized I could be a different type of leader than Bob was. I could keep us chiseling away at the railroad, and out of the law's reach, without keeping them all under my thumb the way Bob had.

I felt a lot better about everything as I kept my turn at the watch, letting Creek and Charley sleep. I didn't regret leaving the gang, it had been time to go. I still respected Bob's talent at what he did; I had to admit he was good, but there just hadn't been any way we'd ever see eye-to-eye. I'd make my own way from now on.

TWELVE

WE CAME TO the Dunns' place in the middle of the night, so there would be less chance of someone seeing us arrive who might be inclined to tell the law. By then we'd seen a paper when we'd gone for ammunition and supplies along the way, and we knew the results of the Adair fiasco. Five men had been hit in total—three during the gunfight outside the train, and two citizens in town. To make matters worse, the citizens had both been doctors—and one of them had died. The three of us got good and quiet when we saw that, and it took us a good long while to start talking again. Men of our calling might shoot someone if we had to, but most of us had an unspoken code about doctors. You never knew when you might need one of them to pick lead out of you, so you left 'em alone.

But, as I'd thought back when it happened, there wasn't a damned thing we could do about it, no way to take it back. Best we could do was try to make sure such a thing never happened again.

Our horses' heads hung low as we urged them up the road that led to the Dunns' ranch house. We'd come a long way and pushed them hard, and we were all tired, too, and saddle-sore and hungry besides. Seeing a real house with bedsteads in it instead of a claim shanty with a hard floor to sleep on made us quicken our pace a bit, and I hoped the Dunns had been sincere when they'd told Creek they'd give us shelter any time we needed it.

There were lamps shining inside the house even though it was late, and the front door opened as soon as we got up to the porch. As we dismounted stiffly, one of the Dunn brothers came out to meet us, but I couldn't tell which one it was since he was back-lit from the lamplight shining out behind him.

"Hello, Creek!" he called, and when he came down the porch steps I saw him better and realized it was Bill Dunn. "Hello Bill," he said to me. "And you too, Charley. What brings you boys out this way?"

I felt a little suspicious; I thought he sounded too jovial, too friendly. Our names were getting more well-known, it seemed, and I was inclined to be wary these days, after Adair, but I was so damned tired I put my suspicions aside.

"We could use a place to hole up for awhile, and

a decent meal, if you can spare it," I said, getting right to the point.

"Our place is yours. Come on in and we'll get you some grub." He went back up onto the porch and stuck his head inside. "Calvin, Dal, come on out here and get these boys' horses put up!"

Calvin and another brother I hadn't met yet came outside and practically bounded down the porch steps. They greeted us enthusiastically and took our horses to the barn after we'd pulled our rifles from the scabbards on our saddles and shouldered our saddlebags. I thought about calling after them to leave the rigs on, in case things went south, but I didn't. The horses were worn out and they deserved to be untacked and rubbed down proper.

We mounted the steps in a group and traipsed inside. The big front room had a long table in it with two lit lamps, and it looked homey and comfortable, with pictures hung on the walls and a horseshoe hung above the front door. A door opened in the far wall and Rose Dunn came out of it, smiling her warm smile at all of us. 'Hello, Bill," she said to me. "Hello Charley." She gave Creek an even warmer smile, and her cheeks went a little pink. "Hello, Creek. It's nice to see you."

"Pleasure's ours, Rose," he told her smoothly, his eyes twinkling at her in the lamplight, and my eyebrow went up, along with the corners of my mouth. There'd been logic in Creek's suggestion that we stay here, but I was pretty sure there was something else, too.

"Rose, you want to see what we can offer them to eat? I'm sure they're starved." Bill said.

She nodded. "Have a seat," she told us cheerfully, "and I'll fix you up something right quick."

"We don't want to put you out none, Rose," I said. It was pretty late and I didn't want to keep a young woman from her sleep, but she waved me off.

"It's no trouble, Bill." She gave me another of her pretty smiles and headed for the kitchen. She was not, I noticed, dressed for bed. None of them were, and I wondered about that, but I held my tongue.

Turned out I didn't need to ask, because Bill explained it. "We get all kinds of folks traveling through here that need a place to stop," he told me. "Sometimes they come late, so we all sort of keep odd hours, in case we need to get someone settled."

I tensed, feeling more awake now—and more wary. "If you got strangers coming around here all the time I don't know if it's the best thing for us to stay here," I said gravely, glancing at Creek and Charley. Charley looked worried. Creek was looking where Rose had gone.

Bill shook his head. "Don't you worry none, Bill.

We got plenty of room, and no one needs to see you. There are outbuildings on the property, and even a big cave out near the back you could hole up in, if it comes down to it." He leaned forward and looked at me square. "I ain't got no love for the law, Bill. You got my word you're always welcome here, and if I hear tell of anyone out after you, I'll let you know." He said it firm and solemn-like, like he was swearing an oath.

I felt some better then, like maybe he could be trusted, and he meant what he said. My worries about him being too friendly seemed silly all of the sudden—the Dunns were a friendly bunch. John and another one of them came to join us at the table, and Bill introduced the newcomer as George. Just as they'd sat down Calvin and Dal came in and told us our horses were put up with fresh hay, and some oats besides.

"I can't thank you enough for your hospitality," I told them. "There ain't enough of it around any more, seems like."

"It's no trouble," Bill said with a smile.

Rose came in with some plates then, and she stopped and frowned at her brothers, all sitting there with us. "I hope you all aren't thinking I'm gonna cook for *you*, too," she said, all exasperated-like, but I could see she was teasing them. "I already did that, three times today." She put the plates down in front of us, and there was crisp salt pork and fried potatoes, and hot coffee and biscuits besides. We thanked her and chuckled at her teasing. I liked Rose a lot and hoped it worked out with her and Creek; she seemed like his perfect match, in spite of her being so much younger.

Her brothers all laughed at her as she rolled her eyes at them. They were a teasing, good-natured family and I was suddenly glad we'd come; it sure was nice to taste home-life again.

We ate her good cooking, while the brothers sat with us and drank coffee. Rose came out after a bit and sat next to Creek, talking softly with him.

Just as I was finishing my coffee, Bill raised an eyebrow at me. "I take it the Dalton boys ain't with you, then."

I sat back in my chair, busying myself with my napkin. "No, they ain't. We ain't riding with them anymore." I saw Creek and Charley glance at me, and I knew they were wondering if it was wise to advertise that fact, but I knew what I was doing.

"Parted ways, eh?" George asked, and I nodded.

"I heard about Adair. Too bad," Bill commented.

"Wasn't nothing we could do about it," Charley said darkly, buttering a biscuit with a little more force than he needed to.

"Things got a little out of hand, for a fact," I said calmly. "But it's done now. Bob Dalton and I don't mix well, and that's the truth of it. But I don't have any ill will towards him, or his brothers. Hopefully their next lark will go some better."

The brothers nodded, and I could tell they weren't going to pry. Suddenly I was so tired I couldn't hardly see straight, and Charley and Creek weren't looking much better off. Rose seemed to sense it and stood up, waving us away from clearing off our plates and showing us to a big room in the attic that had three single bedsteads in it. There was a washstand and shaving mirror, and a table between two of the bedsteads with a lamp on it. There were a few lamps hung with tin reflectors on the walls, besides. It looked like pure heaven to us after so long on the trail, and the old shanties.

"Sleep well, now, boys," Rose told us, and she seemed suddenly older than sixteen. I figured she was going to be a good wife to someone someday, and a good mother too.

"Thank you, Rose," we all said as we slung our gun belts around the footboards, and then we all three practically fell onto the mattresses, not even bothering to take off our boots. I was out like a blown-out lamp before my head even hit the pillow.

That little bit of sleep in a real bed, along with the Dunns' hospitality, made me feel like a new man once I'd woken the next morning. Creek was just starting to wake up in the bed on the other side of the room, pulling his pillow over his head with a groan, trying to shut out the sound of Charley's snoring in the other bed shoved against the far wall. I chuckled softly under my breath and straightened my rumpled clothes as best I could, then went to the wash-stand and poured off some water into the bowl. There was a piece of soap in the dish there and I scrubbed my face and hands good. The water turned black from the trail dust I had caked on, so I tossed it out the window into the yard below.

As I buckled on my gun belt, my mind turned to Edith. I'd had to sort of tuck her away into one corner of it, the last few days, given all that had happened with the gang, but now I knew I needed to see her. She would have read about Adair—there was no getting around it—and I knew she'd be worried. I missed her bad, on top of it, and I needed to make sure the latest yarns in the papers hadn't turned her off me. We were all of us, the Daltons included, wanted for murder now, because of the doctor that had died, and there was a big difference between being wanted for holding up a few trains and being wanted for killing a man. I had to brace myself for the possibility that even though I didn't think I'd been the one that had fired the fatal shot, Edith or her folks might, and that would be the end of it.

I heard a big yawn come from Creek's bed and I turned to see him sitting up and swinging his long legs over the side of the bedstead. He looked half-dead and his copper hair was sticking up like bird's nest. I laughed. "Well, when they called it 'beauty sleep,' Creek, they sure as hell weren't talking about you!"

He woke up good then and laughed right along with me, not bothered in the least by my teasing. "No, they were talking about Charley over there!" He took his pillow and threw it, hard, right at Charley's head. Charley choked on his last snore and sat up like a shot had gone off, Creek's pillow falling to the floor. He looked mad enough to bite and I was glad his gun belt wasn't within easy reach of him.

"Goddamnit, Creek!" he growled. "Ain't you ever gonna get tired of acting like a damn kid?"

"Why the hell would I, when I get that kind of a reaction?" Creek asked, gesturing to Charley's face. He kept laughing, and I did, too.

"Aww, go soak your damn head," Charley muttered, flopping back down onto the mattress and pulling his covers up over his face.

I let my laughter die down and picked up my

Winchester from where I'd leaned it into the corner near the head of my bed. Creek sobered right away, watching me. "What're you gonna do, Bill?" he asked. Over in the other bed, Charley shoved the blankets off his face and looked, too, his irritation set aside.

"I got to go into Lawson," I told them both.

"Edith?" Creek asked, and I nodded.

"She's gonna be worried by now." My voice sounded grim, even to me.

Creek and Charley looked at one another. "You want us to come, or...?" Creek raised one eyebrow at me.

"No. Stay here and let Rose look after you. I'll be back by nightfall, then we can stay on here a bit, maybe scout out the rest of the ranch. Then we can decide what we're gonna do next."

I bid them goodbye, then went downstairs and found Rose in the front room by herself. She was setting out plates on the long table. When she heard my footsteps on the stairs she looked up and smiled. "Morning, Bill. Sleep all right?"

"Like the dead," I said with a chuckle. "A man never thinks he needs a mattress until he goes without one for a time."

She finished with the plates and went to the sideboard, pulling out a handful of knives and forks. "Are the others awake?"

"Sort of," I said, scratching absently at my stubbled chin. I reckoned I either needed to get a shave soon or get on with growing a beard. The thought made me frown a little; I hated to have Edith see me looking like a scruffy mongrel dog, not that it'd bother her any.

"Well, I'm about ready to get breakfast on. Can I get you some coffee, Bill?" she asked me, and I nodded gratefully. We'd gone without it on the trail and I'd found I missed it. It would only take me a half-hour or so to get to Lawson, so I figured I could spare the time.

"You look like you're headed somewhere," Rose said, raising an eyebrow at my rifle as she set a steaming cup in front of me.

"I'm headed to Lawson, just for the day." I cleared my throat. "You know where the Ellsworths have their place?" I tried to sound casual.

She tucked a lock of her hair behind her ear and nodded, and her dark eyes twinkled knowingly at me. "It's about a half-mile from Mud Creek, on the other side of Lawson," she told me. "Mr. Ellsworth's got a big palomino stud he keeps in the pasture at the front of the place. You can't miss him. Hell of a horse," she said in admiration, startling me. I'd never heard a woman use strong language before, not even in the seediest cribs in the red-light district of Dodge

— 141 —

City back in the cattle-drive days, and even if I had I wouldn't have expected it from a sixteen-year-old beauty like her.

She saw it and gave me a saucy grin. "What? You ain't never heard a woman swear, Bill?"

"No, I can't say as I ever have," I replied, feeling my eyebrows raise.

"You got to remember I been mostly raised up by menfolk," she said. "My Mama taught me how to cook good, but just about everything else I know that's worth knowing I got from my brothers. You'll get used to it."

I shook my head a little, laughing under my breath. "You're something, Rose, you know that?"

She nodded at me in complete agreement. "I do know it, as a matter of fact." She let a big grin come out on her face then.

She brought me out a plate, then sat across from me while I ate. "Ain't you gonna eat?" I asked her.

"Already did," she said. "But I'll keep you company, if you don't mind."

"I don't," I said. "You're pretty interesting company, when you get right down to it."

She smiled at that, then fell quiet for a minute, and it looked to me like she was thinking something over real good in her mind. "Bill, are you and Edith going to get married?" she asked me curiously.

I looked up from my food. "I surely hope so, Rose," I said. "Don't know exactly when, on account of I haven't asked her just yet, but I plan to."

"I'm glad. She seems to belong with you, some-how. I thought that when I saw you together at the social. She's got class, and good sense, too." She got real quiet again then, like she was working up cour-age to say something. Then she took a deep breath. "You know Bitter Creek pretty good, right?"

I felt a smile creeping over my face but I kept it soft, so she wouldn't get embarrassed. "Like he was my brother."

She wasn't looking at me; she was picking at some dried candle-wax that had dripped onto the table at some point or another. "I thought so. He doesn't...have a girl like you do, does he?" she asked. Her cheeks flamed and she ducked her head a little more.

I kept my voice good and gentle. "I think he does *now,* Rose, to tell the truth." She looked up, sharp, having missed my meaning and I raised my eyebrow at her, still smiling. "I mean, I think he sort of fancies *you.*"

She bit her lip. "I hope he does." Her voice was real quiet, but there was a shy smile playing with the corners of her mouth.

I got up from the table and picked up my rifle,

then I went for my hat. It was still hanging where I'd left it last night, on the wall by the door. As I passed her I sort of patted her on the shoulder. "Thanks for the breakfast, Rose. I think you could beat the nation cooking."

She looked up at me then and I winked at her, just before I headed outside.

THIRTEEN

GEORGE AND DAL were doing the barn chores when I went to saddle my horse, and I told them I had some business to take care of, but I didn't say where. Something made me hold back from telling them, even though I'd told Rose. I'd kind of gotten in the habit of being cautious about how much I told too many people at any given time—the whole 'wanted for murder' bit made me do that.

My horse had rested up and had his fill of good feed and fresh water, but I didn't push him hard as we headed for Lawson. I never liked to be harder than I needed to on a horse; it just didn't seem fair, what with all the work they had to do on a daily basis. The one I was riding now was a gelding, still strong and fast when it counted but getting on in years, and I figured I'd probably have to see about finding myself a younger one soon.

I moseyed on toward Lawson; it was still pretty

early and I didn't want to get there too soon. Right around eight in the morning I saw a palomino stud cropping grass in a pasture set to one side of a dirt road leading to a small farmhouse, and I had to admit Rose was right—he *was* a hell of a horse, big and sleek with legs a mile long and muscles that rippled under his golden coat. He raised his head as I came down the road past him, but after eyeballing me for a few seconds he swished his tail and went back to eating, uninterested.

The front door of the farmhouse banged open so fast I thought it'd tear off its hinges, startling me, and to my surprise Edith came flying out of it, her skirts bunched up in her hands so she wouldn't stumble over them. She was running toward me, and she looked like she was almost crying. I got off my horse, quick, and tied him to the pasture fence.

She flung herself at me and I put my arms around her, holding her against me, thanking the Lord above she had so clearly missed me and been worried about me. I don't think anything had ever felt so good to me as she did in my arms, just about then.

"I've been so worried," she got out, her voice muffled by the fact that she had her face in my shoulder. "Some of the papers have been saying—"

"Edith, honey, you know the papers get things wrong most of the time," I soothed her. "Everything's all right. Take a breath for me and let me kiss you; I been counting on it for days."

She did, and I kissed her then, a lot longer and harder than I probably should have done. But I couldn't stop myself; I'd been so afraid she'd freeze me out, that she would believe I was a cold-blooded murderer like the papers were saying we all were.

She didn't act like I was taking liberties with her; in fact, she kissed me right back. When we broke apart she put her arms around my neck again. "Thank God you're safe. They said there'd been a gunfight—" She meant at Adair, and I looked her in the eye, knowing I couldn't sugarcoat things. Maybe some men in my position might have done that, but I couldn't. I would leave things out; I would gloss things over if I had to, but I wouldn't outright lie to her.

"There *was* one, Edith. But didn't any of us get hit. I guess we got lucky."

She took a few deep breaths and I kept my hand on her shoulder, afraid the excitement and the tightly-laced corset that wouldn't let her fill her lungs good might make her swoon. But she didn't. Edith was a tough woman, and though she might fly apart for a moment, she always got right back ahold of herself. She looked up at me and gave me a smile that was almost teary-eyed, then she put her soft little hand up and cupped my cheek with it. "I've missed you, Bill," she told me, her eyes shining.

I reached up and took her hand from my face, took the other one too, and then raised them both to my lips and kissed them, one after the other. "I missed you, too, honey," I said. My voice sounded funny to me, sort of husky, like something was wrong with my throat. Seeing Edith took away any of the lingering bad feelings I had about what had happened at Adair.

"Where have you come from?" she asked me, searching my face with her eyes.

"The Dunns' ranch," I said. "Left Creek and Charley there while I came to see you, but I'll go back tonight."

She nodded. "What about…" she hesitated, then up and said it, that name she'd never once spoken since I'd met her. "What about the Daltons?"

If there'd ever been any doubt in my mind that she knew exactly who and what I was, it left me when she said that. She knew, and she'd always known, and yet, somehow, she still cared for me—still loved me. I looked at her square. "We parted ways with them after that night," I said. "We ain't riding with them any longer."

She let out a big deep breath she'd been holding in and nodded, a quick, brisk nod, like that was that.

Then she took my hand and tugged me toward the house. "Come on inside, Bill. Ma and Pa will want to see you."

I planted my heels a bit at that, holding back. If Edith knew about Adair, then so would they. Maybe she accepted me, but would they still agree to, now that all that was out?

She turned back and gave me a serious look, like she knew just what I was worried about. "It's all right, Bill. They'll still welcome you, I promise."

I wasn't so sure, but I let her lead me up onto the porch, and inside the house.

Her folks were waiting for us in the parlor, and I could tell they'd been watching from the window. To my surprise, I saw no trace of fear or disapproval on their faces, only concern—for me, and for Edith.

"Are you all right, Bill?" Mrs. Ellsworth asked me, worry in her eyes, her hands clasped together under her bosom. Her taffeta skirts rustled as she came toward me, looking me over like she wanted to make sure I wasn't hurt. I was surprised at the way she called me by my first name like that, like I was already part of her family. The slightly stern lady I'd met at the social was gone and in her place was a motherly figure that, in a way, reminded me a bit of my own Ma.

"I'm just fine, now I've seen Edith, ma'am," I said, giving her a relieved smile.

She waved a hand. "You call me Ida, Bill, you hear? I'll get us some coffee." she marched past me, heading for the kitchen before I could say anything in response.

Edith gave me a knowing little smile. "She took a shine to you at the social," she whispered to me. I was so surprised I couldn't do anything but stand there.

Mr. Ellsworth came over to me then, putting a hand on my shoulder in greeting. "Glad to see you've stayed in one piece, son," he said, and he looked me right in the eyes. "You're always welcome here, so long as you leave the trouble outside the gate, understand?"

I nodded. He returned it, like we'd settled something, then told me he was going to put my horse up. I protested, not wanting him to go to the trouble, but he waved me off, just like his wife had done. If I'd been surprised by this family at the social, I was plumb bowled over by them now. I reminded myself to start having more words with the man upstairs from now on; I figured He must've been looking out for me for some reason, to have blessed me not only with a woman like Edith in my life, but kindly people like her folks, on top of it.

———— ◦(◉)◦ ————

I stayed with them through supper. Mrs. Ellsworth was a fine cook, on the level with Rose Dunn, and I enjoyed my meal with them even more than the ones I'd had at the Dunns', because Edith was sitting across from me. Once the supper plates were cleared I told them all I needed to head back, and I thanked them kindly for treating me like one of their own.

Edith came with me out to the barn, and I could tell she didn't want me to go, but of course it wouldn't have been right for me to stay. She watched as I tossed the saddle on my horse and tightened the cinch.

"What will you do now?" she suddenly asked, and I looked over at her as I took the bridle from the nail her Pa had hung it on.

"Go back to the Dunns' place and lay low for awhile, I suppose," I said. I was determined not to tell her anything else; knowing that she knew what I was, was one thing. Advertising that I was now the ringleader of my own small-time gang was another. I'd already decided I'd do my best to spare her the worst of anything I might come to do, or be forced to do, in the future. But there was one thing I had to settle before I left.

"Edith, I may not be able to come back here for a while, if things get too hot for me and the other boys.

I ain't gonna take a chance on bringing that kind of trouble to you or your folks. But when I do come back…" I left the horse and came to stand before her, taking her hands in mine, "I'll be bringing you a ring, if you'll have me." I hadn't talked with her Pa yet; I didn't feel I should until I knew when I could make a real life for us, but I had to know if she'd wait.

She smiled at me and reached up to put her arms around my neck. "You didn't even have to ask, you know," she said, low, and tilted her face up. I kissed her, a good long kiss, then another, trying to get my fill since I knew it might be a long time before I could risk coming here so open-like again. When I finally let her go I brushed back a few loose tendrils of that lovely hair of hers, letting my fingertip trail over one smooth cheek, then forced myself to untie my horse and lead it out of the barn. Just before I put my foot into the stirrup she called to me from where she'd been standing at the barn door.

"Bill, be safe."

I swung up into the saddle and met her gaze with mine, giving her what I hoped was a reassuring smile. "I will. I'll see you as soon as I can." Then I lifted my hand in a wave and put my spurs to my horse's sides, taking off at a lope down the road. I didn't look back at her; I knew she'd still be standing there, watching me go.

FOURTEEN

IT WAS A Thursday in '92, when I learned the news. October 6th, the date was, the day when everything changed.

We'd been holed up at the Dunns' spread for a few months by then, letting the fuss over Adair die down some, and enjoying the home-life we'd come to know there. I was in no hurry to do anything until I'd recruited some other men for our cause, and Creek and Charley weren't keen to leave, either—Creek most of all. He and Rose were an item by then, and she'd curbed his restlessness some. I marveled at that; Creek never did like to stay in one place for too long, but Rose was so different than any of the women he'd ever known that he just had to stay around and see what she'd do or say next.

We'd been helping the Dunns with their cattle—in truth, not all of their herd was rightfully theirs; they'd rustled more than a few head, but we didn't comment—and that October Thursday I remember I was coming in from cutting calves when I saw Bitter Creek riding his big black stud up the main road at a full gallop, the horse's hooves churning up dust and throwing dirt clods up into the air behind it.

I felt my heart drop into my boots and my hand went for my gun like it had a mind of its own. Creek had gone to Ingalls that day to play some cards and hear the news, and my first thought was that he'd been found out and the law was on his trail. I put two fingers in my mouth and whistled, sharp and piercing like Bob used to do to get us all off the trains.

He reined in so hard his horse almost sat down on his haunches, then neck-reined him violently to the right, spurring him in my direction. He stopped him hard, slid out of the saddle like a sack of grain and let the horse go where it fancied, the reins dangling on the ground. His brown eyes were glazed over and his face was gray with shock.

"Creek, what the hell's the matter?" I demanded. "What's happened?"

He shoved his hand down into his coat pocket and pulled out a sloppily-folded page from the local newspaper. Without speaking, he shoved it at me.

My brows came together and I took the paper, my gun still in one hand. I unfolded it, holding it taut in my hands against the breeze that threatened to tear it from my grasp.

I didn't see the headline right off; the sun was bright and it cast a glare onto the paper, shining off the ink. Then there it was, the typeface bold and in big letters that must've been an inch tall:

DALTON GANG WIPED OUT.

For a few seconds, I couldn't get beyond that headline; my eyes didn't seem to want to read past those four simple words. I looked up at Creek and found him watching me anxiously. For once, his eyes were not dancing, and his ever-present smile was nowhere to be found. His mouth was set in a hard line and even his copper mustache seemed to droop a little around his lips. I saw him swallow, saw his Adam's Apple bob up and down. Then he spoke, but his voice sounded funny and hollow, like it wasn't his. "Read it."

I slowly dropped my eyes to the paper again and started reading. I had to read it twice; the first time my mind didn't grasp it any too well.

It said that Bob, Grat, Emmett, Dick and Bill Power had ridden into Coffeyville yesterday morning and set to robbing the Condon Bank and the First National Bank—at the same time. The townspeople

had taken up arms against them while they were occupied with pulling the jobs, and had shot them all
to hell when they tried to come out. Bob, Grat, Dick
and Power were all dead. Emmett had somehow sur-
vived—but he was shot up bad and it didn't look like
he was going to make it. He was in custody, the paper
said, and if he lived, he'd answer to charges—and
they'd be murder charges, for some folks in town had
been killed during the gunfight, and the town marshal, besides.

"This ain't right," I blurted out, tearing my gaze
away from the newspaper and looking up at Creek
again. "Is it?"

"I couldn't believe it either, Bill, but it's true. Did
you see what them crazy sons of bitches were trying to *do*?" He jerked his chin at the paper. "Says
they were trying to rob *two* banks at once. And in
Coffeyville, to boot, where the Daltons were raised
up!" He made a snorting noise and shook his head.
"A job that gutsy's got Bob Dalton's signature all
over it. What a damned *stupid* thing to try!"

I didn't answer him, just looked back at the paper,
still trying to make sense of the words printed there.
I knew Creek didn't really mean what he'd said just
now; neither of us had ever thought for one minute
that Bob Dalton had been stupid in any way shape or
form. If anything, he'd been too smart for his own

good. But he'd taken a hell of a gamble and lost, and all I could think about was poor Emmett, full of lead and maybe dying, and all because of something he'd likely wanted no part of, deep down.

We became aware of someone coming toward us, and we looked up to see Charley jogging out across the stockyard, his face full of worry. "What's the matter?" he asked us. "What's that paper say?"

Wordlessly I handed it over to him, watched as his face drained of color when he saw the headline. When he looked up at us his black eyes looked huge in his peaked face and he'd let his mouth fall open aways, just as stunned as we were.

It was the close-call part of it, just as much as the fact that the Daltons, who we'd sort of come to think of as invincible, were dead that kept us standing there like that for a bit as if we'd been struck dumb. If I hadn't soured on Bob when I'd done, and if Creek and Charley hadn't thrown in with me, like as not we'd be laid out in pine boxes right along with them.

I felt myself start to fill up with rage all of the sudden, out of nowhere. I was angry at the bastard lawdogs who'd decided they were going to make poor Em foot the bill that Bob had run up, and angry at the vigilantes in Coffeyville who'd put all that lead in him and probably wanted to string him up on top of it. I knew Emmett, and even without having been there, I *knew* he hadn't been the one killed those men. I knew it in my gut. The paper said that the townsfolk killed had been dropped by a rifle. I'd seen Bob Dalton shoot a Winchester, one-handed and from the hip, and hit whatever he'd been aiming at square in the middle, every damned time. I never saw him miss once. I was *sure* Bob had been the one that done it. But it was Emmett who would suffer for it.

"Bill?" Creek suddenly asked me, and he was looking at me funny, the shock gone some from his face. "You all right?" His eyes darted to Charley's, then back to mine again.

I barely noticed. My fingers closed around the paper, crushing it hard in my fist. I couldn't answer him, couldn't get the words out. All I could think was there was hell coming to Coffeyville, and I'd be the one bringing it. I couldn't leave Emmett to the fate that had been decided for him. I stood by any man I liked enough to consider as family, and Emmett was one of those.

"Rattle your hocks and get ready to ride, boys," I said, and my voice came out cold and dark. "I ain't gonna let this stand. They think Bob brought them hell, but I aim to bring worse." I tossed the balled-up paper to the ground and stalked toward the house, leaving them where they stood.

I went inside, set on getting the rest of my guns and my saddlebags that were up in the attic bedroom. Rose was in the front room, kneading bread at the table, and her head snapped up in surprise as I stomped in. She stopped her kneading, up to her elbows in flour, tendrils of dark hair come loose from her braid hanging down into her face, and called to me. "Bill? You all right?"

I didn't answer her; I couldn't. I took the stairs two at a time, my boots thudding loudly against the wood.

Creek and Charley found me in the attic, loading my revolvers with my back to the door. I heard them hanging back by the doorway, almost like they were scared. I threw a look over my shoulder at them. "Well? You with me, or ain't you?" My voice still sounded hard. I looked down at my guns, my back to them again.

Creek came over to me; I knew it was him from his spurs, since he was the only one of them wearing metal on his boots. He went past me to his rifle and opened it up, reaching into the box of cartridges I'd tossed on the bed and beginning to load them into it. He looked at me square, his gaze solemn, and I knew he was with me, as he always was.

Charley came over, too, and he put on his spurs and his two-gun belt, taking the revolver he'd had tucked up into his vest and sliding it into one of the holsters, then getting the other one out of his saddlebags. Silently he knotted the leather thongs around his thighs, just above his knees, that tied the guns down and I knew he was with us, too.

We gathered our parts and strode back down the stairs, me in the lead. Rose had wiped off her floury hands and had left her bread; she was standing over near the front door with George, Dal, Calvin and Bill, all of them with their heads bent over something John held in his hand. It was the newspaper I'd tossed down outside; he'd smoothed it out and was reading it over. They looked up when we came in, and they must've seen my anger in my face just like Creek had, because their eyes all went wider than normal. Rose looked pale and her brows were drawn together in worry. She seemed to know exactly what was on our minds, without us saying a thing. She went to Creek in a hurry.

"What're you gonna do, Creek? You ain't gonna do anything to answer that mess, are you?" she asked. Her voice had gone shrill; she sounded desperate. I knew it was because she was figuring if Creek went with me, he'd get shot up just like the Daltons had. She grabbed at his arm then and almost hung off him, but he shook her loose.

"That mess *needs* answerin'," he growled, and I

knew then that he was just as mad about Emmett as I was. He wasn't looking at her.

She looked like he'd slapped her, and hurt flooded her face. I was too distracted to feel bad for her, and anyway, if she was gonna love a man like Creek, she had to take what came with it.

The Dunns all looked nervous. "What're you gonna do, Bill?" George asked me.

"I ain't sure yet," I said grimly. "But they ain't gonna like it much, for a fact." I shifted my grip on my rifle and looked at them. "You been kind, to let us hole up here. But we'll be on our way now. We'll look you up once we get back out this way." My voice came out flat.

Bill nodded solemnly at me. "Any time at all, Doolin." The others looked too jumpy to say anything. Rose looked like she was gonna bawl. Creek met her eyes with his; he'd softened his gaze some, but he didn't say anything, just worked his jaw back and forth like he was keeping something back. Then he followed me out the door.

We got the rigs on our horses, quick, and started off. My mind was going forward like a train at full steam as we rode. I wasn't even sure exactly what I was going to do when I got to Coffeyville, except make my fury over the whole thing known. My blood was still running hot, but it'd stopped boiling like it'd been, and I started to see some reason. I knew there was probably little chance me and the others could bust Emmett out of wherever it was they had him put away, and even if we could, he'd surely be too hurt to ride. But I had to at least try to let him know somehow that I hadn't abandoned him to whatever waited for him. I owed him that at the least.

FIFTEEN

I'D ALREADY DECIDED not to see Edith before we left the Territory and headed into Kansas. I felt it was safer for her if I didn't and besides that, I didn't want her to see me so riled up. I'd stopped seeing red after we'd been riding for a few miles, but I couldn't shake the dark thoughts in my mind and I knew it'd scare her. This was my business, mine and the other boys', and she wouldn't understand. I wouldn't hurt her by trying to make her see things from my view, either. Once this was settled, once payment had been made by those that owed it, I'd come back for her.

It worried me some that there were only three of us; I thought it better to have one more. Our fourth man came in the figure of my old ranching compadre, Tulsa Jack Blake.

He'd been drifting in and out of Guthrie; I'd run into him when Creek and Charley and I had played poker at one of the saloons there a few weeks back. He'd been glad to see me and Creek, and Charley, too; their old feud was a distant memory. I knew without question he'd want in on whatever we had planned; he was almost flat broke and was just the sort of fellow who'd be glad to take a train with us if there was any money to be had at it, and excitement besides. I'd already decided I'd pick one for us to go after, once we'd seen about Coffeyville.

We rode hard and got more and more wary as we got closer to Kansas. The papers were gloating good about the Dalton Gang being gone, but Heck Thomas had been seen everywhere nearby, sticking his nose into the Coffeyville affair like he was in charge of anything to do with the Dalton boys. I figured he was trying to save face since he hadn't caught them like he'd planned to do. Well, I thought grimly, he wouldn't catch me or mine, either.

Tulsa Jack wasn't wanted yet like the rest of us, so whenever we needed anything on the trail we sent him into whatever town we came up near. Turned out to be useful, because he'd get newspapers and bring them back to our campsites, and in that fashion we kept abreast of what was going on in Coffeyville. The papers were obsessed with reporting on Emmett's condition, and anything at all to do with the Daltons, and through them we came to learn that William Dalton, the brother that had been tried and acquitted for the Alila job back in California, had arrived in Coffeyville to stand by Emmett and attend to the effects and bodies of Bob and Grat. He'd been in politics back in California, but after the trial he'd been put through he pulled up and left that state, coming back out to Oklahoma Territory. Didn't seem to matter none that he'd gotten off; he was a Dalton and had a black mark struck against him because of it. Wasn't long before the papers in Kansas started to turn on him, too, saying he was shooting off his mouth and swearing revenge for the mistreatment of his brothers' bodies (townsfolk wanting keepsakes of the event had cut away pieces of their clothes and hair while they lay dead in the street), and the theft of property they'd had on them when they arrived, like their guns, their horses and the money in their saddlebags. Seemed from the quotes they had printed that he and I were of like mind when it came to wanting Coffeyville to answer for Emmett's condition, and I started to wonder if we should somehow look him up once we got close. He could deliver our message of retaliation, both to the town of Coffeyville and to Em.

When we got near to the Kansas border, I told Tulsa Jack to get ahold of the schedule for the train that rolled through Caney, a little hole just west of Coffeyville that was about three miles away from where we were camped out. We were low on funds and I wanted to make our presence known besides. The law in the area was still boasting, saying the big-time railroad gangs were a thing of the past now that the Daltons were dead. They didn't reckon on what I had in mind.

We all of us knew Bob had had a knack for planning train jobs, but I was sure I could do just as good. I'd paid attention to how he'd planned things; learned a lot on the jobs I was in on with him, and I knew we wouldn't have any trouble. Caney wasn't much more than camp settlement, and their train depot was set near an outcropping of low hills that would serve well to hide what we were doing, and where our horses were tied. I studied on the schedule for a bit, picked the time, then laid the plan out to Creek, Charley and Jack. We'd pull the job tomorrow night, but before we did, I had mind to get word to William Dalton that I aimed to get payment for what had been done to Emmett.

Jack, of course, was the logical one to go into Coffeyville and hunt him up. It had been five days since the raid and the papers said William was still in town to be at Emmett's side while he was attended by a doctor. They had plans to move him to the jail at Independence soon, which gave us cause to believe he was getting better, against all odds. I told Jack to ride in and find William, and to see if he could get him to leave Em for a bit so he could come out to our camp. Jack rode off early in the morning, and the three of us settled down to wait.

———◦《◊》◦———

"Bill, look there. Jack's coming, and it looks like he found Dalton."

Creek's voice was tense. I straightened up from the map I'd been hunched over and turned to look where he was looking. Jack's roan gelding was coming our way, and there was another rider in tow, in the saddle of a long-legged chestnut with a white snip on its muzzle. They were moving at a canter through the tall dry grass, but when they got within a few hundred feet they dropped to a walk, glancing around cautiously, making sure they weren't being tracked. I put a hand on my hip and waited, Creek and Charley just behind me, on high alert as Jack and William Dalton reached us.

I sized him up as he dismounted. He was shorter

than all the Daltons I'd met previously, and more solidly-built. He had hair the same color that Bob's and Grat's had been, and he was clean-shaven and more well-dressed than I'd expected him to be; probably because he'd been in politics and had the habit. He had a gun belt on and a rifle sticking out of the scabbard on his saddle, and his hat was pulled down pretty low; I figured he was trying to avoid recognition since he'd sort of gone out of the way to make himself unpopular among most common folks in those parts.

He looked at me. "Bill Doolin, I'm guessing?" he asked. I nodded.

"Will Dalton," he said, and offered me his hand. He had a firm grip. "Your boy Jack here says you wanted a word or two with me?" he asked.

"I do," I confirmed. "I appreciate you coming out here; I didn't think it any too bright for me to come to you, considering." He nodded in a knowing way and I could tell he knew of our association with his brothers. I introduced him to Creek and Charley, then got right to my point.

"How's Emmett?" My voice came out hard.

Will shook his head. "He's on the mend, but to tell the truth I'm blamed if I know how. Those bastards put enough lead in him to take down three men. His arm's broke and near to useless, and he can't stand.

They got him with a scattergun on top of everything else. Put him down out of his saddle when he was trying to pull Bob up into it." There was disgust and fury in his voice.

I set my jaw. "Listen here, Will, I ain't gonna lie to you, there wasn't any love between me and your brother Bob; that's why we parted ways awhile back. But I hope he and Grat didn't suffer any too much."

He looked me square in the eye, his expression serious. "I know how my brothers were, Bill. Grat could be hard to get on with; that's the damned truth of it. And Bob was stubborn as hell; it was his way or not at all. I won't hold it against you if you took your leave of them; I figure a man's entitled to his own opinion. Em's talked about you to me, says you're a fair man and a good friend, and I can see you're honest, too. I ain't going to let whatever happened between you and them color my opinion of you any."

I liked him right off, and I could tell he was sharp and he had good sense besides. It relieved me a whole lot; I'd been a bit worried that he'd be another Bob or Grat. My worries were clearly unfounded. "I'm much obliged to you for that," I said, and I figured it was time to tell him what was on my mind then. "Thinking of Em shot up like that and left to answer for the whole thing's got me a bit riled up," I said. "I figure me and the other boys owe Coffeyville a little

more hell on top of what Bob brought 'em already."
My voice came out grim.

Will's eyes started gleaming and he gave me a
knowing sort of half-smile. "I figure I do too, if you
think about it. I'm damned tired of the law in this
country thinking it can put my whole family in coffins, which is what it seems to me they're aiming to
do. They're missing their figure if they think they
can, though, I'll tell you that right now. If they're
betting on putting me away too, they'd be wise to
copper that bet." His voice had taken on a dark tone.

I tapped my fingers against the grip of one of
my revolvers. "When you go back to Coffeyville, if
you'd tell them their bluff's about to be called, I'd be
obliged to you."

He understood me perfectly, and he nodded
slowly. "If you've got no objection, once I see Em
safely to Independence, I'll join you boys. They're
planning on taking him there in two days."

"Be glad to have you along," I said, and I meant
it.

He shook my hand again and headed for his
horse. "I'd best get back. I don't trust that damned
sheriff or any of those guards they got on Em, and I
don't like leaving him alone with them, all helpless
like that." He put his foot in the stirrup and swung up
into the saddle. "It was good to meet all of you," he

said to us. "I'll give Em your well-wishes, and I'll see you soon." He dipped his hat brim to us in a kind of salute, then cantered off, the sun glinting off the rounds in his belt.

Creek came up to my side. "I like him, Bill. He'll be a good man to have with us," he said to me, and Charley nodded as we watched him go.

"Seems so," I agreed. I raised an eyebrow at them. "Let's go over things for our little shindy with the railroad tomorrow one more time, so we're all good and clear."

———✺———

"Keep yourselves steady, boys," I said, low and calm. "Don't jump the gun. Wait for my signal."

It was nearing nine o'clock and we were waiting for the train to pull in to the tiny little station at Caney. There was no station operator to coerce into flagging her down, but we didn't need one. The lines split at Caney and the train would have to stop so the brakeman could get out and pull the lever that would route the train onto the right track. That little detail was part of the reason I'd picked this spot. Jack would surprise the brakeman when he got out and cover him and the outside while Creek and I boarded the engine. Charley would cover us while we conducted our business. I thought it'd feel strange to be waiting on a train like this without Bob there to keep us to task, but it didn't and everyone seemed intent on following my lead.

I checked my watch; it showed eight fifty-six. On cue, we heard the whistle sound out and the low hum of the wheels, and the train pulled in right on time, letting out a cloud of smoke from the smokestack that blotted out the moon for a few seconds. I took out one of my guns; the others did the same, and we crept carefully closer. When we were just out of range, I stopped them all, waiting.

A man appeared in the doorway of the engine, a lantern in hand. He went toward the junction where the two lines met up and set the lantern down.

"Go, Jack," I whispered, and he did. When I saw he had the brakeman at the end of his gun, I signaled the others. "Let's go." We adjusted our masks one last time and headed for the engine.

I bounded onto the step that led into the engine, my gun leveled. Creek was behind me in a similar pose. As it happened, the messenger was standing just inside the doorway of the express car; it was already open. "Evening, boys," I said to him and the engineer, who had his hands raised as Creek urged him back and away from me.

The messenger's face drained of blood and his eyes went big as saucers; he looked at us like we were some kind of spooks. It looked to me like maybe the railroad had let its guard down a little after word came about the Daltons' end. They'd find that was a mistake, by my estimation of things.

"Open the safe, if you would," I said, my tone firm. He stood there for a few seconds more, his mouth hanging open and his eyes looking like they were gonna fall out of his head.

"You're lettin' in flies there, friend, and you're wasting my time. Get to it and we'll be on our way." I punctuated this by deliberately thumbing the hammer back on my gun. The click sounded loud. The messenger started sweating, but still he did nothing. My patience was wearing down pretty quick and I took a step toward him and fired a shot into the floor to hurry him up. "Ain't—gonna—ask—again," I told him, a clear warning in my tone.

He sort of jumped, like he'd been woken up from a nap, and he turned and started twirling the lock on the safe. His fingers were shaking so bad and his palms were so sweaty it took him a few tries to open it. When he finally got it he stood back, quick, almost tripping over his own feet. "Please, don't hurt me. I got a family," he blubbered.

I rolled my eyes. "I ain't gonna hurt you, or

anyone else, so long as you stay where you are. Our business's with the railroad, not you personally." I motioned to Creek and he came forward with the flour sack, reaching quickly for the few stacks of bills set inside the safe. When he was done he backed out, covering the terrified engineer once more. I nodded to the messenger. "Much obliged." Then I turned and ducked out, jumping down quick. I whistled sharp, carrying on Bob's tradition, since it was the best way to get everyone to me. Charley and Jack came out of the darkness, firing a few shots into the air to make sure we got away clean.

We got to the horses and wheeled away into the darkness. My satisfaction with the whole thing rose; it had gone exactly how I wanted it to.

"Damn, that one was easy, wasn't it?" Creek called to me, and I almost hear his big grin in his voice.

"Just like it was supposed to be," I replied. We concentrated on helping our horses keep their footing in the thick grass that came up as high as our feet in the stirrups. Back at our campsite I handed out each man's share, glad to do it, for they'd all shown their sand that night. My gang had pulled its first job and done well by me, and that took away some of the sting from the Coffeyville affair.

SIXTEEN

THEY TOOK EMMETT to the jail at Independence on the eleventh of October, and the next day Will joined us, satisfied, he said, that Em would live. Now that he was sure of that, he told me, he was set to go about making sure the name of Dalton would still be known far and wide—he intended to carry on where Bob had left off, and do some better than he had, at that. The trial he'd gone through after the Alila affair, along with the aftermath of Coffeyville, had turned him off anything and everything to do with the law and he was more than ready to throw in with me and the rest, up for anything we might encounter, and willing to go along with anything I might plan.

By then I had come to grips with the fact that there wasn't any way in hell I was going to be able to do a damned thing about Emmett and his fix. All that trying to bust him out would do would be to get me and the others caught or killed, and I didn't fancy either one. As much as I felt for Em and wished there was something I could do for him, I knew he had to face up to what his blind devotion to Bob had cost him, and he'd have to do it alone.

The law was out for us bad by now, and things were getting hot. The papers published a dispatch sent to the sheriff of Coffeyville by the chief detective of Wells Fargo, saying he and Heck Thomas had gathered a posse to kill a group of outlaws out to rescue Emmett. It was us they meant, our message had been delivered. The paper said the businesses in Coffeyville closed up the day the dispatch came, and the citizens armed themselves to the teeth. I wasn't stupid, I'd stay out of Coffeyville. I didn't fancy getting myself or my gang pumped full of bullets.

The five of us turned our horses' tails to Kansas and headed back into Oklahoma Territory, heading for the refuge of the Dunns' ranch again—but first we had a stop to make. Will had a wife and two children, and they had taken a claim near Kingfisher. Will wanted to see them before he headed for the Dunns' place with us. I agreed, and we came to the house in the middle of the night.

"Will? Is that you?"

We'd been putting up our horses in the stable when the sound of a woman's voice startled us. We turned, all five of us at once, to see the dim outline of a lady standing in the doorway of the barn. She was short and slim, but that was all I could tell about her; it was as dark as a stack of black cats outside.

"Yes, Jane," Will answered softly. We were all trying to keep our voices down in case anyone was watching the house. "Go on back inside. I'll be in a minute. Don't wake the children."

She nodded and turned away, doing as he said. He turned back to me, hanging his bridle up on a nail. "You figure we should go inside in shifts, leave someone on watch?"

"That'd be best." I looked over at the others. "Anyone want to volunteer?" I knew they were all as tired and hungry as I was, but Will was right. We couldn't be too careful.

"I will, Bill," Tulsa Jack said. "I ain't that tired."

I nodded. "I'll spare you in two hours, and we'll bring you out some grub before that. You hear or see anything at all, come get me."

He nodded and settled himself on a barrel set near the far wall, which had a window cut into it. The boards in the barn were full of knotholes and some of them were big enough to get a gun through, if he needed to. He leaned his Winchester in the corner, within easy reach.

The rest of us headed inside, treading quietly so we wouldn't scare the little ones awake. Jane was waiting for us in the front room, which was also the kitchen. She was a tiny little thing, with honey-colored hair run through with streaks of gold. She reminded me of a delicate little bird. We took our hats off, remembering our manners.

Will went over to her and kissed her, then introduced her to us. She didn't seem upset that we were there or scared by all the guns on us; I guessed that she was used to this sort of thing by now, since Bob and Emmett had lived with her and Will for a time back in California. She motioned to the table and told us she'd have coffee and a meal ready for us in no time.

I stopped her when she started to go past me. "Don't go to a lot of trouble, Jane. I figure we've brought you enough as it is, just showing up in the middle of the night like this." I felt bad; I remembered the night we'd come to the Dunns' place in a similar fashion. Seemed like me and the other boys were always imposing on one young lady or another in that manner and it didn't sit well with me.

She gave me a warm, welcoming smile. "Don't you worry about it, Bill," she said firmly, like she'd known me for years instead of minutes. "My husband's family and friends are mine too, the minute they come into this house. It's no bother at all." She smiled again and went over to the stove.

I started feeling pretty miserable then; Jane's kindness made me think of Edith. Like I'd done in the days after Adair, I'd forced myself not to think about her in the last few days; she wasn't with me and there wasn't any help for it. I knew there'd be many times in the coming years I'd likely have to leave her for a time if I kept on with what I was doing, so I needed to get used to it—but sure as hell was hard.

Jane brought us cups of strong coffee and some food, and before I ate mine I asked her for another plate for Tulsa Jack. I took it out to him and he seemed surprised, like he'd thought I'd forget.

"I ain't going to let a man go hungry, Jack, especially not my look-out," I joked gently. "You think you can stay awake?"

He nodded. "Coffee'll see to that. Obliged, Bill."

"See you in a few hours." I headed back inside.

There wasn't too much space in the house; all in all it was only three rooms yet, four if you counted the lean-to. Will told Jane we would bunk down in the front room, and after a bit she went on in to bed, and Charley and Creek turned in, too, using their bedrolls. They were out cold soon as they put their heads down. Will and I sat up together for a few more minutes at the table, a lamp on low between us, talking softly.

He grinned at me suddenly, his eyes dancing the way Creek's often did. "I read about Caney," he said, out of nowhere. "That was you, wasn't it?"

I looked back at him for a minute, then nodded, feeling a funny little smile spread across my face. "Damned straight, it was."

"First one without Bob and the others?" he asked, and I nodded again, taking another swallow of coffee.

"How'd it go?"

"Damned near to perfect," I replied.

"You picked another one yet?"

I shook my head. "Haven't had the time, seeing as how my mind's been sort of fixated on Coffeyville lately."

He nodded and sat back in his chair, looking thoughtful. Then he scratched his chin and gave me a speculating look. "You ever given any thought to pulling a bank job?"

I raised an eyebrow. "Don't the idea of it sort of spook you, after what happened to Bob and Grat?" I asked.

He rolled his eyes. "Hell, Bill, Bob's trouble was he was too ambitious when he came up with that scheme. I ain't saying we should try for *two* of them, like he was set to do. Just one." He paused for a minute to finish his coffee. "You think on it some, mull the idea over. I'm up for whatever you decide." He stood up and bid me to sleep well, then went into the bedroom with Jane, leaving me sitting there, thinking.

We got to the Dunns' in the early morning this time, and they all came out to meet us in the barn, talking over one another so fast I thought their tongues would fall off. They'd all read the papers and wanted to know what we were going to do next, now that we'd been called out so boldly by so many lawdogs. The brothers made a big fuss over Will, too; he was the first Dalton they'd met and of some fame in their eyes because of it. They frisked around the bunch of us like a pack of eager hounds, and I held back from laughing at them as I told their names to Jack and Will.

Rose had come by then, and she made a bee-line for Creek. He picked her up by her waist and swung her around, making her laugh, then he kissed her in his usual bold manner. Her face went pink because we were all watching them, but it didn't stop her from putting her arms around his neck and kissing him back.

"Woo-eee, you got you a live one there, Creek!" Tulsa Jack called with a laugh and a leer. He and Will hadn't met Rose yet.

"Shut up," Creek retorted, but he was smiling.

"Watch your mouth, Jack, or Rose here'll put a bullet in you where it'd count for something," I added, joining in the teasing, my mood lightening. "She's a damned good shot—I've seen it for myself."

Jack made a snorting noise, clearly doubtful. "I ain't never seen a little girl like that handle a shooting iron. You as good as Bill says you are, girl?" he asked Rose.

She gave him an innocent smile. "You care to find out?" she asked. Her brothers all started throwing knowing looks at one another and Creek crossed his arms over his chest, that fox-grin of his spreading out wide across his face.

"Lord almighty, looks like you been called out by a piece of calico, Jack!" Charley started laughing so hard he could barely stand up straight. He knew just as well as Creek and I, and the Dunn brothers, how good Rose was with a gun, but that devilish streak in him was dying to see Tulsa Jack find that out the hard way.

Jack frowned at us. "Are you boys plumb off your nut? I ain't shooting against no little girl!"

Rose put her hands behind her back and sort of sidled up to Jack, her eyes all big and meek-looking. "Why the hell not? You afraid I'll whup you?"

Jack looked like he'd been kicked by a horse right about then, and I knew it was because Rose swore like that. I started chuckling. *This* would be the most fun I'd had in a good long while.

Jack's mouth opened, but nothing came out of it for a minute. He eyeballed Rose for a few seconds, like he was trying to decide if she was for real or not, then shut his mouth and set it in a line, his brow furrowing. "Fine. You want to try to out-shoot me, I ain't gonna shin out or try to stop you, since you seem set on it." He shrugged his shoulders and pulled his six-gun out.

George reached for the Peacemaker he wore strapped up under his left arm and handed it to his sister, one side of his mouth turned up. She took it and half-cocked the hammer, thumbed open the loading gate and checked over the bullets in the cylinder, like she wasn't sure George would've loaded it right. He frowned at her. Tulsa Jack was eyeballing her good again, like he was surprised she even knew how to get a gun open. She ignored him, just tossed her shiny dark hair back over her shoulders and marched herself outside. The rest of us followed, a few of us still chuckling under our breath. Will threw me a look; his eyes were twinkling. I had come to find that Will was just as jovial as Creek most of the time, always up for a laugh, and there wasn't much in life he liked better than a good joke.

"How you want to do this, Rose?" Dal asked, once we were all gathered in the stockyard.

She shot a sly glance at Jack. "Why, however Tulsa Jack over there thinks we should. I don't want to make it too hard for him." Her voice was all sweet.

He glared at her; I could tell he wanted to chew her out bad but it was pretty much branded into us not to cuss at a lady—even if that lady cussed at you first. "Do what you want, I ain't gonna bellyache about it," he muttered.

"Back at my spread in California I used to hang buckskin off of tree branches and use it as targets," Will commented.

Rose turned and faced him, her eyes lighting up. "Hell, this is a cattle ranch, ain't it? We got leather all over the place. That'll do. George, cut off some of that hide you got stretched on the back fence behind the barn. Don't make the pieces too big, either."

He went off to do as she said, chuckling, while Tulsa Jack stood there with his hand on his hip, his gun dangling at his other side. He looked good and irritated. "This is the plumb stupidest thing you three ever got me into," he said to me and Creek and Charley.

"Oh, shut up and get your iron ready," Rose told him primly. "You said you weren't gonna bellyache about it, and that's what I'm hearing."

We started laughing again. "Damn it all, if that girl of yours ain't something!" Will said to Creek, shaking his head. Creek just grinned.

George came back with a handful of strips of cowhide. Each of them were only about three or four inches wide. He started hanging them off the low branch of the cottonwood near the pasture gate, leaving the leather dangling about six feet in the air.

"This is damn stupid," Jack muttered again under his breath. "They ain't even gonna stay still; the breeze is moving them all over the place. We should've used bottles."

Rose rolled her eyes. "Can't you hit a moving target? Quit whining and have your go."

Jack sighed and raised his gun, sighted, and popped off a few rounds. He wasn't a crack shot—among our present group that distinction belonged to me, Will and Creek alone—but most of the time he could hit what he aimed for. Out of the six shots he fired, he hit two of the strips—which was a hell of a lot better than I thought he'd do, when it came down to it. It wasn't an easy challenge.

Rose raised her arm, sighted, and fired, her aim sure, her arm steady. Confidently she emptied her gun, and when she was done, she'd hit five targets in six shots.

Tulsa Jack stared for a few minutes, like it was taking him awhile to realize what had happened. Then his face got all red and his fists balled up. I sobered a little. I knew Jack wouldn't hurt a woman but he'd been pretty damn humiliated, when all was said and done, and a man with wounded pride was something to be wary of. We all watched tensely, waiting to see what he'd do, and Creek started inching himself protectively toward Rose.

Jack looked at the ground for a minute, his arms crossed over his chest. Then we all saw him shake his head, heard a rueful laugh come up out of him. He started chuckling harder and looked over at Rose. "Well, I'm beat," he told her, reaching up and giving his hat brim a tip in her direction. "You got the bulge on me, for a fact, there, missy." It broke the tension and we all started laughing.

"Damn right, I did," she replied, but she favored him with a grin. "Anytime you want a roping or riding contest, I'll take you on."

He shook his head and put his palms out, still chuckling. "I think I'll take your word for it."

SEVENTEEN

"THANK GOD YOU broke it off with the Daltons! if you hadn't left them—"

I could hardly understand Edith's words; she had her face buried in my neck, and besides that, she was crying pretty hard. I could feel her trembling in relief as she kept herself pressed against me, hugging me as hard as she could, like she was afraid I'd up and disappear if she let go of me. I didn't mind though; I just held her tight and put my lips against the top of her head.

"Would you have gone with them, Bill?" she asked me suddenly, pulling back and looking at me anxiously, her tear-filled eyes searching my face like she was reading it over. Her face was splotched and damp and her eyes and nose were red from crying, but she was still the most beautiful sight I'd ever seen. "If you hadn't quit them, and Bob had wanted you to go, would you?"

I reached out and smoothed her wild hair back with both hands, trying to calm her down some. "I don't know, Edith," I said. "It don't matter none, anyway. I didn't."

She pulled in a deep, shuddery breath and hugged me again. "If you had any idea how I felt when I read the papers—knowing you could've been killed right along with them—"

"I'm still here, honey," I interrupted gently. I could see she was trying to get ahold of herself by then and I kept her pulled close, to reassure her.

It was getting dark out; I'd come by her place after supper-time, not wanting to impose on the family. Her folks had greeted me with the same warmth they'd shown me the last time I'd been there, before Coffeyville and everything that followed it, so I guessed my growing infamy wasn't bothering them any—or if it was, they weren't showing it, for Edith's sake. Edith had set to crying right away when she saw me, so they'd left us alone, and we'd come outside together to talk in private. It wasn't that cold out yet, even though it was getting pretty near to November.

I marveled that we were so easy with one another each time we met, even though this last time I'd been away had been our longest stretch apart yet. Once I'd got her good and calm again, we sat together on the porch-swing, talking. She kept ahold of one of my hands while we did.

"I'm sorry about Emmett," she told me, her voice soft and sad. I'd told her about Emmett in the past, and how he'd been a friend to me. "The papers were talking about you trying to get him out; you and the others. Was that true?"

I sighed. "I had a mind to, and that's the truth of it, but I saw reason before I did anything stupid. There's no way on this earth I could bust him out of there. He'll have to bear up to whatever they give him. There ain't nothing else to be done about it." I set my jaw hard and looked away from her for a minute, trying to push down the stubborn anger that still came up in me whenever I thought hard about Em's plight, and how he'd gotten there.

She rested her other hand on top of the one of mine she was holding. It was a simple thing, but it made me feel comforted, and made me know she really cared about how I was feeling. I couldn't help it then, I pulled her close, almost into my lap, and brought my lips to hers. It was a long time before we pulled apart, and when we did she rested her head against my shoulder. She'd started trembling again, but in a different way this time.

I reached into my coat pocket then and pulled out the engagement ring I'd gotten her in Kingfisher just a few days ago. It wasn't any fancy diamond, just a small garnet set into a band of gold. She wasn't the kind of woman that needed a big flashy ring. This one had reminded me of her somehow, lovely yet practical. I didn't make any flowery speech; I knew I didn't need to, and I wouldn't have been any too good at it, besides. Instead I just picked up her slender little hand and slipped it on her finger. It felt like it fitted all right.

Her breath caught a little; I heard it. She lifted her hand and spread her fingers wide, looking it over. I waited, a little nervous she wouldn't like it. I figured she did, though, when she put her arms around my neck again and tilted her face up so I could kiss her again.

"I know it ain't a diamond," I whispered to her, "but—"

"Hush, Bill," she said, putting her fingertips against my lips. She was smiling at me and her eyes were dancing, her tears from before gone. "I don't need a diamond. This is perfect."

"I ain't talked to your Pa proper," I reminded her. There hadn't been a chance to.

She shook her head. "You don't need to. Pa knows you were going to ask me. He talked about it with me. Already gave us his blessing."

I sobered a little, taking both her hands in mine

and holding them between us while we sat sort of facing each other in the swing, our knees touching. "Edith, we got to wait till spring. I'm gonna find a place for us near Ingalls, but I want for us to be able to be settled before we get married, and I got to be able to rest easy about the law, make sure I ain't too easy to find ."

She nodded. "I don't mind waiting, so long as I know it's coming," she said, giving me that pretty smile of hers I loved so much. "Pa can marry us, so no one can use it against you."

My bride-to-be was smart; I hadn't even thought about the fact that her Pa could perform the ceremony. But it would solve things and then some. I had a few things planned for my outfit between now and next year, and the price on my head and the others' would no doubt grow some bigger by then. It would be better for everyone if we were married in secret. "Edith, darlin', you're a wonder. I got plumb lucky when I met you, and that's the truth." I leaned my head against hers and we laughed quietly together.

"You should get on inside. It's getting late," I told her.

"When will you come back?" she asked me.

"I can't say for certain. But you can be sure it'll be as soon as I can." I stood up and walked with her to the front door, escorting her inside.

There was just one lamp lit in the parlor; we'd been outside a long time and it was later than I'd thought. Edith's Ma was nowhere around and I guessed she'd gone to bed. Her Pa was sitting in one of the rocking chairs set near the window, and after Edith had bid me good-bye and kissed him good-night, he came over to me while I got my hat and put it on.

"Have you asked her, then?" he asked me, and I nodded.

"I was aiming to speak to you proper, but Edith said you knew."

He nodded. "You have her mother's blessing, and mine, Bill. My daughter cares for you, and I know you care for her too. I told you once all that mattered was her happiness, and so long as you can give her that and keep her safe, I still mean it."

"I'm obliged to you, Mr. Ellsworth, for seeing it that way," I told him, and I meant it with everything I had.

He put on his own hat and gestured to the door. "Let me come with you to get your horse; I'd like to speak to you just a bit more." He took a lantern from a nail near the door and lit it.

We went outside and headed down the front porch together, and he glanced over at me. "Are you still bent on settling your score with the railroad?" he asked me bluntly, and I wouldn't dance around the subject none; I figured he deserved as much of the truth as I felt I could give him. I owed him that for all the kindness he'd shown me already, and I wasn't even his son-in-law yet.

"I reckon I they still have a debt with me, and the other boys who ride with me," I said evenly.

He nodded shortly. "Well, all I ask is that you try to spare Edith as much grief as you can. She know better than to believe every word the papers say, but when she sees the notices in town, and the articles about you, it's easy to forget that."

"I give you my word, I'll do everything I can to keep her clear of it. I may not always be able to, but I'll try my best."

He met my gaze with his and nodded, saying nothing more. We were at the barn door now, and Mr. Ellsworth opened it, reaching up to hang the lantern on the wall. I stopped, on high alert. My horse was in the stall I'd left him in, but the rig was stripped off. I'd purposely left it on, like I did most of the time now. I threw a confused look at Mr. Ellsworth, but he just gave me a small, easy smile. "Looking for your saddle, Bill?" he asked mildly.

"Yessir. It should be on my horse, so far as I re-member," I said dryly.

"It is." He nodded toward the box stall at the end,

and my jaw just about hit the barn floor, because his big Palomino stud was tied in there, with my saddle and bridle strapped on him. I whipped my head around to stare at him, struck dumb.

"Seems to me that horse of yours is getting a bit worn out. I'd feel some better if you had one I knew could outrun anything that might try to take you away from my daughter, once you're married," he said, motioning me over to the stall door. "His name's Rebel, and you'll find that it suits him well when you get up on him," he said, his voice going very dry. "He's a strong stud, Bill, and *fast*, but he needs a firmer hand than I can give him. He's a younger man's horse. He's yours if you'll take him. Your gelding will suit me fine."

I was struck almost speechless at his generosity, and it took me a good few minutes to be able to form words. "I don't rightly know how I can thank you," I told him, hearing myself stammer a bit. "Are you sure? He's got to be worth a lot." The light from the lantern shone over the Rebel's golden coat, and his cream-colored mane and tail. He truly was one hell of an animal.

He held up a hand. "My daughter's happiness, and therefore your safety, is worth more. I'll rest a little easier knowing you've got him for your saddle-horse."

I stuck out a hand for him to shake. He did, then stood back as I opened the stall door and untied my new horse.

"Don't say I didn't warn you, now," Mr. Ellsworth said, and his eyes were twinkling like his daughter's often did. "He's like a powder-keg with the fuse lit. Keep on your toes and don't let your guard down. I always say a few extra prayers before I ride him."

"I've broken a few horses in my time," I said with a smile. "I'll handle him."

I thanked him again, bid him farewell, then mounted up and lit on out for the Dunns', Rebel's stride eating up the ground as we went.

———— ❖ ————

Even though it was near to ten o'clock at night when I got back, the lamps were all burning and Rose, Creek, George and John were all still awake and in the front room together; the men had a deck of cards out and Creek was teaching Rose how to play poker. Gambling was about the one thing she hadn't picked up from her brothers just yet. They all looked over when I came inside.

"How's Edith, Bill?" Creek asked me.

"Just fine. She was worried, but I set her right

again." I took off my coat and hat. "There's a new stud in your stable, boys," I said to the Dunn brothers, "but don't any of you get any ideas when you see him. He's my new saddle-horse, and he *ain't* for sale. He's a hell of a horse." I flashed a knowing grin at Rose. She looked confused for a second, then seemed to figure out exactly what I meant. She stood up from where she'd been sitting next to Creek and gave me an excited smile.

"Not Mr. Ellsworth's palomino?" she asked me.

"The very same. He gave him to me. Sort of an early wedding present, you might say." I winked at her, then headed toward the stairs.

"You ask her, Bill?" Creek called after me. I could hear the grin in his voice.

"I surely did, Creek," I replied over my shoulder.

"She say yes?"

I paused, my hand on the banister and my foot on the bottom step, and turned to look at him, raising one eyebrow. "What do you think?" I felt a sly grin spread out over my face.

His eye started twinkling and he laughed aloud. "I think she don't know what she's gone and got herself into, that's what I think!"

I shook my head at him, but I was still smiling. I started to climb the stairs.

"Wait, Bill, come on back down here and we'll

have a drink to celebrate," John called. He stood up and went into the kitchen, then came back with a bottle and a bunch of tin cups. He unscrewed the top and poured about a shot of whiskey into each one, and passed them around. He gave one to Rose, too.

"To Bill and Edith," he proclaimed in a grand voice.

"'To Bill and Edith,'" the others all echoed, looking at me and smiling. Creek gave me a wink. I felt a little embarrassed at all the attention, but I lifted my cup right along with them. We all drank, even Rose, and she didn't cough, either. I shook my head to myself. Nothing Rose did ever surprised me anymore.

EIGHTEEN

CREEK AND CHARLEY and I were on our way into Ingalls one Saturday afternoon; we'd missed our old days at the Ransom & Murray and felt like playing a little poker and quenching our thirst. Will had come into town from a spell with Jane and their young ones, and he'd joined us. I had a mind to talk over a few plans with them; we were all of us getting the itch to go out on a venture. Ranch life was getting a bit too tame again.

We'd been riding aways when we caught sight of a man standing alone in the shoulder-high dry grass, his hand raised to his eyes like he was trying to shield them from the sun. He had a kind of frantic about him, like he was searching for something, and as we got closer I could see he was young, and kind of bedraggled-looking, with a few days' worth of scruffy dark beard coming up on his face, like he'd been on the trail for a good long while. The four of us checked our horses, wary that he was some sort of lawman, but he wasn't wearing a badge or gun belt and he didn't look like he was heeled at all, so far as I could tell.

Creek, Charley and Will looked at each other, then looked at me, raising their eyebrows almost in unison. I looked at the young man again and frowned, then nudged my horse forward, my right hand near the gun on that side, just in case. "Hey there," I called to him, and he turned around, startled, like he hadn't heard us come up. "You lose something?" I asked, as the others came up beside me.

"Yessir," he said with a rueful sigh. "My horse."

I cocked an eyebrow at him. "It throw you?" I asked shortly.

"No. I got off to tighten the cinch and the reins slipped out of my hand. He took off and I ain't even sure where he went. I can't see over this damn grass." His voice was tight with frustration and I could tell he wasn't any too experienced at being out alone on the trail. He seemed kind of slow, besides, like he maybe wasn't the smartest fellow in God's creation.

Creek caught my eye and jerked his head to the left. A few dozen feet out I could see a saddled, riderless horse greedily cropping grass. It was a short, stocky horse and standing in a little hollow on the prairie besides, so I imagined it was near to invisible to the man on the ground. "It's over there," I said, pointing, "about a fifty feet out or so."

The young man's frown got bigger and he sort of shrugged his shoulders at me. "I can't catch him," he explained. "He runs when he ain't kept in hand."

I looked at the others, then back at the kid. "Just rope him," I said, reaching to untie my coil. "Here, you can use mine."

He looked even more uncomfortable and his face got kind of flushed, like he was embarrassed. "Don't know how to rope."

I looked at the others and sort of rolled my eyes. Living for so long in cattle country, I was used to near everyone in these parts being able to rope, or at least knowing how, even if they weren't any good at it.

"Creek, Charley, you want to assist me in this?" I asked them, making a lasso. They nodded and neck reined into position, one on either side of me. We trotted forward, and the kid's horse's head shot up. It swung around and broke into a run, its reins dragging on the ground. I kicked Rebel into a canter and readied my lasso; Creek cut sharp to the left and Charley to the right, blocking off its escape route. I swung the rope easy up over my head, then let fly, my loop landing right around its neck, nice and neat.

The horse didn't much appreciate being roped;

he reared up, good and mad. I dallied the end around the saddle-horn quick, then leaned back hard in the saddle, shoving my heels toward the ground. Rebel stopped and sat back on his hind legs, bracing the other horse and pulling the rope taut. I reeled the horse in, pretty as you please, and then ponied it over to the young man, who looked like he'd just seen an attraction in some show. Clearly he'd never worked cattle, nor seen them worked up close.

"I'm much obliged to you, mister," he said gratefully to me as he took the reins, and nodded at Creek and Charley too. Will trotted up, and he was laughing.

"Quite a good show you put on there, cowboys," he said to the three of us. He'd learned to work cattle on his Pa's farm when he was just a boy, but he'd told me it hadn't stuck with him any too good.

I looked down at the kid from my saddle. "What are you doing out here all by yourself?" I asked him bluntly.

He shrugged again. "I ain't rightly sure, if you want the truth. I been looking for work for a time but I ain't found any. I been working on a cotton farm since I came out from Kentucky, but it got foreclosed on and so…" he let his voice trail off. "Anyway, I sure am obliged to you. I would've had to keep going on foot if you hadn't come along when you did." He swung up into the saddle and touched two fingers to his hat brim in thanks, then started his tired horse off at a walk, away from us.

Will looked sideways at me, and I knew what he was thinking. We needed some more sets of hands if we were going to take on some bigger jobs, and a young drifter like this was the perfect recruit. I wasn't any too sure, though; we didn't know a damn thing about this kid and I was sort of getting picky about who I trusted. But I did feel sorry for him, roaming around alone like that with nothing to occupy his hands with.

I nodded at Will. "He can go in for a drink at the saloon with us, at the least," I relented. Will kicked his big chestnut into a canter and caught up with the kid. He stopped him and said a few words, then they both came back over to where Creek and Charley and I were waiting.

"My luck must be turnin' some, to have met y'all," he said. "The name's Oliver Yantis, but most folks just call me Ol."

"I'm Will Dalton, and this here's Charley Pierce, and Bitter Creek Newcomb, and the fella that roped your horse is Bill Doolin," Will said.

The kid's eyes got huge in his head and he looked at us like he wasn't sure we were real. "You tellin' the truth, or just messin' with my skull a bit?" he asked, darting a look at Will, then at me.

"He's telling you the truth," I said calmly, but I injected a very clear warning into my tone. "Question is, what're you gonna do with that information, now you got it?" I let my hand come to rest on my gun, very casually, but I made my point.

He looked like I'd drawn on him, straight out, and he hastily put his palms toward me, almost losing his balance in the saddle. "You ain't understanding me, Mr. Doolin," he stammered in an earnest tone. "I'm honored, and that's the God's honest truth. I've heard a lot about you all, and I admire what it is you been doing."

He was gushing, and I wasn't one to be swayed by flattery, but there was something about this kid that I liked, simple-minded or not. He reminded me of a clumsy newborn calf that needed help figuring out how to stand up and run around on its own. I shot an amused glance at Creek.

Will laughed out loud. "Well Goddamnit, Bill, looks like we got us a stray pup, don't it?" His eyes gleamed.

I shook my head and started Rebel forward. "Don't mind him none," I said to Ol as I trotted past him. "He's the joker in our deck."

"We-ell, look what the cat's dragged in," John Murray, the barkeep and partner at the Ransom & Murray, said loudly as I sauntered in through the doors, the other boys behind me. He was grinning at me wide from behind the bar while wiping a glass on a cloth. He was a jovial, affable fellow and I liked him. Ingalls was becoming known as a refuge for all sorts of men who lived beyond the law, like us, but John didn't care; he just served up the liquor and kept quiet around anyone with a badge that might come snooping around his place. He didn't judge a man by anything except his character, and I admired him for that, because I'd always tried to do the same.

"How are you, John?" I asked him, approaching the bar.

He kept the grin on his face. "Can't complain, Bill. Ain't seen you or yours in awhile. You been keeping busy?"

"Relatively so, I reckon," I replied slyly. He raised an eyebrow at me, like we were sharing in some secret.

"The usual?" he asked me, plucking a bottle of whiskey from the shelf behind him, then handing it to me when I nodded, along with five jiggers.

Creek had picked a table where we could sit facing the door, and get to it in a hurry if we needed to. I refused to sit in corner tables in saloons. I plunked the bottle down while the others got themselves arranged and got their poker chips out of their saddlebags.

We got a game going, everyone flipping in silver dollars to ante. I put another in for Ol, who didn't have one. Ella Mae and Lottie, two girls from the whorehouse at the other end of town, were getting a head start on hunting up customers and started eye-balling us in short order, but I gave them a sharp look and shook my head firmly, warning them off. The boys could seek out company later on if they wanted; didn't make a damn bit of difference to me, but not until I was done with them. As for me, I wasn't in-terested any longer, myself—not with Edith and the ring I'd put on her finger.

Lottie looked disappointed; she had a thing for Creek and looked like she'd been fixing to smooth-talk him into joining her for the evening. Charley was one of Ella Mae's regulars and she usually sought him out when he was in town, knowing he was always good for making her some money. After a few minutes of pouting at me, they moved off to work the other tables.

"You got you a place to stay, Ol?" Creek asked our new addition, never taking his eyes off his hand.

"No; I just been camping along the trail," he said. "Hotels cost money, and I ain't got any at present."

"You ain't gonna win any, either, if I got anything to say about it," Will joked, discarding two cards.

"You heard of the Dunns' ranch, near Lawson?" I asked. "That's where we're staying. The Dunns'll put up any man needs shelter, and they got plenty of room. They won't charge you if you help them out around the ranch."

"I ain't got any skill with cattle, as you probably figured, but I'm good with crops and fence-mending, that sort of work. If you ain't got any objection, I'll follow you back there," he told me gratefully.

Everyone got quiet for a few minutes while they looked over their hands, and I pondered on Ol for a minute. I'd kept it to myself thus far, but I'd picked a bank for us to go after in Spearville, a little town in Ford County, Kansas. I'd formed an idea for distracting the townsfolk while we were engaging the bank, and Ol seemed the perfect man for what I had in mind.

"Listen up, boys," I said in a low voice after Creek had won the pot. "I got an idea."

⋙⋘

"All right, now, every man clear on his part in this thing?" I asked, crossing my arms over my chest and surveying those in my company. They nodded, all of them watching me attentively. I felt my mouth turn up in a satisfied smile.

It was the first of November, '92, and we were gathered around the dying coals of the fire we'd slept by the previous night, in a little concealed hollow just outside of Spearville. Besides Creek, Charley and Will, I had in my company Ol Yantis and a very old friend of mine, Dick West. He'd worked with me at the Hallsal ranch, back when I was Ol's age and just starting out. He'd seen the wanted notices on us and read about our escapades in the papers, and, being of like mind to me about the railroad and the law, had sought me out in Ingalls. He was an easygoing sort of fellow and fitted seamlessly into our little band.

"What a joke this'll be," Will said, chuckling under his breath. "Damned good idea you came up with, Bill," he told me, his eyes twinkling at the thought. "Town won't know what the hell hit it, once Ol does his thing."

Wary of a similar outcome to the Daltons' fiasco in Coffeyville, I had decided that one man in our group would create a fuss to grab everyone's attention while Creek and Will and I were in the bank. Ol would gallop his horse up and down Main Street, firing shots and shouting, to panic everyone so no one would notice what the rest of us were doing. Charley would stand guard outside the bank, and Dick would stay with the horses, to keep an eye on them and to sound an alarm if anyone did anything fishy.

"Let's get on with it, then," I said, tossing the reins over Rebel's head and putting my foot into the stirrup.

We rode toward town, slowing our mounts to a walk and steering them toward a hitching rail set to one side of the last building on Main Street. It was a saloon, so it wouldn't look funny to have a bunch of men ride up to it and leave horses there. I'd also given the boys strict orders not to bring their rifles with them—I was still convinced that part of the Daltons' mistake at Coffeyville was carrying Winchesters so openly into town, hunting season or not.

I'd also decided that we'd spread ourselves out some as we walked toward the bank. Creek and I sauntered along the gallery together, pretending to make small talk, while Will stayed a few paces behind, pretending to be glancing in store windows. Charley hung back even further, minding his own business and carrying a newspaper. I could see the door of the bank just ahead, two stores down the gallery. Ol was sitting in his saddle near the corner of the saloon, watching for us to reach the bank, while Dick leaned against the hitching rail, innocently smoking a cigarette.

Creek and I went inside the bank, and to my relief there was a customer doing business at the counter. This meant the teller was good and distracted, and Creek and I could fake like we were customers waiting for our turn. I looked at Creek, swiftly, and he winked at me, his eyes dancing wickedly.

For a second, everything was still. Then gunshots started going off, and I heard the sound of pounding hooves on the street outside as Ol started his ruckus. The customer at the counter turned to look, and through the bank's front windows I saw men and women coming out of businesses and houses to see what was going on. There were a few screams from women, on account of the gunshots. I saw a heavyset man wearing a tin star go running past the bank, heading in the direction Ol had gone. I looked at Creek and nodded, just as Will came in through the door.

Calmly we pulled our revolvers. The teller saw them first; his face went pale and he slowly raised his hands. The customer looked at him, confused, then looked at us. He went pale, too, and threw his hands toward the ceiling, backing up and almost stumbling over himself.

"You know what this is," I said to the teller. "Clean out the safe and fill her up," I said, handing him a flour sack. "Quickly, now, I ain't got all damn day," I added firmly, thumbing back the hammer so he'd know I meant business. Creek kept the customer covered. Out of the corner of my eye I could see Charley outside the windows, standing guard while pretending to be looking out at Ol, who was still acting like a crazy person, yelling and shooting into the false fronts of buildings as he galloped back and forth. I heard men screaming at him to stop, but of course he didn't.

"Jim, what on earth is going on out—"

Another man had come out of the little office by the vault, and he shut his mouth abruptly when he saw us. "Stop right there and put your hands skyward, now!" I barked at him. "One false move and you won't ever move again."

The teller silently handed me the full sack and took a step backwards, showing me his palms and averting his eyes from mine. I handed the haul over to Will, then backed out with him and Creek, our guns still drawn. Once we were out we motioned to Charley and ducked into the little space between the bank and the feed store, going around the back and running for the horses. I heard the teller come boiling out onto the gallery screaming "*Bank robbery!* Someone get the marshal!"

We high-tailed it to our horses and got up on

them, quick, keeping our guns out. I put two fingers in my mouth and whistled, sharp, to let Ol know we were done. He came running and we took off in a group, leaving the town behind us in chaos.

I knew we would be followed in short order, so once we reached a secluded spot I'd selected beforehand, I divvied up quick—we'd taken almost five thousand—and then told everyone to split up to confuse anyone on our trail. Will and I went in one direction, Creek and Charley in another, and Ol and Dick in still two more.

"Well, *that* was fun," Will commented to me as we loped along together. He started laughing, that big, rolling laugh of his that set everyone else laughing whenever he did it. "I don't figure anyone else's ever pulled a bank job that way, and I bet you that town won't forget us any too soon!"

When we met back up with Creek and Charley at the Dunns' a few days later, George showed us an article on the robbery. It referred to us as 'Bill Doolin and his wild bunch of desperadoes," and Will roared with laughter at that.

"'Bill Doolin's Wild Bunch,'" he said to me. "Has a ring to it, don't it?"

I grinned at him, well-satisfied with how things had gone. "It does at that," I agreed, and it looked like we'd have us a handle from then on.

━━━━━◦((◦))◦━━━━━

Our amusement didn't last long, though. Just a little less than a month after the bank job, we came to learn we'd lost our first man to the law.

It was Dick West that brought the news. He'd been trailed pretty good by a posse, and he'd taken the long way around and waited a while before he came back toward Ingalls. He found us in the Ransom & Murray, and it was there he told us that Ol was dead. He'd fled Spearville and lit out for his sister's farm north of Guthrie. Heck Thomas and Chris Madsen, along with the sheriff of Ford County, trailed him there and surrounded the place. He'd stupidly tried to draw on them when they ordered him out, and they'd fired on him, wounding him bad. They took him to a hotel to heal up, but he'd died from his wounds instead. They propped his corpse up in his open coffin and photographed him so they could gloat about having taken down the first member of the Wild Bunch.

We all got good and quiet when Dick told us, and I shook my head to myself. Poor kid thought he'd be a famous outlaw like Jesse James, and all he got was his dirt nap way before it was due. For a few minutes I felt sorry I'd let him join up with us, but my practical side set in and I shook those feelings off. He'd had a choice, same as every man there, and he'd chosen to throw in his lot with us and come along. I remembered what he said about his luck turning when he met us; I guessed he'd been wrong about that.

NINETEEN

COME THE BEGINNING of March I finally learned the price that Emmett would pay for throwing in with Bob: life in the state prison.

It was all over the papers. They'd convinced Em to plead guilty to the second-degree murder of one of the citizens dropped in Coffeyville, even though he'd kept insisting he didn't even fire a shot that day and that Bob had been the one had done the murders. His attorney and some of his family had told him he was likely to get a lighter sentence, and could avoid a trial, if he made the plea. Then the Goddamned judge had surprised everyone by tossing him in for life, discarding him like he wasn't worth a damn to anyone. Kind, easygoing Em wouldn't leave prison until they carried him out of it, feet-first.

I sat by myself out by the water pump for a good long while after I read the article, trying to make some sense out of it, but I couldn't. I couldn't get my mind wrapped around the hell Em would have to go through, year after year, with no end in sight save for his death. I couldn't help thinking then that maybe he would've been better off if he'd died that day in Coffeyville, beside the brother he'd thought could walk on water.

———⟫⟨⟪———

I found a spread to rent just outside of Ingalls; a little farmhouse set near a creek bed that was furnished with the essentials. The house was shaded by oak trees growing near the creek, but the property around it was pretty wide open, so it'd be hard for anyone to sneak up on. There was a good solid stable built, too. The fellow who owned it was a relation of John Murray's and sympathetic to our way of life, so I knew I could trust him. I figured it was time, then, to keep my promise of a spring wedding.

———⟫⟨⟪———

"You going to church or something?"

I looked up from cinching my saddle to see Rose standing in the doorway of the barn, looking me over suspiciously. I guessed it was because I was gussied up in a new suit, and I'd gone to the barber and had a hair cut and a shave and got my mustache trimmed to boot. A man didn't want to look like a mongrel dog on his wedding day, and I figured Edith would appreciate it, too, even if we were only getting married in her Pa and Ma's parlor instead of some fancy church.

I laughed dryly at her. "It ain't Sunday, Rose." I picked up my bridle and put the bit into Rebel's mouth, standing a good ways away from him so he wouldn't take a bite out of me while I did it. He wasn't fond of being bridled.

Creek came into the barn then, leading Dash, his big black stud, all saddled up. He barked out a sharp word to the horse, who pinned his ears and lunged for Rebel with a squeal. He looked me up and down. "We-ell, you got yourself shined up purty, didn't you?" he said slyly.

I rolled my eyes. "Quit your commentary and let's go." Creek was going with me; we needed a witness besides Edith's folks.

Rose's eyes suddenly widened. "You're getting married today, ain't you, Bill?" she asked breathlessly, putting her hands together in front of her chest. "Why didn't you say something at breakfast?"

I took Rebel by the reins and opened the stall

door. "Because I didn't want to advertise the fact, before the fact. I'll tell everyone when it's done."

Rose looked at Creek. "You goin', too?"

"Every wedding needs a witness," he told her.

She raised an eyebrow at him. "I hope you behave yourself."

He gave her an innocent grin. "Me? I got manners, when the occasion calls for it."

She made an un-ladylike snorting noise. "I ain't never seen 'em." His grin just got wider and I knew he'd given her a devilish wink.

She looked back at me as I mounted up. "Congratulations, Bill," she said softly, her teasing gone. "I'm glad for you and Edith."

I smiled down at her from the saddle. "Thank you, Rose."

She moved out of the way and watched as we headed out of the barn. "Tell Edith if she ever wants some civilized company for a change, she can look me up!" she called after us, teasing again, and Creek and I laughed, our laughter trailing behind us as we trotted toward Lawson, careful not to get any dust on our clothes.

━━◈◈◈◈━━

My mouth went dry when I saw Edith. She had on a dress made of fine white cotton and a little gold brooch pinned at her collar. She had part of her hair pinned into a big knot at the back of her head, and the rest of it flowed down loose to just past her waist like a sheet of black satin. She came almost shyly over to us when we arrived.

"Hello, Bill," she said. Her cheeks went pink.

I took her hands and leaned down to kiss her—on the cheek. I didn't want her folks, who were standing on the other side of the room, to think I was getting too familiar with her before we were man and wife. "You look beautiful, Edith," I told her softly.

Her blush got deeper. She turned to Creek, greeting him warmly, and he leaned down and brushed her cheek with his lips, too. "What a pretty bride you make, Edith," he told her, and I think it was the first time I ever heard him sound completely serious about anything at all.

Mr. Ellsworth was holding his bible in front of him, and he smiled at us as we came over. Mrs. Ellsworth was at his side, and she came over and embraced Edith, and then embraced me, surprising me. I returned her embrace and kissed her on the cheek, then I introduced them to Creek—as George, of course.

"Join hands, if you would," Mr. Ellsworth said,

and Edith and I turned toward one another and did as he said.

I'd robbed trains and a bank by then, shot men, been shot at myself and trailed by lawmen of all sorts, and I'd come through it all cool as you please, but *this* made me nervous. My palms were damp and I was worried about it, but Edith didn't seem to mind. She just smiled at me, her big brown eyes shining.

Her Pa started talking about God, and how He was blessing two of His children in Holy matrimony, but I couldn't really follow his words any too good; I was too busy looking at Edith and thinking how it was a miracle that I'd won her hand, seeing as how I was a wanted man called 'ruthless' and 'vicious' by the papers and 'dangerous' by the law. I thanked God right then that she somehow could see past all that and still care so much for me.

"William, do you take Edith to be your lawfully-wedded wife, for richer or for poorer, in sickness and in health, to love and to cherish as long as you both shall live?" Mr. Ellsworth asked me gravely.

"I surely do," I said, smiling at Edith.

"And Edith, do you take William to be your lawfully-wedded husband, to honor and obey, for richer or poorer, in sickness and in health, to love and to cherish as long as you both shall live?" he asked his daughter.

"I do," she said firmly. Her cheeks went pink again, but she was smiling the loveliest smile I'd ever seen. I pulled her gold wedding band out of my coat pocket and slipped it onto her finger.

"Then, by the power vested in me by God in His wisdom, I now pronounce you man and wife." He smiled at us and closed his bible. "Bill, you may kiss your bride."

I did, and Mrs. Ellsworth started sniffling into her handkerchief. Creek slapped me on the back, and Mr. Ellsworth shook my hand and then kissed Edith. Mrs. Ellsworth embraced us both, kissing our cheeks and welcoming me to her family.

Mrs. Ellsworth had made a big spread for our wedding supper, and the five of us ate and drank merrily while I told them all about the place I'd rented for us. Then her Ma brought out a cake and we had some of that. When it was time to go, Edith's Pa put the trunk with her things into his wagon; we'd hitch Rebel to it and drive to the new house. Creek took his leave with a thank-you to the Ellsworths, a kiss on the cheek for Edith, and a grin and a wink to me, telling he'd see me soon.

Edith's Ma gave her a big basket covered with a cloth; it had a loaf of fresh bread, some butter she'd just churned and the rest of the wedding cake in it. She walked with Edith out onto the porch and they watched while her Pa and I hitched Rebel up and I put my tack into the wagon box. Then I helped Edith into the wagon, climbed up beside her, and we started off, turning back to wave goodbye to them.

"Well, Edith, darlin', we got us a new life to look forward to," I said to her, flashing her a cheerful, loving smile as I drove, careful to keep Rebel at an easy trot. He didn't much like being hitched up to anything and I had to watch him like a hawk.

"Yes, and it'll be a good one," she told me, leaning on my shoulder a minute. "And a happy one, too." Her smile shone out at me in the fading daylight.

"So long as you can put up with me," I teased her. "You married yourself a wild one."

"I know, but I wanted it that way. Keeps life interesting. Besides that, you need someone with good sense to look after you," she said slyly.

"Ain't that the truth," I agreed, leaning over to kiss her. "You're the brains of this outfit from now on."

We were laughing as we reached our new home, and I didn't figure life could get too much better than it was right then.

TWENTY

MARRIED LIFE AGREED with me just fine; going to bed next to Edith every night and waking up with her each morning made me wonder how'd I'd gone so long sleeping by myself. It was nice to be taken care of for a change, to live in a real home with a woman I loved, instead of a claim shanty, a camp or an attic bedroom at the Dunns' shared by men I held up trains and banks with. But even though being a husband suited me well, it didn't alter my activities or my mindset any. The Bunch was in fine form come the middle of '93; we'd honed our craft and our fame got bigger. The gang got bigger, too—besides me, Will, Creek, Charley and Dick West, Tulsa Jack was back with us and he'd brought along three more. There was Bill Raidler, known as "Little Bill" for his short stature, a cowboy who'd worked with us at the Bar X Bar; Dan Clifton, alias "Dynamite Dan," a cattle-rustler who'd come by his handle after he'd managed to blow three fingers off his right hand in an explosives accident; and another of the old Bar X Bar hands—Red Buck Weightman.

I was fine with the first two; Little Bill was up for anything and an interesting fellow to be around, considering he'd had a hell of a lot more schooling than the rest of us, and Dan was affable to a fault and followed my orders without question, but Red Buck gave me pause. I'd never liked him, not from the first, and it was with extreme reluctance that I let him into our little rag-tag band.

"He crosses me too far, he's out," I'd said bluntly to Jack, when he first brought up Red Buck's name. "I mean it, Jack. Am I clear?" My voice had come out hard and cold, and Jack had looked at me in surprise.

"Easy, Bill. He's cutthroat, all right, and damned near to crazy, but he don't flinch when it comes time to get a job done, and he's another gun and another pair of hands."

"We'll see, I suppose," I'd said darkly.

I'd left Edith sewing one afternoon and come to the Dunns' to see the boys, most of whom were still staying there on and off, when Creek told me he had something for me to mull over.

"I came up with an idea for a wedding present for you, Bill," he told me with a grin. He'd been drinking with Will and Charley for awhile before I even showed up, and he was a little lit up by the time I got there. I poured myself some of the whiskey he had left—it'd been awhile, because of Edith—and knocked it back before I answered.

"What's that?" I raised my eyebrows at him and pouring myself some more.

"A train job. The Santa Fe, to be exact, near Cimarron in Kansas. The bank job was fun and all, but I'm sort of partial to trains." He grinned at me.

Will came over to the table where we were sitting and motioned to me to hand over the bottle. I did, and he took an impressive tug before handing it back. "What do you think, Bill? You game?" His eyes were dancing at the very idea. It had been awhile since we'd gone out and they were all getting antsy.

"Why not?" I said carelessly, taking another drink.

Will and Creek gave each other satisfied looks, and we set to making plans.

⸺⊷⦿⊶⸺

"I asked you twice already, and nicely, and now you're trying my damn patience. *Open the safe,* or I'll open my gun into your gut," I snapped, thumbing back the hammer on my revolver as I kept it leveled on the express messenger, the end of the barrel just inches from his vest.

I was standing in the express car of the Santa Fe train—the one Creek had wanted to hold up as my "wedding present." It hadn't been a smooth job thus far and I was in a pretty damned bad mood by then. Instead of complying like most of his fellows did when faced with our guns, the express messenger on this train was either clean off his nut or just plain stupid, because he was refusing my orders.

"He means what he says, friend," Will said, in a warning tone, leveling his Winchester along with Creek. "You fixing to die tonight?"

He looked scared; I could see it in his eyes, and he was sweating, but he drew in a breath, puffed his chest out, and stood firm. "I'm not opening it. You boys'll just have to shoot me."

"All right. Have it your way." I put the gun to his temple then, so mad I could hardly see straight.

He flinched and raised his hands up, squeezing his eyes shut. "Don't shoot! I'll open it! I'll open it, I swear!"

"Then quit blubbering and *do it!*" I roared, striking my boot on the floor for emphasis. I was sweating now, too, because the whole damned thing was taking too long. I heard the others outside firing warning shots, the passengers were panicking good by now.

He turned and dialed the combination, then opened it. There was a good amount of silver inside, and Will scooped it into the bag, quick.

Just as he tossed it over his shoulder, the messenger moved for a shotgun leaned into the far corner of the car. Creek laughed aloud. "Good Lord, man, are you short on brains? You got all these guns in your face, and you think we're gonna let you get to that scattergun?"

The messenger ignored him and kept moving for the gun, so I shot him before he could reach it. He dropped like a stone, blood soaking the floor under him and spreading in a glistening ruby pool toward the toes of my boots. I'd hit him in the heart; he was dead before he even struck the floor.

"Get the hell out of here, all of you!" I growled, thumbing the hammer back again. Will and Creek and Charley hurried to do as I said, startled by my mood.

We sprang down from the train, leaving panic in our wake. I heard the conductor scream for help in the car behind us; he'd heard the shot, and probably found the messenger too. I whistled sharp, then got up on my horse along with the others who'd been in the car with me. Dan, Red Buck, Tulsa Jack and Dick were all coming behind us, and Little Bill brought up the rear.

"What the hell happened in there?" Jack yelled at us, slapping his horse on the rump with his reins, trying to keep up with us.

"Bill shot the express messenger," Creek told him, "and he needed shootin' bad!"

I dug my spurs into Rebel's sides, opening him up to his full stride, and pretty soon I was way out in front of them. I was still furious—with Little Bill and Dick, who'd bungled our entry onto the train when we'd first stopped it, even though I'd given them clear orders; with the messenger, who could've lived if he'd just done what I told him to do; and with myself, for letting that fury get the better of me.

No one said anything else for a good long while; instead, we just ran.

———— ◦◉◦ ————

We were being tracked; I was sure of it. That night when we made camp I couldn't shake the feeling that someone was watching us, and I made the decision not to return to home grounds until that feeling had left me. I didn't sleep at all that night, just sat tensely near our horses, my gun in my lap, my finger inside the trigger-guard. I hadn't let the others build a fire for fear it would be spotted.

We went several days in that fashion, and I hardly slept at all. The third morning, as everyone else was shaking themselves awake, I saw a band of horsemen on the horizon, picking their way down a steep slope and coming toward our little hollow. Creek saw them, too.

"Posse!" he shouted, and grabbed for his reins. The others looked, saw what we saw, and made for their own horses, quick.

"Go, now!" I snapped, and sprang up into Rebel's saddle. He reared, but I sawed at his mouth with the bit and got him back down on all fours. He took off like a shot, Creek following on Dash, then Will on his big chestnut stud. The others came sprinting after us, heading for the safety of the tree-line about two miles out.

I was laid out almost flat over Rebel's neck, and I glanced under my arm, once. The posse had seen us, and they were giving chase. I didn't look behind me again.

We had a pretty good head-start on them, and reached the tree-line well before they did. We zig-zagged among the trees, praying our horses would keep their footing. We came out into a big clearing and kept going. Rebel and Dash were the fastest horses in our bunch, and so Creek and I stayed out in front. Everyone else seemed to be keeping up, but I knew we'd have to breathe the horses soon, or we'd risk getting them so worn out they wouldn't be able to run fast enough for as long as we needed them to.

"Think we've lost them for now, Bill," Creek called to me, and I stood up a little in my stirrups, easing Rebel down into a canter. Creek did the same with Dash, and I threw my hand up to signal the others. They all pulled up, glancing around nervously.

We let the horses breathe, keeping them to a walk as we crossed a narrow, calm part of the Arkansas River. The water wasn't too deep there and our boots in the stirrups stayed dry. I looked behind us, and saw nothing, but that hunted feeling was still dogging me and I knew we weren't safe yet.

"We need to get the hell out of this area, and fast," I said grimly to Will, whose horse had come up behind mine. "They ain't gonna give up."

"Which way you want to head, Bill?" he asked me.

"Toward Meade County and back into the O.T.," I said, "but not near Lawson." My voice was firm. I'd left Edith with her folks while I was gone, and there was no way in hell I was going to risk being trailed there.

Will nodded. Suddenly Creek shouted to me. "Horses coming, Bill!"

I looked behind us again, and I heard the sound

of many hooves on dirt, and men shouting to one another.

"Go!" I cried, spurring Rebel forward. He sprang up the bank with a little squeal and took off, so fast I thought he had a fire at his heels. The others followed suit, and the chase was on again.

<hr />

We ran for over an hour at a gallop; when we hit trees again the horses would go no further at that speed. We'd crossed back into Oklahoma Territory and were in Beaver County; it was night by then. The gang scattered in different directions, taking cover where the bigger trees and underbrush offered it. Creek and Will and Charley had followed me over to some boulders and we got off our horses there, tugging them into the sheltered area as best we could and getting out our guns. I knew the posse would eventually catch up to us, and I was ready for a fight. No lawdog was going to take me down, not as long as I was sucking air and could hold a gun in my hands.

For a few minutes, all we heard were crickets. Some animal cried out nearby as it was caught by a predator. We held our breath and waited. My mind was going furiously, thinking over all possible scenarios. The only consolation I could think of was that their horses were going to be just as tired as ours—but ours had a head start on resting up.

"They came this way!" we heard a man shout, his voice carrying toward us on the warm breeze. I heard underbrush rustling, dry leaves crunching and branches snapping as hooves and boots stepped on them. Next to me, Will raised his Winchester, resting its barrel on the boulders we were crouched behind, its stock at his shoulder. The moonlight shone off the barrel of Creek's revolvers; he had both of them out. I took out my second one, too, and we waited.

"All right, Doolin, we know you're in here!" one of them barked. I saw him about twenty feet ahead of me; he was off his horse. There was a tin star on his vest. "You and your boys ain't gonna get any further! Give up your guns!" A couple more men came out of the shadows then, all of them on foot.

"Send them to hell, boys," I hissed quietly.

It was Will who fired the first shot. He hit one of the posse-members right between the eyes, dropping him quicker than I could blink. The others started firing in our direction, then some of them turned, confused, as more gunfire started popping out from the right of them, where some of ours were hiding.

The lawman with the tin star had ducked down,

but I saw him moving forward toward the boulders we were behind, hunched over, his gun out in front of him. Shots were being fired all over the place by now. Creek aimed for the lawman, but his shot fell short, hitting a tree instead. The lawman returned fire, narrowly missing Creek's head.

I don't know if it was the fact I hadn't had more than about three hours' sleep in three days, or the adrenaline of being shot at, but my normal cautious nature left me right then. I sprang up over the rocks, coming out of hiding, and fired at him. I hit him in the arm, but it was a grazing shot and he kept ahold of his gun. He fired back at me, but his aim was low because of the injury I'd just given him.

The bullet hit me square in the middle of my left foot, and I could tell it didn't go through. The pain was near to unbearable, but I refused to succumb. Wasn't any way I hell I was going to give up, not now or ever.

"Bill, get out of there!" I heard Charley cry hoarsely. He and the others were all going for their horses, having dispatched most of the posse.

I stumbled toward Rebel, the pain from my wound sending tendrils of burning agony up my leg and into my hip. I gritted my teeth and somehow managed to drag myself up into the saddle. Weakly I wove my fingers into Rebel's mane, fighting the pain. My foot felt wet; I looked down at saw my whole boot glistening with blood, the leather soaked through. My stomach turned. I concentrated on staying conscious as Rebel galloped after the others. I heard no one giving chase.

By the time the sun was coming up, my vision was blurred from pain and I felt weak. My boot was dripping blood and my leg had gone numb. I was still trailing behind the others, but they must've sensed something was wrong, because when I came up over a little rise in the prairie I saw Dash and General Sherman, Will's horse, pulled up to a stop ahead of me. Through my fog of pain I saw that both Creek and Will were standing holding their reins, looking toward me in concern.

"You all right, Bill?" Will called.

I tried to speak, but found I couldn't. I felt myself weave in the saddle and I struggled to stay in it. Rebel, thoroughly exhausted, walked up to them, his head hung so low his nose was almost on the ground.

"Jesus Christ!" Creek suddenly exclaimed, seeing my foot. "He's been shot!"

Will came around to look and his eyes went wide. He cursed, violently. "We got to do something, Creek."

My vision blurred again and I felt my stomach heave. Then I felt nothing at all.

⸺◈⸺

"Bill? You hear me?"

I came to on my back in the tall grass, with Creek and Will leaning over me.

"What the hell happened?" I asked. My voice didn't sound like mine; it was weak and quiet and my words came out slurred from pain.

"You passed out," Will said. "We need to get you to a doc, quick."

I shook my head. "Too dangerous," I managed to get out.

"Bill, you got a damn bullet in your foot," he argued. "You *got* to see a doctor!"

"He's right, Bill. What about Edith? You want to make her a widow after only a couple months? Hell, you could die from losing all that blood, or lose your foot to gangrene." Creek's voice was hard.

"Fine," I relented. I closed my eyes and tried to breathe through the pain. I gritted my teeth so hard

I thought I'd break them. "I wish I'd killed that bastard!" I muttered.

Before either of them could reply we heard hooves coming closer. Will and Creek looked up quick, their hands near their guns, but they both relaxed. "It's Charley and Dan," Creek told me.

"What's the matter?" Charley asked, then saw me. "Jesus, Bill, you all right?" He got off his horse.

"Took a bullet in the foot," Will told him shortly. "We got to find a doc."

"We're getting pretty near to Beaver City," Dan said. "Should be a doc there."

Since I'd been laying still for a bit, the pain had eased up somewhat. I managed to sit up. "Wedding present, huh, Creek? You shouldn't have," I said dryly. I managed a rueful smile at him.

He gave me a chagrinned look. "I'll make it up to you," he promised. "And I won't never pick a train again."

I took a deep breath and braced myself as he and Will helped me into a standing position. "I'll hold you to both of those," I told him, then faced the near-impossible task of getting back into my saddle.

TWENTY-ONE

CREEK AND WILL waited with me just outside of Beaver City while Dan and Charley went in to look for a doctor. The rest of the gang hadn't shown; I figured they'd gone their separate ways and would show up in Ingalls down the road.

I hadn't tried to take off my boot; it was so stiff with dried blood I figured it was probably keeping my wound from gushing again. The pain when it came off would be bad, but I'd cross that bridge when I came to it.

Creek handed me his canteen and eyeballed me while I drank. "Well, you ain't gray any longer," he observed. "Figure that's a good sign."

I nodded. My mind kept turning to Edith and I thought about how I'd rather be with her right now instead of sitting slumped in my saddle with a hole in my damn foot. I was determined not to let such a stupid injury take me down, and to get back to her as quick as possible.

After about half an hour we saw Dan and Charley cantering back toward us. They reined in when they reached us. "Found the doc," Dan said. "And we're damned lucky—his place is on the way out of town instead of right in the middle of it. Think we can get in and out pretty easy." He shifted in his saddle and looked at me. "You holdin' up all right, there, Bill?"

"I ain't dead yet, am I?" I replied shortly. "Let's go, if we're going."

They formed a protective group around Rebel as we walked toward town to keep eyes off my injury and to draw less attention to me. We kept our hats pulled way down, but no one even gave us a glance. I was damned glad—I had no energy to high-tail it out of there in a hurry.

The doctor's place was a small house set back aways off the main road, with a little whitewashed fence around it. There was a clothesline run off one side of the house, and a middle-aged woman was standing there, hanging wash. She saw us come up and tie our horses, and she left her basket of washing to come over to the gate. "How can I help you gents?" she asked. She saw our gun belts but didn't appear to be bothered none by them; I'd noticed a lot of men in town wearing them as we'd come through.

"We got a wounded man here, ma'am," Will said, taking his hat off to her. "We're looking for the doc."

"The doctor's inside," she told us. "I'm his wife. I'll take you on in to him."

She watched as I slid gingerly down out of the saddle, holding my bad foot up off the ground like a horse favoring its leg. Creek and Will came to either side of me and I slung my arms around their shoulders so I could limp into the house.

The woman's eyes went to my foot and they widened. "My lord, it looks like you've lost a lot of blood. What happened?"

"Gunshot," Creek said shortly. There was no getting around that, so he didn't bother lying to her.

"Oh, dear. Well, let's get you some help," she said to me. She had a kindly look about her and I tried to give her a smile. I think it came out more like a grimace; my foot was throbbing all to hell and sending shooting pains up into my hip again.

"Stay with the horses," Creek said to Dan, and he nodded.

"Sam?" the woman called as they eased me up the porch steps and into the parlor. "I have a patient here for you."

A man came into the parlor then from another room. He had a full set of black whiskers that were starting to go gray and a face that seemed both stern and kind, at the same time. He wasn't wearing a coat; he had his shirtsleeves rolled up and a watch chain made of thick gold links dangled across his black vest.

"I'm Doctor Brown," he told us all. His gaze went right to my foot. "I would ask you what seems to be the trouble, but I can see it for myself," he said dryly. "Bullet wound?" he raised his eyebrows at me.

"Yessir," I said, clenching my teeth against the pain.

"Let me take a look. Eliza, would you bring me a basin and some hot water, please?" he asked his wife, and she nodded and left the room.

The doctor looked at Creek and Will. "Bring him in to the examining room, please." He went into a room off the parlor, and they walked me in after him. Charley stayed in the parlor.

The room was small and had a cabinet on one wall that held glass bottles of all shapes and colors, and some instruments were laid out neat on a little table below it. A big thick book with the lofty title of "Bramwell's Practical Medicine and Medical Diagnosis" stamped on its cover was set out on a bookstand near the window, and there was a washstand in one corner. There was a long table in the middle of the room, and he bade me to get up on it and lay out flat on my back. I did and stared up at the ceiling.

The doctor came over to the table. "You boys can

wait in the parlor, if you please," he said to Creek and Will.

"I'd rather they stay, Doc," I said, and he nodded.

"All right. What's your name, son?" he asked me.

"William," I said, using my full name, just in case. It was such a common name I figured I didn't need to bother with an alias unless he wanted my last name, too.

He didn't ask me, though. Instead he looked down at me and frowned. "Well, William, I'm going to have to get your boot off so I can look. I don't imagine I need to tell you that it's going to hurt."

"I kind of figured, Doc," I replied, gritting my teeth again. I heard the door open and the sound of skirts swishing.

"Here's the water, Sam," Mrs. Brown said, and he thanked her and murmured something to her under his breath. She opened the cabinet up and I heard her take some things out of it.

I felt the doctor take ahold of my boot heel, and I braced myself. Those boots fit me good and they'd sort of formed to my feet. I had trouble getting them off without a bootjack as it was.

He pulled the heel toward him and I about took out my gun and shot him, just so he'd stop it. I started to sit up without thinking, and the doctor made some sound in his throat, motioning to Creek and Will.

Will came forward and I felt him pin my shoulders down with his hands. "Got to stay still, now," he told me gravely. For once his eyes weren't dancing; they were sober and still.

I squeezed my eyes shut. "I wish you'd buffa-lo me with your gun butt, Will," I managed to get out. "Then I wouldn't have to—" I stopped talking abruptly and bit down, hard, on the inside of my cheek as the boot came off. The pain was searing me like my foot was on fire, and I couldn't feel my hip. I fought the urge to cuss out loud; I knew the doctor's wife was still there, so I just did it in my head.

"The bullet didn't go through, but I'd imagine you knew that already," the doctor told me. I heard him wringing out a cloth. I kept my eyes shut. "The boot and your sock slowed it down a bit. I'm going to clean it up now. This is just water, to start with." I felt him wiping the bullet hole. Will kept me pinned down, and it was a damned good thing he did.

"The bullet is lodged in your foot, William, but I think I can remove it. I can give you a little chloro-form before I do."

"Will that put him out?" Creek asked, and I opened my eyes and raised up my head a little to look at the doctor.

"Yes, briefly."

I shook my head. "I don't want that. If you got

something for pain, I'd be much obliged to you, but don't go putting a cloth over my face." I didn't want to risk it. If I were to be put out and the law were to show up, I wouldn't be able to get away.

The doctor shared a glance with his wife. "All right, if you insist. I'll give you some morphine for the pain, but it won't kick in right away."

"That's all right. Just do it, Doc." I laid my head back down, and Will put his hands on my shoulders again.

Mrs. Brown brought a cup over to me and told me I needed to drink what was in it. It was morphine in water and it was as bitter as hell, but I drank it. She supported my head while I did. Then the doctor pulled up a chair to the end of the table and started his work.

I kept my mind on one thing while he did it— Edith. I kept focusing on her, picturing her face, hearing her laugh in my head, seeing her pretty smile. I imagined the feel of her soft little hand on my face and it helped distract me some, but the pain still made me want to air my lungs in a way Mrs. Brown—and likely Doc Brown, too—wouldn't care to hear. I wished I'd pass out again, like I'd done earlier—but I didn't.

After what seemed like a year's time, I felt something pop out of my foot, and heard something metal drop into the basin Mrs. Brown was holding. She set it aside and brought him another bowl, and he cleaned the wound again, with alcohol, this time, which made me resume my mental cussing right where I'd left it off. Then he put some sort of ointment on it and packed it with a poultice. After he was done he started winding strips of bandages around my foot. He didn't stop until my whole foot was covered up to my ankle, leaving only my toes sticking out.

"You'll have to stay still for a bit to let everything clot up," he told me, standing up and wiping his hands on a towel his wife handed him. "I'll give you some ointment to put on the wound every day so it heals, but I must warn you that you will have a limp for the rest of your life. The bullet shattered one of the small bones in your foot, and I can't set it like I would a leg or an arm. You'll have to keep off of it as much as you can."

By then the morphine was making me feel funny and I didn't really respond to what he was saying. Someone asked, "when can he ride?" and I wasn't sure if it was Will or Creek, because their voice sounded strange, distorted somehow.

"He can't ride with that injury," the doctor said gravely. "The wound will start to bleed heavily again, and he could die of blood loss. Furthermore, he can't put his boot back on. He'll need to stay here at least until nightfall; the morphine may cause him to hallucinate. If you must leave, you'll have to take him in a wagon and go slowly."

"Can he rest here while we go see about a few things?" Whoever-It-Was asked.

"Of course."

"I'll stay with him," someone else said. "You and Charley go on."

I heard the sound of footsteps leaving the room, and the sound of someone pulling up a chair next to the table. By then my eyelids felt like they were made of lead, and I let them close.

———— ((◉)) ————

The boys hunted up a wagon somewhere and put a bed of straw in it, and they found a gentle mare to pull it. I figured they probably borrowed her without the owner's permission; probably did that with the wagon, too, but I didn't ask them. By dawn I was feeling more like myself save the near-intolerable throbbing in my foot, and we all decided it was time to push on. I knew we'd wounded a lot of the men in that posse, but that wouldn't stop the law from looking for us, not with the express messenger, and all.

They paid the doctor with some of the silver and

told him we were heading out, and he watched as Creek and Charley eased me up off the bed I'd been occupying in their back room and walked me gingerly into the parlor.

"You boys might want to take the east road out of town," he suddenly said, very calmly.

"Why's that?" Creek asked. He wasn't looking at the doctor; he was watching out the front door while Dan drove the wagon up to the gate and Will readied the saddle-horses.

The doctor's voice stayed good and calm. "Because if you take the west road, you'll have to go right past the sheriff's office."

That drew Creek's attention—and mine and Charley's, too. We stared at him for a few seconds, all of us speechless. I saw Charley's hand creep toward his gun automatically; I shook my head at him, sharp, and gave him a fierce look. He dropped his hand.

I swallowed hard, desperately trying to think of something to say, at a loss for just about the first time in my life. It sounded like he knew *what* we were, if not *who*, and it also sounded to me like he was of a mind to help us. I looked him straight in the eyes, seeing nothing of malice there. Looked like maybe I'd been lucky enough to get myself helped by a doc sympathetic to our little war with the railroad, like the one lived in Ingalls was. Before I could say a word, he spoke again. "As far as I'm concerned, you're a man come to me in need of my help. I don't know your surname; I don't care to. I don't know how you took that bullet; I don't care to. And that's what I'll say if anyone asks." He nodded toward the wagon. "Make sure they take you as slowly as you can. If that wound starts to bleed bad again, you'll be in trouble." He stuck out his hand, and I shook it, firmly, giving him my thanks. Creek gave him a nod, too, then he and Charley helped me hop-step like a three-legged dog to the wagon. I laid flat in it, like the doc had said to.

Creek latched the wagon gate and tied Rebel to it, good and secure, then got up on Dash. Will edged General Sherman up next to the wagon box and looked down at me. "You all right in there, Bill?" he asked me with a grin. His eyes were twinkling again.

"Well, Will, my foot hurts like hell, if you want the truth," I said dryly.

"This'll be a funny story one day to share with all them little ones you and Edith are gonna have," he teased, a wicked grin on his face.

I rolled my eyes. "I can imagine it now: 'let's hear how Pa got his bum foot by sticking it under a lawdog's gun after he robbed the Santa Fe train.' Quit shooting the breeze, damn it, and let's go." There was a smile toying with the corners of my mouth—even though I was about ready to start cussing good from the knife-like pain creeping up on me again. One thing I could say for Will—he always knew how to lift a man's mood up out of the muck.

Will laughed and looked up at Dan. "Let's get on with it, then."

Dan gave a "giddyup" to the mare and flicked the reins across her back, and the wagon started forward. I gritted my teeth; the movement was none too comfortable. I laid there and tried to stomach it, and all the while I kept trying to think how the hell I was going to explain this to Edith.

TWENTY-TWO

"JESUS, TOM, YOU look like you're about two steps away from your grave."

Creek's voice was dry as he glanced up from his hand of cards, his gaze falling on the newest member of the gang.

Roy Daugherty, who preferred to be addressed by his alias of "Arkansas Tom Jones," shrugged his shoulders and forced a wan smile at Creek in response. "What're you talking about, Creek? I'm right as rain."

"'Course you are. That's why you got the complexion of a bedsheet," I replied. I plucked a few chips from one of my stacks and tossed them on top of the pot in response to Creek's bet.

Tom was a cowboy who'd latched onto us a few months' back, after I'd gotten through my convalescing from the Cimarron disaster. He hadn't done much cowboyin', when you got down to it, since he

was just shy of twenty-three—besides that, he preferred our company to that of working cowhands.
He hadn't gone on any excursions with us yet, either; my foot wasn't up to snuff and I didn't want
to take a chance on being caught during a job on
account of my injury.

Tom was normally a lively fellow, fun-loving
and eager to get in up to his ears into anything we
could think up, but today he looked just about ready
for the undertaker's. He'd been sick for several days,
laid up with a fever and chills, and he'd been staying
at a hotel next door to the Ransom & Murray, trying
to shake whatever ailed him. When he caught word
a big group of us had gathered at the saloon, he'd
come to join us, but he was swaying in his chair and I
figured if he stayed too much longer he'd be done in.

Charley tossed in his own bet and shot a glance at
Creek and me. "Quit harping on how sick he looks,"
he said. "I want him to keep playing—he's losing
every hand."

Will raised an eyebrow at Charley. "What do you
care? He sure as hell ain't losing to *you*!" He gave us
all a smug look. "I call."

"Aww, hell, I fold," Dan said, tossing his hand
down in disgust.

"I don't!" Creek said. He laid his hand down, and
he had two pair of fives. Red Buck let out an annoyed

grunt and tossed his hand down, too, reaching for the bottle of whiskey set in the middle of the table.

Creek looked at me. "Bill? You in or out?"

I laid my hand down, face-up. I had two pair, too—of sevens. Creek's mustache drooped as he frowned, first at my hand, then at me. I just gave him a sly smile and leaned back in my chair, my arms crossed over my chest.

"Charley?" Will asked, his eyes twinkling. Charley glared at him and showed his hand. It was only a pair of twos.

"And you, Mister Two-Steps-From-Your-Grave?" Will asked Tom. He shook his head and folded without a word, looking a little less pale now and a little more green around the gills.

"Well, that leaves me, don't it?" Will said nonchalantly. He showed his hand, and it was a straight flush. Everyone groaned as he triumphantly leaned forward to scoop the pot toward him.

"God damn it, I ain't playin' you anymore," Red Buck said sourly to Will. He glanced over at me. "You aiming to have us do something soon?" he asked me bluntly. "I'm gettin' damned tired of doing nothing but play poker for hours on end."

Then get the hell out of our company, I wanted to say sharply. I still had not warmed to Red Buck; he made my skin crawl whenever he was near me—there was just something in his head that wasn't right and I had a feeling he'd end up causing us trouble, sooner or later. I had to admit, if even just to myself, that I was hoping it would be sooner, so I'd have an excuse to cut him out of the gang.

"I'm workin' on it," I replied coolly, raising an eyebrow at him and giving him a warning look. "Cool your heels, Weightman. If you're so damned eager to get back out there, you're free to go, any-time—by yourself."

The others were throwing uneasy looks at me, and at Red Buck, and next to me I saw Creek's hand move to rest on the handle of his gun in its holster, under the table.

For a few tense seconds, there was silence around our table. Then Red Buck let out a frustrated breath and shoved his chair back from the table, heading for the bar.

"I thought he was gonna draw on you, for a sec-ond, Bill," Creek commented, low.

"If he ever does, I'll put him down faster than you can blink," I growled, keeping my voice low, too. "That son of a bitch is asking for trouble, and if he pushes me too far, he ain't gonna like the outcome any too well."

Will glanced over at Red Buck, who had his back to us. "Well," he said thoughtfully, sticking a cigar in his mouth and pulling a match out of his vest pocket, "he's a little short on brains if he thinks he can challenge you, Bill. Maybe you ought to send him packing. Wouldn't bother me none if you did. He's damned crazy." Before I could answer, Will frowned at Tom, whose face was inching closer and closer to the surface of the table, like he was nodding off. "Damn it, Tom, will you *please* attend to yourself and turn in? I ain't aiming to miss out on the next hand because I had to go ride for the undertaker to clear your sorry corpse out of here." He flicked his wrist sharply to extinguish the match, and exhaled a cloud of smoke toward the ceiling.

Tom looked up, and his eyes were a little glazed over. "Maybe I should go up to bed for a bit," he agreed weakly. He pocketed his chips and got unsteadily to his feet. "I just need to sleep awhile, and I'll be just fine." He trudged toward the door and headed for the hotel.

Tulsa Jack was sauntering in just as Tom went out, and we all saw Jack eyeball Tom with a raised eyebrow. He said something to him, and Tom shook his head and kept going. Jack came over to our table and plunked himself down in the chair Tom had vacated.

"He looks about ready for his grave," Jack

commented after greeting us all. "Kid's pretty sick, by the looks of it."

"Seems so," I agreed. "Sleep'll do him some good, I reckon."

We all flipped in antes and Charley started dealing out new hands. As we were all looking over our cards, a short, skinny old-timer came in the doors and walked right up to our table. He was a local around Ingalls; I recognized him as one of the old bachelors that frequented the saloon's faro table—and the saloon girls, even though he was probably old enough to be their grandpappy. Everyone knew him as Old Jenkins.

"Mister Doolin, I got a message to deliver to you and yours," he said gravely in his rusty voice. His tobacco-stained gray whiskers dangled limply from his chin and wagged as he spoke, and he had a chaw in one cheek that made his craggy face look misshapen.

I raised an eyebrow. "Go ahead." I leaned back in my chair a little, waiting, and trying to hold back a smile.

"I was out by the edge of town a bit ago, and I come up on a couple covered wagons heading this way. Man driving the lead wagon had a tin star on; looks like he's a deputy marshal, or some such. There were a bunch of other men holed up in the wagons, besides. Looks to me like maybe they're aiming to try to take you boys into custody."

I let out a short laugh. "That's what they're aiming, is it?" I glanced at the others, amused, and not the least bit concerned. "Listen here, friend. I'd be much obliged if you'd ride back on out there and tell them if they think they can get us, they're sure as hell welcomed to try it. As for me and the others, we just got dealt a fresh hand, so we'll just set in here and attend to our game."

"What do you say, Jenkins?" Creek asked jovially, grinning wide at the old man. "You want to be our appointed messenger to the United States Government?" His eyes were twinkling mischievously.

Jenkins nodded, not even cracking a smile. He scratched at his chin. "I figger I can handle that." He gave us a little salute and headed back outside.

I started to laugh. "This'll be fun," I commented to the others. They were all chuckling, too.

"You figure we should scatter a bit?" Tulsa Jack asked me, a little nervously.

"Jack, they ain't gonna get us," I said firmly, tossing some chips into the pot. "I bet twenty-five."

"We got friends in this town, and enough guns on us to take down anyone who comes in and tries anything," Will added breezily. "Charley, it's your bet."

"I see your twenty-five, Bill, and I'll raise you ten."

"I ain't gonna let some damned lawdogs come in

here and try to drag me out," I said, tossing two more chips into the pot. "This is our town, boys, and we'll make a stand if we got to. I ain't running."

"I'm with Bill," Creek said firmly to Jack.

"So am I," Charley said. The others nodded, and Jack pursed his lips.

"Guess I am, too," he said. "I fold."

<hr />

"I'm gonna go take a look around, Bill," Creek said about an hour later, after we'd played several more games and shared a second bottle of whiskey. We'd seen no sign of Jenkins or any lawdogs.

I cocked an eyebrow at him as I drained the last swallow of whiskey from my glass. "You sure, Creek? That may not be a good idea."

"I can't just sit here," he said, sounding agitated. "If they're coming, they need to hurry the hell up. Otherwise, I'm heading out to see Rose."

I shrugged. "Suit yourself. See you later, then." He picked up his Winchester and headed out the door.

A few seconds later, I heard a gunshot, then a few more. I shot to my feet, toppling my chair behind me, and the others did the same, drawing their revolvers or reaching for their rifles. The few other patrons in the saloon dove under their tables, and behind the bar, John Murray reached for his own Winchester.

I ran, in a crouch, toward the front windows, and without hesitation I used my rifle stock to break one of the glass panes so I could stick the muzzle through the window. On either side of me, the others were doing the same. We could see men crouched here and there along the street, guns pointed toward the saloon, and we opened fire almost simultaneously. I couldn't see Creek anywhere. Outside, people started screaming; I could hear it in between the volleys of gunfire.

The marshals returned fire, and bullets started smashing through wood and flying through the rest of the glass left on the windows. Bottles behind the bar started exploding as stray shots hit them. At the hitching rail in front of the saloon, a horse tied there let out a scream of pain as a bullet hit it, then dropped dead. The horse alongside it jerked its head up so hard it broke its reins, then wheeled away from the rail in terror.

We hit the floor, gritting our teeth and firing back, but I knew we were outnumbered. The whole front of the saloon was being shot full of holes and I figured it was a small miracle none of us had been hit yet. The shooting stopped and I heard a voice call out, "give up your guns and surrender, Doolin! We got you outnumbered!"

"Go to hell!" I shouted back, firing off a few more rounds. The lawmen answered them and I knew it was time to go. "Get out, now!" I yelled to the others, scrambling for the back door of the saloon and hearing them follow me. If we could make it out that back door, we could get to the livery, where our horses were put up.

As I burst out the back door, I saw John Murray leap over the bar, his rifle in one hand, and noticed he was heading for the front door. He was defending his saloon—and defending us. "John, get down!" I called back over my shoulder, gritting my teeth at the pain starting up in my bad foot. More shots rang out, and I saw Murray crumple in the doorway, his rifle dropping to the floor with a clatter. I looked away.

As we ran, I heard more shots being fired from somewhere above us, and when I looked up I saw the end of a Winchester sticking out one of the hotel windows. Tom had apparently decided to get in on things, and from that angle he had an advantage on the small army of lawmen. I was damned glad of it as I saw a shot from his rifle drop one of the marshals like a buck at the hunt. The others in his party dove for cover.

We drew our revolvers and fired at the remaining lawmen as we made for the stable. Someone's shot went wild and I saw it hit a kid running down the

gallery, trying to take cover in one of the other saloons. The kid fell and lay still. I heard more screaming and horses whinnying in terror.

We made it into the stable and grabbed wildly for
our horses, vaulting ourselves up into the saddles and
kicking them into a gallop. I wasn't sure everyone
was still with me; I didn't take the time to check.
Rebel was in the lead as we went flying, hell-bent for
leather, down the street amidst a fresh hail of bullets
and running bodies, all obscured by clouds of gunsmoke and dust churned up by the horses' hooves.

I heard a horse scream behind me, heard a ruckus
right after, and I checked Rebel and turned him back
just in time to see Will go flying out of his saddle
as General Sherman collapsed under him, one of his
forelegs gushing blood. I saw bone glistening white
and jagged in the center of the horse's wound and I
knew his leg had been shattered by the bullet. Will
rolled clear of him just before he would've been
pinned underneath and started running for cover.

One of the marshals rose up from behind a water trough then and ran for Will, his pistol aimed for
Will's chest. I raised my revolver and shot him, killing him before he could kill Will. Another deputy
came up over the body of a dead horse in the street,
cornering Will behind a fence with a shotgun. I saw
Will take aim and drill him right in the chest, and he

dropped like a stone into the dirt. He wasn't dead yet; he was moaning and clutching at his chest, but I figured he probably would be, soon.

I dug my spurs into Rebel's sides and made it over to Will, reaching a hand down to him. "We got to get out of here, now!" I said hoarsely. He took my hand and I hauled him up into the saddle behind me. Rebel took off like a shot, running hard to catch up with the others. All around us, bullets were still raining.

We made it to the top of the little ridge at the end of Main Street, and we all turned our horses and fired some departing shots, more out of anger than of thinking we were gonna hit anyone. Out of the corner of my eye I could see that Dynamite Dan had blood soaking the shoulder of his shirt; looked like he'd been hit but I didn't take the time to comment. Everyone scattered then; I didn't bother to call any of them back. I was too intent on getting myself and Will to safety.

Rebel was good and spooked and he ran wild for a few minutes. Will hung on behind me. Suddenly we came up over a little rise and caught sight of a big black horse, long-legged and with a white snip on the end of its nose, standing idle in a patch of dry weeds. The saddle on its back was empty and the reins dangled down to the ground.

"Bill, that's Dash," Will said tensely, and I checked Rebel, hard.

"What the hell…?" I let my voice trail off. I heard a moan come from the brush on the other side of Dash, and saw a hand raise weakly up out of them, reaching toward us. The sun glinted off a head of coppery hair half-hidden in the weeds.

"Jesus Christ!" I slid out of the saddle and let Will have the reins. Creek was laying on his side, his face white and twisted with pain. There was blood glistening on his right thigh and pooling in the dirt beneath him. I cussed under my breath and crouched at his side. "Creek, you been shot!"

"I couldn't ride no farther, Bill," he said to me, and his voice was so weak I could barely hear it.

I looked up at Will. "I got to get him out of here or he ain't gonna make it," I said grimly. I reached down and gripped him under the arms, pulling him up off the ground. He gasped in pain but I kept on, dragging him toward Dash. "Help me out here, Creek," I said around clenched teeth, shoving him up toward the saddle. He reached up and gripped the saddle-horn, and between the two of us we got him up there, somehow. I climbed up in front of him and he slumped against me, his whole weight on my back.

"Hang on, Creek," I said grimly, and I gathered

up Dash's reins as Will took off on Rebel. Behind me, I could hear horses coming. I didn't know if they were ours or the law's—and I didn't wait to find out.

———◆———

We rode for mine and Edith's place; it was closer than the Dunns' ranch and they were less likely to track us there, since the law was already suspicious of the Dunns and their knowledge of us as it was. Will pulled Rebel up around the back and took him by the bit, forcing him into the stable. He was a recognizable horse and both Will and I knew we couldn't leave him tied outside where someone might see him.

The front door banged and Edith flew out onto the porch, gasping in shock as she saw me get off of Dash and pull a nearly unconscious Creek down out of the saddle. His britches were soaked through with blood by then.

"Oh, my Lord, what *happened?*" she cried. "Oh, God, Bill—"

"He's been shot. Edith, get a bowl of water and whatever cloth we got for bandages. Hurry up, honey. I'm all right." I wasn't looking at her right then; there wasn't any time for explanations.

Her face was white, but she turned and ran back inside. Will came over and together we walked Creek inside, one on either side of him, his arms slung around our shoulders. By the time we got him up the porch he was nearly sapped of any strength.

"That wound's bleeding bad," Will said grimly.

"Bullet's still in there," I replied. "I got to get it out of him or he'll be bad off."

We got Creek into the bedroom and laid him out on the bed; I knew the quilt Edith's Ma had made for our wedding present would be ruined but there wasn't anything for it. She came in then, carrying a bowl and pitcher and a bunch of towels.

"Will, hold his shoulders down. Edith, I need you to hold onto his legs, now, so he can't twist away from me." I looked up at her, once, met her eyes with mine. Her face was still pale but her gaze was steady; without questioning me she went to the foot of the bed and took ahold of Creek's ankles with both of her hands.

I pulled my knife out of the scabbard I kept hidden in my boot and cut the leg of Creek's britches open, then wiped the blade down with a wet cloth and dug it into his leg. He let out a cry of pain and tried to jerk away from me, but Edith was proving to be surprisingly strong and she held him fast, bearing all her weight down to brace him. Sweat broke out on her brow and little tendrils of her hair started sticking to her neck, but she kept at her task as I worked.

Creek kept up his howling, but I kept on going. I felt the knife blade hit against something metal and I managed to pop the bullet out. It hit the floor and rolled off somewhere. Creek's screams died down and trailed off into big gasps for air. He was sweating and there was no color to his face. Water was squeezing out of his eyes.

"I can't take no more, Bill!" he whimpered. "Just leave me be and let me die!"

"You ain't gonna die, Creek," I told him firmly. My hands were slick with his blood, and there was blood all over the bed and the floor and my clothes. The front door banged and I heard running steps; Charley and Tulsa Jack suddenly appeared in the doorway, their faces going white at the sight of Creek laying bloodied on the bed and me leaning over him with my knife.

I didn't waste time in enlisting their help. "Jack, come over here and take over for Edith. Edith, I need you to find a sheet and tear up some strips for me; I got to bandage this leg up, quick." She nodded and rushed out of the room once Jack had come over to take ahold of Creek's ankle, her skirts swishing against the doorframe in her haste.

"They got Tom, Bill," Charley told me, and I

looked up at him, noticing for the first time that he had a blood-stained bandage wound crudely around one arm. Looked like he'd been shot, too.

"Killed him?" I asked shortly.

"No. Took him into custody. Sons of bitches just let him run out of bullets and then they went up and hauled him out."

I didn't answer him. "You're shot," I commented, helping Will and Jack hold Creek down, who was fighting us again.

"Just grazed. I'll be all right." He looked at Creek and his black eyes filled with worry. "You think he's gonna make it?"

"He will if I have anything to say about it," I said shortly. I looked up at him. "Someone should go ride and get Rose. Maybe having her here will help."

"Charley and me'll go," Jack said quickly, "if you two can manage him all right."

Edith came back into the bedroom with a muslin sheet and her sewing scissors. She made cuts along one edge of the sheet, then started ripping it into long strips. Creek started cussing at us all then, his pain was making him crazy.

"God damn it, Creek, shut up!" I snapped. "You're gonna make yourself bleed to death!"

He kept carrying on and he was moving around too much, so I took one of my revolvers out of my holster and wound a towel around the butt. I met Will's eyes with mine and he nodded, rolling Creek's body toward him so the back of his head was exposed. Then, moving swiftly, I cracked the butt of the gun across the base of Creek's skull, knocking him out. Edith let out a gasp but raised both of her hands to her mouth to stifle it.

We all let out our breath in relief, and I straightened up, looking over at Edith. "It's all right, honey. I just knocked him out. He's got to stay still so I can bandage him up." She didn't answer me, just nodded and took a big, deep breath as she brought me the bandages, and some tincture to put on the wound.

Jack and Charley left to go get Rose, and I asked Will to bring me some of the thick clay from the creek bank out back. I'd have to pack the wound with it before I bandaged it or it wouldn't stop bleeding.

When Will left, there was only me and Edith left in the room with Creek, who was still out cold. She touched my arm, hesitantly. "What happened, Bill?" she asked softly.

"God-damned lawdogs," I said shortly, my voice hard, my eyes on Creek's prone form. "They tried to take us all down while we were in Ingalls."

Before she could say anything, Will came back in with the mud in a bowl, and I started packing it onto Creek's leg. Then Will lifted it up a little and I started winding the bandages around, tightly. It took a hell of a lot of them, but we finally got his leg to where there wasn't any blood showing through.

I straightened up and wiped the clean part of my wrist across my forehead to stop the sweat from coming down into my eyes, then let out a breath of relief. "Think that'll do it," I murmured under my breath, more to myself than to Will or Edith.

Creek was coming to by then and he was moaning; shivering, too. He had a fever and I told Edith to get extra blankets so we could sweat it out of him.

As we were piling them on him, I heard horses coming up to the side of the house, and I looked out the window, quick. It was Jack and Charley and Rose, and Rose was in the saddle of George's big gray stud. As I watched, she scrambled down in a flurry of skirts and petticoats and tossed the reins at Jack before she ran for the front porch. A minute later we heard her come inside.

"Bill? Edith?" she called, her voice sounding more high-pitched than usual.

"Back here, Rose!" I called. "Go to your right and down the hall."

She came into the bedroom and her face drained and her hand went to her mouth when she saw Creek laying there prone under the big pile of quilts and my buffalo overcoat laid over the top. She ran for the side of the bed and reached under the blankets for his hand. "Creek?" You hear me?" He didn't answer her and she looked up at me, her eyes huge in her peaked little face. "Is it bad? Could he die?"

I rubbed at a sudden crick in my neck. "He was hit in the thigh. I pulled the bullet out but he's lost a hell of a lot of blood." My voice came out grim and she bit her lip, looking back down at him.

I wiped my bloodied hands on a wet rag. "He's a fighter, Rose. He'll pull through."

"Thank you," she whispered. "Thank you for doctoring him up."

I nodded, then motioned to Edith and Will, and we left them alone for a bit. I was suddenly parched and I went to the kitchen for water, Edith trailing behind me. Will took up his rifle and went out onto the porch to assess things and to talk with Jack and Charley. He was worried they were tracking us.

Edith stood in the doorway and watched while I drank. I turned a little while I was drinking and met her eyes with mine, then I put the glass down, went over to her, and pulled her against me. She sort of sank into my embrace and buried her face in the hollow of my throat. We both knew she was getting blood all over her dress from the stains on my clothes, but neither of us cared. "Bill—" she started to say, then choked on the rest of her sentence and fell quiet.

"I'm sorry, honey," I told her, kissing the top of her head. "I'm sorry I brought all this here and got you mixed up in it. But there ain't anything for it. I couldn't let him die."

"No, of course not," she mumbled. "It's just... oh, God, Bill, it could've been you, instead of him."

"It wasn't." I took her by the shoulders and gave her an encouraging little shake. "I'm all right, honey. And you did a damned good job of helping me in there."

She looked me in the eye. "Do you really think he's going to be all right?" she asked me in a small voice. She liked Creek a lot; she'd told me once that she would always be grateful to him for coming with me to that first social, and for standing up for us at our wedding.

I nodded. "It's gonna take more than one bullet to the thigh to take Creek down," I said firmly. I cupped her face in both my hands and kissed her hard then, grateful beyond measure to have been spared injury, capture or death in that fight, just so that I'd been able to come home to her again.

TWENTY-THREE

BY THE TIME nightfall came, Creek's fever had broken, and he was calmer then. Rose didn't want leave his side, but he insisted she go get herself some of the supper Edith had put together for all of us. While she was out of the room, I sat with Creek, and he told me what happened to him.

"I was walking along the gallery," he said, his voice still sounding like a shadow of its usual self, "and I had my Winchester in my hands. I wasn't but ten steps or so from the saloon when this son of a bitch came up from across the street and fired on me. It hit my rifle and blew the damned thing apart. Then he fired again and hit me. I pulled my revolver and got of a couple shots, but I knew by then that there were a hell of a lot of them and I knew I needed to get out of there. I wanted to warn you and the boys but there wasn't time." He swallowed and winced against a stab of pain, then licked his lips and kept talking. "You know how I came into town after the rest of you today?" I nodded. "I didn't put Dash up at the livery. I tied him 'round back of the hotel because I stopped in to see how Tom was faring. So I got to Dash and managed to get up on him, but pretty soon I got too weak to ride, and I remember falling off. That's where you found me."

I sighed. "They got Tom, Creek. Charley said they arrested him at the hotel after he ran out of bullets."

Creek's eyes closed for a second, and when he opened them I could see regret in his expression. "He saved my life, Bill, just like you done. He drilled that son of a bitch before he could kill me."

"I know. I wish he'd been able to get away." I fell silent, thinking things over in my mind. For a few seconds I thought about trying to bust Tom out from wherever they had him locked up, but then I abandoned the idea. I knew I wouldn't succeed. We had lost another man—but there were still a hell of a lot of us left. I felt a grim determination well up in my gut. I'd stayed out of the law's grip up until now, and I'd continue to do so, no matter what.

—————— ((●)) ——————

The outcome of that bloodbath in Ingalls was

pretty much what we thought it would be—three marshals died and two townsfolk, too. John Murray wasn't killed, just wounded bad, and they arrested him for harboring wanted criminals. Made me good and mad when I heard that—as far as I was concerned, a man had a right to fend off people who were shooting his saloon all to hell, and he'd just been doing his job by serving us whiskey and letting us play poker in his place. There was talk of lynching Arkansas Tom, but in the end, they just threw him in prison. Just a day after the fight, the new U.S. marshal for the Oklahoma Territory, one E.D. Nix, sent out proclamations into the papers saying he and his remaining deputies were going to get me and mine come hell or high water. I laughed aloud when I read that. Let 'em try.

"Bill? Are you out here?"

Edith's voice was just a faint whisper, and I could barely see her silhouette as she slipped out the front door onto the porch around ten o'clock the night after the fight. It was pitch-black outside and I had a feeling we were in for some rain.

"I'm over here," I replied, speaking in barely

above a whisper myself. I was heading for the stable, treading slowly in the darkness.

She came down the steps lightly and followed me into the stable. As we went in the horses all let out throaty nickers, hoping for more food. I closed the door behind us, then reached up for the lantern and took a match to it; its glow filled the building and illuminated her worried expression. She had a shawl pulled around her shoulders and she was worrying the edges of it with her fingers as she watched me.

I took down the collar from the stable wall, and gathered up the traces and the rest of the harness. She saw me and her worried look got deeper. "What are you doing?" she asked in alarm.

I slung my arm through the collar and slid it up on my shoulder to carry it over to the stall where the gentle mare we kept for pulling our wagon was housed. "Edith," I said seriously to her, "we can't stay here. It ain't safe. After what happened yesterday, they're gonna be looking for us all over hell. And I won't let anything happen to you, you hear me?" I went in with the mare and slipped the collar over her neck.

Edith came closer to the stall, still clutching her shawl tight. "Where will we go?" Her voice was small.

"I ain't sure. But we need to go tonight. The law

could be out any minute." I motioned for her to hand me the diving bridle, and she did.

I glanced at her as I took the headstall and slipped the bit into the mare's mouth. I knew she'd been though a hell of a lot in the last twenty-four hours, but there was something else the matter; she wasn't acting right.

"You all right, honey?" I asked her.

She bit down on her lower lip and lowered her eyes from mine for a second, and I felt a sudden wave of fear crash over me. Had all this been too much for her, made her change her mind about me, about us? "Edith?" I prompted, my voice coming out funny— sharp and higher-pitched than usual. I stopped fussing with the mare and came out of the stall. "What is it?"

She took a deep breath and looked at me square. "This isn't the time to tell you, I know, but…Bill, I'm going to have a baby. I was going to tell you yesterday…before all this happened."

There wasn't too much in the world that could shock me anymore, but that did. I'd always figured we'd start a family one day, but I'd figured on it being down the road aways, when I was ready to swear off my vendetta and when I'd gotten ahold of enough money to never have to worry about it again. To have it happen now, when the stakes were so high, struck me speechless for a few minutes.

She swallowed hard and her fingers started working the shawl's edges again; I could tell she was worried I'd be upset about the news. In truth I was far from it, but the timing of it was what was giving me such pause. I came to from my shock and quickly put my arms around her, pulling her close.

She spoke before I could, going limp in my arms, like she was relieved. "Oh, Bill, I was so worried you'd be upset," she said, into my vest.

"Edith, honey, I ain't upset. I'm happy, I promise you. I been wanting us to have a baby, and that's the God's honest truth. It's just that I'm gonna worry double about you, now, and I got to get you someplace safe." I pulled back from her aways and stroked back the little tendrils of her hair that always wisped around her face, then kissed her, first her lips, then her forehead.

She kept her forehead leaned against mine and I saw her throat bob. "Will you stop now, Bill? Now that you know the baby's coming?" She put her hands against either side of my face, pushing her fingers into my hair. They were shaking.

My whole body went tense and I took her by the shoulders, stepping back from her against the stall door and holding her out at arm's length, looking her straight in the eyes. "Edith, there are men out there that are trying to *kill* me—kill the others, too. You understand? If I do nothing it's the same as if I'm just setting out in the open waiting for them to come and get me." My voice came out hard, but I couldn't help it. I knew she heard the rage there, but I didn't apologize for it. Lord knew I'd tried my best to spare her as much as I could, but as far as I was concerned, this was all-out war, now. They'd taken two of ours and they aimed to take more. Now we'd taken some of theirs, and they'd called me and mine out. I was damned if I was going to surrender; I'd always said I'd fight for my freedom until the day I took my last gulp of air.

She had tears in her eyes and I rubbed her upper arms gently with my hands then, trying to make her see reason. "Edith, you got my word, when everything's settled and when I've found somewhere safe, I'll give all this up. But not a damned day earlier than that." I clenched my jaw and let her go, then went back in with the mare. "Best get you on inside, and gather whatever you want to take." I buckled the breastcollar on and fastened the traces, then turned back to her, sensing she hadn't moved from the stall door.

"It'll be all right, honey. I promise you. You got to trust me." My voice was good and soft now, and, I hoped, reassuring. I reached over the stall door and ran the backs of my fingers over her cheek, lightly.

"I do trust you, Bill," she said. Her words came out choked. She ducked her head and turned away from me, quick, heading out into the night and back to the house.

————— ((•)) —————

I got the mare hitched up and hobbled her near the side of the house so we could load the wagon up easy without making it too obvious. Just as I'd picked up my rifle and was preparing to head back in, I heard the jingle of bits, the low squeak of leather, and the sound of horses coming up at a canter. I cocked the rifle and moved into the darker shadows made by the house, ready to shoot whoever it was out of their saddles.

A whistle came; it was Charley's. He and Jack were in the lead, and they had Dick West with them, who was ponying another horse under saddle. "It's us, Bill," Charley called quietly. He dismounted and tossed his reins over the porch railing.

I relaxed and came toward them, my gait hindered by my bad foot, which had been giving me grief ever since the fight. "We came to get Creek," Jack said to me, dismounting, too. "We thought we should split up some for a time, if you agree."

I tucked my rifle under my arm. "I do," I said. "Edith and I ain't staying here. It's too dangerous. We'll shake the law off our tail, and then when Creek's healed up, we'll get ourselves back to it." My voice was firm.

Dick spit tobacco juice off into the bushes, then shifted in his saddle. "He fit to ride, you reckon?" he asked me, jerking his head toward the house.

"He's complaining every ten minutes about me making him stay in bed, and I was about ready to tie him to the bedstead, if you want the truth. But his leg hasn't bled again, and he ain't spiked a fever since the first one."

"Well, if he's bellyaching like that, and if his leg ain't bleeding any, then he's fit to ride as far's I'm concerned," Charley said. "Bill Dunn's got a one-room dugout aways out from the ranch. We'll take Creek there, hole up awhile. When you're ready, you come get us, and I'll get ahold of the others."

"Best go get Dash out of the stable, then; get him saddled," I said.

Will came out onto the porch then; he'd been sleeping in the stable until we came up with plans. He'd wanted to ride out to his claim and be with Jane and the children, but I'd told him to wait a few days in case the law was tracking us. Last thing I wanted was for Jane or his little ones to get harassed by

Marshal Nix's men, or the Three Guardsmen them-selves, if they managed to follow Will there.

We told Will what we'd discussed, and I looked up at him from where I stood at the base of the porch steps. "What do you figure, Will? Sound like a plan you can live with?" I asked. I'd been counting more and more on him the last few months as a confidant for any plans I made; I knew he wouldn't hesitate to tell me if he thought I'd made a wrong choice.

I saw him nod in the thin moonlight. "Count me in. I'll go saddle Creek's horse."

"Heard what happened to General Sherman, Will," Dick called suddenly. He nodded toward the horse he was ponying. "Damned shame. This one ain't near the horse he was, but I figured he'll do you all right."

"Much obliged, Dick," Will said. He headed off toward the stable.

I looked at the others. "Come on in and let's get Creek situated." I headed inside without waiting for an answer.

Edith was moving around in a flurry, packing up food and supplies from the kitchen. I went over to her and stopped her in her stride, leaning in to place a soft kiss on her temple, hoping to reassure her a little more. Then I went on through to the bedroom, hearing the others come inside and take their hats off to Edith, greeting her quietly.

Creek was sitting up in bed, propped up by pillows. His color looked better than it had been. "Creek," I said, "you think you can ride?"

One of his eyebrows rose. "Of course I can, if I got to. And I'm guessing I got to, or else you wouldn't be asking me." He gave me a ghost of his old grin.

"We think you should, Creek," Charley said, coming into the room, Jack and Dick behind him. "We got a place to hole up for a bit, let that leg of yours heal up. It ain't too far away."

Creek nodded and shoved the quilts back, gingerly moving himself toward the edge of the bed. Jack and I moved forward to help him stand, and his face went a little pale when he did it, but he stayed upright and I saw no red seeping through the thick layer of bandages.

We managed to get him dressed; I gave him a pair of my britches to wear since I'd shredded his old ones all to hell. Then we walked him slowly toward the front of the house.

"Just a minute," Creek said suddenly, when we were almost to the front door. "Where's Edith? I got something to say to her."

"I'm right here," she said, coming to the doorway

that led from the kitchen to our front room. "What is it, Creek?"

He hopped on one foot to angle himself toward her, Jack and I shifting with him since he had his arms slung over our shoulders. "Edith, I sure am indebted to you for doctoring me up and letting me stay here like you done, and I'm sorry I got all that blood all over your fine quilts and floor and whatnot." He looked ashamed.

My wife smiled her lovely smile at him and came over to lay her hand over his that was resting on my shoulder. "Don't you worry none about that, Creek, and you know our home is always yours. Although I have to say I do hope that the next time I see you, it will be under better circumstances."

"I sincerely share that hope," Creek replied with a chuckle. "You take care of Bill, now."

She laughed. "I always seem to," she said, giving me a look. "Rest up and get well." She patted his hand again and went back into the kitchen.

We got him out to the porch and found Will waiting there with Dash, saddled up and ready. Gingerly Creek put his foot into the stirrup, and Charley and I helped support his weight as he dragged himself up into the saddle. His face twisted in pain and he went pretty white, but he stayed up there and gathered up the reins.

"You gonna be all right?" I asked him soberly, looking up at him.

"Don't got a choice, do I?" he replied. He grimaced. "I'll manage." He gave me a look. "You watch your back."

"I will. You do the same."

He leaned down a little and extended a hand to me, and I took it, giving it a good squeeze.

"Let's go," Will said shortly, trotting up on the horse Dick had brought him. He looked down at me as Charley and Jack mounted up. "We'll see you soon."

I nodded and stood on the bottom of the porch steps, watching as they cantered off into the darkness.

TWENTY-FOUR

"THAT'S IT, I'M taking you to your Ma and Pa's place."

My voice was grim as I came around the wagon one morning to find Edith hunched over in the grass, wiping her wrist across her mouth, loose strands of her hair straggling around her pale face. She'd been getting sick like this every morning since we'd left the old house, and even though she never complained, I knew she was miserable, having to bed down in the wagon every night, with me always on edge and on the lookout for the law.

"I'm all right," she protested weakly. "This is normal."

"It may be, but being out here like this without any comforts ain't helping any." I went over to her and crouched at her side, resting the stock of my rifle in the dirt and putting my other arm around her shoulders. "I'll take you to your folks' place tonight, then come back for you when I figure out where we're gonna settle down."

She let her breath out and lifted a hand to push her hair out of her face. "How long do you think that will be, Bill?" she asked me wearily.

"You know I can't answer that," I replied softly, leaning in to kiss her temple softly. "But I ain't gonna let you spend another night out here like this."

She let out another shaky breath and avoided my eyes. "I'll get breakfast going," she said. I rubbed her back as I stood and helped her up.

"I'll do it," I said. "You go and rest."

"I'm not dying, Bill," she snapped at me, sharp. "I'm fine." She shook bits of grass and dust off her skirt and headed for the water bucket set near the ring of stones where our campfire had been. She took a long drink from the dipper, then went to the wagon for the coffee pot and the skillet she used for cooking our meals outdoors.

I ran my hand across my eyes, feeling helpless. I knew she wasn't really mad at me; she'd been having wild mood swings since the night she'd told me we were expecting. But the strain of worrying about her and the baby, while also worrying about the law catching up with us, was starting to weigh heavy on me. I knew she wanted to stay with me, and I didn't want to up and leave her again, especially when she was sick like this and scared for my safety, but I had to do it.

We'd been traveling around the Territory for a few weeks while I tried to get shed of the feeling of being hunted out like a game animal. We'd stayed clear of towns so far, but we were running low on provisions and I knew I'd have to chance it pretty soon. All the more reason to get her to her folks' place as soon as possible.

My mind made up, I picked up my rifle and went to bring the mare and Rebel in from where I'd picketed them out to graze.

———— ◈ ————

I kept the wagon to the most secluded trails I knew about; narrow ones that wound into quiet wooded areas, offering less chance of running into anyone else, and less opportunity for the law to sneak up on us. Traveling the way we were made it much slower going, but I refused to take any chances. By noon Edith was feeling some better and stopped looking like she was gonna keel over every time the wagon wheels went over a rut or a rocky place. As we were heading down a gentle slope back toward a stretch of prairie she put her hand on her middle, which wasn't starting to show anything just yet, and looked over at me as I kept the lines in play between my fingers. "What should we name the baby when it comes, Bill?"

I glanced at her with a soft smile. "We can't name it yet, honey; we don't know what it's gonna be, boy or girl."

She rolled her eyes at me, but she was smiling as she did it. "I know that; I just wanted to hear what names you like for each. It's sort of fun to think about, don't you think?"

I felt a smile come out over my face as I looked thoughtfully out over the trail. "It is, at that," I agreed. "Makes you think about what kind of person he or she'll turn out to be, once they come." I nudged her shoulder with my mine, gently, as she sat close beside me on the wagon seat. "If it's a little girl she'll be pretty like her Ma."

She lifted a hand and brushed at the hair blowing around her face in the breeze. "More than likely it'll be a boy, and he'll be a devil like you." A loving tease was plain in her voice.

"Well, if he is, you'll be some prepared for that, seeing as how you've managed to put up with me thus far." I made my voice good and dry when I said it and she laughed.

She got quiet for a few minutes after that, like she

was thinking something over. I waited for her to tell me the names she'd thought about, but she didn't. Instead, she leaned her head to the side a little and looked at me, thoughtful. "Bill, you mind if I ask you a question?"

"'Course not," I said, keeping the mare to an easy trot. "What is it?"

She tucked her hair back off her face again and bit her lip softly. "When the time comes, and you're done with all this—I mean, when you feel you've evened up the score enough with the railroad—what are you going to do? Have you thought about it at all?" Her voice was careful, like she was afraid I'd be upset she was asking.

I slowed the mare up to a walk, because we were coming to a creek crossing, and then I answered her, keeping my eyes on the path ahead and the low place the wagon would go over the water. "I've thought about it," I said. "Easy there, Sally," I murmured, soothing the mare when she balked a bit. "You know I've never known much but cows; seems to be what I'm good at, besides…what I been doin'." I cleared my throat a little and slapped the reins gently across the horse's back.

"But there's so little call for working them, seems like, from what you've told me," she said, reaching a hand back to hold firmly onto the wagon box as the mare started across the creek, Rebel coming along easy behind the wagon, where I had him tied.

I shook my head. "Don't mean working them for someone else, honey. I'd raise them. Start up a spread of my own." It was the first time I'd ever actually said it out loud, to her or to anyone; in truth I think I'd just said it to ease her mind a bit, but the more I thought about it, the more I liked the idea. I wasn't ready to do any such thing just yet; I still had some plans for the Bunch that needed doing, but it was nice to entertain the thought of a life after all this, once I was ready to stop.

We got across the creek and came up into a grassy area, and with the fall sunshine pouring over us and the breeze caressing our faces, and thoughts of children and a ranch down the future in our minds, I think we both felt a little better about life as a whole right then. Things might be tight for the two of us right now, but they'd get better.

TWENTY-FIVE

AN ICY WIND whipped across the plains, driving the cold into my bones as if my heavy wolf's fur-trimmed coat wasn't even there. Flakes of snow started coming down from the steel-gray sky, adding to what was left over from the last storm. I ducked my head a little against the wind and tapped my spurs to my horse's sides; he was balking at heading through the deepening snowdrifts.

It was January of 1894 and I'd only just come back toward Council Creek, hunting out the dugout the boys had taken Bitter Creek to after the fight in Ingalls. I'd left Edith safe and sound with her folks in Lawson, but I'd had a hell of a hard time doing so. It'd been so tempting to just stay there with them, but I knew better. I'd been warned that Bill Tilghman had been seen in the area often, and I had to stay ahead of him. I didn't tell Edith, but I had dreams about staying and him coming to her folks' farm in the middle of the night and rooting me out of there, leaving Edith in misery and our baby without a Pa. I counted those dreams as a premonition of sorts, and I'd forced myself to go, telling her I'd come for her as soon as I could, glad that I could at least leave her with family.

With a lot of reluctance, I'd left Rebel there, too; too many lawdogs had seen him in Ingalls and I knew they'd be looking for a palomino. I bought a tall black stud named Black Devil off a rancher outside of Enid who was as fast as Rebel and about ten times as ornery, but I got him in hand and pretty soon I had him gentled down enough so he didn't cause me too much grief.

The snow started coming harder and the only sounds I heard were Devil's snorted breaths and the soft plopping of his hooves in deep snow as he picked his way through. I could see faint tracks out ahead of us, two or three horses from the looks of it, and in the distance, near a sharp rise in the terrain, I could make out a thin plume of smoke wafting up from what appeared to be a snowbank. I knew better, though; I figured I'd found the dugout I was seeking. By the time I got close my coat and hat and Devil's mane and forelock were dusted with a thick layer of flakes. I eased him up and stopped him, and he fought the bit, pawing at the snow with one hoof.

"Settle down there, you ornery old cuss," I muttered absently to him, standing up in my stirrups a little to better peer through the falling flakes. I could see a door cut into the little hill before me; that and the smoke coming up out of the smoke-hole were the only signs that it wasn't an ordinary hill. Holding Devil firm, I whistled, my old two-note whistle the boys knew well, hoping they'd hear it through the door. Then I waited, ready to flee if need be. Someone was in the dugout, that I was sure of, but I couldn't be sure *who*.

The door opened and a short, bulky figure came out of it; he had a heavy bear-skin coat on, a scruffy beard masking his face and his hat pulled down practically to his eyeballs, but when he straightened up I recognized him easy. "Well now, if it ain't the Notorious Bill Dalton," I said, addressing him by the moniker the papers had stuck him with and crossing my wrists on the saddle-horn.

"You sure are a sight for sore eyes, Doolin," he told me, traipsing through the snow toward my horse as I dismounted. "We been waitin' on you, but we were starting to get worried, to tell the truth, seeing as how it's been awhile and then some."

"Well, I had some things to see to, and I didn't want to come here before enough time had gone by. Tilghman's out like a damn bloodhound."

He reached out and shook my hand. "You see Edith to safety?" he asked.

I nodded. "Her and our baby." His eyes widened, then his brows came together in confusion. Before he could say anything I chuckled. "It ain't born yet, Will. She told me the night after the Ingalls mess."

He smiled. "I'm happy for you, Bill. Ain't nothing in this world like being a father."

We started working our way through the snow, Black Devil prancing agitatedly behind me. "Where the hell's a man supposed to put up his horse around here, anyway?" I asked Will, choking up my hold on the reins a bit.

Will jerked his head off toward a fuzzy shape in the distance, obscured by the snow. "There's a sod stable there. It ain't too big, but there's an empty stall yet." He eyeballed my horse. "Where's Rebel, and where'd you come by this undertaker of a stud you're riding?"

I laughed shortly. "I left Rebel back with Edith's folks for a bit. Figured he was too easy to spot. Bought this stud up near Enid; he ain't as hard to handle as he looks."

Will looked him over again. "Damned fine-looking horse, but it looks like a man's got to keep his wits about him good to ride him any too well."

"I got him handled pretty good by now," I said.

Will got the door of the stable opened and I led Devil inside, noting Dash in one stall, and Little Bill Raidler's gelding in another. There were three other horses there I didn't recognize and I threw a look at Will over my shoulder as I tied Devil in. "Who's here, Will?"

"Bill Dunn, with the bay, and that gray stud there is mine. He ain't General Sherman, for damn sure, but he's pretty close."

I raised an eyebrow, waiting. When Will didn't say anything else I jerked my head toward the leggy buckskin in the middle. "And?"

He sighed. "Weightman showed up a few days ago," he admitted.

I set my jaw and felt my hands form fists, like they had minds of their own. Red Buck. "Damn it all to hell, I thought he'd go off on his own, since he seemed to think I was too slow to pick jobs."

Will lifted his shoulders in a helpless shrug. "I'd hoped so, too, Bill, but like it or not, he's here. I let him stay; I was afraid he'd go to the law and try to make some deal for himself in exchange for blabbing about this place, if I told him to get out."

I sighed and came out of the stall, reaching for the pitchfork sticking out of the hay pile. "I hadn't thought of that," I admitted, "but it sounds like the sort of thing he'd be liable to up and do." I pitched a few forkfuls of hay to Devil. "How's Creek?"

Will stuck his hands deep into the pockets of his coat. "Doing well. His leg's healed up so good you wouldn't ever know he'd been shot up. Hardly even limps." He gave me a sly grin. "Maybe you missed your calling, Bill. Should've been a doc. Ain't too late."

I rolled my eyes. "I'll take it under advisement, Will." I limped toward the stable door. My foot was aching bad from the cold; it didn't ever give me any rest from the torment when the weather was like this.

"Now that you're here, maybe we can get out of this hole and look up the others," Will commented as we trudged toward the dugout.

"That's my intention," I replied. We went inside, Will ducking through the low doorway first.

The dugout was one long, narrow room, as dug-outs usually were, and even with the fire going at one end and two lamps with a tin reflectors hung near the door, the inside was dark. I could make out the crouched forms of three men near the fire, and a fourth sitting in one corner, near the rough-hewn table. There was a stew-pot hanging over the fire and I smelled food cooking.

"Boys, look who I found playin' in the snow," Will said with a chuckle, and two of the crouched men stood and came over to me. They were Little Bill Raidler and Bill Dunn. The man in the corner stood stiffly up and headed over, and he was Creek. He reached for my hand and pumped it enthusiastically, then clapped me on the shoulder.

"I'm sure glad to see you, Bill!" he said, grinning at me as of old, his eyes snapping sparks in the lamplight. "Now we can get the hell out of here—no offense, Dunn."

Bill Dunn lifted his hands, palms out. "None taken, Newcomb." He nodded at me. "Good to see you, Bill."

I nodded back, but it was an automatic gesture with no real meaning behind it. I suddenly had a funny prickling sensation moving up my spine, like a spider crawling up a fence post, and it was Bill Dunn causing it.

My eyes narrowed a bit as I watched him move back toward the fire to toss another chunk of wood on it. The man who'd remained there when the others had come to greet me sat back on his heels and lit a cigarette; I knew it was Red Buck and I didn't care a continental about him giving me the cold shoulder. He was walking a fine line with me, and he knew it. I'd deal with him later. Right then I was more concerned with Bill Dunn. Those old nagging suspicions I'd had about him that first night I'd ever set foot on his ranch, the ones I'd thought long out of my mind, were suddenly back and it was irking me all to hell that I couldn't figure out why. There was just something off about him all of the sudden, like he wasn't real happy we were all there in his place.

Creek had sobered beside me and he was looking at me sharp, like he'd sensed my sudden change in mood. "You all right, Bill?" he asked me, keeping his voice low.

"I'm fine, Creek. Hungry as a bear, though, if you want the truth." I looked him in the eyes then and just barely shook my head, warning him off. I wanted to keep my suspicions to myself for now, until I figured out exactly what they were.

"We can fix that," Will said jovially. "Little Bill, let's rustle up some of that stew and them biscuits for our fearless leader."

Little Bill got a tin plate and spooned up some stew from the pot over the fire, and handed it to me along with a fork and a biscuit from a basket on the table. The biscuit was light and fluffy, and I recognized it right off. "Got Rose doing some biscuit-baking for you, seems like," I commented around a mouthful, grateful for the hearty meal.

Bill Dunn nodded. "She sent over a batch with me when I came out a bit ago."

Will, still standing near the door, put a hand on his hip and looked toward the fireplace. "What's the matter, Red Buck, ain't you glad Bill's back? Means we can get ourselves going again, like you been bel-lyachin' about every damn half-hour since you got here." His voice was good and loud and the sarcasm in it was plain. I chewed, swallowed, and waited to see how things would play out, my free hand creeping toward one of my pistols. I had to admit I hoped he'd draw on Will so we'd have an excuse to put a few pieces of lead in him; Lord above knew, if ever a man needed shooting, it was Red Buck. But I knew he wouldn't do it; drawing on any man in such a cramped, dark space would be suicide, never mind the fact that Will could drill a dime at ten yards. Red Buck may have been an arrogant son of a bitch and a killer, but he wasn't stupid.

"It's about time you showed up, Doolin," Red Buck replied crossly in his Texas drawl, standing up and reaching for a bottle of whiskey set out on the table. He yanked the cork out with more force than was necessary and knocked back an impressive swallow. "Took your own God-damned time; I suppose you ain't picked anything for us to go after yet, either." He wiped his wrist across his mouth and plunked the bottle back down.

I calmly set my plate down on the table and deliberately crossed my arms over my chest. "I have at that, Red Buck, but I'm not sure I'm gonna tell you about it, nor invite you along, seeing as how your attitude ain't exactly to my liking." I let my words hang a minute, then raised one eyebrow at him while the others watched warily. "Now, seems to me I've told you this before, so this is gonna be the last time, and you're gonna listen for once: you don't like the way I do things, there's the God-damned door. Either you can walk yourself through it and not come back, or you can sit down on your sorry ass and shut the hell up; I don't care which. But from now on, if you stay, you don't speak until you're spoken to, 'cause I ain't taking any more of your bullshit. You follow me?" I made my voice good and hard and kept my eyes on his, never flinch-ing. I remembered what Will had said to me about him turning on us, but I brushed it aside—Red Buck was wanted just like the rest of us, and Marshal Nix and his like were too proud to give a man wanted for murder any sort of deal he'd consider taking. I knew Red Buck's type; he'd rather die than belly-crawl to the law and beg for mercy, even if it meant the rest of us would be hunted out.

For a few tense seconds, there was silence. I could feel the fury coming off him, I could tell he wanted to take his gun out and shoot me dead right there—but I also knew he wouldn't do it. I waited, and he clenched his jaw and slowly put his palms out toward me in an apologetic gesture. I could tell it just about killed him to do it. "I follow you." I had to strain to catch his words, they were so mumbled.

"Good." I picked my plate up and started eating again. Out of the corner of my eye, I saw Will give me a brief nod of approval, a slow smile tugging at the corner of his lips.

⸺◈⸺

I could not, of course, dare to sleep after that little exchange; if I let my guard down Red Buck was likely to put his gun to my head in the middle of the night—and the others' heads, too. He bore no loyalty to any of the men there, and between his love of killing and the dressing down I'd given him, we'd be perfect targets for his homicidal tendencies. So as tired as I was, I volunteered to stand the first watch that night, and with the daylight beginning to fade outside, I positioned myself in one corner, my rifle across my knees.

Just as Bill Dunn was making ready to take his leave of us and head back to the ranch, the hair on the back of my neck stood up and that old hunted feeling started creeping back on me. Over the sound of the wind outside the door, which was the only part of the dugout sound could penetrate, I thought I heard horses snorting. I tensed and crept toward the door, motioning to the others to get down and be quiet.

There was a large knothole in one of the wide planks that formed the door, and I knelt and glanced through it. The harsh wind outside was scouring away all the snow that normally would've drifted up against it, and in the twilight I could make out the shape of two horses stopped just a few dozen feet from the dugout. They weren't members of the gang; how I knew that, I couldn't say for sure, but I knew it just the same.

"Someone's here, and they ain't ours," I hissed in a whisper. "Get back, all of you!" I moved against the wall, my rifle cocked.

Creek, Will, Little Bill and Red Buck all got their rifles at the ready, crouching into the blackest shadows of the corners, while Bill Dunn sat down in a chair near the table, trying to look like a man minding his own business, alone in his dugout. None of us dared to breathe, seemed like, for fear we'd be found out.

We heard the jingle of spurs, and then a knock came, loudly, at the door. Without waiting for an answer, it opened, and a man came inside, brushing snow off his heavy frock coat with gloved hands.

I looked him over from where I was crouched. The dim light, his hat and the thick muffler wound around his neck made it hard to see his features clear. I could tell he had a heavy mustache.

"'Scuse me, friend, I'm sorry to disturb you, but I'm looking for the Dunn Ranch," he said pleasantly to Bill.

"Who's asking?" Bill asked tensely.

"The name's Tilghman. I'm with the United States Marshals Service. I'm hunting out some cattle rustlers said to hide out at the Dunn place and you'd be doing me a great help if you'd point me that way." His voice was polite. My heart about fell out of me and for a second I thought it might stop beating altogether.

"I don't know exactly where it is. Afraid I can't help you any." Bill's voice was brisk and dismissive, and he turned back toward the table, pretending to be busying himself with the lamp. I had to admire him for not falling all to pieces when Tilghman had introduced himself.

Tilghman paused for a moment, clearly surprised by Bill's rudeness. I collected myself quickly and kept my cool head; my freedom depended on it. I kept my rifle leveled, but I didn't fire. Tilghman may have been a lawman, but he was an honorable one, and as long as he wasn't slapping shackles on my wrists or any of the men in my company, I'd leave him be.

"Well, thank you anyway," he said after a few seconds, touching his hand to his hat brim and abruptly leaving.

As soon as the door had shut completely, Red Buck suddenly lunged out of the shadows, drawing his revolver and heading for the door. I shot to my feet and stepped in front of him, leveling my Winchester at his chest, barring him from going any further. "Leave it," I hissed under my breath.

Red Buck's thumb went for the hammer on his gun, cocking it back with a loud click. "That's *Bill Tilghman* out there, God damn it!" he hissed back at me. "He and that bastard Thomas are the ones that put me in prison all them years back—I ain't letting him go! I owe that son of a bitch a bullet, and that's what I aim to give him!"

"You'll only get yourself shot and give the rest of us away," I growled. "And lawdog or not, Tilghman's too decent a man to get shot in the back by the likes of *you*." I managed to inject a good deal of scorn into that remark, ready to take the stock of my rifle to his jaw just to get shed of the sight of his face in front of mine.

"He's right, Buck," Little Bill whispered hoarsely. "Use your damn head!"

Red Buck hesitated, then gritted his teeth and released the hammer on his pistol, angrily shoving it back into his holster and turning away from me.

For a few minutes, no one spoke. Then I went over to the table, ignoring Red Buck. When he crossed me again—and I had no doubt that he would, eventually—I'd send him packing. "How much ammunition do you boys have?" I asked, leaning my rifle against the table and checking the guns in my holsters.

"I got an extra box in my saddlebags," Creek said.

"I got two," Will said. "Why, Bill? What are you thinking?"

"I'm thinking we need to quit this place, tonight," I said grimly, "and I want every man armed to the teeth."

"You think that's a good idea? Tilghman might be laying in wait." Creek's voice was doubtful.

I shot him a look. "He ain't gonna lie in wait in this kind of weather," I said, jerking my thumb back toward the door as I re-holstered my guns. "And I believed him when he said he was looking for cattle rustlers. His mind's on something else. We can slip out, easy. I ain't staying here, not with him being so close."

"Did he have a posse with him, Bill?" Will asked me.

I shook my head, reaching for my saddlebags.

"Didn't see one. There were only two horses out there, so far as I could tell." I slung the saddlebags up over my shoulder and took my rifle in hand. "Much obliged for the meal and the shelter, Bill," I said over my shoulder to Bill Dunn, then made for the door, hearing the others follow. I still had a bad feeling about Dunn, and there wasn't any way in hell I was going to say anything about the job I'd planned in front of him.

We made for the stable, being good and cautious, but there was no sign of anyone around and we got in and got tacked up, quick. Black Devil nearly took a chunk out of me when I was bridling him, but I ducked out of the way before he could.

"You have to break that stud in yourself, Bill?" Creek chuckled as he tossed his saddle onto Dash's back and reached for the cinch.

"Just about," I replied through clenched teeth as I dodged a hoof thrown in my direction.

Will laughed. "Maybe I missed the mark earlier when I told you you could've been a doc, Bill. Maybe you ought to have been a lion tamer."

I shook my head at them both and led Devil out of his stall, ready to outrun the law again—and more than ready to get back at what I seemed to do best.

TWENTY-SIX

"SO, WE GONNA rob the Santa Fe train again, you figure?"

I had been toying with a silver dollar, standing it up on its edge and spinning it around on the table-top, but when Will spoke I let it fall onto its side, leaning back in my chair and appraising him and the others, who were positioned here and there around the room, all of them waiting on my answer.

It was late April and we were holed up in an old abandoned cabin Will and I had come across after we'd left Bill Dunn's dugout; we'd used it after we'd successfully held up the Farmers & Citizens Bank in Pawnee back in January. It was a small one-room place made of sturdy logs, old as the hills and shabby to boot, but the walls were too thick for bullets to go through and it had enough brush grown up around it that I felt like we were pretty safe there. Whoever had abandoned it had left a rough-hewn table and two rickety chairs inside. There was no floor laid and there were clumps of weeds pushing up through the hard-packed dirt, and the chinking between the logs was flaking off. It was the kind of place no one would give a second glance to, let alone go near, which was what made it so perfect for concealing us all. There were so many in the gang now that finding good hiding places we could all squeeze into was getting tiresome. I knew we couldn't chance using this one for too long; I'd vowed to keep us moving before the law could hunt us up, but for now it would do nicely. I'd been avoiding our other favorite hideout, the big cave near Council Creek that lay on the Dunn property; I hadn't forgotten that funny feeling I'd had about Bill Dunn the last time I'd seen him and I didn't want to put myself in his or his brothers' vicinity just yet.

"Not the train," I answered Will, who had the other chair. "Just the station; the one at Woodward."

Tulsa Jack let out a short laugh from where he was leaning against the wall near the fireplace. "Where the hell's the fun in that?" he asked.

I gave him a look. "That station's got money in it, Jack. Why bother with the damned train and the chance of bungling it if we can get what we want from the station?"

Creek lifted his shoulders in a little shrug. "You got a point there, Bill."

"Why all the care-takin', Bill?" Dick West asked me curiously. "You getting tired of holding up trains?" He was sitting on the floor, idly dragging the tip of his bowie knife around in the dirt.

"Hell no," I said irritably. "But think about it: we pulled off that bank job earlier this year in Pawnee; we got them murder charges on us for Ingalls and Cimarron; our names are all over the place and Marshal Nix's raised the rewards on our heads. Things are hotter than hell for us. We want the railroad's money, don't we? The law'll be expecting us to take it from the train. So we'll take it from the station instead. All comes from the same place, don't it?"

"Suits me," Dynamite Dan said from one of the corners. "Hell, cash is cash."

"Woodward, huh?" Will said, scratching his whiskered chin. "Guess we better get riding, then." He gave me a sly grin. "It's aways between here and there, and if we wait too long in between jobs, people will quit talking about us and all our hard-earned fame will be for naught."

I felt a little pang then of some feeling I couldn't identify right away. Then I realized it was wistfulness. I didn't really regret anything I'd done so far but I was starting to get a little weary of the notoriety that came with it. Maybe if I wasn't so famous,

I could go home to Edith for a good long spell, and get myself used to the idea that in a few short months there'd be someone in the world who would call me Pa.

———◆———

"You know, Doolin, there's so many of us now that we could just shoot this place all to hell and leave no witnesses," Red Buck muttered to me as we cautiously dismounted from our horses aways away from the Woodward train station at dusk on the tenth.

I shot him an irritated glare as I pulled my neckerchief up over my face. "Why in the hell would I agree to that?" I retorted in a low voice. "There ain't any reason to shoot anyone at all, so long as they're doing what we tell them and ain't trying to put us under. You want to kill something just to kill it, go hunting." I drew my revolver and motioned the others forward. Red Buck obeyed me, as he'd been doing ever since I'd stopped him from shooting Bill Tilghman in the back, but he didn't look happy about it. I wondered for about the fiftieth time why the he stayed with us since we didn't seem to do enough killing for his tastes, but I put it out of my mind since I had better things to think about just then.

Leaving Tulsa Jack with the horses, we sauntered into the station. Creek and Will were on either side of me and they leveled their rifles at the man behind the counter in unison. Dan, Charley and Little Bill stood just outside the door on guard, and Dick and Red Buck came in behind us, revolvers at the ready.

"Evening," I said pleasantly to the railroad man, who looked like an animal caught in a trap, his arms raised stiffly toward the ceiling, palms out. He wasn't very old and I figured he hadn't been working there any too long. "Hand over all the cash you got, if you want to keep on sucking air." I motioned to Creek with my free hand and he pulled the sack out of his coat with a flourish. He tossed it to the man, who let it fall to the counter, his hands still raised. He looked too scared to move and I cleared my throat.

"You deaf, son?" I asked warningly, drawing back the hammer on my gun.

He shook his head, his eyes staring right down the barrel of my gun. He still didn't move.

"You got a death wish, then?" My patience was starting to wear dangerously thin.

He shook his head again.

"Then *fill up the damn sack,*" I growled, and took a step closer.

I guess I got through to him then, because he

started like he'd been jolted awake and snatched up the sack, opening the safe behind the counter. It was nice and full, I noticed. He emptied it into the sack and tossed it back onto the counter, then backed up, his hands raised to the ceiling. He almost fell over the chair he'd been sitting in and his pale face was drawn into a scowl. He hadn't said a single word the entire time.

"Smile, son!" Will commanded in his booming voice. "You can tell the papers and your Mama you got held up by the Wild Bunch and lived to tell about it!" He took his hand from the stock of his rifle and tipped his hat to the kid; his eyes were dancing devilishly and I could tell he was grinning under his neckerchief. I rolled my eyes at him and headed out the door, the others backing out after me.

As we were riding away past the nearby town, dropping to an easy trot and minding our own business so's not to attract too much attention to ourselves, I caught sight of a few people walking along the gallery toward the lighted-up church on the outskirts. It was a man, dressed nice, with a woman on his arm. His wife, I supposed. At his other side he had ahold of a little girl's hand, probably only about four or so, carefully helping her walk along with them. The street lamps set along the gallery illuminated them as they went.

At first I didn't know why I'd noticed them, or why the sight gave me pause—so much so that I checked my horse a little and almost drew him to a stop so's I could look longer. Then I realized I was imagining myself and Edith and our child, walking along in a town like a normal family, instead of a man wanted for murder and robbery, and a woman who had to hide her marriage from all but a few folks. It was a simple thing I suddenly realized I might never be able to know, if I pushed my luck too far. Thinking such a thing out of nowhere surprised the hell out of me, and I stopped Devil short, watching the family go inside the church together.

"Bill?" Charley suddenly asked, low, from near me. He'd seen me dawdling and falling behind, and he'd circled back to me in alarm. Up ahead, I saw some of the others stopped and waiting, too, uneasily looking back at me and likely wondering what the hell I was doing. "What're you looking at?" he asked me, in just above a whisper.

I shook my head and shut my eyes for a minute, to try and clear the strange thoughts from my mind. "Nothing. Thought I saw something out of place, is all. Let's get out of here while we still can." I tapped my spurs to Devil's sides, and he started forward with a little grunt of protest. I put him into a lope, going past the others, pushing on into the underbrush and away from all them law-abiding folks, and that town, and that family.

When we felt it was safe to make camp I divvied up the spoils of our little to-do. We'd taken over six thousand dollars—a good haul; seemed I'd picked this one right, but even as we were on the move from there I was already thinking about the next job we'd pull. If I occupied my mind with planning our excursions, it stopped me from missing Edith so bad, stopped me from thinking about that little family I'd seen, and stopped me from thinking too hard about why all these things were bothering me so much all of the sudden.

TWENTY-SEVEN

"HOW'RE WE GONNA answer this, Bill?"

Will tossed a newspaper down on the table in front of me as he spoke and pointed to a headline and article. He'd just come back to the cabin after going out for supplies, and he was riled up pretty good over whatever the paper said. He started pacing the small room while he waited for me to read it.

It was just after sunset in mid-April, and there was only me, Will and Creek present in the little cabin that evening. Charley was outside, acting as our lookout. The others had scattered after our last time out had ended up in a shoot-out with a storekeeper in Pottawatomie County who wasn't too keen on being robbed. All we'd gotten out of the whole mess was a wounded member—Creek had been shot in the shoulder and we'd been forced to flee from there with nothing to show for our trouble. Red Buck had shot the storekeeper but he'd lived, and identified us.

The bullet had gone through Creek's shoulder clean and his wound was almost healed now. The others were set to join up with us pretty soon so we could head to Missouri to take a bank I'd picked out. The storekeeper incident in Sacred Heart had put me in a pretty damned bad mood and I was anxious to make the next time out a success. I wasn't used to failure and I didn't like having to admit to it.

I picked up the paper and scanned the article. It went on about how the law had just about had its fill of us and how Marshal Nix had sent out a directive to his deputies that we were all to be brought in dead if necessary. I raised an eyebrow at Will, puzzled as to just why he was so upset about the article. To me, it was more of the same—Nix shooting his mouth off and sprouting fancy statements to the papers to make folks think he was getting somewhere in his pursuit of us.

"Don't it stick in your craw, Bill, to hear him say plain he aims to have us murdered if he or his cronies get the chance?" Will asked me, his voice hard.

I shrugged. "He's been talkin' that way since he got his commission, Will, and so has every other law-dog in the territories. It don't mean he's gonna take us down, now or ever." My voice sounded weary, even to me, and Will and Creek heard it. Will stopped his pacing and gave me a look, his brow furrowing. Creek glanced at Will, then looked back at me.

REBECCA ROCKWELL

"What the hell's the matter with you, anyway?" Will asked suspiciously. "You changin' your mind about all this, now?"

I rolled my eyes. "No, Will. But if you want the plain truth of it, I'll tell you: I got a wife I don't get to see more than a few weeks or months at a time, seems like; I got a baby on the way and I don't even know if I'll be there when it's born, or when I'll get to see it. Hell, you're in the same fix with your family; seems to me you'd understand."

"Jane knows how it is, just like Edith does." Will's voice was like iron and I heard that famous Dalton stubbornness in it, plain as day. "What I'm talking about is being called out by some God-damned, big-mouthed U.S. marshal sitting behind some fancy-Dan desk in Guthrie. I do what I please, same as you and every man we ride with, and I'll be damned all the way to hell if I'm going to let myself get put into a coffin just so the government'll figure he's worth what they're paying him."

I sighed. "I know how you feel, Will, but I'm just starting to think that maybe it's time to figure on pulling a few more big jobs and then being done with it all before Nix and his like get their way."

Ever since the job in Sacred Heart had gone so wrong—and ever since I'd seen that little family outside of Woodward—I'd been thinking more and more

— 314 —

about getting out of the gang. Something in me had begun to change. My old rage at the railroad was beginning to cool a little—and I knew it was because of Edith and our baby, and all those thoughts I'd been thinking about living respectable and peaceable, sooner rather than later. I was getting tired—of the notoriety, and the risks, and having to leave Edith most of all. But I hadn't figured on saying anything to anyone just yet. I surprised myself that night, coming out with it like I did.

Will didn't answer me and I wasn't surprised, when it came down to it. From the beginning, he'd been in it for the fame more than anything else. Something in him had been triggered that day when Bob and Grat and Emmett met their fates in Coffeyville; some deep desire to make the name of Dalton live on in infamy even more than it already would. He wanted to be the Dalton that got away with it all, the Dalton that was remembered as smarter and luckier than Bob. And as much as I respected and liked him, I somehow knew, that night in the cabin, that he'd keep on going until the law put him under, family or no. And I knew right then and there that I didn't want the same for myself.

Will clenched his jaw in frustration and went outside abruptly, like he thought I'd suddenly lost my mind and couldn't be talked sense into. I let him go, the silence settling in around me and Creek.

I shifted uncomfortably in my chair and raised my eyes to Creek's. He was looking at me soberly and I wondered what was going on in his head. I sighed. "I suppose you think I'm off my nut, too," I said.

He shook his head slowly, still looking seriously at me. "No, Bill. I see where you're coming from. I see where Will's coming from, too. The two of you've got different priorities now, is all it is. From where I'm sitting, seems to me Will wants people to be talking about 'the Notorious Bill Dalton' a hundred years from now. And there ain't nothing wrong with that in my book. You've wanted to make a point to the railroad for ruinin' our livelihood, and seems to me the bunch of us have done a pretty good job of that so far. Every man's got a limit to what he can stand. If Will wants to answer Marshal Nix, let him. And if you want to go back to your pretty bride and your baby, well, seems to me that's only fair. We didn't none of us say we'd do this for the rest of our lives, did we?"

His voice was mild. I ran my fingers through the dust on the table-top, tracing mindless patterns there as I took in his words. "What *did* you think you'd do for the rest of your life, Creek?" I asked him wryly.

He shrugged. "Work cows. Hell, I got on at my first ranch when I was barely twelve. Never thought

I'd do anything else with my time—never wanted to, at that. But times change, and you got to change with them. I figure I can either stop robbing trains and banks and stores right now and be stone-broke for the rest of my life while I dodge the law, or I can keep doing it and enjoy the fun and the profits while they last. But that's me. I don't got the ties you do, and I don't intend to have them. I don't intend to take a wife or have a family proper like you done. But I ain't gonna look down on any man—especially my friend—who has."

I let my eyes meet his again and gave him a half-smile. "You been a good friend to me, Creek," I said quietly.

He gave me his familiar grin. "Just returnin' the favor, is all."

I stood up, stiffly; my bad foot was plaguing me all to hell again. "I'm gonna go talk to Will a minute."

I went outside and found Will smoking a cigarette out by the corral where our horses, all still under saddle, were penned. In the moonlight I could see Charley sitting on the far side of the fence, his rifle across his lap, keeping an ear and an eye out in the darkness.

"I thought I had you figured, Bill," Will said to me as I came up beside him. "Never thought I'd hear you say one word about quitting."

I let my breath out and crossed my arms over my chest. "Well, I never thought I'd have a family, Will. I thought I'd work cows until I was old and die on some ranch. And then when I married Edith I thought I could stand leaving her to go all over hell like I done. But it turns out I can't stand it like I thought I could, and now that I got this baby on the way it makes it all the harder. I ain't sayin' I want to quit tonight. Hell, I still got some jobs planned for the gang yet. But I *am* sayin' I don't want to be doing this forever."

He turned at looked at me then, his expression still hard. "You think they're gonna leave you be, once you stop, Bill? You ain't never gonna be shed of the things you've done. None of us will. You know they'd rather shoot themselves dead than drop the charges they got on you."

"I know that. But I *can* quit while I'm ahead, and maybe someday I can start over, like I promised Edith." I paused. "The cattle trade ain't never gonna come back like it was in this country, Will. And no matter how many trains or banks we hold up, the railroad'll keep on doing what it does. We've made a mark on it, we've hurt it some, and I guess that's gonna have to be good enough for me, when all is said and done."

Will was quiet for a minute. He took a deep, slow

drag off his cigarette; the end flared up bright for a second. "I've always respected you, Bill. Still do. But I just don't see things the same way."

I nodded. "I know. We're pretty different, you and I, when it comes right down to it. I won't begrudge you none if you decide you want to keep on going after I'm done with the whole thing. All I'm saying is we got to be more careful than ever now. There's too many of us, and we're gonna be too easy to find, especially now that Nix is raising all the rewards on our heads. Every man from here to Mexico will be out to get those bounties."

He was quiet for a minute, and so was I. I watched him toss the remnants of his cigarette down on the bare ground around the corral fence and crush it out under his fancy snakeskin boot. Will always did favor flashy boots and big spurs. "You got it right, there, for a fact. The gang's gotten too big." He leaned his arms on the top rail of the fence, looking out at the horses. When he spoke again his voice was as near to empty of any joking or teasing as I'd ever heard it. "Maybe it's time we split up, then. I'll go my way and you go yours, each with the others' blessing. I've learned a hell of a lot from you, Bill, and maybe it's time I put it to use for myself."

There was no ill will or anger in his tone, nothing to make me think he was wanting to part ways because we'd had a disagreement about what our ultimate goal was. He was simply suggesting what he thought was best, and though I'd miss riding with him, I knew he was right. "If that's what you want, then you got my good wishes."

He turned to me. "Been a hell of a ride, ain't it?" He was grinning now, wide, his eyes twinkling in the bright moonlight.

I laughed. "Sure has. And I'm sure it will keep on as such, for a time." I paused. "You sure you don't want to come with us to Missouri when we go?"

"No, I'm aiming to head for Texas. Maybe I'll shake some of them government bloodhounds off your trail when I do." He stuck out a hand to me. "So long, Bill."

I shook his hand, good and firm. "You take care of yourself, Will. Give 'em hell."

His grin got bigger. "I'll give 'em so much hell they won't be able to handle it all," he bragged, and I knew he believed it. "Good luck, Bill."

"You too." I stood back and watched as he ducked into the corral and untied his horse. I didn't bother asking him if he wanted to say good-bye to Creek; I knew he didn't. It was that old Dalton trait of being bad at good-byes. He led his horse out of the corral and put a foot into the stirrup, throwing his leg over the saddle. I saw Charley turn to look, and Will lifted his hand to him. I knew Charley had likely overheard everything we'd said, but he didn't comment. Instead he just waved back, and the two of us watched Will canter off into the wild terrain with the moonlight flicking off his horse's shoes and the bright bullets in his gun belt; Charley up on the fence, and me standing by the gate. I found myself remembering the unceremonious way he'd put himself into our company, back after Coffeyville, and I thought it fitting that he was taking himself out of it in just the same way.

When we couldn't see or hear him any longer, I turned and went back inside the cabin, leaving Charley to resume his watch. I was going over the plan for Missouri again in my mind, taking Will out of it. Whatever he ended up doing, I wished him luck, and I didn't doubt his fame would continue like he wanted—I just hoped it would turn out to be worth it to him, in the end.

TWENTY-EIGHT

AFTER WILL HAD gone, I tried for almost two weeks to lay low and focus on our upcoming plan, but I found I just couldn't set my mind to getting started on it until I'd seen Edith—and the baby that I was pretty sure would've got itself born by now. I'd ride hard and get to the folks' farm in the middle of the night, then leave the following night to meet up with the boys and head for Southwest City, where the bank I'd picked waited for us to come clean out its vault.

Creek walked outside with me to my horse, when I was ready to leave the cabin. He stood back and watched as I untied Devil and tossed the reins up over his neck.

"I don't know, Bill," Creek said soberly to me, shaking his head. "You sure you're gonna come back?"

I shot him a look. "Why the hell would you think

I wouldn't?" I asked him indignantly, leading Devil over toward the corral gate.

He gave me a knowing look, one side of his mouth going up in a half-smile under his mustache. "Because as bad as you been missing your wife, what's to say you won't get yourself back there and then just decide to stay with her, and your little one, if it's come?" His voice was uneasy and I could tell he was afraid I'd do just that, and leave him and the others hanging in the wind.

I looked at him square. "Creek, you got my word, I'll be back just when I said I'll be, wind and weather and lawdogs permitting. I planned this little adventure, and I aim to see it through. Besides that," I added, picking my way through the corral, muddied by yesterday's rain, "when I *do* decide to give all this up, I'd better have a damned good cushion in my pockets, don't you think?"

He leaned his arms on a rail of the corral and watched as I came closer through the sticky mud. "You'd better, at that," he agreed, looking relieved.

"Well," I replied, "seems like a bank's a good place to get one, don't it?" I flashed a knowing grin at him, which he returned. He moved to the gate and opened it for me.

I mounted up and pushed my hat down, low. I'd let a full beard come up over my face, and it'd come out a darker blond than the hair on my head. With it hiding my features good, and the hat and my bulky coat to disguise my form somewhat, I figured I looked different enough from all the descriptions the law had out on me to downplay my chances of getting recognized while I traveled.

Devil snorted and dipped his muzzle, eager to run. When I checked him he put out a hoof and started pawing at the ground, wound up like a coiled rattlesnake set to strike. I made him stay put, though, long enough to look down at Creek. "We'll meet up here in five days and be on our way," I said firmly. "And when we get to Southwest City, they won't know what hit 'em."

Creek stood back against the fence, out of Devil's way. "Keep yourself clear of Tilghman and the like, and have yourself a nice *meaningful* time with the missus." He gave me a wicked grin.

I tried to frown at him but found I couldn't hold back an answering grin. "I figure I'll make the most of things," I said breezily. "I got a talent for that. See you soon." And I put my spurs to Devil's sides and gave him his head, bracing myself in the saddle as he took off like a shot.

When at last I reached it I approached the Ellsworth farm carefully, from the back, creeping up to it like an animal stalking prey instead of running up and flying inside to see Edith, as I wanted to do. I wasn't certain the law even suspected I was married; Edith kept it a secret as best she could, taking off her wedding ring every time she went out among folks and using her maiden name, but I couldn't be sure word hadn't gotten out about us. I saw nothing amiss. The night was mild; the weather was warming up a bit. The moon was bright and it threw a silvery glow over the house and the pasture fence, and the big, dark rectangle of land Edith's Pa had plowed out for grain. There was a dim little light, not bright enough for a lamp, coming through the lace curtains in the window of Edith's bedroom; I figured she had a candle lit. The rest of the house was dark and quiet.

I rode Devil at a walk up to the stable; he was good and tired out from our straight trip there so he didn't make a fuss at being held back. Quietly as I could, I led him inside and he followed me easy, his head hanging low. The darkness inside the stable was pierced here and there by shafts of moonlight coming in through knotholes in the lumber; I used them to see by so I could lead Devil into a stall. Good old Rebel thrust his head over the door of the loose box and eyeballed me suspiciously, then nickered, low in his throat, when I spoke a soft word to him. I made up my mind then I was taking him when I went back out, recognizable or not. I'd gotten used to Devil but he couldn't hold a candle to my palomino.

I stripped my bridle and saddle off Devil and curried off some of the sweat he had on him from keeping up such a brisk pace, then drew up a bucket of water for him from the water-barrel by the door and pitched him some hay from the pile at the end of the stable. I was so eager to see Edith that the simple tasks seemed to take forever and a day, but at last I finished and slipped back out of the barn, easing the latch shut slowly so it wouldn't rattle. If Edith's Pa heard me he could take me for a horse-thief; and I had no intention of getting shot down accidental-like by my own father-in-law, after everything else I'd come through alive. I bent down and jerked open the buckles of my spur-straps, taking them in hand so they wouldn't jingle.

Instead of going to the porch I went around to the back, and when I got close to her window I gave a soft whistle, different from the one I used with the gang. All those months ago, when I'd had to leave her there, I'd told her that if I ever had to come back in the middle of the night, that whistle would be my signal to her. I just hoped she'd hear it. I stood back a bit in the shadow made by the house, off to one side of the window, and waited, my heart going a little faster than normal.

I saw the lace curtains move wildly as her hands fumbled with them, hastily drawing them aside as she opened the window, and in the candle-light her lovely face appeared behind the glass, her long hair tumbling loose over her shoulders as she bent down to look outside.

"Edith," I whispered, just loud enough for her to hear me.

"Bill?" she asked, her voice quavering, like she was going to cry. I stepped out of the shadow into the moonlight, and her face lit up when she saw me. "Oh, thank God!" She was whispering but her voice sounded choked up. "I'll let you in through the lean-to," she said, and without waiting for an answer, she darted away from the window.

I hurried to the lean-to and when the door opened I went in, right into her arms. I pulled her so tight against me that her bare feet came up off the ground, and I kissed her so hard her head bent back. I felt her hands slide up into my hair, pushing my hat off and letting it fall where it might as she kept my mouth against hers. I would've kept that kiss going for a year if my lungs would've let me. I wanted to ask about our baby; somehow my mind registered that her figure was as little as ever so it must've been born, but I couldn't seem to stop kissing her long enough to ask her anything at all.

When we finally did pull apart, she started talking in a near-whisper, fast and shrill, and so breathlessly I could barely understand her; all her sentences were run together in a big jumble of words. "I've missed you so much! I've been watching the papers; I know you say they get things wrong but I couldn't help myself, Bill, I was so worried something had happened to you. And now you're here and you can see our baby… it's a boy and oh, Bill, he's an angel! He's already grown so much—"

"Shh, shh, honey," I soothed huskily, a little loving laugh coming up in my throat as I kept her pressed up against me, all ghostly-white in her night-gown with her black hair shimmering in the glow from the lamp she'd carried into the lean-to with her and set down on the shelf there. My eyes kept drinking in the sight of her and my throat had a lump in it. "We had us a boy? Is he healthy?"

She nodded, her face aglow with the smile I loved so much. "Healthy and strong, even though he came a little early. I'm fine, Bill," she added, seeing my eyes traveling over her swiftly as I stepped back from her just a little ways. "Ma helped me and I didn't have any problems. He was born just three weeks ago. He was small but he's grown fast." She paused, calmer now, and looked at me, putting a hand to my face and running it over my thick beard, then moving it to my shoulder. "You're thin, Bill." Her voice was small, now, and worried. Her slender eyebrows drew together and her smile faded.

"I'm all right, now that I'm here with you, and about to see my son," I told her, smiling. "And I don't much like the beard, either," I teased her, knowing she'd rather I looked like I usually did, clean-shaven with only my mustache, "but I needed some means of disguise."

She raised her chin a little and her smile came back. "Well," she told me, stroking back a lock of my hair that had fallen down into my eyes, "Pa's got a razor you can use." Her eyes were twinkling at me as of old.

I didn't have the heart to tell her I couldn't stay longer than a day, on account of Missouri. That news could wait. Instead I kissed her again, good and thorough. Then I let her take my hand and lead me, quietly, into the darkened house and back to her bedroom, carrying the lamp with us.

The room looked the same as I remembered it; the bed covered with the blue and red quilt Edith had made when she was a girl, and the thick braided-rag rugs on the floor. There was a candle lit on the dressing table and against the wall near the bed stood a cradle draped with soft blankets. Edith set the lamp back into its holder on the wall, and letting go of my hand, she went to the cradle, bending to gently draw back the top blanket. With my heart going in a strange flutter, almost like I was nervous, I tip-toed to her side and looked down, for the first time, at my son.

He was smaller than I thought he'd be, dressed in a little cotton shift over his diaper. His tiny, perfect little fingers were curled into miniature fists as he slept, and his little lips were parted as he drew in soft breaths. I watched his chest move up and down, saw his long eyelashes quiver against his cheeks, and I couldn't speak for the wonder of it. I stretched out a hand and laid it, feather-light, over his tiny head, feeling the downy softness of his hair under my palm. It was blond, just like mine. As I touched him he worked his little mouth in his sleep, and it made the muscles in his temples move; I felt it and I thought I might fly to pieces. He was real, this tiny little boy that was half me and half Edith. The enormity of it was hard to get my head around.

Edith was watching me; I glanced over at her and saw her lips curve up in a soft little smile. Her eyes were moist as she watched me with him. "I named him Jay, Bill," she said. "I hope you don't mind it. I couldn't leave him without a name when I—when I didn't know when you'd be back." Her voice caught on her last words.

I drew in a lungful of air; seemed like I hadn't really been breathing while I was touching the baby, and drew my hand back. "Jay Doolin," I said quietly. "It suits him," I told her gently, giving her my blessing for not waiting for me to decide about it. "You named him well, honey." I slid my arm around her shoulders, my eyes looking back down at my son. Seemed like I'd never get my fill of looking at him. I wanted to hold him but I didn't have the heart to wake him up.

"He's a good baby," she told me, her voice low. "He sleeps well for me most of the time—except tonight. That's why I was awake when you got here." She smiled at me.

"I'm glad you were," I replied. "I didn't much fancy waking your folks."

"I'll tell them you're here in the morning," she said, turning to face me. I slid both arms around her then and found her mouth with mine, certain now that I'd done the right thing in coming back here before the gang's next time out. I didn't think I'd get my fill of being with her and my son before I had to leave again, but I could sure as hell try.

The rooster crowing in the chicken coop near the barn woke me the next morning, just as the sky was starting to get light. I'd slept more soundly than I'd done in a long while—once I'd gotten to sleep—and the night had gone by in a flash. I rolled onto my back and ran a hand sleepily over my eyes, then opened them to see Edith sitting in the rocking chair in the corner in her nightgown and wrapper, the baby cradled to her breast. The laces at the front of her nightgown were loosened and his little fingers were curled into the folds of muslin around him. I could hear him making soft little smacking sounds as he nursed. One of her hands was cradling the back of his head, the other supported his body, and she was looking off toward the window, a distant expression on her face.

"What are you thinking about?" I said, keeping my voice low. Even so, she started at the sound of it, then looked at me, her lips curving into a smile, her lashes sweeping downward for a minute, almost like she was suddenly shy of me. I thought I saw her cheeks go a little pink.

"I didn't know you were awake," she whispered.

"I wasn't, until just now," I said, leaning up a little on my elbows. "You didn't answer my question."

She closed her eyes a minute and gave a soft little sigh, the smile fading a bit from her lips. "Just thinking about how good it is to have you home—and how you haven't told me how long it'll be for."

I set my jaw a little, not having wanted to tell her just yet. Being back with her, and with Jay, had been a little bit of Heaven for me and I wasn't ready to shatter that mood. But I couldn't lie to her. "I didn't want to bring that up last night," I admitted, sitting up fully, the sheet and the quilt pooling over my lap. The morning air was cold, even inside the house, for the stove and the coal heater hadn't been lit yet, and I reached for where I'd tossed my clothes carelessly onto the floor last night. Without getting out of bed, I pulled on my undershirt, but when I reached for my shirt Edith stopped me.

"I've made you a few new ones, while you were away," she told me. Jay had finished, so she laid him down into his cradle and went to the chest of drawers, reaching into one and pulling out a crisply-ironed, neatly folded shirt she'd made of dark blue checked calico.

"Thank you, sweetheart," I told her with a smile, drawing it on. She watched me critically while she tied the laces of her nightgown back up.

"I suppose it's too big for you, now you've gotten thinner," she commented.

"It's just right," I told her, and it fit me well. We both heard footsteps in the hallway, and a moment later came the sounds of stove lids rattling.

"The house will be warm in a few minutes," Edith told me, reaching for her chemise and her corset.

We dressed quickly. Once I'd pulled my galluses up over my shoulders and buttoned my vest I went to the bowl and pitcher and scrubbed my face, then combed my hair as she pinned hers up. I frowned at myself in the mirror; my beard needed trimming pretty bad and I hated to face Edith's Ma looking so ragged. "You got any scissors in here?" I asked her, and she brought the pair from her sewing basket.

"Here, let me," she said, and sat me down on the edge of the bed, giving me the bowl to hold on my lap to catch the trimmings. She worked quickly, standing back every few seconds to examine my face. "I'd rather shave it off," she teased me softly, her eyes twinkling.

"I know you would, and I'd let you, except that it hides my face good," I told her.

She sobered again. "So when *are* you leaving, Bill?" she asked, taking the bowl away from me and motioning to the mirror. I stood up and admired myself; she'd done a good job.

"I'll have to go tonight, honey," I said, catching her eyes through the mirror. I saw her head bow, in the reflection, and she turned away quickly to lay away the scissors. She was biting her lip, hard.

I turned away from the mirror and faced her, reaching out to take her gently by the shoulders. "Edith, listen to me. I knew it was going to upset you, to have me stay for so short a time, but I just had to see you and meet our baby before I'm due to meet up with—"

"I don't want to know!" she suddenly said, interrupting me. She kept her voice low so her folks wouldn't hear her but the impact on me was the same as if she'd yelled. "I don't want you to tell me anything anymore, Bill. Not unless it's got to do with you coming home for good." She drew in a shaky breath. "I can't take any more worry, and every time you tell me something like that it just adds to it. So you just keep your plans to yourself, and do what you have to do." There was no rage in her voice at all, she wasn't scolding me, but she *was* about to cry— she started blinking fast and she wouldn't look at me square.

I took a good, deep breath before I spoke again. "Edith, sweetheart, it won't be too long before I come home for good, and that I can promise you. I been plannin' on it for awhile now, and now that we got us a baby I'm more ready than ever. There are just a few things yet that need doing, and then I'm gonna take you and Jay away from here and we're gonna settle down like a normal family. I just got to have enough money for it. That's the only thing keeping me from staying right now."

She held back her tears, that strength she'd always had in her bracing her and helping her get ahold of herself. She looked up at me then, her dark eyes searching mine like she was trying to read something in my face. "You mean it?" she whispered.

I nodded. "I've always told you, you had my word on it, and I meant it each time." I pulled her against me and she didn't resist; she just put her face against my chest and slipped her arms around my waist. I laid my cheek against her hair. "I wish I'd met you sooner than I did," I told her, suddenly speaking words I hadn't had any intention of telling her, then or ever. "If I had, I wouldn't ever have started—" I stopped talking before I could finish my sentence. There wasn't any use in saying it; doing so wouldn't change anything. I'd believed wholeheartedly in my little cause when I'd started out and enjoyed it all besides, but I hadn't known what it was I'd really wanted out of life, those few short years ago. Now all I wanted to do was be done with it all and settle down. I would be thirty-six soon. Maybe I was getting too old for outlawing—or maybe it was just that being a husband and father was finally winning out over everything else.

She kept quiet; she seemed to know that there weren't any words of comfort she could offer to what I'd been about to tell her. Instead she just pulled away from me and took my face in her hands, her thumbs sweeping over my whiskered cheeks. Then she stood on tiptoe and kissed me on the mouth, softly. We heard soft cooing noises coming from the crib, and Edith smiled. "I think you should hold him now," she told me. "He's good and awake." She stepped away from me and went over to the crib, and talking softly to Jay, lifted him out and handed him to me, before I was even ready.

"Support his head, now," she told me softly, love for him, and me, sounding out plain in her voice. "There you go." She smiled down at Jay. "Your Papa's got you! Isn't that something?" She bent over him and tapped a finger gently on his tiny nose, playfully, and he smiled and waved his fist. His eyes were the same color blue as mine.

I didn't realize it at first, but I was holding my breath the first few seconds I was holding him. He was heavier than I thought he'd be, his little body warm and soft in my arms, and he looked straight up at me like he knew I was his Pa, his little head nestled in the crook of my elbow. I let my breath out, swallowing hard against everything I was feeling. I didn't think I had enough room in me for all those feelings. "Well, hello there, little fella," I said to him, very softly. "Aren't you a fine boy!"

Edith had straightened up and she was watching us, still smiling, and her eyes were shining. Suddenly there was a knock at the bedroom door that startled us.

"Edith? You all right in there? Breakfast's almost on," her Ma called.

Edith reached out and patted my arm. "You keep on holding him. I'll go out and let them know you're here." She went toward the door before I could say anything. "I'm just fine, Ma," she called, and slipped out the door, shutting it behind her.

I looked back down at the baby. "Well, son, seems it's just you and me, for a bit," I told him, unable to stop smiling at him. I felt a little silly, talking to him like that, but he seemed to like it. He sort of smiled up at me and kicked his little legs and waved his hands, letting out a noise that sounded almost like a giggle. I leaned my head down and tickled him with my beard, and he made it again, a little gurgling sound.

We were still laughing, the two of us, when Edith came back into the room. "Looks like you boys are getting along just fine," she told me, beaming. "Come

on out and see the folks; they're glad you're here."
She shook her head when I made motions to hand
Jay over to her. "You keep him, Bill. You should hold
him as much as you can, as long as you're here." She
turned and led us from the bedroom.

"Bill!" Mrs. Ellsworth said warmly when we
emerged into the parlor. "Welcome home," she
told me simply, coming over to give me a kiss on
the cheek and lay a gentle hand on Jay's head. She
frowned at me, looking me over critically. "That's
quite a beard you've grown," she commented in her
usual outspoken manner. I could tell she didn't much
approve of it.

"Yes'm, it is at that," I replied, smiling at her.
"Edith trimmed it for me this morning; otherwise you
might have thought you had a bear for a son-in-law."

Mrs. Ellsworth examined my face critically for
a moment. "She did a decent job, but John's got a
razor you may borrow—which I think you should,
after breakfast."

"Ida," Mr. Ellsworth groaned, coming inside
from taking care of the stock and overhearing her,
"for goodness sake, my dear, show some tact." He
smiled at me. "Hello, Bill. Glad you've come back
all right."

"Mr. Ellsworth," I said, nodding to him. His
smile got a little wider when he saw me holding Jay.

"What do you think of your little man, there?" he asked me, hanging his hat up.

"I think he's the handsomest baby I've ever seen," I said truthfully. "Takes after his Mama, luckily." I shot Edith a sly look and winked at her.

"Well, he's got your coloring, and your eyes," Edith replied, "but it'll be awhile yet before he'll get the beard." She grinned at me and went to help her Ma set the table.

Mrs. Ellsworth made a sort of clucking noise with her tongue. "I still think you should get rid of it," she told me stoutly. "A handsome young man such as yourself shouldn't hide his face behind all that hair."

I gave her a smile to show I wasn't bothered at all by anything she was saying. "It serves the purpose well, though," I pointed out mildly. She looked a little uncomfortable then, like she'd forgotten about why I should have need of such a beard, until that moment.

Mr. Ellsworth raised an eyebrow and smoothed over the awkward moment. "Pay her no mind, Bill," he told me. "She's always got an opinion at the ready on just about anything." He softened his words with a smile, then raised his coffee mug to his lips.

"What's the good of having opinions if you keep them to yourself?" Mrs. Ellsworth retorted good-naturedly as she set a platter of hot pancakes down on the table, along with a pitcher of warmed-up molasses, and a plate of bacon and hot biscuits. It felt wonderful to be making ready to sit down to a good meal with family.

"Here, Bill, let me take him while you eat," Edith said, sitting down at her place and reaching her arms out for Jay. I handed him off to her, surprised at how reluctant I was to do so. She settled him into her lap, keeping him secure with one hand while she deftly managed her fork with the other. I marveled how easy women seemed to adjust to having a miniature little person to take care of, day in and day out. I pulled out the chair next to her and sat down, thanking Mrs. Ellsworth for the coffee she'd set out before me. Together we ate and talked, lingering at the table well longer than normal. I didn't know as I'd ever enjoyed a meal more than that one—more for the company, than the food—although the food was pretty good, too.

⸺◉⸺

All too soon that day was over, and as the sun fell I knew I had to think about getting on my way. Just before supper Mr. Ellsworth had told me in confidence that on his last trip to town he'd heard rumors that Bill Tilghman and Chris Madsen were focusing

their search for me on Logan and Payne Counties—
which meant I needed to make myself scarce from
there, and soon.

Edith kept finding excuses for me to stay just a
bit longer, but finally there were none left she could
make. I had been sitting with Jay on my lap, finding
different ways to make him give his little giggle at
me, and when I handed him over to Edith he reached
out a little hand toward me, like he wanted me to
take him back. That nearly broke me and if Edith's
Pa hadn't told me about Tilghman closing in, I probably would've abandoned my plans and stayed.
Edith put him down in his crib for the night, after
I'd kissed him gently on his little forehead, and then
she'd come outside to the barn with me after I'd said
goodbye to her folks. While Edith had been putting
Jay to bed, I'd discretely slipped her Pa some money,
for all the care he'd been providing for Edith and Jay,
and for Rebel, too. I told him if it was all the same to
him I'd leave Black Devil there and take Rebel when
I left.

Edith followed me silently to the stable, and
waited in the dark while I lit the lantern and hung it
up on the wall. Then she stood outside the loose box
while I tacked Rebel up. I felt her eyes on me as I slid
my rifle out of the saddle scabbard, checking it over,
then buckled my gun belt snugly around my waist.

Pretty soon there wasn't anything left for me to do, so I came out of the stall to say goodbye to her.

I pulled her almost roughly to me, bending down to kiss her good and long since I knew it'd probably be awhile before I could be with her again. Her body bent back a little, and I felt her go limp in my arms before she started kissing me back, almost desperately. "I know you have to go, Bill," she whispered shakily to me in between kisses, "but, oh, God, I wish you didn't."

"I know," I said, tightening my arms around her and inhaling the sweet scent of her hair. "I don't want to leave you but I got to. It's not safe for me to stay here right now, and I won't let anything happen to you or Jay as long as I'm breathing."

She had tears in her eyes when she pulled back to look at me, but she didn't let them spill over. "Just stay safe. Promise me."

"I promise. I love you and our little boy, and I'll be back for you as soon as I can." I kissed her once more, then let her go, quick, and went into the stall to take Rebel in hand. Edith stepped away from him and stood back as I led him from the barn, then she came outside with the lantern and stood against the latched door as I put my foot in the stirrup and threw my leg over the saddle. I looked down at her as I gathered the reins, and found I couldn't speak, so I just pulled my hat down low and tapped my spurs to Rebel's sides. Just before I put him into a lope I looked back and lifted a hand to her. She waved back, strands of her hair tossing around her face with the breeze.

I cantered off, forcing my mind to turn to Missouri and the gang. I didn't look back again.

TWENTY-NINE

"THINK THAT JUST about concludes our business here," I said breezily to the teller at the bank in Southwest City. I slung the bulging feed sack over my shoulder, my revolver aimed in his direction, then took a couple of steps backwards, the rowels of my spurs jingling in an almost merry manner. "We'll be on our way now, boys," I said to the others, who were all still covering the bank's manager and the three customers who were kneeling in one corner, their fingers laced behind their heads.

The teller raised his head a little and looked me straight in the eyes for a split second, then lowered his gaze back to the floor as he stood next to the open vault. Something in that fleeting glance made me think he just might be foolish enough to try something stupid—even with all them guns in his face. I cleared my throat warningly. "Keep your hands where I can see 'em. No need for things to get messy."

Glancing to my left, I caught Creek's eye and jerked my head toward the door. He gave a short nod and cautiously but quickly got out of there, followed by the others. I was the last man out, keeping my eye—and my gun—on that teller. His hands stayed raised, the customers stayed kneeling. Satisfied, I backed out the door, ready to make for the horses and turn their tails on the town.

Just as my boot heel hit the planks of the gallery outside the bank, I heard Creek's voice exclaim, grimly, "Oh, hell—*everyone get down!*"

Before I could react or even turn fully around, I heard the sharp popping of gunshots ring out from the street. Bullets started splintering the wood of the pillars that supported the awning over the gallery where we were, and just above my head the glass of a lantern shattered as a bullet struck it, showering glittering shards onto me and onto Creek, who was closest to me. I dropped like a stone onto my stomach, using the bag of money as a shield, then raised my revolver up over it, sighting out into the street and squeezing off shots. All around me the others were ducking behind posts or water troughs, trying to inch their way toward where we'd left the horses, all the while returning fire. Every Goddamned person on the street seemed to have a gun they were emptying in our direction, all out of nowhere. *Jesus*

Christ, it's Coffeyville all over again, I thought, my heart sinking.

Most of the others were still scrambling on ahead toward the horses, and I couldn't tell if anyone had been hit or not. Behind me, the panes of glass in the windows of the bank were exploding as bullets hit them, and the people we'd left inside were crying out in panic, laying flat on the floor and covering their heads and necks with their arms. Up and down the street, townsfolk ran screaming to take cover, and horses whinnied in terror, throwing their heads up and jerking at their tethers, trying to flee.

"Bill!" Texas Jack suddenly shouted at me, over the din, and I looked over at him as I got to my feet and managed to find some manner of cover behind a pillar. His eyes were wild, his face was streaked with sweat and the muzzle of his pistol was smoking. "Over there!" he was saying frantically, motioning with his gun as he began reloading it, shoving bullets into the empty cylinder with fingers that shook. "Get those sons of bitches over there!"

I looked where he was looking and saw two men running right toward us, one in front of the other, the sun glinting off the guns in their hands. The rest of the gunfire seemed to have slowed for a moment. I raised my gun on them, but before I could fire I heard a shot and saw both men suddenly stumble, falling to the street almost in unison. Out of the corner of my eye I saw Little Bill lower his Winchester from his shoulder, smoke wafting from its barrel. Looked to me like he'd gotten them both with a single shot, the bullet passing first through one man, then striking the other.

I didn't linger in my looking, though. *"Go!"* I roared to him and to Jack, turning away and sprinting for Rebel. My bad foot had been giving me more and more trouble over the last few days, but at that moment I felt no pain from it; in fact I felt nothing at all other than the desire to flee. Something whizzed past my head and struck it near my hairline, right above my ear, and I felt a wetness begin to trickle down from my temple and run into my beard. As I lunged for Rebel's reins and vaulted myself up into my saddle, red-hot stabs of pain began throbbing at my forehead. Some of that wetness oozed down into my mouth at the corner and I tasted blood. I spit it out, violently, and spurred Rebel like the Devil himself was chasing us. My whole head was aching now and the place at my temple was stinging like mad; I realized I'd been shot. I gritted my teeth against it and kept going, my right arm beginning to feel the heavy weight of the bag of money I'd somehow managed to hang onto.

There were riders coming after us; I heard

pounding hooves and shouted demands for us to stop, but of course we just rode on all the harder. In front of me I saw Creek laid out almost flat against Dash's neck, and I whipped my reins back at Rebel's flanks, asking for more speed. He gave a little grunt and opened his stride up some more. I glanced back under my arm and saw about five or six riders giving chase. Then I heard a gunshot, and I stopped looking after that. We were too far out ahead of them for the shot to find its mark, but I was going to do everything I could to make the distance between us even wider. On either side of me, Little Bill, Tulsa Jack, Red Buck, Dick West, Dynamite Dan and Charley were all following suit, some of them on stolen horses; I guessed the ones they'd come with had been hit in the exchange of bullets.

The horses were all good and lathered by the time we could no longer hear the posse behind us. We were fleeing into the Neosho River Valley, out of Missouri and back toward the Oklahoma Territory, and home turf. My mind was racing—even though we'd lost the posse for now, the law would be hot on our trail, and more feverishly than ever.

"We got to breathe them!" Creek called out, pulling an exhausted Dash up from a canter, which was the fastest he'd go at that point. I pulled up Rebel, too, and one by one the others reined in. Everyone was still together, I noticed, as the great cloud of dust our horses had kicked up began to settle around us.

"Jesus, Bill, you been shot!" Dick suddenly exclaimed, reining his gelding alongside Rebel and leaning in from his saddle to peer closer at me. The others all looked, too, and Creek rode Dash over, his mustache drooping around his mouth as he frowned.

"Just grazed, I think," I managed to say. The pain was coming on pretty good again and I bit down on the inside of my cheek to distract myself from it. There was blood drying in my hair and beard, under the edge of my hat and all down the sleeve of my shirt. There were big splotches of it on my thigh and my saddle, too.

"You'd better wash it off some, let someone take a look," Creek said soberly. He craned his neck a little and his brow furrowed as he peered at my forehead from where he still sat in his saddle, trying to see under my hat brim. "Looks like maybe more than one piece of lead hit you."

"I'll look at it later," I said shortly, gritting my teeth. "It ain't safe for us to just be sitting out here in the open like this. Let's push on." I squeezed Rebel with my legs and he started walking, too tired to trot. His head hung low as he walked.

"Well, I'll be damned," Charley suddenly said with an amazed little laugh as he set his horse to following mine, "if you didn't manage to save the haul! I figured you'd dropped it during that fracas—I know *I* would have!"

I looked down at the heavy bag, the weight of which was making my arm go numb. "I figure we sort of earned it, don't you, Charley?" I replied wryly. "Here, *you* carry it for awhile, seeing as how you ain't got any holes in you like I got."

He trotted his stud up next to Rebel and grinned at me as he took the heavy sack. "Feels like we got us some riches here, boys."

"I figure there's a few thousand in there, at the least," I said, kicking Rebel into a trot. Charley put the bag reverently in front of him in the saddle, cradling it with his right hand like it was a child in need of protection. We pushed on, the bunch of us, heading for the cover of trees and making our way toward Indian lands.

"Buckshot," Creek announced grimly, as he crouched next to where I sat against some boulders on the bank of a clear little stream. He was peering closely at my forehead with the aid of a lit match. I winced and dipped my handkerchief back into the water, wringing it out before putting it back against my wounds. The bleeding seemed to have stopped but I knew I couldn't leave all that dust and sweat caked on there. Taking my hat off had been hell; the drying blood had made it stick to the wounds.

"Doesn't look like any of it stuck in you, though, but I can't tell for sure." Creek continued. "One of these looks pretty deep to me. Bled a whole hell of a lot. Your hair on this side looks the same color as mine. Your beard, too." He tossed the match into the water.

"Maybe I secretly wanted to take after you, Creek," I joked, but it was a pretty feeble effort. "God damn it," I swore under my breath as I drew the bloodied handkerchief away. "Hurts like hell."

The others were getting a little fire going with Tulsa Jack at the watch; the sun had gone down and we'd found a secluded area to lay low in, just long enough to rest the horses and see about my wound.

"You're damned lucky it just grazed you, Bill. Scattergun wound ain't nothing to take lightly," Dynamite Dan said, coming over to us and dipping his canteen into the water. "If it'd hit you square—"

"If it had hit me square, Dan, I wouldn't be breathing still," I finished for him, my voice dark. "I'd like to know who the hell in that town started that whole mess. Could've been another Coffeyville, easy."

"I think that was their intention," Dan said dryly, "only without leaving any survivors among ours, and without any of theirs dying." He put the cap back on his canteen, his disfigured hand working just like it would've if it had all five of its fingers still, instead of just two.

"I think those two Little Bill hit are done," Creek commented, a little soberly.

"We should've just killed the whole God-damned bunch of them," Red Buck muttered, filling his own canteen. I rolled my eyes, declining to answer.

"If you want to go on back there and take the entire damned town on, Buck, by all means, go ahead," Creek said, standing up. "Personally, I'd rather keep on living than commit suicide. We got the cash and we got away, so that's enough for me and everyone else here, 'cept you, seems like."

Red Buck didn't answer, just screwed the cap back on his canteen and went back over to where Dick and Little Bill were building the fire. Aways out, Tulsa Jack sat tensely on a boulder framed by shrubbery, at the watch, his Winchester cocked and ready across his knees and both his pistols loaded full.

I let my breath out and leaned back against

the hard boulder, closing my eyes a minute. When I opened them I saw Creek watching me warily. "Lucky you had your hat on, Bill; seems like it sort of slowed the pellets down." He raised an eyebrow and peered in to look at me close. "You gonna be all right?" he asked me.

"I'll be fine," I told him firmly. Now that I had little Jay waiting for me along with Edith I was more determined than ever not to get myself shot into my grave after some robbery. "I don't think we should head straight back into the Territory. We should head into Arkansas a bit, then maybe double back, to throw them off."

Creek nodded. "We'd better see about some kind of bandage for you, though, before we get going too far. If that starts gushing again you'll be in a bad way."

I winced as I drew the handkerchief away again. "There's a shirt rolled up in one of my saddlebags ain't never been worn," I told him, suddenly remembering the other one Edith had given me before I'd left the farm. It was the only clean cloth I'd be likely to find for a while—I wasn't going to risk seeking out a doctor this time around. I'd been lucky, that time in Beaver City. Wasn't any way in hell I was going to push that luck. "You can cut some strips from it, and I can use my hat to hold them good once you've tied them on."

Creek nodded and took out his knife, and he stood up and went to Rebel where he was tethered to a low tree. A moment later I heard the sound of cloth tearing and I winced again—this time from knowing Edith's careful, loving work was being ruined. I knew in my heart she'd be glad of it, though, if she knew it was going towards saving my life.

As Creek was working, I raised my hand up and put it against my vest, where the inside pocket was, and I felt the piece of folded-up paper I'd tucked inside. Later on when I was bandaged up with strips of crisp white muslin from the shirt, my hat drawn snugly down over it and my head throbbing something fierce, I drew that well-worn paper out of my vest and unfolded it, quietly, while the others ate roasted bits of a rabbit Little Bill had shot and counted, then re-counted, their shares of the haul. Even though I was sitting a good ways away from them the fire threw enough light my way for me to read the words written there in Edith's flowing hand—though I didn't need to read them; I had them memorized:

Good-Bye.
How often by that lonely word
Our pleasures have been driven.
Good-bye is often said on earth
But never said in Heaven.

She'd found the verse, she'd told me, in a book she was reading once, and the words had somehow made her think of me. She'd written them down on a scrap of paper and kept it tucked away in her dressing-table, and when I'd left her off at her folks' farm that time last year, after the fight in Ingalls, she'd given it to me. She'd told me she wanted me to carry that simple verse with me and know that if anything ever happened to take me away from her, all the good-byes we'd ever said over the time we'd known and loved one another wouldn't amount to anything once we were reunited in Heaven. I wasn't one to be moved much by poetry; in truth I'd never read much at all, but that verse—and the meaning behind it—stuck with me and was never far from my mind.

"You ready to push on, Bill?"

It was Dick West's voice that broke me out of my contemplation of those words, and I quickly folded the paper up and put it back in my vest before I looked up at him. "Yes, we'd best get moving, 'fore the night gets too old." I got stiffly to my feet, my head and my foot aching, and trudged over to Rebel while Little Bill and Dan put out the fire and the others got to their horses. I paused before I put my foot in the stirrup, expecting to feel blood start soaking through my bandage, but I didn't.

THIRTY

WE MANAGED TO evade the posse by heading into Arkansas, planning on taking the roundabout way back to the Territories over the period of a few weeks' time, but by then I had a fever and the chills, on top of my wounds, and I didn't much care where we ended up.

Red Buck grew antsy and one night he convinced Little Bill and Dynamite Dan to go off somewhere with him, likely to some red-light district or to stir up trouble, but Dick, Charley, Creek and Tulsa Jack stayed with me. Creek tried his best to get me to eat, and kept forcing water into me, but instead of getting better I got worse. Finally one night came where I was so delirious from fever I forgot where I was and who I was with. I didn't know how much time passed, but the next thing I knew I was waking up in a strange room, laying in a narrow bedstead with a brass frame. Swallowing slowly against my throat that felt sore and swollen, I looked around a little without moving my head.

The room was small and the walls weren't papered or painted; they were just narrow boards that were still the bright golden color of new lumber that hadn't had time to weather gray yet. There was a wash-stand with a shaving mirror and a bowl and pitcher in one corner, and a plain chest of drawers, and hooks hung up on the wall opposite the bed for clothes and hats. My coat was hung up on one of them, and my hat on another. My rifle was leaned into the corner near the door, and my saddlebags were slung over the footboard. When I turned my head a little bit to the right, I saw Creek sitting in a chair set near the window, the sunlight that was coming through it throwing a big square of light onto the floor at his feet, intersected by the shadows cast from the strips of wood in between the panes of glass. He was reading a newspaper and hadn't seen my eyes open.

I swallowed again and licked my dry, cracked lips, and managed to croak out, "Creek?"

He looked up, quick, over the top of his paper, and then he quickly folded it back up and tossed it onto the floor, his face breaking into a relieved grin as he leaned forward a little toward the bed. He looked tired; there were big shadows under his eyes and his mustache looked limp. He had a few days' worth of stubble coming up on his face, too. "Well, now, look who's decided to wake up! You gave me a scare, Bill. Wasn't too sure you were gonna make it, for awhile."

I drew in a breath that hurt my lungs. "Where the hell are we?" I asked, weakly. My body felt sore all over, like I'd been beaten.

"We're in Bentonville," he told me, "at a hotel. We been here a few days, while you were deciding whether you were gonna live or die on us. You've got the grippe, on top of them buckshot wounds." His voice was grave.

I gave him a look. "If I got the grippe, then why in the hell are you sitting in here with me? You'll get it, too." My voice sounded like a shadow of its normal self, even to me.

He shrugged. "I had it once, a few years back, and I lived through it all right. Besides, I been sitting in here with you for three days now, and I ain't got it yet, do I?" He sat back a little in his chair. "You doctored me, Bill, and sat with me when I had that gunshot wound; if it wasn't for you I'd be dead now. I wasn't gonna just leave you here alone." His voice was a little indignant.

I tried to manage a smile. "Much obliged, Creek."

He gave me a short little nod and went for a water glass set on the chest of drawers, bringing it to me and watching almost critically as I took a shaky sip. When he was satisfied I could manage for myself, he sat back down in his chair. "A doctor's been by to look at you," he told me, and held up a hand when he saw me tense up. "Don't get riled up. He don't have the slightest idea who you are, or I am, and he don't care, neither. He's a young doc that sees to some of the Indians in the area. He took a quick look at your forehead, too, and dressed it proper. Didn't even ask me where you got it; I think he was so sure you were gonna die from the grippe that he figured it didn't matter none. But damned if you didn't beat it!" His eyes were twinkling at me, now.

I let my head fall back a little against the pillow and sighed, suddenly lacking the energy to keep my eyes open. "Don't count your chickens, Creek. I feel like shit."

He plucked the glass out of my hand and set it on the little table next to the bed. "Maybe so, but you're talkin' to me and you ain't got a fever, so that's a sure sign you've turned a corner."

I struggled to stay awake. "Where're the others?"

"Charley and Dick are playing poker in the saloon downstairs, and Jack's hanging around the outside of the hotel, on watch, like he's been since we got here." Creek chuckled under his breath. "He reminds me of a bulldog, Bill, always on guard."

"Good thing, too," I murmured. "We can't be too careful."

"Ain't that the truth." He stood up again and went to the window, glancing out of it. "You still got some healin' up to do, before you'll be fit to ride. We'll stay on here till you feel strong enough to go."

I nodded, my eyes closed again. "What day is it, Creek?" I asked him sleepily.

"Tenth of June," he told me. He was quiet for a moment, and I could almost feel him debating with himself about something. Before I could ask he pulled a folded piece of newspaper out of his vest pocket. "I been keeping this to show you, once you were well enough," he told me. "I ain't sure you're well enough now…maybe I should show you later," he hesitated, and I knew something bad was in that paper.

"What is it, Creek? Just tell me," I said, opening my eyes again, feeling less sleepy and more wary.

He was still looking out of the window and I saw his jaw move back and forth, then clench. "Will's dead, Bill."

He said it blunt like that, and I felt like I'd been slapped. I must've looked that way, too, because Creek didn't wait for an answer, just started talking again.

"Happened two days ago," he said, "near

REBECCA ROCKWELL

Ardmore. He and some others took a bank in Texas,
I guess, just a little more than ten days after we took
ours. The law trailed him to the place he was staying
at with Jane and their little ones. The article says he
jumped out the window with a pistol and refused to
stop when they ordered him to, so they shot him."
Creek's voice was full of disgust. "His *babies* were
there, Bill. Had to see their Pa die like that." He suddenly thumped his fist, hard, against the wall near
the window-frame. "God-damned lawdogs. Sons of
bitches probably didn't even give him a chance to
surrender, like they're sayin' they did."

"You know he wouldn't have surrendered,
Creek, whether they gave him the chance to or not,"
I pointed out, but I felt rage and sorrow coming up
in me, too, through all the aches from the grippe.
Will Dalton—my *friend*—was gone, just like that,
and so quick after he'd left us. Strangely, my mind
turned to Emmett, wasting away in the penitentiary
at Lansing, and I wondered if he knew yet. Another
brother put under the daisies. I bowed my head suddenly, squeezing my eyes shut. I hoped that somehow Will, who'd always been so restless in the time
I'd known him, was at peace now. I felt like I usually did after I lost a friend—like I needed to rise
up and get revenge, somehow, even though I knew
it would be all I could do from here on out to keep

myself and the friends I had left from meeting the same fate.

Creek was looking at me now, watching me struggle with the news, and he was quiet for a minute. Then he spoke again. "They say folks are coming in droves to look at him, so they can brag they've seen the corpse of the Notorious Bill Dalton." Creek's voice still sounded disgusted. "Just like they did with Jesse James, when he died."

I remembered seeing the photographs of Jesse's body, sold as souvenirs all over the country, after Bob Ford murdered him back in 1882. The morbid curiosity of folks had made me shudder, and the first thing that'd kept coming up in my mind was how terrible Jesse's wife and children must've felt, just like these last few days must've been hell on earth for Jane and her children. Thoughts entered my mind then about how the law would likely do the same to all of us, if they ever got us, and nausea welled up in me then.

Creek let out a heavy sigh. "Well, if he aimed to live on forever in some way, I guess maybe this'll do it," he said, sadness in his tone as he stared back out the window again, one arm leaned on the windowsill, the other hand resting on his hip. I didn't answer him; I suddenly felt like I was a hundred years old.

We let the silence stretch out a bit between us, both of us thinking about Will, and about Bob and

Grat and Emmett, and, I was sure, thinking about what might become of us down the line, sooner or later. Finally, Creek broke it. "You want to read this?" he asked me, holding the still-folded piece of newspaper. I shook my head. He'd told me enough; I didn't need to read the reporter's gloating words. He put it back in his pocket.

"You'd better get some food in you, if you think you can," he suddenly said, changing the subject. My stomach turned at the idea, but I knew he was right. I'd never be able to get out of bed, much less go back on the run, if I didn't try to get my strength back.

"Suppose you're right," I said with a heavy sigh.

He left the window and took up his hat, then slid into his frock coat to hide his guns a bit. "I'll bring you up something; tell the boys you're aiming to live while I'm at it." He gave me a ghost of a smile, then left the room. I heard his spurs jingling softly as he moved off down the hallway.

When he'd gone I pushed back the blankets a bit and saw I was wearing only my britches and my undershirt, and I looked around, in a sudden panic, for my vest and realized it was hanging on the hook next to my coat. Feeling weaker than a newborn kitten, I somehow got out of bed and managed to make my way over to it, putting out my hand and feeling for the pocket. Relief flooded through me when

I felt the little square of paper still tucked inside. Edith's verse was still there. Somehow I felt that if I lost that connection to her, I'd lose my mind along with it.

————))(())((————

Creek came back up with Charley and Dick in tow; they brought me up some biscuits and a cup of tea from the restaurant downstairs. I was surprised to realize that I was hungry, after all, and as I ate they milled around and talked back and forth about Will, and the job in Missouri and the gunfight afterward. It was then I learned that the two men Little Bill had shot with one bullet had been brothers—and one of them had died. To make matters worse, the dead one was J.C. Seaborn, a former State Senator of Missouri. Seemed to me we couldn't do a damned thing any-more without someone getting killed by our guns, or some of us getting shot up. All the more reason, I thought to myself, that the time to stop was nearing. But I said nothing to the others. What mattered now was getting myself well enough to push on, and get back to Edith and Jay.

Always one to reach a goal when I set one out in front of me, I recovered faster than the other boys figured I would and just three days later we were on our way out of Bentonville.

———•((•))•———

Some two weeks later we rode our tired horses over the Territory line into Oklahoma, having ventured into Kansas for awhile after leaving Arkansas to throw the law off our trail. By then I was fully over the grippe and my wounds from Southwest City were healing so well I didn't need to dress them anymore—a damned good thing, in my mind, since folks were more likely to look twice at a man with a bandage around his head. By the time we drew near to the outskirts of Newkirk, we were running low on provisions and hadn't had much luck hunting, so we decided to stop at one of the farmhouses we came across to see if we could pay for a meal.

We did that often in those days; a lot of the time we could convince the farmers were just travelers on the move in need of a home-cooked meal; once or twice we were even so bold as to pretend to be members of a posse seeking out our own gang, and we got pretty convincing at it, too. Creek and I got laughs for days out of such ruses. Sometimes I was certain the folks we ate with knew exactly who we were, but either sympathy for our cause or fear of us kept them from saying or doing anything about it.

The farm we stopped at outside of Newkirk was one of those that feared us; I could tell that right off. The farmer was a tall, thin man with skin tanned brown from the sun who said little to us, just eyed our guns nervously as we sat around his table and got served up supper by his wife. She said nothing at all, not even when we thanked her, and though me and the other boys all used our best manners, I could tell we weren't gonna get anywhere with her. She was drawn up tense the whole time she was waiting on us and her mouth was set in a hard line.

They had three children, two daughters who were on the verge of womanhood and one little boy. The girls helped their mother in the kitchen and kept their eyes away from ours, and the little boy sat on the edge of a bed that was set in the corner of the big front room and stared at us with round eyes, his mouth open a little ways in an awed expression. Not a one of them said a single word. When we were done I thanked them politely for the meal and gave the farmer the twenty-five cents apiece he said he'd charge us, then tipped my hat to the women and headed out the door, anxious to be off. I figured if we kept going I could be back at the Ellsworths' farm in just a few days. The thought gave me new energy and I turned to Creek as we collected our horses.

"When we get closer to Payne County I want to pick a place to meet up later," I told him.

He gave me a sideways look as he tightened the cinch of his saddle. "Thought maybe you were done, Bill," he said quietly.

"Not yet," I said firmly, tightening my own cinch. "I ain't aiming to have that mess in Southwest City be the one we go out on."

Creek nodded. "Good," was all he said, but I thought he looked relieved. As much as the noose was beginning to tighten around the gang, we were all of us proud and stubborn men, and given our feelings toward the law, none of us wanted anyone to think we'd stopped our activities because the law was making things too hot for us. When I stopped, it would be on my own terms.

THIRTY-ONE

"THINK THAT'LL BE all, boys," I said to Creek and Charley as I slung the heavy, awkward sack of money over my shoulder, my gun still aimed straight at the heart of the express messenger on the Rock Island train at Dover. He cringed and looked at the floor, his hands still raised, palms out as he inched backwards, moving away from the safe we'd just cleaned out.

Creek and Charley ducked fluidly out of the express car, their boots thudding onto the platform as Tulsa Jack, Little Bill, Dynamite Dan, Red Buck and Dick West crowded around, their guns still in hand. I kept the express messenger and the fireman who stood near him covered for a few seconds more, then jumped out myself, unable to hold back a smile as I did so. Wasn't another group of men in the country more practiced at holding up trains than my Wild Bunch. The whole damned lark hadn't taken but ten minutes, if that, and we'd come off with a good haul, if the weight of the sack was any indication.

"Let's get a move on," I said almost breezily to the others as I stepped up into Rebel's saddle. Wasn't any need to vault myself up there like I had a fire under me anymore; the company men and passengers were too scared of us to try anything, and by the time they came around from the stupefied state that looking down our gun barrels left 'em in, we were long gone from there.

We headed west, in far less of a hurry than we used to be after we'd pulled train jobs. The bunch of us felt even more invincible than usual that day; I think it was because for all their big talk, neither the Three Guardsmen nor the great Marshal Nix had been able to get anywhere close to laying a hand on even one of us since Southwest City—and it had been nearly a year since that job.

Staying wary out of habit, I kept my mind on getting a good distance between the Dover station and our group, but once I felt we'd reached relative safety I started thinking, turning over plans in my mind. I'd been saving up money here and there in banks and at the home farm since the year before, and with what I'd take from this job, I thought I might have enough, finally, to leave the Territories and get myself out of the robbing business for good. The thought of getting

Edith and Jay somewhere safe and setting down with them brought a smile to my face—such a large one that Creek, riding at my side, noticed. He gave me a look. "What's got you looking so chipper?" he asked me, his eyes dancing.

"Nothing. Think we got us a pretty good haul, is all," I said quickly. Now wasn't the time to bring up retirement.

———◦(◉)◦———

By mid-afternoon the next day, we'd crossed into Major County, and there we stopped near a stream off the Cimarron to camp for a bit and divvy up, all of us still feeling pretty damned good about how the whole thing had gone off and figuring we were far enough away from the scene of the holdup so's we didn't have to draw our revolvers at every little sound. We milled around, talking, filling our canteens at the stream and adjusting our horses' tack in between counting and re-counting our money. Only Tulsa Jack, acting as lookout, sat near a gnarled old tree trunk with his rifle at the ready, his whole body drawn up like a rabbit on the watch for a pack of wolves.

When the first shot came, I thought I was hearing

things. My eyes met Creek's and Charley's where they stood together near an outcropping of rocks, and they looked just as stunned as I felt. Then another shot came, and with it the sound of pounding hooves, and as if in a dream I saw Tulsa Jack throw himself to the ground, cocking his rifle in mid-fall, firing off an answering shot as he hit the dirt. I looked where he was shooting and saw a group of men on horseback, all flying straight toward us, the sun gleaming off the guns in their hands and the spring breeze carrying the sounds of their excited yells to our ears.

"We found you, you God-damned sons of bitches!" one of them screamed hoarsely. "You ain't getting away this time!"

"Give it up, Doolin!" another one called, less wild excitement and more grim authority in his tone than the first. "You and your boys are caught! Don't make this end badly!" He drew his horse to a stop with a dramatic tug on the reins; the nag slid a few feet on all fours and sent a spray of dirt out ahead of it, throwing its head skyward. Through the wafting dust I saw the sun catch on the badge its rider wore on his vest, and then my brain seemed to start working again, and I found cover behind the same boulders sheltering Creek and Charley. Around us, Little Bill, Red Buck, Dick and Dan were finding whatever cover they could, too, and then all hell broke loose.

"You boys are done!" one of the posse-members gloated, sliding ungracefully off his horse in excitement and jerking a second pistol from his other hip-holster, aiming them both in the direction he'd seen us take cover. He wore no badge and I gathered he'd been after some thrills when he'd volunteered to come out after us; too bad all he'd get was lead out of my gun.

"Like hell we are!" I snarled back, sighting and firing, my aim true. The bullet hit him in the forehead, spraying blood and brains all over the place. The horse he'd just come off of shied and reared, turning and fleeing, the stirrups flopping against its sides, its reins dangling in the scrub.

The marshal I'd seen dove off his horse and took cover, and some of his men followed suit in an almost practiced fashion. Those, I figured, my mind working at a furious pace, were the trained lawmen. The ones that just sat on their horses gaping at the body of the man I'd just put a hole in were likely more volunteer vigilantes, out to be heroes or collect rewards. I jerked my other revolver and set to work on them, Creek, Charley, and the others all following my lead. The lawdogs fired back and pretty soon I couldn't see a damned thing for the gunsmoke hanging thick in the air.

I ducked my head down and began yanking

bullets out of my gun belt, reloading my Colts with quick, practiced fingers. Nearby, I saw Creek reach for his Winchester, leveling it over the top of the rocks we were behind and squeezing the trigger as the lawmen kept on emptying their guns at us. I heard a horse scream and saw the bay mare Dan had been riding crumple over, and I felt my fists clench even tighter around my guns in dismay. The horse might have been hit by a stray bullet instead of on purpose, but even so, it might give them ideas. We might be able to hold them off for awhile longer; we had enough ammunition and enough guns, but if they started shooting our horses, we were done for. Wasn't any way we could escape on foot; they'd catch up to us, sooner or later.

I swore violently and inched myself closer to Creek and Charley. "We got to get out of here, 'fore they take our nags out!" I called, shouting to be heard over the din of gunfire. As I spoke a bullet hit the branch of the tree just above where Little Bill was taking cover, sending a shower of splintered bark down onto the brim of his hat.

Our horses were in a frenzy, rearing up what little ways they could and tugging at their tie-downs in an effort to get away from where we'd tethered them in some scrawny trees. Dick had hobbled his gelding instead of tying it, and the horse almost toppled over, fighting the hobbles from fear. I saw Dick lunge for its front legs, producing his knife and slicing the rawhide that joined the ankle straps. He was up in the saddle in short order and fleeing from there before I could blink, shots still whizzing past him from the posse's guns.

"We got to chance it, Creek!' I called, and he nodded.

We dug in and ran, keeping as low to the ground as possible, somehow making it to the horses. Charley followed, a scattergun blast narrowly missing his back. He grabbed for his horse and got on. Then Creek reached Dash, and Little Bill got to his dapple gray, reaching down a hand to Dan and helping him get up behind him, since Dan's mare lay dead in the grass a few feet away. Red Buck got up on his stud. All the while, the lawdogs and their posse were still firing away, bellowing at us to stop and surrender—like there was a chance in hell we'd consider it.

There was no calming Rebel and I had to be quicker than a rabbit to stay out from under his flailing hooves as I yanked his reins loose from the branch I'd tied them to. I got myself into the saddle and sawed at the bit, getting him clear of the others as they all began to gallop off.

I started to follow them, but something made me pause, even with shots still ringing out here and there from the guns of our would-be captors. Tulsa Jack still hunched behind a tree-stump, taking aim at the marshal I'd noticed at the beginning of the fight. "Jack!" I hollered, struggling to hold back Rebel, who was bucking out with his back legs, sweat pouring off his flanks and the white part of his eyes showing all the way around.

Jack looked up and saw his roan gelding whinnying in fright and fighting his tether, and then he saw me, motioning to him to give it up and flee. He turned back, fired at the marshal without success, and made a break for it.

The marshal raised his arm, and I heard another shot. I saw Jack stumble; saw bright red blood come spurting over his white shirt. He fell, and didn't rise, and the posse's guns went silent as if their owners were holding their breath, waiting to see how bad they'd got him.

My eyeballs were stinging from all the gunpowder and the acrid smell of it burned my nostrils. I knew Tulsa Jack was dead. I couldn't do anything for him now, only get myself out of there. I gave Rebel his head and he shot forward, streaking after the others and leaving the remains of a friend behind me.

THIRTY-TWO

I DIDN'T HAVE time to mourn Jack, those first hours after the gunfight. We'd let our guard down too far and we'd paid for it, and barely escaped with our lives at that. To top if off, two of our horses—Red Buck's and mine—came up lame after only an hour or so on the run.

At first, I thought Rebel had thrown a shoe, from the way his gait faltered. But when we slowed down to breathe them I knew it was more serious than that—somehow he'd damaged one of his forelegs and by the time I felt it was safe enough to stop for a few minutes, he couldn't bear any weight on it.

Red Buck's stud had put his hoof in a badger hole while we were fleeing, and we'd all heard the crack of his cannon bone breaking. Red Buck's sour expression didn't change a bit as he calmly got down out of the saddle, cocked his Winchester, and put it to the horse's low-hanging head. As he pulled the trigger I looked quickly away, and I saw Creek wince and do the same. Funny how we could watch a man die from a bullet I'd put in his forehead, but couldn't bear to see a horse go that way.

"You gonna shoot yours, Doolin, or you want me to do it for you?" Red Buck asked me bluntly, reaching down and pulling the saddlebags off his saddle where the horse lay in a heap in the grass, throwing them unceremoniously over one shoulder and leaning his rifle on the other.

"Hell no, you ain't doing it!" I snapped back, venom in my tone. "You ain't putting so much as a finger on this horse." My voice sounded strange, choked up and hoarse, and for a minute my vision wavered, like the way the air did when heat waves showed in it. I wanted to put my gun to *his* head, like he'd done to that poor horse, and now wanted to do to mine.

"Jesus Christ, it's only a nag," Red Buck muttered. "You want to get away from them sons of bitches, or don't you? You ain't gonna be able to go anywhere on that stud, and he'll only slow us down."

"Damn it, Buck, shut your God-damned mouth," Charley snarled, low in his throat, like a dog warning off someone he was about to tear to pieces.

I didn't listen to Red Buck's answer. Instead I stared sorrowfully at Rebel and examined his leg one more time. He let out a little noise of pain, like a squeal, when I put my hands to it, and drew away from me, baring his teeth and throwing his head up as he tried to hobble on three legs, sweat pouring off him.

My chest felt like it had a rock sitting on it; I couldn't seem to draw in a deep breath. The shock of seeing Jack die like he had, combined with the certain fact that I'd have to lose the best riding horse I'd ever had, made me feel as near to crazy as I'd ever felt till then.

I knew what I had to do; as much as I hated to admit it, Red Buck was right, and Rebel was suffering. We were out in the middle of nowhere and I knew that posse would be trailing us still. I reached over gingerly and drew my rifle out of the saddle scabbard. Rebel eyeballed me, but his head had drooped and the proud spark that had always been in his eyes was gone. All I saw was an animal in pain. At least, I thought grimly, I could ease that pain. Rebel had served me damn well, and I couldn't repay him by letting him suffer. I took a shaky breath, cocked the rifle, and brought the barrel to his wide forehead.

Dash started at the sound of the gunshot, and Creek pulled back on the reins and checked him before he could spook. "Whoa," he said, low. He was averting his eyes from Rebel's body as he did so.

I kept my eyes on my saddlebags and, like Red Buck had done, I unbuckled the straps and pulled them free of my saddle. My fingers were shaking while I did it. I took them in hand, and then had no choice but to haul myself up behind Creek. Reluctantly, Charley let Red Buck come up behind him, and we started going again.

There was no time to say anything; we'd lingered too long, in my mind, as it was. We pushed on, fleeing farther west, and I tried not to think about the bright red blood soaking the front of Jack's shirt, and the image of Rebel dropping in a swirl of gunsmoke from my rifle.

———— ◉ ————

"Look there, Bill, there's a farmhouse," Creek said tensely, after we'd been riding for over two hours and were still in the middle of nowhere. I craned my neck around him and saw a small, lonely little house about a mile out, with smoke coming out of the stove-pipe and some horses in a corral nearby. It was nearing sunset and the bunch of us, and the horses we had left, were exhausted and famished. We needed food and as many fresh mounts as we could get our hands on, and it looked like we'd have to steal both at gunpoint unless the farmer was willing to give them to us. Otherwise, we weren't gonna make it.

We headed for the front of the place, stopping our lathered horses in the little road made by the farmer's wagon-tracks. In the dying light we could see four horses in the corral, and another one in the little yard built onto the back of the barn behind the house. There was a saddle sitting on the top rail of the barnyard and a bridle on the fence post, like they had just been taken off the big bay inside.

The front door opened, and an older man came out of it. He was tall and thin, with a silvery beard dangling down off his chin. He reminded me of an undertaker in his severe black suit of clothes.

"What do you boys want?" he asked us suspiciously, and I saw his eyes darting to each of us in turn, his gaze on our guns and our gun belts.

"We need a meal, and some fresh horses," I answered, keeping my voice even.

"You won't get either, here," he said firmly, crossing his arms over his chest and narrowing his eyes. "I don't cater to men who break the law—man's law or God's.""How do you know we've broken either one?" Little Bill asked him, a glare clouding his face.

"There's no call for all those guns you've got on you unless you have, and you've been running from something, by the looks of your horses. You say you need a meal, but what I think you need is to ask God for forgiveness for your sins," he said stoutly, his steely dark eyes glittering at us defiantly and his chin raising up a little.

"You a preacher or something?" Charley asked him doubtfully.

"Yes, I am," he replied. "Now be on your way."

Red Buck got down from behind Charley. "You aiming to be closer to God, Preacher-Sam?" he asked mockingly. "Hell, I can fix it so you can *meet* Him, right now!" He took out his revolver and aimed straight for the old man's heart, a cruel sneer on his face.

"No!" I cried hoarsely, but my voice was drowned out by the gunshot. The preacher crumpled to the ground, dead before he hit it.

"Damn it, Weightman, what the hell did you do that for?"

"*Jesus*, Buck!"

"What the hell's *wrong* with you?"

Creek's, Charley's and Dick's voices all spoke out at once and Little Bill looked pale. Red Buck ignored them; he just laughed under his breath and holstered his revolver.

My gaze went red and something in me snapped. I got down from behind Creek and pulled out one of my guns. "That's it," I hissed, my eyes boring into Red Buck's broad back. "You ain't riding with us any more." My fist clenched so hard around the handle of the gun that it began to hurt. I took a step toward Red Buck and thumbed back the hammer, wanting to drop the son of a bitch the same way he'd dropped that innocent old man.

"Bill," Creek said in alarm, but I ignored him. Red Buck turned toward me and his brows drew together as he saw my gun coming up to stare him in the face. It was too late for him to answer my draw; I'd drill him before he'd get his gun out of the holster and he knew it. He froze where he was, his face bearing a cold, dead expression.

"You going soft on us, Doolin?" he sneered at me, but his voice sounded hollow, almost like he was actually afraid. I felt a humorless smile tug at the corners of my mouth. Just as I'd always thought— the bastard was a yellow dog when he didn't have a cocked gun to hide behind.

"I should kill you right here, you sorry son of a bitch," I growled at him, "but I ain't gonna stoop to your level. Get yourself a nag and get out of my sight, and if I ever see you in my vicinity again, I promise you, I will *put you under*."

For several tense seconds, everyone held their breath, waiting to see what Red Buck would do, and what I would do. None of them tried to interfere; they knew this was between the two of us. Finally, Red Buck walked over and pulled the saddle off the barnyard fence, tossing it onto the back of the bay horse. Silently, he tacked up, fuming all the while, and all the while I kept my gun on him.

"Why the hell don't you just shoot me, Doolin?" he asked me tauntingly, as he led the horse out of the barnyard. "Or ain't you got the sand to?"

"I ain't wasting a bullet on your sorry ass," I replied icily. "Get going."

He put his foot in the stirrup and got up on the horse, and then checked it, roughly, staring down at me. "You'd better watch your back from now on," he warned, punctuating his words by spitting off into the grass. "If I ever see you again, you'll answer for this, and it won't be quick and painless, neither."

I just smirked at him and drew my other revolver, cocking the hammer back and aiming them both straight at him. I wasn't afraid of Red Buck or his threats; I never had been. He kept on glowering at me for a minute, then, letting out his breath in disgust, he slapped the horse's rump hard with the reins and galloped off.

Behind me, I heard one of the others let their breath out in relief. "Good God-damn riddance," Creek said in a hard voice.

I drew in a deep breath and put my guns away, trying not to look at the body of the preacher, laying sprawled face-down near the open front door. Then I started for the barn. "We need to see if there's any other tack here," I said over my shoulder to the others. The hair on the back of my neck was standing on end; somehow I knew we didn't have much time to linger here.

I went into the barn and looked around quickly, my eyes straining to see in the dim light. I spied a couple saddles hung on one wall, and a few bridles, and some saddle-blankets. I grabbed one of each and lugged my load back out to the corral. Dick, Charley and Dan, whose horses were the most exhausted, were following my lead. Little Bill kept his gray and Creek stayed mounted on Dash; I knew he wouldn't give him up, tired out or not. He was peering tensely off in the direction we'd come from, watching and listening for any signs of the posse.

I grabbed the halter of the first horse I got near, a chestnut, and got the headstall on it, quick. The bunch of us were silent as we tacked up. Dick was cutting up a rope he'd found in the barn, fashioning a hackamore out of it like we'd used to do back on the cattle ranches. There weren't enough saddles or bridles for those of us taking horses, so Dick would have to ride bareback.

Little Bill had gone inside the house to search for any food we could take with us, and he came out with a loaf of bread. He broke the loaf into pieces and handed them out, just before we got on our way again. I ate mine, but it tasted like dust in my mouth and I had to force it down. I wasn't hungry any longer; somehow I thought I might never be hungry again, nor would I ever be rid of the memories of all the deaths I'd seen that day—Tulsa Jack, Rebel, and that feisty old preacher.

———✦———

We split up soon after leaving that place, knowing we'd be harder to track that way. Creek and Charley came with me, but the others scattered and went off in separate directions. Not one of them had asked me about the next time out, but I wouldn't have said anything if they had—there wasn't going to be a next time. I knew I was done, after this day. Holding up trains would never hold the same excitement for me that it once had, only bad memories. After today, it wasn't fun, or a joke, or even a strike back at the thing that had taken away our livelihood anymore. It had become something dark and terrible for me, and I wanted nothing more to do with it. I wanted to go home to my wife and son and let happy memories take the place of all the ones I'd made today. I'd do what I needed to do to stay free, but nothing more than that.

Creek and Charlie were grim, too, and there wasn't a lot of conversation between the three of us as we stopped to rest the horses in a little outcropping of tall rocks we'd found after riding for another four hours straight. We were all thinking about that man that Red Buck had so senselessly killed, and wishing Tulsa Jack would've made it. And maybe it was silly of me, but I was mourning the loss of my horse, too.

"What are we going to do, Bill?"

Charley's voice, low and sober, startled me out of my silence and I looked up at him. "I'm going home," I said. "I got a wife and child that need me, and I ain't going to miss out on being with them any longer." I shifted my weight from one boot to the other while I held the chestnut's reins, letting it crop grass.

Creek was leaning against a boulder that rose far above our heads, one boot crossed in front of the other in a casual posture while his horse ate next to mine. He was staring at the ground like he saw something interesting there, but I knew he was just deep in thought. Then he cleared his throat and looked up. "Do you mean you're done, Bill?" he asked quietly.

His eyes weren't dancing in jest, the way they so often did; instead they were still and sober.

"Yes," I said firmly. "It's like I said to Will, before he left us: we've hurt the railroad some and we've made sure they ain't going to forget about us any too soon, but I ain't gonna push my luck anymore. I've got enough money now to make a new start somewhere, and that's what I'm going to do."

Creek nodded slowly. "I can't blame you for wanting to," he told me, giving me a half-hearted smile. "I guess we've had us a pretty good run, when you think about it." He reached into one of his saddlebags and pulled out a flask of whiskey. "What would you boys say to a drink?"

I smiled at him and held the flask up to them when he handed it to me. "To the Wild Bunch," I said a little sadly, knowing nothing would ever be the same again, and knocked back a good tug. The liquor burned my throat and warmed me, bracing me a little. I passed it to Charley, and he repeated my little toast before drinking, then Creek did the same.

Pretty soon we were ready to go. Creek looked at me. "Guess we'll head for the Dunns'," he said, glancing at Charley, who nodded.

I frowned. "Creek, are you sure that's a good idea? I got a bad feeling about the whole bunch of them."

His brow furrowed and he looked at me like

I'd gone off my nut. "You mean you still think Bill Dunn's up to something?" he asked. "He ain't never tried anything before, and you know they've always offered us shelter."

"That was before the damned rewards on our heads went sky-high," I reminded him grimly. "The Guardsmen think they're in with us as it is," I continued. "They could be waiting for some of us to show up there, especially after word gets out about that preacher back there." I jerked my thumb in the direction we'd ridden from, feeling rage come up in me at Red Buck again.

"I don't think the Dunns would tolerate the law hanging around on their place," Creek replied, tossing first one rein, then the other up over Dash's neck. "Hell, they'd have to hide just about their whole herd of cows—you know how many they been rustling nowadays?" He grinned wickedly at me and tightened his cinch. "The Dunns ain't any angels, and the law knows it. Every damned one of them could be brought up on charges, easy."

I sighed. "Just watch your back, Creek. You too, Charley."

Creek chuckled under his breath. "You worry too much, Bill." He finished with his tack and turned toward me, sticking out his hand. "I know we'll see you around, but in case it gets to be awhile…"

I knew what he meant. If I took Edith and Jay away from the Territories, as I planned to do, it would likely be a long time before I saw them again—if ever. I gave him a half-smile and shook his hand, laying my other one on top of his and squeezing firmly. I'd miss the old devil, and the many good times we'd had together; somehow I didn't think I'd ever have another friend as good as he'd been in this lifetime. "You take care of yourself, Creek."

He smiled back at me, his eyes dancing again in their familiar, fox-like way. "You too. And take care of that family of yours."

Charley stepped forward and shook my hand, too, looking solemn. "Thanks for the good times, Bill," he said. "Hope we'll see you again someday."

They got up on their horses and I got on mine, and we put our spurs to them, cantering off into the night that was just barely beginning to turn into day—me in one direction, and them in another. I was riding away from a way of life I'd known for nearly five years—but today it felt like fifty. I rode hard for home, my bad foot aching in the stirrup and my head throbbing, and I felt like I was a hundred. There had been a time I'd thought robbing trains and banks would keep me feeling young forever, but maybe, in the end, all it had done was age me faster.

THIRTY-THREE

"BILL, WAKE UP! You're having a nightmare."

Edith's voice, soft and calm, and her hand on my shoulder, woke me from yet another night of troubled sleep. In my dream I'd been reliving that last day with the gang, only this time the bloom of blood I'd seen come out over Tulsa Jack's shirt had come out over mine as I was shot instead of him. And when I'd felt the bullet hit me, I'd looked up to see not the smug face of a lawman but that vicious sneer of Red Buck's, at the other end of the smoking gun. And then I'd watched him shoot the others one by one, first Creek and Charley, then Dan, and Little Bill, and Dick. I'd felt the blood pouring out of me and my life fading with it, and just before I hit the ground I'd seen him smile and turn his gun on Rebel, calling out to me, "look here, Doolin, I saved a shell for your God-damned nag!"

I let my breath out and put a hand over my face,

disturbed by the vividness of my nightmare—the same one I'd been having for weeks—and exhausted from too many nights interrupted by it. When I put my hand down and opened my eyes I saw Edith sitting there next to me, worry in her big dark eyes. She'd left a lamp burning low on the table by the bed. She did that a lot these days; she knew that either Jay was going to wake her with his fussing or I was, with my nightmares. But good mother and wife that she was, she didn't ever complain about any of it. Instead she just rocked Jay back to sleep, or soothed me until I felt calm enough to lay back down.

I'd been a sorry sight when I'd shown up at the folks' farm, after parting company with Creek and Charley. I was dirty and bedraggled and downtrodden, sick over everything that had happened and yet filled with a feverish desire to firm up some kind of plan in my mind to get us away from there. I hadn't intended to tell Edith anything about those last few days, but when she'd come to meet me at the barn she'd watched me pull the tack off the bad-tempered chestnut mare I'd stolen, and she'd asked me where Rebel was. And I'd told her how I'd had to shoot him after he'd ruined his leg, fleeing from a posse, and how Tulsa Jack had died and how I'd decided I was done with the gang. I didn't tell her about Red Buck, or the preacher. Wasn't anything in the world I could say that would make her understand *that.*

She'd just listened to me, saying nothing. And when I'd finally stopped talking, she'd come over to me where I stood outside the chestnut's stall, and she'd put her arms around me, silently. We'd stood there like that, holding each other, until she finally pulled away and took my hand, leading me to the house.

I'd bathed after supper, but even as I washed away all the dirt and grit on me I found I couldn't make my mind feel clean. My thoughts were tangling themselves into a giant snarl and I couldn't sort any one of them out. That night I'd had the nightmare for the first time, and it seemed I was destined to be plagued by it from then on.

"Are you all right, now?" Edith asked me, her hand gently stroking the back of my neck. Her voice brought me back to the present and I nodded slowly, taking a good deep breath. When I looked at her again I saw her eyes searching my face, like she was looking for something there. "You've got rings under your eyes, Bill," she said in a small voice. "You *must* get a good night's sleep, sooner or later."

I gave her a wry half-smile. "Think it's bound to be later, honey, based on the way things've been going." She didn't smile back; she clearly saw nothing funny about the situation. In truth neither did I, but I had to make light of it, or I'd lose my mind.

I pushed the quilt back and stood up, going in my long nightshirt to the crib and peering in at Jay, who was sleeping soundly, for once. He was just over a year old now and starting to say words, and his days of sleeping so well for Edith seemed to have passed, likely because I slept so poorly and was always waking him up. I knew I risked waking him up now, but I couldn't help myself—only Edith's soothing touch and the sight of Jay sleeping peaceful could calm me down enough, after the nightmare, to go back to sleep myself.

I watched Jay for a minute, then went to the window, standing just to the side of it as I peered out, rather than square in front of it. I always did that now, whenever I was in a building, in case someone was waiting outside to shoot me. The hair rose on the back of my neck and I peered hard out into the darkness, straining my eyes to see something that wasn't really there.

In the bed, Edith still sat, leaning back on one hand she had pressed into the featherbed behind her, as she watched me. "Bill," she said quietly but firmly, "come back to bed. There's nothing out there that's not supposed to be."

I looked again, anyway, then came back to bed,

getting back under the quilts and laying there, stiffly, until I finally began to relax. Edith lowered the wick of the lamp so it was barely lit, then laid back down beside me, facing me, her hand laying over mine in between us. Just before I drifted off I put my other hand against my chest, half-expecting to feel the warmth of my own blood seeping through the muslin of my nightshirt.

THIRTY-FOUR

"BILL, I THINK you had better come inside," Edith said to me soberly on the third of May, just before the noon hour.

I turned in the stall I'd been mucking out and leaned the pitchfork against the wall of the barn, alarmed by her grim tone. Gently slapping Mr. Ellsworth's bay mare on the hip to get her to move over, I came out of the stall and refastened the rope that closed it off.

"What's the matter, honey?" I asked her, lifting up my hat and wiping my wrist across my dampening brow.

Her expression got even more grim. "Pa's just come back from town, and he's brought the paper," she told me. "There's an article there you need to see, right away." She was twisting her hands in her apron as she spoke. I felt my stomach drop a little. Clearly, whatever was in that article wasn't any sort of good news.

When we came out of the barn I pushed my hat as far down on my head as it would go, hunching over a little to hide my height and better conceal my features. I knew I couldn't stay indoors all the time; there were chores to do and stock to take care of, but I was trying to be as inconspicuous as possible whenever I did go outside. I'd seen nothing suspicious around the farm since I'd arrived there, but even so, I couldn't shake the feeling that I was being hunted out somehow, like an animal.

Mrs. Ellsworth was in the parlor when we came in, holding Jay on her hip and standing with Mr. Ellsworth. They both shot quick, guarded looks at one another, then at me. Neither of them said anything. Edith looked at her Pa and asked, "where is it?" He gestured, silently, to the little table in between the rocking chairs, and on it sat a copy of the *Guthrie Daily Leader.* Edith picked it up, but instead of giving it to me, she headed for our bedroom. Puzzled and even more worried, I hung up my hat and went after her.

Edith stood aside to let me pass into the room, and once I was inside it she shut the door and faced me. I felt my brow furrow as I watched her. "Edith, what in God's name—"

"It's Creek and Charley, Bill," she said very quietly. "The paper says they were killed yesterday."

Her big brown eyes stayed locked on mine, and they were full of sadness, and sympathy.

I felt the blood drain from my face. "Then the paper must be wrong," I shot back at her, quick and firm. My heart felt like it was beating a little faster than usual.

She kept looking at me with that pitying expression. "It isn't, Bill. It says their bodies were brought into Guthrie this morning, and they've been identified by several people." She was holding out the paper to me, but I didn't take it. I just stood there, rooted, unable to get what she was telling me through my thick skull. *Not Creek.* Anyone but Creek.

"They were shot up when they arrived at the Dunn place," she told me, and I felt the blood start to pound in the vein at my temple. *The Dunn place.* Just like I'd predicted.

Edith was still talking, but all of the sudden I couldn't stand it any longer, to have her tell me how Creek and Charley died, in that calm, sympathetic tone of voice. I put my hands up, quick, stopping her in mid-sentence.

"Don't...don't tell me any more of what the God-damned paper says, Edith," I managed to get out, but my voice came out choked and rough, a tone I never had used with her before. She went real still, her eyes huge in her peaked face, and shut her mouth in a hard line. I swallowed so hard it hurt. "Just put the paper down, and I will read it for myself," I said, in a harsh voice that was just above a whisper.

I saw a flash of hurt in her eyes as she put the paper down on the edge of the bed, but I couldn't tell her I was sorry. I couldn't do anything right then, except stand there while she quietly left the room, shutting the door behind her after her skirts swished through the doorframe. I heard her footsteps receding up the hallway toward the front of the house. Once they'd faded, I reached over and picked up the paper. The headline read:

Lucky Lay of the Last Looters.
Outlaws George Newcomb and Charley Pierce
Succumb After Battle.
Cleverly Surrounded and Filled With Bullets.

Numbly I read over the long article, but I only retained bits of it: Creek and Charley, bought to-gether in a covered wagon to Marshal Nix's office. Creek shot five times, Charley filled with so much buckshot they didn't bother to count it all. Charley's eyes still open. Creek's skull blown apart, his brains showing. Even their horses had been shot. Some up-start, newly-commissioned deputy marshal I'd never heard of named Sam Shaffer was smugly claiming responsibility for it all—and thereby claiming the rewards on their heads. The paper said he'd walked into Marshal Nix's office and asked for "just one trial at those fellows." Nix had deputized him right then and there, then likely put his city-shined boots back up on his fancy-Dan desk and waited like a king on a throne while this Shaffer bastard did his dirty work for him. I tossed the paper down and staggered over to the wash-stand, hunching over and heaving my guts out into the bowl.

My stomach kept on turning over long after it was empty, and it was a good long while before I stopped retching into the bowl. Water was pouring out of my eyes and I felt dizzy, like I was going to keel over. I'd seen my share of death in this lifetime; I'd even caused some myself when I'd had to, but somehow none of it struck me quite the same way reading those callous, gloating sentences did. Creek and Charley had been my *friends*, both of them, and now their corpses were being put on display for the public to gawk at, just like they'd done with the Daltons, and with Ol, and Tulsa Jack, and Will. Shakily I shut my eyes against the image and stood against the wall, trying to steady myself. Then I slid down it until I was sitting against it, on the floor be-tween the bed and wash-stand, my knees drawn up against my chest.

I stayed there like that until my head stopped spinning and my stomach stopped flopping around. Then I got slowly to my feet and rinsed out my mouth and tossed the contents of the wash-basin out the window. Afterward I picked up the paper again and tried to read everything I hadn't been able to take in the first time. The paper had a completely fictional account of the Dover job, and it said Creek was the one had killed Preacher Godfrey when we were fleeing. It also accused Creek and Charley of vile intentions toward two young women at a farm-house they were said to have stopped at after Dover. I felt rage come up in me at that until I was crushing the edges of the paper in my hands. Marshal Nix knew that such disgusting lies were what the masses wanted to hear; no doubt the son of a bitch had told the paper to put that lurid little bit in. And they *were* lies—I'd never once seen Creek or Charley treat a woman disrespectful—not even the whores in the cheapest cribs in Ingalls. The article mentioned me, too, gloating that I was now the sole remaining member of the "original Dalton Gang" and implying that I would be next.

I took the front page of that paper and crumpled it up into a ball, then put it in the wash-basin. I pulled a match from the little tin next to the lamp, and I touched it to the paper, watching as the flame slowly consumed it and turned it to soot. *Like hell,* they would get me next!

For a long time after the paper had burned down to ashes in the basin, I paced the bedroom floor, my mind working furiously, my anger and sorrow at Creek and Charley's deaths simmering just below the surface of my thoughts, pushing their way stubbornly through the plans I was trying to make. I still couldn't believe that big-hearted, devil-may-care Creek, with his great rolling laugh, his dancing eyes and his hunting-fox grin was gone, just like that. It seemed sort of fitting to me, in a way, that surly yet loyal little Charley had died alongside him, since they'd always been in each others' company as long as I'd known them.

I stopped in my pacing for a minute and shut my eyes, drawing in a big lungful of air. Just like with Will and Tulsa Jack before them, there was nothing I could do for Creek and Charley now, except to remember them for their good friendship and the loyalty they'd always shown me, and to keep myself out of the grip of those that had taken them down and now wanted to put me under, too. Someday when I was old, and if I ever got the charges on my head cleared somehow, if anyone ever asked me about Will or Tulsa Jack or Creek and Charley, I'd tell them what good friends they'd all been to me. Maybe in doing that I could bring some humanity back to their memories, instead of letting folks remember them as cold-blooded, murderous robbers who'd got what was due them for their crimes.

Feeling like I had come to terms a bit with the shock of it all, I resumed my pacing, and my planning. The article had said they thought I was hiding in Payne County; they knew I was nearby, it seemed. If Marshal Nix was deputizing any God-damned Tom, Dick or Harry that came into his office and asked for a commission, then anyone and their brother could try his hand at taking me down and claiming the sizeable reward on my head. The time had come to get Edith and Jay away from Lawson—and I'd wait no later than that very night to leave.

I went over to where I'd left my watch on the dresser, and opened the case. It showed two-fifteen, which shocked me a little; seemed I'd been pacing and fuming over Creek and Charley for over two hours without realizing it. I'd missed dinner, but I didn't care. I strode over to the bedroom door and went out, coming up the hall to the doorway of the front room. Edith was sitting in one of the rocking chairs, her face tilted downward as she held Jay on her lap and rocked him, and her Ma was sitting in the other one, knitting on something, her head bent over the swiftly-moving needles that made soft clicking noises as she worked.

I cleared my throat. "Edith, I need to speak with you a minute," I said almost briskly. Her head came up quick and she looked at me in surprise, her expression a little guarded, like she wasn't sure what she might see in my face. Her Ma looked up, too, and her eyes went from my face to Edith's and back again, her knitting needles frozen in her hands.

Edith stood up and quickly came to me, and I turned and led the way into the bedroom, letting her in and then shutting the door behind her. She set Jay down in the middle of the bed and turned to face me, her eyes warily searching my face.

"We're leaving here," I told her abruptly. "Tonight."

Her eyes widened, and her face went a little pale. I saw her take in a steadying breath before she spoke. "You're taking us with you, this time?"

I had been getting out the box of bullets I had hidden in the chest of drawers to fill up my gun belt, but at her words I stopped and felt myself, for the first time ever, begin to feel impatient with her. "Of course I am, Edith! For God's sake, I ain't going to leave you and Jay here—the three of us are leaving for good! I ain't aiming to stay and let that smug son of a bitch Nix send his deputies out and fill me up with lead the way they did to Creek and Charley!"

Her face crumpled and she broke into tears, raising her hands to her face, and I felt lower than the lowest creature in God's creation right about then. I put the box of cartridges down and went over to her, taking her by the shoulders and drawing her against me, putting my arms around her and resting my chin on the top of her head. "I'm sorry, honey. I'm sorry I was sharp with you. But I can't take being away from you and Jay any longer, and it ain't safe for me to stay here anymore. You read that paper, same as me. You see they're saying plain as day that I'm the one their aiming to put away next." I kept my voice low and soothing. "So I got to take you with me. We're going to start us a new life, honey, like we talked about. Remember, when we were coming here before Jay was born?" I kept stroking her back as I held her.

I felt her nod. "I just hate to see you so angry, Bill," she told me in a small voice, her tears slowing some. She wouldn't look at me.

"I know, sweetheart," I told her, taking her face in both my hands and pressing my lips to her forehead. "I don't much like being angry, either. But they're killing my friends, and calling me out, and there's only so much I can take."

She took in a shaky gulp of air and put her hands up to my face, same as I was doing to her. I felt her soft little palms against the stubble of beard that was starting to grow back over my jaw, and her eyes, still wet around the edges but filled now with that steadying, loving gaze that had always braced me in hard times, locked onto mine. "I'll start packing, and we will be ready to leave whenever you say," she told me, quietly yet firmly.

I leaned in and kissed her then, quickly, on the mouth this time. "We'll need to travel pretty light," I told her. "Pack up some clothes and whatever else you and Jay can't do without, and I'll speak with your Ma and Pa. We'll leave after supper," I told her.

As I was going out the bedroom door she called softly to me and I turned back. "I'm so sorry, Bill," she told me softly, "about Creek and Charley."

I looked away from her and collected myself before I answered, "so am I." Then I went out, closing the door behind me.

＝＝＝((()))＝＝＝

Late that night Edith's Pa helped me put the wagon-bows and the canvas cover onto our wagon, and hitch our old mare, Sally, and the stolen chestnut mare from the Dover job to it by the poor light of the moon and a single lantern hung near the barn door. We needed a team of horses to make good time, and I wouldn't leave the stolen mare at the Ellsworth's farm in case the law came snooping around and somehow recognized it as belonging to the old preacher, Godfrey. While we got the harness on them and backed them into place, Edith stood on the porch with her Ma, Jay bundled up in a blanket in her arms.

Mr. Ellsworth didn't say much as we worked, and he had a deep furrow between his brows. I knew he was worried about what would happen to Edith and his grand-baby, but he knew that we had to go. Staying would be the same as suicide, for me.

"Whoa, Sally," I murmured, fastening the traces. The ornery chestnut mare, who Edith had started calling Lady, pinned her ears and tried to nip at her, but I stopped her with a sharp word.

Once we got them hitched up proper, I started bringing the valises and bundles of bedding and putting them in the wagon box. Then I put in our food and cooking supplies, a bag of oats for the horses, and my tack. Last of all I put my loaded rifle under the wagon-seat where I could reach it quick if I needed to. Pretty soon there was nothing left to do but leave, so I went to the porch to get Edith and Jay.

Edith was talking softly with her Ma, and when I came up onto the porch with them they hugged each other tight, somehow managing not to crush Jay between them. Mrs. Ellsworth had tears in her eyes; I could see them by the light of the lamp hung by the front door. She leaned down and kissed the top of Jay's head, then ran her hand over his soft blond hair. "Good-bye, my darling little boy," she said tearfully. "You be an angel for your Ma and Pa." She looked up at Edith and kissed her softly on the cheek. Edith gave her a sad little smile and turned to hug her Pa.

Mrs. Ellsworth turned to me then and I wondered if tonight would be the night she might finally take to disapproving of me, seeing as how I was fleeing her home in the middle of the night and taking her daughter and grandchild away with me. But like she'd always been since I'd married Edith, she was nothing but warm. She embraced me and let me kiss her cheek and thank her for all she'd done for us.

"I'm sorry we have to go like this," I told her quietly, "but I can't see any way around it."

She looked at me square in the lamplight, raising her chin a little in that bold manner she had. "You must stay safe, so of course you must get away from here," she said. "I've never told you this before, Bill, but I simply cannot believe what the papers have said about you. I know you're a good man who hasn't done what they say you have," she added stoutly.

I couldn't help affording myself the wry little smile that came up on my face when she said that last bit. If she only knew! But it warmed me to know that like her daughter, this good woman somehow saw something in me that was worth caring about, in spite of my pretty blackened reputation. I caught her eye again. "I promise I'll keep them safe," I vowed, and I meant it. She gave me a short nod, fingering the heavy gold cross she wore around her neck as she did so.

Mr. Ellsworth had finished hugging Edith, and after kissing her on the cheek and Jay on the top of the head, as his wife had done, he turned to me and held out his hand. "I will pray for you," he said gravely, as I shook it.

"Thank you. I expect I can use as many of those as I can get," I said dryly. He seemed unable to say more, so I held out my arm to Edith and began to escort her to the wagon. She settled Jay down in the little bed she'd made for him, just behind the spring-seat.

Just as I'd helped her up onto the seat, I heard Mr. Ellsworth's voice behind me from the porch, after he'd cleared his throat. "I'll keep Black Devil for you, for when you get back out this way," he said, and I turned and threw him a smile. I knew we might not be back out this way for a long time, if ever, and I knew *he* knew it, too—but I let him hold onto the hope.

"Much obliged," I said. I got up onto the seat beside Edith and flicked the reins across the horses' backs, and they started off. Before we got too far down the road, Edith turned and leaned around the wagon-cover to wave at them, and I knew they were still standing on the porch, watching us go.

After she'd turned back to face the horses and had looked into the wagon box to check on Jay, who'd already fallen asleep, she looked over at me. "Where are we going, Bill?" she asked me, keeping her voice real soft to keep from waking Jay.

"Kansas," I told her, then clicked my tongue at the horses and put them into a trot.

THIRTY-FIVE

LONG AGO DURING my cowpunching days, when I took the herds to Abilene or Wichita on the big drives, I would pass through a section of Crowley County in Kansas that I liked. There were acres of farmland there, the nearest neighbors were many miles away from one another, and life seemed to move at a slow, unassuming pace. Folks there stuck to their farms, only venturing into town when they had to, and they didn't seem to pay much attention to anything but their crops or their stock. I thought I could blend in there, pass for nothing more than another farmer and his family on the move to good, fertile land. Now that the Wild Bunch was a thing of the past for me and so many of the men I'd ridden with were in their coffins, I was holding out hope that in time Nix and the Three Guardsmen might find other things to focus on, if I kept to myself and stayed on the right side of the law. We would camp there until things died down a bit. Eventually I could plan for our new life in Mexico or South America, and we'd leave the country, but for now, the farmland near Burden would do nicely.

It wasn't easy going, in the beginning. If I'd thought traveling with a woman expecting a baby had been trying, I found out pretty quick that traveling with a one-year-old child was even harder. Jay was a good little boy, most of the time, but there were limits, and when he got tired or in a temper it was often all Edith could do to quiet him enough so's he wouldn't wake the dead with his screaming. I knew all children had those times but it made me nervous, because I was afraid the sound of his cries would call more attention to us than I wanted.

On top of it all, I couldn't rest easy until we were well away from all of the gang's old haunts. During the day I drove as far as I dared push the horses, stopping only for mealtimes and to water and feed the team. At night I kept watch, all four of the guns I owned at hand, while Edith and Jay slept in the shelter of the wagon-cover. It wasn't long before this arrangement started to wear on me, and one day as we'd just crossed the Arkansas River into Osage County, I found myself fighting to stay awake. In fact, I nearly fell off the wagon seat until Edith caught my arm and hauled me back into an upright position.

"Bill, stop the horses," she said firmly, and, shaking myself back awake, I did. "This must stop— you've got to get some rest," she told me. "Lay down in the wagon and I'll take the reins," she said, no room for argument in her tone. Her face, far back in her sunbonnet, was set in determination.

"Sally's all right but Lady's a lot to handle, Edith," I protested weakly. I wanted to sleep so badly I could hardly bear it, but I didn't want her getting hurt.

She gave me a look. "I've been driving horses and mules all my life, Bill," she chided. "I can handle her." And she reached over and took the lines from me, deftly weaving them between her fingers.

I was too tired to protest any further, so I crawled into the wagon box and laid down on the bed that Edith had fashioned out of a straw-tick and some quilts. Jay was sitting up on its edge and he scoot-ed himself toward me, stretching out a chubby little hand. "Papa," he said clearly.

I smiled. That had been his first word, and though he'd said it dozens of times since, along with "Mama" and a few others that didn't always make a lot of sense, I never grew tired of hearing him say it.

"Join your Pa for a nap, Jay," I said drowsily. I settled him down next to me, and just before I closed my eyes I saw Edith glance back at us, smiling affectionately at the sight, before she started the horses forward again.

⸻ ⟨◉⟩ ⸻

Things got a little easier after that; Edith often drove during the day so I could rest up enough to keep watch at night. But I didn't always sleep well; the old nightmare didn't come anymore but it had been replaced by a new one in which I felt my body get pierced by dozens of bullets at once, fired by a lawman whose face I could never see clearly. Edith was always in the dream, running toward me and screaming with grief as I fell, but too late to do anything. I always woke up before she reached me.

Edith was worried about me; she fussed over me even more than usual, watching like a hawk to make sure I ate well and got as much sleep as our traveling—and my nightmares—would allow. Crossing into Kansas helped ease my mind some, and in the evenings after that I stopped being so keyed up and jumpy while we ate or rested after supper.

One night after Jay was asleep in the wagon, Edith and I sat together in the grass by the fire, finishing our coffee. I'd had a few days' peace from my nightmares, and we were making good progress toward our destination, so my mood had improved a sight by then. I teased her as we sat together, feeling like a little bit of the weight I'd been carrying around on my shoulders from being hunted out had started to lift.

Before long, though, I noticed that Edith's answering smile didn't reach her eyes and she had little lines of worry in her forehead. Something was bothering her pretty good; I could tell, and instead of getting ready to keep watch for the night I reached over and took her hands, making her face me. "Edith, what's the matter?" I asked her, keeping my voice good and gentle.

She went still for a minute, looking away from me, then set her mouth and looked me in the eyes. "Would you ever consider turning yourself in to answer the charges against you, Bill?"

I stared at her in total shock. Never in my wildest imagination would I have thought she would ever ask me something like that, and it took me a good while before I could get my voice to work proper so I could answer her. "Edith—"

"I've been keeping something from you," she burst out, more distressed than I'd ever seen her, and I let go of her hands, feeling my body stiffen as I stared warily at her.

"What?" I asked softly, but my voice sounded

steely and sharp, like the edge of a knife blade. The hair rose up on the back of my neck and my pulse started to race a bit.

She took in a breath; I could see she was trying to compose herself. She wasn't crying, but her voice sounded like she wanted to pretty bad. "Back when you brought me home, after...after Ingalls," she said in a rush, "a man came out to the farm in January, asking to speak with me. I'd never seen him before, but I knew he was a lawman. He had a badge."

The night sounds, the crickets and the cicadas and the crackle of the flames in the little fire, seemed to fade in and out of my ears in a queer fashion, and I felt my palms dampen. She kept talking, fast. "It was Marshal Tilghman," she told me. "He questioned me about you, said that he'd heard in circles that I knew you, and that some had even told him we were married. He told me that I should speak to you and tell you that the Department of Justice wanted you to turn yourself in and have your day in court for what happened that day in Ingalls. He wanted me to convince you to do it." She was wringing her hands in her lap, twisting her wedding ring around and around her finger as she spoke. "I took my ring off before I spoke with him, I had a shawl on that hid...my condition. I told him he was misinformed, that I had never met you, nor even seen you before. He believed me, Bill,

I could tell he did. He went away and never came back to bother me again."

I had to work pretty damned hard to find my voice, and when I did it came out real soft. "Why didn't you *tell* me?" I demanded, thrown for such a big loop I didn't think I'd ever recover from it.

She kept twisting her ring around; it sparkled in the firelight and she fixated on it, so she wouldn't have to look me in the face. "I didn't know where you *were,* Bill!" she replied, that tear in her voice getting bigger. She blinked a few times, fast. "And then when you *did* come home, Jay was born, and I'd missed you so much—" she choked and bowed her head a minute before continuing, "I couldn't bear to worry you any more than you already were," she said. "I know I should have told you then, but I knew if I did you'd leave us again…and I just couldn't bear to have you go that way. I was afraid you'd be angry with me for speaking with him at all—but I *had* to, Bill! If I refused to speak with him he would've surely suspected that I was hiding something!" Her eyes were good and wet, now.

"It's all right, Edith," I heard myself say, and I was surprised how calm my voice sounded. Some of the shock was wearing off a little and I knew she was right—there was nothing she could've done but what she had. And I'd been in Pawnee that January, holding up the Farmers and Citizens Bank with the rest of the gang. There was no way she could've told me so it would've made any difference.

She stopped twirling her ring and looked at me, her eyes still brimming with tears but now filled with hope. "It is?"

"Of course it is, honey," I told her with a sigh, reaching out and folding one of her hands in both of mine, trying to reassure her. "You did the only thing you could've done."

She came and sat close to me, and leaned her cheek against my shoulder while I put my arms around her. "I'll tell you true, Edith: back when I was first starting out, there wasn't any way in hell I would've even thought about turning myself in. I would've rather died than surrender." I put my hand up and stroked the silken strands of her hair as I talked, unable to help myself. "But now that I got you and Jay, I'd like to clear my name, some-how; not have to live like this anymore. But I don't know if that will ever happen, sweetheart. It may be that we'll have to leave the country one day, to get away from it all. And I want us to be prepared for that." I turned my head awkwardly and kissed her temple. "We'll have us that cattle ranch yet, honey. I just don't rightly know where it'll be, at the moment."

Later on, as she was settling down under the quilt beside Jay, I told her softly, just before she went to sleep, "from now on, if anyone asks, our name is Wilson. Tom and Lillian."

THIRTY-SIX

"WILL THAT BE all, then, Mr. Wilson?"

I turned from where I'd been glancing out the window of the general store in Burden and faced the counter, and the storekeeper. "Yes, that's everything," I answered evenly, watching as he took his pencil from behind his ear and wrote up the charges for the supplies I was buying—bacon, coffee, flour and cornmeal.

While he wrote I discreetly watched the other customers in the store; two men and an older woman. The men never glanced my way; they were examining the new plows the storekeeper had ordered from back East, but the woman, I thought, was stealing too many glances at me for my liking. I looked back at the storekeeper, wishing he'd hurry the hell up so I could get back outside, where Edith and Jay were waiting, bundled snugly in the wagon tied at the hitching rail.

In truth I knew I was making mountains out of molehills; we'd been living outside of Burden for over six months now and I'd never been bothered before. I came into town every few weeks for supplies, usually buying them at this very store, and I'd never felt like anyone was looking at me funny, the way I did today. I knew I looked a little bedraggled; I was thin, my coat was getting pretty threadbare and my heavy beard needed trimming badly besides. I'd been saving every dime I could since we'd left Oklahoma, going without new clothes and other luxuries so I'd have that much more money toward getting us our new life. We'd had a quiet and peaceful time in Kansas with no sign of the law, so I felt like the uproar over Creek and Charley's murders, and over the gang itself, might be dying down just a little.

The law sure as hell hadn't forgotten about us, though; we were still being hunted down like animals, one by one. It had been with dismay that I had learned Little Bill Raidler had been arrested by Bill Tilghman in September after he'd been shot up in a gunfight with the marshal near Pawhuska. They'd put him on trial, wounded though he was, and he'd been convicted for his part in the robbery at Dover. They'd given him ten years. When I'd read that, I'd set to firming up my plans to flee the country.

I planned to leave Kansas in spring, when the

weather was better, and travel through Socorro County in New Mexico, where I knew we'd find a measure of safe haven as we headed for the border. So far we'd had a pretty mild winter all in all, but I didn't fancy traveling so far in the cold and snow, not with Jay being so young and my bad foot plaguing me all to hell. My rheumatism was at its worst in weather like this and there were some mornings I could barely walk, the pain was so bad. It seemed to get worse every year. The Cimarron train robbery and the gunfight I'd gotten it in seemed to have happened a lifetime ago, instead of just two years.

"Looks like it might snow," the storekeeper commented to me, as he added the small column of figures, drawing my attention again.

"Looks that way," I agreed, glancing back out at the iron-gray sky, then letting my eyes drift to the wagon. Edith was holding Jay on her lap, though he really was getting too big for that now, at almost two. He was watching a perky little black-and-tan dog that was trotting along the gallery, and he had a big grin on his face. I smiled affectionately, then noticed the older woman watching me again as she drifted toward the dry goods. I looked uncomfortably away and shifted my weight from boot to boot; the movement sent tendrils of agony up my bad leg and I winced.

"You ever thought of taking the spring treatment for your foot there, Tom?" the storekeeper asked me as I handed him some money. "They got bathhouses in Arkansas that are supposed to work wonders for rheumatism."

I nodded as I took the paper-wrapped packages by their string ties. I'd seen a doctor in Burden a few weeks back for my foot, unable to bear the agony as I'd always done. He'd mentioned the sulfur baths in Eureka Springs, too, as the best chance I had at relief. "I'll have to try it, sometime," I told him. "Much obliged, Frank."

"You take care, now," he answered, and turned to help the woman, pulling down a bolt of flannel for her to look at. I left the store as quick as my foot would let me, but I couldn't shake the feeling of her gaze on my back.

Edith reached down to take some of the packages and put them in the wagon. She glanced first at me, then at the store, then back at me again, worry in her eyes. "Is everything all right?" she asked me in a low voice, seeing the disquiet on my face.

"Everything's fine," I told her, not wanting her to worry. I went around to the other side of the wagon, preparing to climb up on the seat after I'd untied the team.

"Papa, look!" Jay said to me, pointing enthusiastically

at the little dog as it continued on its way, its nose lowered busily to the planks of the gallery, its tail stuck straight in the air.

"That's a fine little dog, Jay," I said to him, chucking him under the chin as I gathered up the reins. "We'll have to get you a pup of your own, one of these days." I flicked the reins across the horses' backs, and they started forward, heading out of town and back toward our camp.

⸻ ((◍)) ⸻

"Bill, there's a wagon coming."

Edith's voice was tense and her hands, holding onto the sides of the washtub where she'd been washing our clothes, were white-knuckled. Jay, who'd been playing with some rocks nearby, looked up at her, puzzled.

I tensed, too, and looked up from where I'd been cleaning my guns, just inside the tent made from the canvas wagon-cover. About a quarter-mile out I could see a wagon being pulled by a matched team of bays, traveling straight toward our camp. There was a woman driving it, and another sat on the seat beside her. When they got a little closer I recognized the woman sitting beside the driver—it was the older woman who'd been staring at me in the general store the previous week.

I reached for the revolver I'd just loaded and laid down on the straw-tick inside the tent, flat on my stomach, out of sight of anyone outside. We rarely saw folks pass by our little hollow, and the fact that that woman who'd been eyeballing me was in it had me good and worried. "Edith, stay calm and act natural," I told her hurriedly, drawing a quilt up over me and staying as still as a stone. I cocked the hammer back, slow, on the gun and waited, holding my breath.

The sound of horses' hooves on hard ground came closer, and the rattle of wagon-wheels. After a bit I heard a woman say, "whoa," and the creak of a wagon-brake being set.

"Good afternoon," I heard a female voice say pleasantly. "It's Mrs. Wilson, isn't it?"

"Yes, good afternoon," Edith replied evenly.

"We've never been introduced, have we?" the stranger said. "I'm Elizabeth Howard, and this is Eva Moore. Her husband is the Reverend at the church in town, and my husband Frank owns the general store where you folks get your supplies."

"Nice to meet you both," Edith said, still managing to sound completely normal. I was proud of her. "I'm Lillian."

"Is your husband here, dear?" the Reverend's wife asked. I thought she sounded suspicious, but my mind could've been playing tricks on me.

"No, he's gone hunting," Edith said smoothly.

"You're probably wondering why we've come to see you," Mrs. Howard said kindly. "The fact is, Eva and I and some of the other ladies have seen you and your family when you come into town, and it's clear you're in need of a little neighborliness. We felt bad, knowing you're roughing it out here like this, with your sweet little boy, and, well, we took up a little collection for you at church last Sunday. We'd like you to have it; perhaps it will make things a little easier for you. Times are so hard these days, it's sometimes difficult to get by without some help."

There was a short silence in which imagined I could feel Edith's shock—and embarrassment. "That's very kind of you," she stammered, "but it's not necessary."

"Of course it is, dear," Mrs. Moore said firmly. I could tell by her tone and the volume of her voice that she was a hell of a lot pushier than her companion, and probably wore the britches in her family to boot. "Good Christians help one another in times of need."

"Oh, but really, I don't think—"

"Don't you say another word about it," the

Reverend's wife said in what I thought was a pretty condescending tone. "Our church-members have donated supplies and warm clothes, and there is some cash here besides. It does us all in the congregation some good to know we've helped out a neighbor; makes us feel as though we're doing the Lord's work properly, as is His will."

Damned old pea-hen, I thought in irritation. *She ain't even hiding the fact that she's doing this more for herself—to score points with the Almighty—than she is for us.* My fingers curled more tightly around the handle of my gun.

"Well—thank you," Edith said weakly, wisely deciding not to fight the old bat any further on the subject. I was getting mad—and more than a little spooked, besides. Seemed like folks were paying a bit too much attention to us—and it seemed like my little idea of keeping ourselves to ourselves wasn't going to work any longer.

"No thanks are needed, honey," Mrs. Howard said. "Perhaps when you've decided to settle down, you'll come and join us one Sunday. The Reverend Moore gives the most inspiring services."

'My husband and l will surely consider it," Edith said politely. I chanced moving just a little bit and peered out of the tent at them, still clutching my revolver in a death's grip. The two women were getting up into their wagon, and a minute later Mrs. Howard clucked her tongue at the bays, starting them off in the direction of town. Edith just stood there, watching them, her arms crossed over her chest. There was a big bundle at her feet, along with a dry-goods box and a little cloth sack. Jay was standing close by her, hiding behind her skirts as he, too, watched the wagon grow smaller. Pretty soon it disappeared around a strand of trees, and I slowly let the hammer down on my gun and got to my feet, ducking out of the tent.

Edith turned and looked at me with a disturbed expression as I came up beside her. "I suppose you heard all of that," she said softly.

"Yes, I heard it," I said grimly, sliding my gun back into the holster I wore under my left arm. "And I didn't much like it, for a fact."

"Will we push on, then?" she asked me. I narrowed my eyes a bit as I watched the empty road, half-expecting a posse to appear where the wagon had been. I felt gooseflesh raise on my arms and my trigger-finger itched in a way it hadn't done since the last gunfight I was in, after Dover. There was more to this than simple charity. How I knew, I couldn't say, but I was suddenly sure of it.

"No, Edith," I said, my voice still grim. I moved back toward the tent and reached for my gun belt, which I'd left laying just inside the door. I fastened it snugly around my waist. "I'm leaving here, tonight, and after a while's gone by, you and Jay are getting on the train to Lawson," I told her, my voice coming out hard. "You're going back to the farm, without me, for a time."

"What?" she cried, one hand going against her throat and her eyes growing round in surprise.

"This ain't just a case of folks thinking we need their damned charity," I said insistently, digging my saddlebags out from where I'd stashed them under our extra quilts. I threw them over my shoulder and limped over to the back of the wagon, taking out my extra boxes of cartridges and beginning to load up my Winchester. "The law's out after me, still, and if we stay here like this, all of us together, Tilghman or Thomas or Madsen is going to hunt me up. I'm sure of it." My voice came out hard.

She put a hand to the top of Jay's head as he clutched at her skirts and leaned against her hip, watching me with big eyes and putting his fingers in his mouth. Edith was too distracted to move his hand away and pull them out, as she usually did. "But Bill, they were just women from the church in Burden," she pointed out, her voice coming out a little shrill. I could tell she was panicked at the idea of leaving for home without me but I had to send her back—and hope that the lawmen dogging my heels would follow her, so I could get away. I had to run, to stay free. Staying and making a fight would only mean a long nap in a coffin—or prison. Neither one appealed much to me.

"I don't understand, Bill," Edith said to me in a small voice, coming up to my side and touching my arm. "You said you couldn't take being away from us any longer. That we were going to finally start a new life."

I finished loading the rifle and snapped it shut with a sharp flick of my wrist. "I know I did, honey. And both of those things are still true. But I thought we could stay out of folks' minds here, and it looks like we can't. I ain't aiming to leave you at the home farm for long. Just long enough to throw the damned lawdogs off the scent."

She heard what I was saying, but I could see she didn't agree with me none. She tightened her grip on my arm, and I felt her fingers digging into my flesh. "Let's just go, then," she said urgently. "To Mexico, or farther. Like we were planning." There was a pleading note to her voice.

I stopped messing with my guns; I set the rifle down on its stock and leaned it against the wagon. Then I reached over and gently pried her fingers from my arm, turning to face her and holding her hand so she'd look at me. "Edith, listen to me. There's someone after me; I can *feel* it. If we leave together, and we're tracked, they'll catch us. They'll lock me up so fast it'll make your head spin—or worse. We won't be able to outrun them, traveling with the wagon this way. But if they watch you and Jay, think you're going to lead them to me, I can get away from here. I'll go to Arkansas, up to them sulfur baths the doc told me about. I'll take a bit of that cure for my foot, and after a few weeks' or a month's time, I'll come for you, and we'll go. You got my promise, Edith." I took her slender shoulders in my hands and leaned down a little so I was looking her straight in the eyes. "Don't you trust me, darlin'?"

She bit down on her lower lip. "I've always trusted you, Bill," she told me, almost whispering, "but… I just don't want to go another year without seeing you, and wondering if you're safe. I don't want you to miss out on all of the growing up Jay's going to do." She reached down and hugged him to her with one hand. Tired of being petted, he squirmed against her and ducked out of her grasp, no longer interested in what his Ma and Pa were doing. He went back to his game near the washtub.

Neither of us called him back. I hugged Edith and kissed her. "It ain't gonna be that long," I told her firmly, and I meant it. "I got nothing in this world but you and Jay," I said, "so I'm damned if I'm going to risk leaving you without a husband and Jay without a Pa. It's got to be this way."

She squared her shoulders and composed herself, showing me that strength she always managed to find inside her when times got hard, and she gave me a nod. "If you think it best," she said, "then we'll go to Lawson when you say."

"That's my girl. Take this." I handed her the thick stack of bills I had in my saddlebags. "Keep it safe, Edith. It's everything I've saved."

She frowned at the money. "I will, but you must take some of it with you," she protested.

I gave her a half-smile and picked up the little cloth sack the two women had left. I felt bills in there. "The Burden congregation will pay my way, it seems," I said dryly.

She looked a little disapproving, but I didn't apologize. We couldn't very well give the money back, and she knew it. I knelt down and untied the bundle. There were some women's clothes and some little boy's things, too, but I was most interested in the overcoat folded up at the bottom. It didn't show hardly any wear and was in a hell of a lot better shape than my old one. I stripped off the one I was wearing and put the new one on, glad to see it was a frock-style and hid the two pistols on my hips. I wound the warm woolen muffler Edith had knitted me around my neck and tucked its ends under the coat.

Edith was putting up some food for me to take along. "When will you leave?" she asked me, struggling to hold back her sadness. Her wedding ring caught the dying sunlight and sparkled as she reached up and tucked a stray lock of hair behind her ear.

"In the middle of the night, when it gets good and dark," I told her. "I'm taking Lady. You'll have to leave the wagon and the old mare in Burden," I told her, speaking softly. "Wait a few weeks, then drive into town. Put them up at the livery and see if the owner will buy them. After that, get on the train to Lawson. I don't dare write you, but I'll be back for you and Jay as soon as I can."

———— ◉ ————

Late that night, after the moon had risen and the coyotes were yapping eerily in the brush, I carefully dropped a kiss on the top of Jay's head as he slept soundly, then crept from our tent and led Lady over to the tree nearby, tying her lead line to a low-hanging branch and beginning to saddle her up. Edith checked on Jay one last time, then came out to stand at Lady's head and watch as I cinched the saddle snugly.

She was quiet as she stood there; there wasn't much to say. She didn't want me to go and I didn't much want to, either, but we both knew I had to, and that was that. I brought the headstall over and slipped the bit between the horse's teeth, then tied the saddle-bags and bedroll behind the cantle. Finally, I slid my rifle into the saddle-holster.

When I was done I turned to face her. "I'd better go, honey," I told her softly. "Are you good on clear on what to do?"

She nodded, collecting herself, then stepped closer to me, putting her hands to the back of my neck and drawing my face down for a long kiss. When we parted she slid her hands down against my vest, and she felt the folded-up piece of paper in my vest pocket.

"That's your verse," I told her with a smile, my voice coming out a little husky with emotion.

She gave me a weak smile in return. "I didn't know you were still carrying that," she said, her thick lashes fluttering as she blinked rapidly to hold back tears.

"Of course I am," I told her. "You told me to keep it with me, so that's what I been doing." I put my fingers under her chin and tilted her face up. "You got to be brave for me, honey," I told her quietly. "Keep yourself and Jay safe, and if anyone comes around asking questions, you just keep on with what you told Tilghman the first time. Understand?"

She nodded. I put my hand beneath my coat and drew out the small revolver I'd been wearing under my left arm. "I want you to keep this," I told her. "You'll need protection while I'm gone, just in case. There are shells for it in the tent."

She took the gun a little gingerly, but I knew she could handle it proper if she needed to—I'd taught her how to use it, just after we'd first left Lawson. "I got to go now, Edith."

"Wait a minute." She put the gun down just inside the tent, then came back over and put her arms around me again. I held her close against me, kissed her long again, then reluctantly let her go and untied the mare, putting my foot into the stirrup and mounting up, ignoring the stabs of pain that crawled up my leg at the action.

"I'll see you soon," I told her, looking down at her as she stood back against the tent, a dark shape against the white canvas.

"Stay safe," she replied.

"I will," I told her, then gathered the reins. Pointing the horse's head toward Arkansas, I kicked her into a lope and cantered off, knowing I was doing what I had to do—but hating like hell to do it.

THIRTY-SEVEN

"MAY I HAVE your name, mister?" the young clerk at the Davy Hotel asked, his pencil poised and ready over the register as he waited for me to answer. He had one eyebrow raised at me, and I knew it was because of the way I looked. I made a mental note to visit a barber as soon as possible and get my beard shaved off, so I'd draw less attention to myself.

"Tom Wilson," I answered evenly, shifting my weight to my good foot. The pain in my bad one was so bad after my long journey that it took me twice as long to walk anywhere as usual, and once I got to wherever I was going, my foot would go numb. The short walk from the livery to the hotel had been hell.

"Looks like you've come a long way," the clerk said in a friendly manner as he wrote my alias down, then reached for the key to my room.

"I have, at that," I agreed, and wished he'd hurry up. I didn't want to say too much, but I didn't want to be too surly, either, or else he might get suspicious.

"Have you come for the spring treatment?" he asked, sliding the key across the counter to me. "I couldn't help but notice your limp."

"Yes," I said. "I've heard it works wonders."

He nodded. "Folks come to Eureka Springs from all over the country to take the cure," he said. "You're in fifteen."

I took the key and pocketed it. "You got a barber nearby?" I asked.

"Yessir, just four stores down," he said, pointing toward the other end of town. "Supper's at six in the dining room, if you'd care for a meal," he told me.

"Much obliged." I nodded to him, then limped up the stairs, slowly, to my room.

It was small but neat, with a brass bedstead in one corner and a marble-topped washstand under the window. I tossed my saddlebags onto the bed after taking out my money and tucking it into my vest.

I didn't dare wear my gun belt in town; I hadn't seen a single man wearing them and I knew I'd stick out, going around so heavily-armed. I unbuckled it and tossed it down beside the saddlebags—but not before I'd tucked one of the revolvers into my shoulder-holster. I figured I'd have to go heeled the rest of my life, at the rate my fame—and the price on my head—was growing.

I caught a glimpse of myself in the mirror hung over the wash-stand and I paused a minute, examining my reflection with a frown. Besides the shaggy beard covering the whole lower half of my face and creeping down my neck, and the unruly tendrils of hair poking out from under my hat, I saw lines at the corners of my eyes that I didn't remember ever having been there before. There were dark rings under my eyes, too, and they looked less blue to me than usual—paler, somehow, like the color was fading out of them. *Jesus Christ, I look like I'm eighty,* I thought to myself. Being hunted was starting to show in my face, it seemed. Well, a good shave and a haircut would fix most of it.

As I turned to leave I thought of Edith and Jay with a pang that actually made my chest hurt. I prayed they had made it safely back to her folks' place, and that she hadn't had any trouble along the way. Then I forced myself to put them out of my mind. I hobbled gingerly out of the room and locked the door behind me, tucking the key into my vest pocket along with the money and Edith's verse.

<hr />

Getting my chin scraped, my mustache trimmed and my hair cut lifted my mood considerably, and after a quick meal at the hotel, I hobbled down the gallery to take a look around. Snowflakes were drifting lazily down from the sky, and my breath misted out white in front of me as I walked. The gas lamps along the street were lit, and piano music tinkled out from one of the saloons. As I passed it I got a sudden craving for a drink, so I went inside the swinging doors.

"Evenin,'" the barkeep said, moving down the bar toward me and taking a cigar out of his mouth. He seemed a jolly fellow and he gave me an easy smile. "What'll you have?"

"Whiskey sounds good," I said, coming up to the bar and taking off my hat. There were a few other men in the saloon, but they were busy playing faro and didn't spare me a second glance. The one lone customer seated up to the bar was way down at the other end from where I was, and he just gave me a friendly nod and went back to his drink. The whole air inside the place was mellow and easygoing. Eureka Springs didn't see much in the way of rowdiness, so I'd heard, and it was so unlike the towns I was used to that it gave me pause at the beginning. I felt like I needed to hold my breath and wait for something to happen, but nothing ever did.

"Here you are." The barkeep set a jigger of whiskey in front of me, and I knocked it back. It burned my throat pleasantly, and sent tendrils of warmth through me that took my mind off my foot, some. I put the jigger back down and nodded at it, and he poured me another.

"New in town?" he asked me, as I knocked the second one back and then reached into my coat pocket for some coins.

"Yes, just arrived," I said. "Here for some relief for my rheumatism."

He nodded. "Well, you came to the right place. Them springs are miracle-workers. You want another?" He motioned to the whiskey bottle.

"Two'll do me just fine," I said. I put my money down, then took up my hat. "Much obliged."

"You take care, now," he said in his friendly way, and went to put the bottle away. I put my hat on and went back out, breathing in a few deep lungfuls of the sharp, cold air. I was feeling pretty good as I made my way, slowly, back to the hotel. I might not have my family with me for a time, but it sure looked like maybe I'd made the right choice in coming here.

By the time I'd been in Eureka Springs for a few weeks, I was positive that coming there had been one of the best decisions I'd ever made, because the spring treatment gave me the first real relief from the pain I'd ever felt. It didn't cure me completely, but it helped a whole hell of a lot, and I started going to the bathhouses every day. I would take the newspaper and read it over while I soaked, and no one ever bothered me or looked at me twice. By the fifteenth of January I decided that I'd stay another two weeks, then be on my way back to Lawson. When I went I'd travel by train since I'd sold the stolen mare and tack to the livery. As much as I objected to the railroad in principle, I had to admit that it would get me back to my family a hell of a lot faster than a horse would.

That morning I took my paper in as usual and sat down in on the camel-backed sofa in the men's waiting room to wait until a bath was free. Around me, other men waiting for their turns at the baths read papers, too, keeping to themselves.

"Morning, Mr. Wilson," the attendant said as he passed by with an armful of folded towels.

"Morning," I replied, unfolding the newspaper. I was glad for the warmth of the wood stove that was heating the room; it was colder than usual out today.

The door opened with a creak, and heavy footsteps thudded in from the gallery as their owner stomped the snowflakes off his boots. I looked up from my paper—and almost fell off the sofa. I recognized the gray-mustached man who had just come inside; it was a man I'd only ever seen in person once before, but had hoped never to see again in my life: U.S. Deputy Marshal Bill Tilghman.

He didn't give me a second glance; instead he just strode through the waiting room like he owned the place, passing me and the others by and calling for the attendant as he went into the room where the baths were. I stayed still as a statue, watching after him, my mind beginning to race, along with my heartbeat.

My gut told me to get the hell out of there, to run. But I couldn't run anywhere with my foot the way it was, and getting up and leaving would look suspicious to all the others in there with me. I looked down at my coat and for a moment considered unbuttoning my vest and getting my gun out, but before I could do anything, Tilghman suddenly came around the stove, the gun in his hand aimed straight at my heart.

"All right, Doolin, throw up your hands and surrender!" he ordered, thumbing back the hammer on the gun.

I stood up, quickly. "What are you talking about?" I demanded automatically. "I've done nothing wrong!" My hand went for my revolver like it had a mind of its own. Maybe I could get the bulge on him.

Quick as a rattlesnake striking, he grabbed my wrist. His gun went from my heart to my head and he spoke in a tone underlined with iron. "Throw up your other hand, Doolin, or I will shoot you down. You're caught."

While he was speaking, the others in the room had all shot to their feet and were fleeing hastily out the door, their faces pale. In about thirty seconds there was no one left there but me and Tilghman, and we stood at an impasse, me wanting to get my gun out, him wanting to disarm me but unable to do so with one hand.

I heard him let out a frustrated breath, and, still leveling the Colt at my temple with his right hand and squeezing my wrist so hard I thought he'd snap it like a twig, he turned his head toward the door that led to the baths and roared for the attendant. "I am an officer of the law and I need your assistance with this," he said to the other man, who was cowering like a whipped dog in the doorway. "For God's sake, man, get over here and help me," he snapped. If it hadn't been me he was latched onto like a tick on a dog's ear, I might have laughed, because he looked damned ridiculous, strong-arming me like that.

The attendant came timidly over, his eyes as round as silver dollars, and reached for the buttons on my vest with a shaking hand as I stood there smirking at them both. I didn't try to get away; I knew Tilghman meant what he said, that he *would* shoot me, and shoot to kill. As enraged as I was about being captured at last, I wasn't in any mind to commit suicide. My life wasn't worth a damn to Tilghman, or any other lawdog—Nix had made it clear that the reward on my head would be paid no matter if I was alive or dead when I was brought in to his office.

The attendant's fingers were trembling so violently that he couldn't get the buttons of my vest open, and I rolled my eyes and looked at Tilghman, fighting a sudden urge to laugh. "Why don't I help him? Otherwise we're going to have to stand like this all day."

Tilghman set his jaw, clearly finding no humor in the situation, but he nodded. I undid the last few buttons, then raised my hand back up.

Tilghman looked at the attendant. "Get his gun," he ordered. *"Now."* The attendant swallowed so hard I saw his Adam's Apple bob up and down, and gingerly reached into my vest and pulled the gun from my holster. "Now take it outside."

The attendant did as he was told, holding my gun out at arm's length like it was a living thing that would bite him if he let go of it.

"Look at me," Tilghman ordered. "Do you know who I am?"

"Yes," I replied evenly. "Marshal Tilghman. Were are Thomas and Madsen? Seems like you three are joined at the hip."

"They're around," he replied, "but they've got your partners to track down. I made you my special project."

"I'm honored," I replied sarcastically. "Kinda dogged, ain't you?"

"That's my job, Bill," he said simply. "Now, as you know, I must take you back to the Territory." He brought my hands together in front of me and fastened shackles around my wrists. "Will you go peaceably?"

I looked at him. My gun was gone, my hands were chained, and my bad foot made it near to impossible for me to move anywhere quickly in weather this cold. "I don't got much of a choice, now, do I?" I asked, arching an eyebrow at him.

"You *do* have a choice, son," he replied stoutly. "You have a choice of resisting me and making your days numbered, or you may act a man's part and face the charges against you in court."

I sighed. "I won't resist you. You got my word."

He nodded approvingly and motioned me forward. "We'll go to your hotel and get your effects," he said.

He put his revolver away and walked me out the

door, then took my gun from the still-shaking bath-house attendant and put it in his coat. I noticed folks looking at us in alarm as they noticed the irons on my wrists.

"Tilghman, would you consider taking these off? You've caught me square, and I'm reconciled to that. You got my word I won't make a move, and my word's as good as my life," I said earnestly. For some reason, the idea of respectable folks seeing me in chains like a captured animal almost bothered me more than knowing I'd been caught.

He glanced at me as we walked, and then, to my surprise, he stopped and looked me in the eye, then pulled out his keys and unlocked them. "I will take you at your word," he said quietly, "but you may be certain that if you make a single move, Doolin, I *will* drop you, and it'll be before you can even blink."

I nodded, and rubbed at my wrists, grateful to be free of the heavy, uncomfortable shackles. "I have money in the bank, here," I told him, as we started to pass it. "I'd like to get it before we leave."

He nodded. "You may. But be quick. I don't want to linger here."

You'd like to get my head onto a platter and deliver it to your high-and-mighty Nix as soon as possible, I thought sourly, but I didn't say it. Instead I went into the bank, with him close behind me, and I withdrew the one hundred dollars I had put there for safekeeping. I had to admit to myself that it was a little strange to be standing in a bank and conducting a transaction, instead of watching from behind a gun as the teller cleaned out the vault. My days of bank-robbing seemed long ago to me, now.

We went to the hotel and collected my things, and Tilghman took my other revolver and my rifle and my gun belt. He let me take my saddlebags—but only after looking inside them to be sure I had no gun hidden there.

THIRTY-EIGHT

WE TOOK THE train back to Guthrie with Tilghman's deputy, a quiet man named Kelley, and true to
my word, I didn't try anything. I'd always heard that
Bill Tilghman was an honorable man, and I'd seen
for myself that he was. The fact that he'd taken my
irons off when I'd asked said a lot about his character, and he deserved my cooperation for that, the way
I saw things. I knew I was caught, and so I'd decided
that as long as I could see no real opportunity for
freedom, I would behave myself.

When the train first rolled out of the station, I
could think of nothing but Edith and Jay. Edith
would know of my plight soon enough—I knew my
capture would be all over the papers come morning.
Tilghman had wired Nix with the news, and no doubt
Nix would want to gloat about it to the public, since
I was now called "the most notorious and desperate
outlaw since Jesse James."

My heart was sick at the thought of not being able to see Edith and Jay as I wished, and I stayed silent as I sat in front of Tilghman, who, I knew, had a gun within easy reach. Outside the telegraph poles flashed by, the wires strung on them swooping down in between each one, their green glass knobs glittering brightly in the sunshine.

"You will want to contact your wife, once we reach Guthrie," Tilghman suddenly said, and I tensed up.

"I am not married," I said quickly and firmly. I didn't want Edith mixed up in this mess—it might be dangerous for her. Tilghman didn't say anything, but I could tell he didn't believe me for a minute.

<hr />

"Well, I'll be damned."

I started awake at the sound of Tilghman's voice above my head, and I straightened up from where I'd been slumped uncomfortably in my seat. I'd dozed off awhile back, and now I felt the train slowing as it approached the depot at Guthrie. Tilghman was half-standing in his seat and peering out of the windows at the platform, his bushy brows drawn together in a 'V' over his sharp eyes.

I looked where he was looking and was surprised to see a huge crowd of people—many hundreds of them, by my estimation—standing on the platform, all of them with their heads swiveled toward the train, craning their necks to see through the windows into the passenger cars.

"What the hell is *this*?" Deputy Kelley asked tensely, leaving his seat and coming over to us. He put his hand on the back of my seat, bracing himself as the train rolled to a stop, puffs of steam wafting up and blocking out our view of the crowd for a moment.

"The news is out," Tilghman said, giving Kelley a sideways glance. "Everyone wants to get a look at him." He nudged Kelley. "There's Nix and Hale."

I tensed up at the sound of Nix's name, and looked where they were looking. Two men in expensive suits with thick gold watch chains glinting across their vests stood on the platform, out in front a bit of the crowd of people. One of them had had a waxed handlebar mustache that curled up on the ends and a ramrod-straight posture. He stood with his hands behind his back and his chest puffed out in importance, a glittering badge displayed prominently on his coat lapel. Nix himself. I felt rage come up in me at the very sight of him, this bastard who I blamed for Creek and Charley's deaths and the fact that'd I'd had to keep my family in squalor for the last six months. But I forced it down, and I got calmly up and let Tilghman and Kelley walk me to the door of the car. I walked slowly, hindered as usual by my foot. They had given me a cane to use, but I'd refused it. I was thirty-seven, not eighty-seven, and I was damned if I'd let them see me leaning on a stick like an old man. I may have lost my freedom for the moment, but I still had my pride.

I had known I was of some fame in both Indian and Oklahoma Territories, but nothing had quite prepared me for the sight of all those people, pushing and shoving and jostling to get a glimpse of me as I stepped down off the train. The image flashed through my mind of people crowding the undertaking parlors to look at the corpses of my friends in the same manner and my stomach turned. I kept an easy smile on my face in spite of it, determined to take all these damned lawdogs down a few pegs by showing them that they didn't mean a damn to me, and that I wasn't afraid of them, or whatever fate that awaited me.

"Mr. Doolin, I believe?" Marshal Nix said to me as I was walked up to him. He looked me over from head to foot. I could almost hear his thoughts: *you ain't so much.*

"Marshal Nix," I replied through clenched teeth,

struggling to keep my tone polite. Never in my life had I wanted a gun in my hand as much as I did at that moment, and I fought the urge to spit in his face.

"You have given us quite a trial, Mr. Doolin, but now it's time to arrange yours," Nix said. He gestured to the man at his side. "This is Chief Deputy Hale. He and I and Deputy Marshal Tilghman will take you to the Marshal's office now. This way." He turned and headed to a closed carriage that was waiting just beyond the edge of the platform, the horses hitched to it bobbing their heads and pawing with their front hooves in impatience, spooked by the noisy crowd.

I got in it and Nix, Hale, and Tilghman crowded in with me. There was another man already inside; a reporter from *The Guthrie Daily Leader.* He did not try to ask me any questions; just stared at me with a wondrous expression as if he wasn't convinced I was really there in front of him. As he stared, his pencil moved rapidly against the small pad of paper he had balanced on his knee. I looked at him once, my face impassive, then knitted my fingers together in my lap and stared straight ahead as the carriage started forward, plunging through the narrow gap in the massive crowd of people. I realized with a pang that along with my longing for Edith and Jay, I already missed the open space of the prairies, the feel of a horse under me going where I told it to, and the weight of a gun on my hip—and I hadn't even seen the inside of a jail cell yet.

———•《◉》•———

There were still more people crammed into Nix's office, all of them standing there like it was some kind of receiving line and I was some high-up politician or otherwise famous person set to walk down it and shake their hands. There were a few gussied up ladies, some men in suits, and a few more lawdogs, all with their badges spit-shined and their gun belts slung around their waists. One by one I was introduced to "Mr. or Mrs. So-And-So, a leading citizen of Guthrie" who was "pleased to meet such a famous figure of the current times." I towed the line and greeted each one politely, not knowing or caring who they were and puzzled as to why they found it necessary to shake my hand in person.

I started paying closer mind when I got to the other deputy marshals; these men had been stalking me like prey since the first train job I'd ever pulled with the Daltons. Two of them in particular caught my attention, a man around Tilghman's age and a another one about mine. The first man had a tough yet wise look about him, with sharp eyes that seemed to miss nothing; he was Heck Thomas, one-third of the Three Guardsmen and the sworn enemy of my gang and the Daltons before us. He crossed his arms over his chest and gave me the once-over like Nix had done, saying little. A funny prickling sensation traveled up my spine and the hair on the back of my neck stood on end when his eyes met mine. I held his gaze, though, refusing to be cowed. I'd never had much love for the law, for a fact, but I sure as hell wasn't afraid to face it, or the men that claimed to enforce it.

The younger man leaning casually against Nix's polished walnut desk was Frank Canton, in town from his post at Pawnee. I'd heard tell of him; he worked alongside the Guardsmen but unlike them, had a pretty colorful reputation. I'd heard his morals could be a little skewed and he wasn't above corruption if it benefited him in any way. He gave me a completely different sort of look than Thomas had, and the smirk on his face made me want to put my fists to him—but of course I didn't.

For over an hour I was made to stand there as crowds of curious gawkers streamed through the room, moving in through the front door and out the back, every damned one of them staring at me like I was some sort of attraction in a traveling show. Miserably I thought again that this must have been how people filed through the funeral parlors to view the bodies of Will, and Tulsa Jack, and Creek and Charley as they were roped crudely to undertaker's boards—only I was still alive to be humiliated by it. But, by God, I'd never let the people or the law know it bothered me—not for a minute.

By the time they'd all finished eyeballing me, I was famished and thirsty, my foot was throbbing so bad from standing in one place that I thought I might pass out from it, and my face hurt from keeping a fake smile stretched across it for so long. Nix opened up his watch case, saw it was near to two o'clock, and got up from behind his desk, where he'd been at his leisure while I was on display. He put his hat on with the air of a king donning a crown. "Let's get the man some dinner," he said to his men, "before we book him into his cell." He swept past me, taking his overcoat from the coat rack and sliding majestically into it as two of the other deputies dogged his heels like bodyguards.

My blood was running pretty hot at the way he kept talking about me like I wasn't standing there in front of him, or else I was too low and common for him to address personally. Tilghman came over to me and took my arm above my elbow, moving me forward. "Let's go, Bill; I'm sure you could use a meal, like the rest of us," he said in a pleasant tone, and I thought to myself that if there was one lawdog in the bunch I could tolerate breathing the same air as, it was him.

As we walked toward the door he threw a look over his shoulder at Thomas. "You coming, Heck?"

Thomas shook his head and lit a match for the cigar he'd stuck in his mouth. "I'm on duty," he said shortly, and Tilghman nodded and kept walking me toward the door.

"You figure we should put the irons on him, until we get to the hotel?" Canton asked Tilghman, glancing sideways at me as I hobbled forward.

"Frank, he's been unshackled since just after I arrested him, and he's been true to his word about not trying anything. You'll continue to do so, won't you, Bill?" he asked me, and I nodded shortly.

"Well, I don't suppose you'd get very far with that bum foot of yours, anyway, would you, Doolin?" Canton pointed out in a breezy manner as he put on his hat. "All the same, though…" he pushed one side of his coat back and put a hand pointedly on the handle of the gun he wore at his hip, and grinned so wide at me I saw every tooth in his head.

I gave him a deliberate look. "You'd better be damned thankful I ain't heeled, Canton," I told him evenly, keeping my voice low. "If I were, I'd drop you so fast you wouldn't even have time to jerk that pistol."

"Enough," Tilghman said sharply. "Frank, leave it alone. Bill, come along now and keep your mouth shut."

THIRTY-NINE

I ATE MY dinner in the Royal Hotel, seated at a long table with two deputy marshals parked on either side of me like guard dogs—yet another strange turn of events in what was turning out to be the strangest day of my life. I pictured Creek's and Will's dancing eyes and heard their big laughs in my mind, and I wondered what the hell the two of them would say if they could see me now. Nix and some of the others tried to ask me questions, like where I'd been hiding out or when I'd last seen any of the gang members that were still sucking air and living free—but I didn't tell them a damned thing. I just kept insisting that they had it all wrong, that I hadn't done anything, and that it was only because I'd known most of the other boys back on the ranches during our cattle days that my name had grown connected to theirs. I knew they didn't believe me, but I stuck to my story. If I were to have a chance in hell of getting shed of the charges against me in court, I knew I couldn't admit to so much as a misdemeanor. I guess they must've realized I wasn't going to crack, because by the time we'd finished up, they'd stopped pestering me.

"Time to go," Nix announced, dabbing his mustache with the corner of his napkin and tossing it down on his empty plate. He pushed back his chair and stood, his watch chain swaying across his brocade vest. "Bill, if you'll do the honors, as the arresting officer, I'd be much obliged," he said to Tilghman. "I got work to get back to. You and Frank take him over to the jail, then report to me. The man from the *Leader* will want to speak with you and get your side of the story for the paper." He swept out of the dining room with his guard-dog deputies, never sparing me a second glance.

"Let's go, then," Tilghman said. He tipped his hat at the girl who'd served us the food—she looked like she was going to swoon at any moment from being in the presence of an infamous outlaw—and marched me out the door, Canton planted at my other side.

At the jail they searched me and took my watch and my money, but it was only when they got to my vest pocket that I realized I would lose the only connection I had left to Edith—the verse of poetry she'd given me. Tilghman unfolded the battered paper and read the lines in Edith's feminine hand, then glanced up at me with a knowing look. I looked away so he wouldn't see the agony in my eyes, but I must not have looked away quick enough, because I thought I saw a flash of sympathy in his expression. Then I thought that surely I must have imagined it—I wasn't ready to give any lawdog on this earth credit for being capable of such an emotion.

———◉———

After they'd booked me in, Tilghman turned to me and told me he would take me to be arraigned before the judge in Stillwater for the murders of the deputies in the Ingalls fight three years ago, and he would be back before that to discuss my plea and an attorney to represent me. Then he thanked me for being so cooperative a prisoner while in his custody and left Deputy Canton to take me to my cell.

"Well, Doolin, looks like it's just you and me, now," Canton said, chuckling under his breath. He made a sweeping gesture toward the iron door that led to the most secure of the jail cells. "After you."

I took a deep breath. Never in my life had I seen the inside of a cell before, and it was hard to believe it had come down to it now, after everything I'd seen and done—and gotten away with. But there wasn't a damned thing I could do about it, except face it and wait for the chance to change my circumstances.

Canton started whistling as he prodded me toward a cell. "Kind of cheerful for the line of work you're in, ain't you?" I remarked bitterly, standing back as he opened the door to the dark, iron-barred hole I'd call home for the foreseeable future.

"You don't seem to realize what an historic day this is, Doolin," he said. "You got any clue how much manpower the Marshals Service has put into making this day happen?"

"I have a pretty damned fair idea," I replied dryly, stepping into the cell and standing impassively as he almost gleefully swung the door shut.

"That's why every available deputy in the Territories came into town to see you for themselves, once they heard," he continued, as if I hadn't spoken. "Madsen's off trailing what's left of your partners in crime, or else he'd be here, too." He shoved the key into the lock and turned it; the click seemed to echo through the cell block.

"Where's the great Deputy Shaffer, or didn't his commission continue after he murdered Bitter Creek Newcomb and Charley Pierce?" I asked scathingly.

Canton gave me a long, calculating look as he pulled the key out of the lock, then twirled the ring once around his finger with a flourish before shoving it into his britches pocket. "Hell, Doolin, you ought to know better than anyone not to believe everything you read in the papers," he told me condescendingly, one corner of his mouth going up in a funny little smile.

"What the hell are you talking about?" I asked warily, on edge now.

"Sam Shaffer ain't a real person, Bill," Canton said. "It was one of the damned Dunn brothers, in a cheap disguise. Nix just gave that story out so it wouldn't be known how they *really* died. Your Deputy Shaffer is nothing more than John Dunn in a fake beard." There was a lot of disgust in his tone, alongside the triumph, and I could see he was torn between talking down the Dunns, whom he clearly despised, and throwing their misdeeds in my face for the sake of seeing my reaction.

"There wasn't any gunfight at the Dunn ranch. The Dunns just hid in their barn like cowards and shot Pierce and Newcomb all to hell when they got off their horses. They admitted the whole thing to us when they brought the corpses in. They wanted those bounties—and they wanted Nix to drop all the cattle-rustling charges on them. We've been pestering them for years to give you and the others up; guess the time finally came when they decided harboring your kind wasn't worth the federal charges they'd face if we caught them doing it. It was just our bad luck that you didn't take the bait, too."

He leaned in close to the bars, taking two of them in his hands. "You and your boys have caused my organization more than a few headaches, Doolin. We don't care at this point how we get you, and what state you're in when we do. Makes less work for us and costs the government a hell of a lot less if your type are dead, rather than alive, when they're finally brought to justice. But in your case, what with you being the king's prize and all, I think the U.S. government won't mind spending the money to put you behind prison bars nice and legal—or have you strung up with a rope necktie." He grinned wickedly at me. "You enjoy your accommodations, now." Whistling, he walked off down the hallway to the office, shutting the heavy iron door behind him with a loud *clang.*

I sat numbly down on the thin mattress on my bunk, trying to get my head around what he'd just told me. *The Dunns* had killed Creek and Charley, not the law. The family we'd counted on for so long for shelter and a safe haven had betrayed us, just like I'd feared they would. I felt like a fist was closing around my lungs, preventing me from taking in enough air. My grief at their deaths suddenly felt as fresh as the day I'd learned they'd been murdered.

I thought of Rose then and the sick feeling I was fighting off got stronger. *Had Rose known?* Had she stayed in the house and watched Creek ride up from the front windows, listening for the gunshots that would trade her brothers' freedom for his life? Had she watched him and Charley bleeding in the stock-yard, or seen her brothers put their bodies in the wagon that would bear them triumphantly to Guthrie, as if they were hunting trophies? I shut my eyes and put my head between my hands, trying to stop imagining it. I couldn't bear to think of Rose, who had seemed to love Creek so well, stooping to such a low deed. But how could she *not* have known, as close to her brothers as she was?

I must've pondered on that for hours, pacing the length of my cell until I thought I'd wear a hole in the floor. Finally, around the time I heard them bringing supper, I thought I'd better stop thinking about it or I was liable to lose my mind.

Spur-punctuated footsteps coming down the cell-block distracted me, and I went to the bars to look out. Tilghman was coming toward my cell with a guard in tow, and I stood back and waited as he un-locked the door and came in with me, leaving the guard on watch outside the cell.

He took off his hat and cleared his throat. "May I speak with you?" he asked me. I nodded.

He came over and settled himself on one edge of the bunk that hung suspended from heavy chains fastened to rings in the wall, and I sat on the other edge, watching him warily. "I'd like to clear up this business about your wife, Bill," he said.

I shook my head. "I told you, I'm not—"

"Come, now, be truthful," he said, cutting me off. "I know you're married to the Ellsworth girl from Ingalls, and I know that you have a child with her. I spent over a month surveiling the two of them after you disappeared from Burden, thinking you would return there, before I tracked you to Eureka Springs." His tone was surprisingly kind. "You've been married for some time now, haven't you?"

"What does it matter?" I asked weakly, looking at the bars of my cell instead of at him.

"Because I've been wired by other deputies in the Territory that she and your little boy have left Lawson and are on their way here to Guthrie," he told me. "She will arrive to nothing but scrutiny— which I know you don't want. But there's no help for it."

I felt my heart sink at his words. I'd figured Edith would come to Guthrie, now that word was out of my arrest; I hadn't thought of the publicity she'd face once she got there, the questions from the blood-hound reporters at the *Leader* and the interrogations

REBECCA ROCKWELL

by the marshals. I pushed down the fury that had risen up in me at the idea of her being hounded and looked Tilghman in the eye. "Will she be allowed to see me?" I asked him soberly, and he nodded.

"Yes, we'll allow it," he said, just as gravely. "Perhaps she can secure an attorney for you."

I nodded in defeat, wishing he would just leave me there to wallow in my blackening mood—the strangeness of that day was beginning to wear off and it was finally sinking in, what the future likely held for me.

He seemed to sense my desire to be left alone and stood up, holding his hat upside down in one hand. "The *Guthrie Daily Leader* will be sending someone in to speak to you, before too long," he warned me. "The papers are pretty damned interested in your career." He gave me a sideways look, then put his hat snugly on his head and left the cell, locking the door securely behind him.

FORTY

FIVE DAYS AFTER I'd first been put in that cell, I heard a commotion of sorts coming from the office, the noise carrying through the barred window in the door that separated the cells from the rest of the building. I heard the sound of keys in the lock, and the heavy door swinging open, and even though those were sounds I'd grown used to in the week I'd been languishing there I somehow knew that Edith had arrived, and they were about to bring her to me.

"You may have some time to speak with your husband, Mrs. Doolin," I heard Tilghman's voice say, "but you may not enter the cell with him. I will allow you some privacy and stay in the office, but there will be guards at the end of the hall at all times. Do you understand?"

"Yes," I heard Edith reply.

"Where's Papa?" Jay's little voice demanded, and I felt my chest contract almost painfully at the sound. I'd missed them both so much I could hardly bear it; and now our reunion would be spoiled by the presence of the guards, and the thick bars in between us.

"We are going to see him, Jay, like I promised you," Edith said gently, her voice artificially cheerful. "Come along, now."

I got up and walked to the bars, putting my hands around two of them and pushing my face in between them. Edith and Jay were coming down the hallway, dressed up in Sunday clothes. Edith had her hair knotted up in a heavy mass under a hat that matched the dark blue fabric of her dress, and a plaid woolen shawl drawn around her shoulders. Her hands in their knitted silk mitts guided Jay forward, and when her eyes found mine they grew moist with tears. "Bill," she said, and choked on the word. I saw her bite her lip and bow her head a minute, then square her slender shoulders as she got ahold of herself.

"Hello, darlin'," I said huskily in a soft voice as she came up to the bars, putting her hand through them to take mine.

"Ma'am," I heard one of the guards say gently yet firmly from the end of the hall, "we can't allow you to have contact with the prisoner."

Edith drew her hand back quickly, bowing her head again and choking back another sob that threatened to escape her throat. Jay ran to the bars the minute he saw me. "Papa!" he called with a smile. He seemed delighted to see me and unable to understand why I was not coming out of the funny-looking room I was in to pick him up and swing him over my head to make him laugh, as I usually did.

"Hello there, Jay," I told him, trying to sound cheerful. I knelt down to his level, barely brushing his hand with one finger as he gripped the lowest cross-bar of the cell's front. I couldn't help trying to touch him. The guards stayed silent, so they must not have seen it. "How's my boy?"

"Good," he told me stoutly, then put his fingers in his mouth as he stared at me.

Edith reached down and gently pulled his hand away. "He's missed you, Bill. He's been asking about you every day since you left our camp."

I swallowed hard; my eyes were stinging pretty good and my throat felt closed off. I stood up and looked at her, feeling like I'd gladly give my life if I could just be allowed her familiar embrace, one time. "Have you been getting along all right?" I asked her, keeping my voice low.

"Yes, until I heard…the news," she told me. "Oh, Bill, I thought I'd die when I heard!" Her voice rose in distress.

"I know, honey, but it's done now, and they've

been treating me just fine, so far," I told her, trying to cheer her as best I could. "I'll just have to make the best of things, and you will, too." I gave her a weak smile. "Where are you staying?"

"A boarding house not far from here," she said. "I…I registered under Mrs. Tom Wilson," she told me. "I was afraid to use my real name."

I sighed. "I don't think it matters none, at this point, Edith," I told her. "The papers already know we're married." I looked her in the eyes. "They'll probably be around to pester you, before too long."

She bit her lip again, then took a deep breath. "I'm going to see about a lawyer for you this afternoon," she told me.

"That's good, honey. I'll beat these charges before you know it; they've got no proof of the things they've accused me of," I replied encouragingly. In truth I knew that wasn't the case; there were plenty of witnesses from Ingalls to identify me; I hadn't exactly been discrete when I'd shot the marshal who'd been hell-bent on killing Will that day. But I'd never told her the details, and I wasn't planning on doing so now. She had enough to worry her, at the present.

She blinked back more tears. "This wasn't how I wanted to see you again," she told me in a whisper, her voice breaking.

"Me, neither," I told her. "Please, Edith, don't cry.

I can't stand it when you cry. Everything will be all right. You've been so brave for me, honey; you got to keep on being brave. It's the only way I'll be able to bear things." Even though I knew it was against the rules, I put my hand out and quickly cupped her cheek, unable to help myself.

"Won't warn you again, Doolin," the guard called sharply, in a far less gentle tone than he'd used with Edith. I bit back a hot retort and pulled my hand away, gritting my teeth.

"Will you, Edith? Be brave for me?" I asked, never glancing at the guard.

'Yes, Bill," she replied, in a voice I could barely hear.

They let her and Jay stay with me for another half-hour, but finally we heard the door open and Tilghman came up to Edith, his hat in his hand. "Ma'am, I'm afraid that's all the time we can allow you today." His voice was respectful and gentle when he spoke to her.

She nodded and reached a hand down to rest on Jay's shoulder. "You must say good-bye to your Papa, Jay," she said gently.

Jay looked up at her, then back at me, his eyes going wide. "Papa isn't coming with us?" he asked in his little treble voice. I heard panic creep into his tone.

"No, son, I got to stay here," I told him, being real gentle when I said it and crouching down to his level again. "I need you to be my little man and go with your Mama now, and I'll see you soon, all right?"

"Papa, I want you to come," Jay said, huge tears pooling in his eyes and his face scrunching up.

"Jay, I know you don't understand, but I can't go with you," I said, agony coming out plain in my voice, though I tried to hide it. I looked up at Edith and saw that her eyes were about to pool over. She swallowed hard and rubbed her hand over his little back in a comforting caress. I noticed she had her wedding ring on.

"Come on, sweetheart," she said to him calmly, doing her best to soothe him. "We will see Papa again very soon, I promise." He began to cry anyway, and she gave in and picked him up, even though he was too big for it. He clutched at her shawl with his little fists and buried his face in its folds, crying noisily, and almost killing me.

Edith threw a last look at me, over the top of his head, her eyes saying everything she couldn't speak in front of Tilghman. "Stay well, Bill," she told me, and headed for the office, her back straight and her shoulders square.

Tilghman put his hat on his head, turning his head to give me a long look, just before he followed them. This time, I couldn't deny the sympathy in his expression, no matter how hard I tried.

"Another one of yours down, Doolin!" Frank Canton's booming voice sang out cheerfully to me one morning in early March. I sighed and pulled my thin, lump-ridden, threadbare pillow over my head, turning my face to the wall of my cell, ignoring him—though, I had to admit, I *was* curious who they'd gotten.

It was a pretty mild curiosity, though, since I found it pretty hard to care too much about anything those days. I hated jail-life so much that I often felt like just giving up and letting myself waste away, and I *would* have, except that I was desperate for the chance, however slim it might be, to be acquitted in court and return to my family; their visits kept me sane. Now they'd gone back to Lawson at my insistence to await my court proceedings—if they ever came. I'd been holed up in the same God-forsaken cell now for close to three months, and they hadn't even arraigned me yet. Sometimes I thought that Thomas and Canton and Patrick Nagel, the new Territorial Marshal who had replaced Nix, were purposefully delaying it, just so they could all sit around in their nice, comfortable office and gloat to one another about how I was rotting behind bars.

"Did you hear what I said, Bill?" Canton insisted, standing now at the bars of my cell. "We got another of your precious Wild Bunch yesterday." The glee in his voice was plain.

"I heard you the first time," I said icily, still laying under my thin blanket, the pillow over my head muffling my voice. "Since your life seems to depend on it, I'll ask you: who is it?"

"George Weightman, alias 'Red Buck'," he said. "Posse got him near Arapaho."

"Red Buck ain't any friend of mine," I muttered. "He go peacefully, or did he shoot the posse all to hell?" There wasn't much interest in my voice.

I heard Canton's boots shift and his spurs rattle. "Oh, he went peacefully, all right—peacefully roped to an undertaker's board!" He chuckled.

I pulled the pillow off my head and sat up, then looked at him square, my face impassive. "He's dead, then?" I asked calmly.

"Deader than a doornail," he said with a smile, watching me closely for a reaction.

"Good." I stretched back out on my bunk, lacing my fingers together on my stomach, and stared serenely up at the ceiling.

Clearly, that wasn't the reaction Canton had been hoping for, and it must've surprised him, 'cause he stayed quiet for once. I kept on looking at the stone ceiling above me—even closed my eyes after a bit— and he must have gotten my point, because I heard his boots and spurs retreating down the hallway.

Inwardly, I breathed a sigh of relief. I'd never been scared of Red Buck, but I'd always worried that he might take his sadistic hatred for me out on Edith or Jay, if he ever found out where they were, especially since word was out that I was behind bars. Red Buck had been pure evil, in my mind, and a man that evil wasn't fit to live. I hoped he'd pay, somehow, for all the innocent lives he'd ruined without cause— and enjoyed ruining, to boot.

———— ◈ ————

One evening the following month I got a visit from Tilghman, who asked to speak with me, as he always did, like he was asking to enter my home. He came in the cell with me and watched as I finished the last swallow of bread that they'd given me with my supper, then spoke. "I've come to speak to you about your arraignment," he said.

"About time," I replied darkly. "Didn't figure

you were every gonna get around to that." I took a swallow of water from the tin cup sitting on the floor at my feet.

"Yes, it's been awhile, I know. But the time has come; I'll be accompanying you to Stillwater on the first, where you'll be formally charged in the deaths of the marshals at Ingalls." His voice became coaxing. "I've come to see if you'll consider taking a plea that will put aside the need for a jury trial."

I almost laughed; I couldn't imagine them offering me any deal worth taking "What kind of a deal?"

"Fifty years, in the state prison," he said, watching me for a reaction.

I *did* laugh. "Tilghman, I'm thirty-eight now," I told him plainly. "Why the *hell* would I agree to take fifty years?"

His face stayed sober. "Because if you take your chances at a jury trial, you will likely be put to death."

I cocked an eyebrow at him, staying silent. His mention of a death sentence didn't shock me, like he almost seemed to think it would. I'd always known the noose was on the table.

"Bill, think of your poor wife, and your son," he told me, his voice raising just a bit. "Do you want them to read of your hanging?"

I stood up and started pacing the cell, while he

stayed leaning against the bars, his hat in his hand. "If I'm in the God-damned penitentiary for fifty years, that ain't gonna do them much good, is it?"

"But you will be *alive,*" Tilghman insisted. "And there is always a chance at parole."

I laughed at him again. "You think they'd give *me* parole? After all they're saying I've done? After all them headaches I caused you and yours, while you were trying to slap shackles on me? You're off your nut." My voice came out good and bitter.

"All I am saying," Tilghman said in that calm way of his, "is that you should consider it." He put his hat on his head and looked me in the eye. "Bill, I believe in reformation. I believe that a prison sentence can serve its purpose. You have been nothing but well-behaved in my custody, and you have caused us no trouble while you've been here. I would like to think that if you accept this deal, and *do* get granted parole one day, that you could enter back into society a changed man."

I sighed. "I appreciate the sentiment, Tilghman, but I think you're the only one in your line of work that's of that mind." I turned my face away from him, my mood darkening.

"Think about it," he urged again, then motioned to the guard, who unlocked the cell and let him out. "I'll speak to you about it again the night before we are to go to Stillwater. Perhaps you'll have changed your mind." He walked away toward the office without waiting for an answer, as the guard turned the key in the lock, then went back to his post.

FORTY-ONE

THOUGH I'D THOUGHT my mind had been made up, it turned out that I *did* think about it. I thought about it constantly, until I thought I might lose my sanity. My gut told me not to take the deal, that there was still some chance that though my charm and the lack of proof beyond witnesses, that I might get off and emerge from my trial cleared of the charges against me. But then I'd thought of Little Bill, wasting away in the very same jail as me, and how they'd given him ten years just for his part in the Dover job. If they gave him ten years for *that,* then they'd surely make me swing from a gallows if they found me guilty of murder. In that respect, maybe Tilghman was right. Maybe I *should* take the deal, and count on his influence and the good behavior I knew I was capable of, if the occasion called for it, to get me paroled.

I went back and forth about it for days, but when

Tilghman came to see me the night before they took me to Stillwater, I'd made up my mind as best I could. I told him I would take the deal and plead guilty.

We took the train to Stillwater, Tilghman escorting me, as he'd promised. He led me, shackled for propriety's sake, into the courtroom, and the judge glared down at me from his bench, passing judgement as if he were the Almighty Himself. "William M. Doolin, you have been charged with the deaths of three deputy U.S. marshals on September first, eighteen-ninety-three. How do you plead?"

The few seconds between the end of his sentence and my reply seemed longer than a year to me. Maybe Tilghman was right, maybe I *would* get paroled; maybe not. But last night as I'd lain awake thinking, I'd come up with an alternative, a plan forming with sudden clarity in my mind the way the train and bank-job plans used to. Maybe I wouldn't have to count on parole—or acquittal—after all.

"Not guilty, Your Honor," I said firmly.

Beside me, Tilghman tensed in surprise, and the lawyer representing me did, too. I saw the judge's brow furrow; he'd been expecting the other plea, too, since Nagel had wired him when I'd accepted the deal. I stayed impassive and calm.

"This is your final plea, Mr. Doolin?" he asked me, raising one eyebrow.

"Yes," I said.

"Very well. Your trial will be held the middle of next month, in this courtroom. Deputy Tilghman, the prisoner is surrendered back into your custody until the time of his trial. Court is adjourned." He banged his gavel.

Tilghman put hand on my upper arm, his grip like iron. "Come along, Bill," he said quietly, and led me, limping, outside to the train, ignoring the people and newspaper reporters gathered there to watch. He led me to a seat and sat in it next to me, and when the train started going he turned to face me.

"You went back on your word, Bill," he said, his tone laced with disapproval. "Why?"

I looked at him. "Well, I'll tell you true, Tilghman: I thought about it some more, and when it comes down to it, fifty years is a mighty long time." I folded my still-chained hands in my lap and looked out the window at the countryside going by. I could tell he was looking at me in exasperation—but I just let him stew.

———— ◈ ————

The jail at Guthrie had a big communal area in its center that the guards and the inmates called the bullpen; all the secure cells surrounded it. During they day they let all the inmates out into the bullpen to be at their leisure, then locked them up in their cells at night. As long as I'd been there, they'd kept me in my cell at all times, because of my fame—or infamy. A man didn't have a chance in hell of escaping from one of those, even with a gun—which of course I didn't have. But maybe, just maybe, if I could get myself moved into the bullpen, I could gather some other men for my cause, and we could pull off a jail-break—the biggest job I'd ever pull, if it worked. After all, I was good at that—both the gathering men part, and the pulling a job part.

And if it *didn't* work—well, I knew for a fact at this point in time that I wanted to be free and in the company of my wife and son, not locked up like an animal, even if it wasn't forever. Life without Edith and Jay was no kind of life for me, and I knew in my heart that I'd rather be nailed into a coffin than be, quite literally, barred from their presence.

——◉——

"All right, that's the third meal in a row you've skipped," Joe Miller, one of the night guards, said in an exasperated tone as he stood at the door of my cell, frowning at the tray of supper still sitting un-touched where he'd left it—after taking away my untouched dinner. The day-jailer had removed my uneaten breakfast at noon.

I stayed where I was, curled into a pitiful little ball under my blanket, even though it was the end of June and it was hot and uncomfortable inside the jail, no matter the time of day. I didn't acknowledge him; instead I kept my breathing sort of shallow and my face, half-hidden by the blanket, longer than the Cimarron River. I had to play this right from the first, or else it wouldn't work. If I acted like I had some-thing catching, all that would get me was prodding by a doc and further isolation, instead of what I wanted.

"Doolin, you ill, or something?" Miller asked me, his brow furrowing deeply as he took a step closer.

"I don't feel right, for a fact," I told him in a small voice.

"Eating something might help. You want me to leave your supper tray for a bit?" There was suspi-cion in his tone.

I shook my head. "I ain't hungry," I told him. It was the truth, at that moment—I was not hungry. The plan I'd been mulling over in my mind for the last few days had kept me so distracted I forgot about everything else.

"You want a doctor?" he asked shortly.

"No," I said with a heavy sigh.

"All right, go hungry, then. Don't bother me none." He unlocked the door and picked up my tray, then took it out and locked the door behind him.

For the next three days, I kept up my starvation routine, even though I was beginning to get pretty damned hungry by then. Once or twice different guards came by to stare at me while they talked under their breath to one another, and finally I got a visit from Tilghman, Heck Thomas, and the prison doctor.

"He's not eating, you say?" the doctor asked, after Tilghman had led him to my cell one morning. "For how many days?"

"Four, now, the guards tell me," Tilghman replied as they stood outside my cell. "Bill, are you sick? Is that why you're not eating?"

I gave him a sorrowful look. At this point the game was easy—I knew without seeing a mirror that I looked like hell. I was feeling so weak from hunger by then that I couldn't stand without getting dizzy, but I made myself bear it. Today might be the day.

"I just ain't hungry," I told him. "Being here, in

this dark little place, without getting to move around good…it's just wearing on me. I been getting dizzy, and I ain't sleeping well, either." I looked at the floor.

"What the hell are we babying him for?" I heard Thomas demand in a sharp whisper to Tilghman, still loud enough for me to hear. "If he wants to starve himself to death, let him! It will save the taxpayers the cost of his trial, and good riddance besides. We need to make an example of him—we will not tolerate any more of his type in these Territories. All of this train-robbing and holding up banks and shooting up of innocent folks has got to stop, and stop *now,* with him rotting behind bars."

Hatred for Heck Thomas made my chest feel suddenly tight, but I shoved it down and gritted my teeth. *Come on, now, Tilghman,* I thought, *show that merciful side I know you got.*

"Heck, be reasonable," Tilghman said disapprovingly. "We must show our prisoners the proper way to behave, by our example, and we must give them their day in court, no matter their fame, or the crimes they have been charged with. You know that as well as I do."

Thomas let out a breath in frustration and I heard him shift his weight from boot to boot; his spurs jingled like little bells. "Fine, it's up to the doc. I got more of his lot to track down, anyway. He's your captive, Bill," he said, speaking to Tilghman. "Do whatever you think best. Nagel will go along with it." He walked away then, heading for the front of the building.

"I don't think his problem is necessarily physical," the doctor commented quietly, once Thomas had gone. "I think he needs a change of scenery from the constant confinement in this cell, or he *will* become ill. Have you considered allowing him into the bullpen for the day?"

"I've been thinking about it," Tilghman replied slowly, "and I think I'll allow it. For awhile, anyway." He cleared his throat. "How about it, Bill? Will you behave yourself?"

I nodded, forcing myself not to look overjoyed. "Yessir," I said solemnly.

"All right, then. Tomorrow morning, we'll give it a try." He paused. "Will you eat breakfast, now?"

"I'll do my best," I replied.

Only when they'd gone to tell the guard to fetch my breakfast back did I allow myself the smile that had been waiting on my lips. At this rate, I'd be home to Edith and Jay before those fool lawdogs knew what hit 'em.

FORTY-TWO

"BILL DOOLIN!" I heard a familiar voice call from the other end of the bullpen just a few days later, and I turned to see none other than Dynamite Dan Clifton moving through the other inmates toward me.

"Dan!" I said in surprise, thrown for a loop to see him there. "What the hell...? When did you get here?"

He came over to me and shook my hand, quickly, with his two-fingered one. "Just today. Son of a bitch Canton got the bulge on me in Texas and brought me in for the Ingalls fight," he said sourly. He was thin and bedraggled-looking, and stubble was beginning to cover his face. He had shadows under his eyes, too.

I raised my eyebrows. I'd heard Canton was off trailing other members of the gang, and I'd been glad, since it meant he wasn't around to antagonize me every time another one was caught. I was sorry he'd gotten Dan, though. "Damned shame," I said. "Sounds like maybe you could've made it to Mexico, almost."

He shrugged. "That was my intention. I'll tell you true, Bill, that Canton's a snake if I ever met one. He thinks like a longrider—if I didn't know better, I'd say he'd been one, once." He looked me up and down and spoke again before I could answer. "You holding up all right? I was shocked as hell to hear they got you."

"I'm dandy, now I'm out of solitary confinement, during the day," I told him in a low voice. "And I'll tell you what: I'm aiming to get back to my wife and child a hell of a lot sooner than they're figuring I will," I murmured, jerking my chin at the guards, and at Canton, who was standing outside the bars, talking with them.

Dan gave me a questioning look, his brow furrowing, but I shook my head ever-so-slightly. "I'll tell you later, after Canton's gone," I said, low, out of the corner of my mouth. He caught my meaning and nodded.

"You heard about Creek and Charley, I suppose," he asked me, a note of regret in his voice.

"Yes, I heard," I said shortly, my voice coming out like steel. "And someday I aim to hold them that done it responsible. You got my word on that."

There was no time to talk any more; Canton was shooting looks in our direction, clearly annoyed that we were speaking with one another. I shot Dan a look and drifted away from him, heading over to a small table in the corner to join in a card game with three other prisoners I'd been friendly with during my time in the bullpen by the name of Jones, McLain and Killian.

———————

Little by little over the next few days I revealed my plan to Dynamite Dan and the three others I'd enjoined to help me: Killian, McLain and Jones. After going over things with them methodically and carefully and discussing all possible scenarios we might encounter, I decided we were ready, and from then on we watched and waited for the right moment to act.

It was a Sunday, as it turned out, and by locking-up time that night, we were in position. I kept picturing Edith's lovely face, and her verse kept coming to my mind: *how often by that lonely word / our pleasures have been driven. Good-bye is often said on earth / but never said in Heaven.*

Determination welled up in me, hotter than ever;

seemed to me I could feel it coursing through my veins instead of blood and bracing me. I wasn't going to let that verse ring true for Edith and me, not yet. I'd hold her in my arms again—as a free man. I could not—and *would* not—bear another day in that cage. I figured I had a reputation to live up to, and it was time for all them lawdogs and reporters I'd met to learn just what I was capable of—and how low I'd gotten their guard down, with all my talk of peaceable surrender and being eager to face my trial and clear my name.

Miller, one of the two night guards, was coming toward the bullpen, right on schedule, his keys in hand. As we all watched, he took his revolver out of his hip-holster, as he did every night, and put it in the box set to one side of the bullpen's front door, so he wouldn't be heeled when he came in amongst our crowd of unsavories. Then he unlocked the door and came inside, shutting the door behind him, ready to herd us all like a bunch of cattle into our cells, like always.

I waited, making no move. Neither did McLain, Jones or Killian. George Lane, the inmate we'd recruited to strong-arm Tull, the other guard, waited tensely near the door by the water-bucket set just beyond it, ready to spring our little trap.

The prison trusty who always carried the light for Miller was taking much longer than usual to show up, and I took that as a good sign that maybe we actually did have a chance in hell of pulling this lark off. Miller moseyed on through, apparently unconcerned with the trusty's delay, heading right for the back of the bullpen like I'd known he would do and getting farther and farther inside. When he was almost at the end of it, the trusty and his lantern finally appeared, coming in amongst the crowd to join him.

Quickly, I turned and caught Lane's eye, giving him a sharp, quick nod. He nodded back and went up to where the water bucket was, reaching through the bars and pretending to reach for the dipper, something we all were allowed to do anytime we were thirsty and wanted a drink. As I watched with narrowed eyes, holding my breath, Tull came over toward the bucket, after Lane complained that he couldn't reach the dipper. I saw his head swivel downward as he started to lean down and reach for it—thereby taking his eyes off the unlocked door, which he was supposed to have been guarding.

Before I could blink, Lane had suddenly rushed the door of the bullpen, throwing it open, and tackling Tull like a wildcat pouncing on prey, pinning his arms to his sides. Quick as a flash, McLain, Killian and Jones rushed out and mobbed him, Killian jerking the revolver out of the holster under Tull's arm after a desperate struggle.

"Miller!" Tull yelled, his voice shrill with shock, "get out of th—" McLain's hand over his mouth cut off the rest of his words.

Out of the corner of my eye, I saw Miller and the trusty turn, their forms going rigid in the dim light, and start to run for the door. I let one corner of my mouth go up in a smile, stepped out the door, and locked it before they could even get half-way across the bullpen.

"God damn it, Doolin, what the *hell* are you do-ing?" Miller screeched, slamming into the bars and gripping them so hard his knuckles went white. He gave the bars an ineffectual shake, his eyes aflame as they met mine.

I smirked at him triumphantly, adrenaline shoot-ing though my veins in the same way it had every time I'd held up a train. "What's it look like I'm do-ing, Miller?" I asked sarcastically. Then I turned and ran for the box containing Miller's revolver. The oth-er prison trusty came running to help Tull, but I buf-faloed him across the back of his skull with the butt of the gun, swift and sure, knocking him out cold.

While I was doing this, the others had dragged Tull over to the door that opened the individual cells. Dan was in one of them, along with some of the other prisoners the marshals wouldn't allow in the bullpen. Canton had recently decided he didn't want

Dan in my company, so he'd put him away in solitary. McLain held Tull's revolver up to the guard's temple and thumbed back the hammer. "Open it," he ordered, his eyes gleaming in the lamp-light.

"No," Tull replied, without hesitation, his voice sounding calm.

"I said, open the damned door!"

"And I said, I won't do it!" Tull retorted. "You bastards are all out of your God-damned minds, thinking you can get away with this!" There was sweat coming out on his temples; I could see it glistening on his skin. The others all looked at me for direction, none of them wanting to deviate from the plan I'd so thoroughly driven into their skulls, night after night.

I picked up Miller's revolver and strode over to Tull, my boots thudding sharply on the stone floor, and shoved the gun against his heart, more to scare him into doing what I wanted than anything else. "Tull, open the door. *Now.*"

His face paled; I saw that clear, but he shook his head.

"Shoot him, Doolin!" Killian urged eagerly, as the others watched me with looks half-way between nervousness and morbid curiosity. None of them were big-time criminals; their offenses were petty ones, like whiskey-peddling and counterfeiting.

They'd never had occasion to kill another man, and even though they wanted their freedom bad, I knew they'd look to me to handle any of the evening's messier business rather than finding the sand to do it themselves. I wanted to roll my eyes at the bunch of them—I wouldn't kill Tull; I needed him alive if I wanted that combination open, but evidently they were too short on brains to realize it. Again, I ordered Tull to open the lock. Again, he refused.

"Hell, I ain't got time for this," I growled under my breath, and lowered the gun, grabbing Tull by the vest in the same instant. With a grip like iron, I hauled him away from the others and dragged him over to the bullpen, unlocking it and shoving him inside. Then I reached for an astounded Miller and hauled him out with the bunch of us.

"Jones, lock that door back up," I ordered over my shoulder, and prodded Miller toward the cell-block. "You're going to open it, Miller, and you're going to get one minute to do it. If you don't, I swear to God, I will use this, and it won't be just a flesh wound if I do." I cocked back the hammer with an ominous-sounding click.

Miller was sweating, too, and I could see he was torn between doing his duty and saving his life, but he could tell I meant what I said. He drew in a few shuddery breaths and started opening the combination lock, setting his mouth in a hard line. I could tell it just about killed him to do it. I kept my finger on the trigger, sweating now myself. The whole thing was taking longer than I'd wanted it to, but there was nothing for it. I wasn't going to leave without giving Dan the chance to go, too. I owed him at least some of the same loyalty he'd always shown me during his time in the gang.

Miller finally got the damned lock open, and we shoved past him and got the guns the day guards had left in the boxes. Then I called to Dan, who ran to join me. "Any man who wants to go is free to come along!" I hollered, shooting a grin at Dan as the two of us made for the front doors after locking a furious Miller in one of the cells.

Some of them came behind us; others stayed. I didn't care a continental who got out and who didn't; I was in this for myself first, but I figured it wouldn't be fair if I didn't give the others in the bullpen a chance, too. Dan and I got the key away from Tull and set free anyone who wanted to leave. Just as before, some of them stayed, and others left. By the time we'd fled out the front doors of the jail, there were a dozen or so, by my estimation, fleeing behind me, into the darkness of Guthrie's streets.

FORTY-THREE

FOR A GOOD long while once I was out, I did nothing but run, ignoring the steady, bone-jarring pain in my foot. The streets were darkened and quiet, with nobody out to see us flee, and by some unspoken signal we all headed north for the railroad tracks that led out of town.

I shoved Miller's revolver into the pocket of the coat I'd found hanging on a hook near the jail doors as I ran, and beside me, Dan stuffed the gun he'd gotten ahold of into the waistband of his britches. My heart was beating so hard I thought it might burst, and my lungs were burning from running so long and so fast. After we'd gone a good half-mile, I knew I would have to rest, and I staggered to a stop, struggling to catch my breath. At my side, Dan stopped, and one by one, all the others did, too, still looking to me for direction.

It was pitch-black out, with no moon nor stars

to light our way, and only the track alongside us to give us direction. Cicadas were humming in the brush alongside the tracks, and the warm summer air pressed down on us, sweltering even at the late hour. I sat down at the place where the dirt cleared next to the tracks met the grass and shrubs of the wild land beyond, then laid down flat on my back, too exhausted to go on, for the moment. The others, all panting like worn-out, overheated dogs, followed suit.

With ears still honed for the sound of men on our trail, Dan and I listened tensely as we rested, but we didn't hear anything other than the usual sounds of night. I supposed the lawdogs and the off-duty jail guards were just now getting the word about us busting out, but once they'd gotten over their shock and gotten themselves organized, they'd be out like bloodhounds, Nagle's fury at our escape prodding them on like a whip at their backs. Such a thing would be an embarrassment to him and the whole Marshals Service, and I knew he'd spare no expense, nor lose any time, in tracking us down. We could ill afford to linger anywhere near Guthrie.

"What do we do now, Doolin?" one of the inmates asked weakly in a near-whisper, clearly losing some of his nerve now that he was actually out of the jail and at large.

"Whatever you've a mind to," I responded

dismissively, sitting up and brushing the dirt and dry grass out of my hair. "As far as I'm concerned, it's every man for himself, now. I got enough to worry about as it is."

Dan, getting to his feet nearby, showed no concern at my words; he knew he and I would stick together, at least for a time. But we owed nothing to the others with us, now, and wouldn't have them hold us back from reaching our goal of getting the hell out of Guthrie and into a place we could hole up until I figured out the next stage of our escape.

"You gonna leave Oklahoma, Doolin?" one of them asked me curiously.

"Not without my wife and child," I replied, my voice firm.

With my breath finally caught and my heartbeat back to normal, I stood up and started walking north, Dan hurrying along by my side. Behind us the others hesitated, then split off into small groups, going off in separate directions.

"What are you figuring on, Bill?" Dan asked me quietly as we walked, all our senses on alert.

"We got to get ahold of either saddle horses or a rig and get out of here, quick as we can," I told him in an equally soft voice. "Nagel will call out every lawdog from here to Indian Territory and farther, once they've told him what's happened."

After a bit we heard the sound of hooves and wheels, and we looked over to see a buggy coming, the horse pulling it held to a lazy walk as it was driven towards town. There were no other horses or rigs in sight, so this one would have to do. I looked over at Dan and pulled the revolver out of my pocket and thumbed back the hammer, and he reached for his gun, too. The buggy was about forty feet or so from us, so we crouched in some brush to wait until it got closer.

There was a soft rustling behind us and I whipped my head around, ready to put a bullet into whoever was there. Just before my finger squeezed the trigger, I got a look at the man and recognized him.

"Jones! What the hell are you doing?" I demanded in a barely-audible whisper, the anger plain in my tone nonetheless. "I almost drilled you." I lowered the gun off him.

"Let me come with you, Doolin," he pleaded, so soft I could barely hear him. "If you're aiming to take that buggy, I can help. I'm armed, too." He showed me a small hatchet he'd taken from the jail. His voice had a desperate note to it and I figured he had no idea what to do next, or how to stay free.

"Fine, suit yourself," I agreed hastily, turning my face back toward the buggy. It was nearly on us now and I had no time to argue with Jones. I'd let him come with us, for a bit anyway. After all, he *had* helped me pull the whole thing off clean.

"Let's go," I murmured, and quick as a flash, Dan stepped up to the side of the buggy, his revolver aimed for the driver.

"Don't try anything stupid," he said firmly, as the buggy stopped. Jones and I went smoothly around to the other side, our weapons at the ready.

Inside the buggy, the woman sitting behind the driver stifled a scream and shrank back against the man, whose mouth was hanging open as he gaped at Dan—and the gun he had leveled at his gut. The woman started to fumble at the bodice of her dress and I saw the gleam of a gold watch pinned there as the clouds above parted aways, revealing the moon. She was either trying to hide it or trying to hand it over, I couldn't tell. I shook my head. "We just want the rig and the horse, nothing else," I said to them both, trying to stay calm. "Hurry up, now, get out."

The man who'd been driving got out of the rig so fast the buggy swayed and the whip jiggled; the horse tossed its head up and snorted, spooked by the sudden movement. Jones went quickly around and grabbed its bridle, holding it fast. The driver went around to the side I was at, his body rigid with fear, and, rather clumsily, helped the young woman out.

Even in the low light I could see her face was drained of blood until it was near to colorless.

"We ain't gonna hurt you, we just need the buggy," I said again, keeping my gun on them. They said nothing, backing away from us, the woman clutching the man's arm, stiffly, and almost stumbling over the hem of her skirts.

I looked over my shoulder and got into the buggy, quick, and Dan and Jones got in with me, squeezing into the small space. I took up the reins and reached for the whip in the whipsocket, getting the nag going at a run. As I turned the horse to the north I caught one last glimpse of the man and woman, still standing there agape, watching as we fled into the darkness.

<hr>

I turned the rig east at the first road we came to, the horse still running at a good clip, its flanks starting to gleam with sweat in the thin moonlight and its breaths coming out in measured grunts. The light buggy flew behind it, jostling over the ruts made by countless other wheels, and I gritted my teeth as I kept the lines in play, praying we wouldn't hit any deep ones. If we did, the whole damned outfit was likely to go sailing up into the air, or topple over.

After a bit, the horse grew too tired to run any longer, and I braced my feet against the dash and hauled back on the reins to breathe it. It dropped into a trot, then a walk. My thoughts were racing like a steam-train at full throttle as I worked out what to do next.

I had a mind to head for Cowboy Flats, where I'd lived with Creek and Charley on Creek's claim, which now seemed like a lifetime ago. I knew the law would probably hunt for us there, but I also knew it was full of good places to hide and men who were of like mind and lifestyle to the three of us, who wouldn't alert the law if we were spotted. I knew that area like the back of my hand; I figured we'd be safe enough there for a short time until we could push on out of the Territory.

I hadn't thought of Edith or Jay since before the jailbreak; my mind had been wholly focused on getting myself out of there and away from Guthrie. Now, it seemed I could think of nothing else. I had an ache in my gut, seemed like, from missing them and I wanted nothing more than to turn the nag toward Lawson and get them—but of course I couldn't. Lawson and the home farm was the first place they'd look. I'd have to be patient and wait for the right time. Somehow, I had to get word to Edith—though she'd know, come morning, what had taken place.

It would be on the front page of every paper in the Territory.

We crossed the Cimarron just as the sun was rising, and hid out for a while in the scrub. I unhitched the buggy and left it, knowing the man and the woman would have reported its theft to the lawdogs, and they'd be on the lookout for it. I pulled the harness off the horse and turned it loose to fend for itself; one exhausted horse with no tack wasn't going to do the bunch of us any good.

"Where're we gonna head, do you figure?" Dan asked me, looking warily around as I stripped the gear off the horse, who stood with its head hanging so low its muzzle was practically in the dirt.

"Into Morrison," I told him, naming a town not too far away.

"Why Morrison?" he asked me, in a low voice. He threw a look over his shoulder at Jones, who was crouched at the water's edge, cupping water from the river in his hands and splashing his dusty face with it.

I gave him a sideways look, feeling my jaw clench up a little. "We need money, Dan. We're gonna have to pull a job to get some, like the old days. Ain't no way around it, as far as I can figure." My tone of voice was resigned. "We'll pick something, a saloon or a store..." I let my voice trail off.

He nodded. "What about him?" he asked,

motioning ever-so-slightly to Jones with a jerk of his chin. "I ain't sure about letting him come, Bill. He don't know either one of us any too well, or the way we do things, when you think about it, and he don't seem like he's the sharpest fella I ever met, neither."

I nodded and gave the horse's rump a gentle slap, encouraging it to run off and graze. "We'll send him on his way, once we get to Morrison," I told him, watching as the horse plodded off into the underbrush. Then we started walking.

⸻ ◈ ⸻

The area was fairly swarming with lawdogs. We picked our way, mile by agonizing mile, through the area, moving so slowly I thought I'd go out of my mind with frustration. We saw men on horseback, obviously looking for us, almost every time we turned our heads, and more than once we had to lay flat on our stomachs in brambles or creek beds and all other manner of terrain, holding our breath as we waited for the threat of discovery to pass us by. I kept us to the most secluded, wild places I'd known when Creek and Charley and I had hidden out in the area after train jobs with the Daltons, and after almost a full day of travelling this way, we finally saw a few buildings that meant we'd come to the edge of Morrison.

It was night again, now, and we were all three exhausted and dirty and hungry, the constant threat of capture weighing on us. At least, it was weighing on Dan and me. Jones was so happy to be out of jail and away from Guthrie that he decided to go into town on his own and get into whatever trouble he could find for himself. "Obliged to you for letting me help you with that little shindy back there, and for letting me tag along with you this far," he told me, shaking my hand. "Hope you can stay clear of the law."

"So long, Jones," I told him, and after a goodbye to Dan, he headed off, walking toward town like he didn't have a care in the world.

Dan shook his head and made a sarcastic sound in his throat. "He's a damn fool if I ever saw one. You'd think he didn't have an ounce of brains in his skull, the way he acts."

I shrugged. "He served his purpose. Come on, let's go. There's a saloon right on the edge of town; I figure that's the one to hit."

FORTY-FOUR

WE CREPT THROUGH the darkness toward
Owen's Saloon, skulking in the underbrush like animals on the hunt. I was going over things in my mind,
recalling the way the place looked on the inside. I'd
spent some time there, on and off, during furloughs
from my activities with the Daltons; in fact, it had
been in that saloon that I'd first been introduced to
Bob. It was liable to have a good amount of cash in
it; there were a lot of drinking men in the area, and
it was late at night, so a good deal of 'em would've
spent their money there by now and be good and
lit up besides. All the better, in my mind—it would
make them less liable to interfere in our little venture.
I needed to scrape together enough money to get another rifle, a gun belt and ammunition to replace the
ones Tilghman took, a new hat to hide my face, and
a new wagon and team for taking Edith and Jay out
of the country. I hoped like hell Edith still had a good

amount of the money I'd given her before I'd left Burden—I'd known she would've had to spend some of it, by now, to live on and to pay the attorney she'd secured for me in Guthrie. I wanted to have enough to get by on for a time in Mexico or South America, without having to shove a gun in someone's face to get more. I'd do it once more, tonight, because I had to—but I wasn't aiming to ever do it again.

"You figure we'll just go on in and hold up the bartender?" Dan asked, shifting his weight back and forth as we stood half-concealed by the trunk of a tree. He pulled the gun from his waistband and thumbed it open, checking the bullets there.

I nodded. "Keep it simple. Hopefully there won't be anyone else heeled in there that'll try anything."

He glanced at me. "I'll cover you, Bill. We'll make out all right. Just like old times." He threw me a grin, and it was tinged with a little sadness. It made me think again of the friends I'd lost along the way, Will and Charley, and Tulsa Jack—and especially Creek. Then I forced it all down and pulled the jailer's revolver out of my coat.

Calmly, as if we were regular townsfolk instead of wanted men, Dan and I sauntered over to the saloon and stepped through the doors. In the three seconds or so before anyone noticed us, I scanned the room, assessing things. There were four men at a poker game near the back, a half-empty bottle of whiskey, next to another empty one, on their table beside the pot. From the way a few of them were swaying in their chairs I figured they were good and drunk, and they weren't wearing gun belts. The only other people there were two men sitting up to the bar and the bartender himself, who was smoking a cigar and shooting the breeze with them. There was no register on the counter than ran behind the bar; it was an old saloon and I knew the money was kept in a box under the counter.

I looked at Dan and nodded shortly. We raised our guns in unison, Dan covering the poker-players, me aiming for the bartender and the two at the bar. I cleared my throat, loudly, and they all looked up, their eyes going wide in shock.

"All right, everybody stay where you are," I barked, my voice like the lash of a whip in the suddenly silent room. On the staircase that hugged the back corner of the place I saw one of the girls from the brothel upstairs start to descend into the saloon, but she stopped short when she realized what was happening, her hand clutching the banister, her face going white.

I advanced toward the bar. "Put your hands where I can see 'em, all of you," I ordered. I thumbed the hammer back on Miller's revolver and met the eyes of the bartender. "Get out your cash-box, and hurry up."

"All right, all right, take it easy there, son," he stammered, his face flushing bright red. He reached under the bar and I watched him like a hawk, my finger on the trigger. If he came up with a gun, I'd drop him. I'd gone through too much in the last couple of days to have my chance at freedom spoiled by a small-town saloonkeeper who was too heroic for his own good.

He quickly handed me the contents of the cash-box, and I stuffed the stack of bills into my coat pocket, my gun leveled at him all the while, my narrowed eyes never leaving his. I could tell he recognized me by the look on his face; word was out about us by now. "Obliged," I said shortly. "Now, put your hands back up where I can see them, nice and slow." He hesitated, and I felt my jaw clench. "I ain't playing around, mister. I've been in a pretty damned bad mood for a couple of months now, and so I'd advise you not to try my patience." Behind me, I heard Dan's boots shift on the worn plank floor and I knew he was just as impatient as me for the job to be done.

The bartender put his palms toward me, slowly, looking like he was going to raise them up as I'd ordered. Suddenly he said, in a hard voice, "to hell with your patience, you got a reward on your head the size of—" He was reaching down again as he spoke, his hand moving under the bar. The muzzle of a shotgun appeared as he tried to bring it into position to shoot.

I squeezed the trigger before he could, knowing if I didn't it would mean our freedom and our lives. My bullet went through the bartender's arm, rendering it useless. I heard a clatter as the shotgun fell to the floor, and he let out a howl of pain. The saloon girl on the staircase screamed, and the two men at the bar dove to the floor in a panic. The mirror behind the bar cracked dramatically as the bullet I'd fired passed into it after going through the bartender's body.

Dan still had the poker-players covered; they too had hit the floor when I'd shot the barkeep. I jerked my chin at the door, the muzzle of my gun still smoking. "Let's go!" I hissed, and he ducked outside. I followed, satisfied that no one else was going to try anything stupid.

There were a few saddled horses standing at the saloon's hitching rail; Dan and I reached for the first two we got to and yanked their reins free, vaulting ourselves up into the saddles and putting our heels to them, hard, ignoring the screams and shouts of people who'd come out of neighboring buildings to see what the ruckus was. I leaned over my horse's neck and lit out into the summer night, Dan close behind.

It wasn't exactly how I'd wanted things to go, but I'd done what I felt I had to—and at least I hadn't killed the damn fool.

———— ⊶⟨◉⟩⊷ ————

We ended up in Clayton, just west of Ingalls, and when we got there I went into a general mercantile and bought an older-model Winchester the storekeeper was selling cheap, a black hat with a wide brim, a couple boxes of shells, a gun belt and a canteen so I'd be able to carry water with me in case I had to hole up someplace where I couldn't get any for a time. I was good and bedraggled-looking by then but the storekeeper, a wizened, bespectacled old man who was even harder of hearing than he was short on eyesight, didn't seem to find anything questionable in my appearance, and he took the money I handed him cheerfully. Dan stayed outside with the horses, preferring to hang on to every dime of his half of the money we'd stolen from the saloon.

I'd been thinking things over in my mind, and I was debating the wisdom, or lack thereof, of heading toward Lawson and trying to sneak onto the farm, just for a night. I was pretty wary about going back there, since Tilghman knew where the Ellsworths' farm was—and knew how devoted I was to my wife and son—but my desire to see them was greater than my fear of taking the chance. A colder man than me might have just abandoned them there and fled the country alone to save his hide and his freedom, but I couldn't do it. As much as I wanted to believe that we'd make it somewhere safe together, I knew in my bones that my future was uncertain—all the more reason I was desperate to see Edith as soon as possible. I knew one thing, sure as I knew my own name: I was *not* going to go back to that jail, nor any other. I'd die before I'd see the back-side of bars again—because if they put me back there, they'd never let me out. Any chance of parole would be lost forever now, because of what I'd pulled off that Sunday night in Guthrie.

"What are you going to do, Bill?" Dan asked me later, as we were camping out in a sheltered, hidden little place outside of Clayton. He was skinning a rabbit he'd caught, while I kept an eye out for any trouble.

"I got to try to meet up with Edith, just for a night," I said firmly, settling my rifle more comfortably across my knees.

"How?" he asked me, looking up as he pulled the hide free of the rabbit's flesh. "If you've a mind to take her out of there—"

"I don't, not yet," I interrupted. "I didn't get this far just to get myself caught again. But I got to try, just for a short while, and then as soon as I can I'll rustle up a wagon and team and get her and my boy out of the country for good." My voice was firm.

Dan was quiet for a minute as the rabbit roasted on a twig spit he'd fashioned. "I guess that's what we're all going to have to do; get out of the country. Those of us that are left, anyway." He shook his head. "I still can't believe those lawdog sons of bitches got Creek and Charley like they did."

I clenched my jaw and swallowed hard against the rage I still felt—and always would feel—against the Dunns. I wanted to seek them out, the murdering bastards, and shoot them full of holes the same way they'd done to Creek and Charley, but I knew I'd probably never get the chance. "The law didn't get them, Dan. Not the way you think, anyway."

He looked up, quick, a wary glitter in his eyes as the firelight hit them. "What are you talking about, Bill? I saw the paper, same as everyone else."

I shook my head. "The paper lied, Dan. Those God-damned, yellow-bellied, greedy Dunn bastards did it. They hid in their barn and shot them off their horses, and Nix knew it. He deputized John Dunn in disguise as Sam Shaffer and let him and his brothers take them down. Frank Canton told me about it, the first night I was in that hole in Guthrie."

Dan looked first stunned, then furious. "After all that bullshit about hiding us and giving us shelter anytime we needed it, and Bill Dunn saying he'd never give us up to the law…" his voice trailed off, like he was too mad to keep talking.

"Guess all their cattle-rustling caught up with them and they decided to save their good-for-nothing yellow hides, and collect the rewards on us besides," I replied bitterly. "You can mark me, Dan, if I ever see any of them again, I'll make them square their debt with me." My voice came out with a growling note to it and my fists clenched. I wished like hell I could ride onto their place and do just that, but I knew I couldn't. Canton had told me I was on their list, too—which meant they were probably laying in wait there to see if I'd show up. No, I told myself, I had to focus on Edith and Jay. Bill Dunn and his brothers would get what was coming to them, someday. I had to believe that, and be content with it.

FORTY-FIVE

AFTER A COUPLE days of slow, cautious travel, we made it to one of our old hideouts on Mud Creek, not too far from Lawson, and found Dick West there, laying low. He was thrilled to see us both and clapped me on the back, hard.

"You are without a doubt the *cleverest* son of a bitch I've ever been acquainted with, Doolin!" he told me with a grin when I'd gotten off my horse. "No one but you could've pulled off a jailbreak like that!"

I gave him a lopsided smile. "I got lucky, I guess," I said.

He chuckled. "I know you, Bill. Luck didn't have a damn thing to do with it. I'll bet you planned it to the letter and then pulled it off clean, just like you always do." He shook his head, still smiling. "I'm glad. I didn't figure jail would much agree with you."

"No, it surely did not," I confirmed. "And I ain't aiming to go back there ever again."

He looked at me soberly, his grin fading. "You going to take Edith and your baby and run?"

I nodded. "I figure we'll end up in Mexico or South America. I just got to get a team and wagon together and wait for the right time to go. But in the meantime, I'm aiming to see them—tonight."

He darted a look at Dan, then looked back at me. "You sure that's a good idea? They had all them stories in the papers about Edith and you, and where her Pa and Ma live. Don't you figure they'll be looking for you there?"

"They've only got so many deputies, Dick," I said stubbornly. "They'll be so busy running all over hell that they'll have folks in the area be on the lookout for me—but none of them will squeal, even if they do see me. You know they've always covered for us in the past. Besides, I'm aiming to get there at night and sneak into the house. The lean-to's always unlocked. Edith started leaving it that way for me, back before Southwest City."

Dick still looked sober. "You sound pretty confident, Bill," he remarked. I could hear the doubt in his voice, plain as day.

I busied myself with reloading my gun, and felt the muscles in my jaw clench up. "I got to be, Dick, or else I'll bungle things, or lose my nerve. And I'll tell you right now I ain't going to go another day without seeing my family. I got to take the chance."

There was a silence as the two of them watched me loading bullets into my rifle and Miller's revolver. Then Dan spoke. "Well, Bill, if you're aiming to try it, we wish you luck. Lord knows you've always had it on your side."

I nodded shortly and shoved the revolver into my holster. Dan was right—luck always *had* been on my side. I just had to hope—and pray—that it would stay that way for a little while longer.

———=••(●)••=———

After a couple hours of nervous pacing and waiting around, I finally figured it was late enough and set out for Lawson about nine o'clock, on the horse I'd stolen. It was eerie out; clouds had gathered thick overhead and there was no sign of the moon or any stars. The warm, damp air seemed to press down on me as I rode, keeping the horse to an easy trot so as not to arouse the suspicions of anyone who happened to be out in the area, though I saw no one. Everyone was holed up indoors, scared of the threatening feel of the weather. A late summer storm was coming, and before I made it halfway to the home farm the skies had opened up and rain came pouring down on me, soaking me to my bones, seemed like. Thunder rumbled off somewhere, and I saw quick flashes of lightning pierce the darkness. My horse pranced uneasily underneath me every time it thundered, but I held him fast.

I crossed the bridge over Eagle Creek, anticipation welling up within me until I couldn't hardly stand it. All I could think about was Edith, and how much I'd missed her and Jay during the months they had me locked in that hell-hole of a jail. Pretty soon the house came into view and I fought the urge to simply get off the horse and let it roam where it might in the rain, just so's I could get inside to her faster. Instead I put him up in the barn, being quiet as I did, hastily stripping the wet saddle off him and tossing some oats into the feed-box. Then I crept out of the barn, hunching down low in the tall grass as I made for the lean-to.

It was open, just like Edith always left it, and I wondered if she just did it now out of habit, or because she actually had hope that I'd make it there to her someday soon, now that I was out. I ducked inside the tiny, dark room and stood for a minute, glad to be out of the weather. I had rainwater dripping down off me and pooling on the floor, and

I was muddy and bedraggled besides—but I was *home*.

Before I could do anything, I heard footsteps, swift and light, in the hall outside the lean-to, and the door swung open, letting in a glow that that pierced the darkness so suddenly that it blinded me and I blinked, unable to see who was holding the lamp. I heard a sound that was a half-gasp, half-sob, and I knew it was Edith who was standing there.

"Oh, God!" she gasped, bursting into tears and setting the lamp down on a shelf so fast the kerosene sloshed violently and the flame flickered in protest; for a minute I thought she'd broken it. Then she flew into my arms, burying her face in my neck and almost knocking me over, her slender body shaking with sobs.

"Edith, darlin'," I choked out, my voice husky with emotion, and held her as tight against me as I could, even though I knew I was getting her soaked and dirty. I lowered my face into her silken hair, breathing in her familiar scent. After a minute she took in a few big, deep gulps of air and pulled back from me just enough to put her hands to my face, feeling the planes and hollows of it and stroking my sodden beard and hair like she had to be sure I was really there. I felt water spill over my lower eyelids and I knew it was tears; they mixed in with all the rainwater on my face and I tasted their saltiness on my lips when they tricked down there.

"I can't believe it," she gasped, struggling to get ahold of herself. Her face was flushed in the lamplight. "I can't believe you're here, and safe..." She stopped talking and pulled my face down, kissing me like I was the air she needed to breathe.

"You should know by now, Edith, that I'm always bound to come home to you, honey," I told her huskily in between kisses. We finally broke apart when we couldn't breathe properly any longer, and I started shivering then, so hard my teeth chattered. The rain that had soaked me had chilled me to the core.

"Oh, Bill, you're drenched," she said, like she'd only just now realized it.

"I got caught in the storm," I told her, trying to stop shivering. "Got you all wet, too..."

"I don't care," she said firmly, shaking her head. "I'll heat up water for a bath, and fetch you some dry clothes."

I nodded, bending down to pull the bootjack out from under the bench set near the door. Clumsily I pulled my boots off as she went hastily out of the lean-to and ran for the kitchen, her muddied, dampened skirts flaring against the doorframe as she went.

She came back a few minutes later with a quilt; she helped me strip off my wet clothes and wrap the heavy quilt around myself. The tub was already in the lean-to and she made me sit and rest on the bench while she came back and forth with the big kettle, slowly filling the tub with steaming water.

I heard the muffled voices of her folks as they came out of their bedroom to see what she was doing; Edith put a finger to her lips and left me a minute to go tell them I was there. There were some surprised-sounding exclamations from them both, but I couldn't make out their words through the walls.

"Jay's awake, Edith," I heard Mrs. Ellsworth say clearly; she must've moved closer to the lean-to.

"Please, Ma, will you look after him? I must take care of Bill."

I heard footsteps go off toward the small bedroom next to Edith's as her Ma went to comfort Jay. Soon Edith came back and set towels and a clean nightshirt out for me, along with some soap, and I sank gratefully into the steaming water, figuring as I did that next to being in her arms, this was likely as close to Heaven as I'd ever get.

She sat in there on the bench while I bathed, unwilling to leave me alone for even a few minutes. I didn't mind a bit. I washed all the dirt and mud off me while she talked to me about Jay, and how shocked she'd been when she'd read the paper the morning after my escape.

"Were you afraid, Bill? While you did it?" she asked me softly as I lathered soap into my hair. I scrunched myself down awkwardly in the steel tub and ducked my head into the water to rinse off the soap before I answered her.

"No, Edith," I said. "The only thing I been afraid of this whole time is not being able to see you and Jay again."

She blinked back fresh tears as she looked at me from across the small room and a wobbly little smile crossed her beautiful face. "That's what I was afraid of, too," she said. She took a deep, shaky breath and collected herself, then handed me a towel. "I'll go turn down the bed while you dress," she told me almost shyly, standing up and moving toward the door.

"Edith?" I called back, wrapping the towel around myself as I stood up.

She turned back, her hand on the doorknob. "Yes?"

"Why are you still dressed?" I asked her. It was near to ten o'clock, best I could figure, but she still had her dress on and her hair pinned up.

She gave me a look I couldn't decipher. "I was waiting up," she told me. "Somehow I had a feeling you would show up here tonight," she said in a funny-sounding voice. "I had a dream last night..." her voice trailed off and she shook her head a little, like she was shaking off a memory. Then she was gone, heading toward our bedroom.

————⟨⟨◉⟩⟩————

Late that night I laid awake on my back, staring up at the ceiling, in a strange state of contentment mixed with apprehension at what might lay in store for us until we were safe. Edith lay in my arms, her body pressed tight against mine, her cheek against my heart. Her hair was loose and I kept running my fingers gently through it, letting the long, soft strands of it pool over my bare chest like black silk. She didn't wake up when I did it; she was sleeping soundly for what I suspected was the first time since she'd heard of my arrest, back in January. One of her hands was resting on me up by my shoulder and I reached over and covered it with mine, running my fingertips lightly over it, unable to stop touching her.

Outside the rain was still coming down in a steady roar, but the thunder seemed to have stopped. I closed my eyes a minute, feeling the rise and fall of Edith's body against mine as she breathed the slow, even breaths of sleep, and I thought that it had all been worth it—all of the planning and waiting and running after the escape, even holding up that saloon in Morrison—because all of it had helped me end up back here, like this. And I knew that if something happened to me down the road, at least I'd had this night with her, and the last time I touched her in this life wouldn't have been that swift, forbidden touch we'd shared through the bars of my cell in Guthrie.

FORTY-SIX

I WOKE WELL before dawn, and though everything inside me was screaming to stay curled in Edith's embrace under the warm quilts, I knew I had to go. I'd promised myself that I wouldn't spend more than one night at a time at the farmhouse, between now and the time I left with them, for good. It would be too easy to be spotted there, and then the law would be on me so fast my head would spin. I felt safer at the old hideout on Mud Creek with Dan and Dick, and I swore an oath to myself to be back there before the sun came up.

Carefully I got out of bed without waking Edith, and I dressed in the clothes she'd laid out for me before we'd gone to bed. I was buckling on my gun belt when she stirred and woke, turning over to see me sliding the gun into my holster.

"Bill?" she asked sleepily, yawning as she did so. "What time is it?"

"It's early, sweetheart." I glanced over at the clock on the chest of drawers. "It's not even four, yet." I was whispering; the rest of the house was still asleep.

"Why are you dressed?" she asked in alarm, more awake now. She sat up, the quilts wrapped around her, her tousled hair tumbling in an unruly mass around her shoulders. It was so dark in the bedroom that I couldn't see her all that well.

"Edith, honey, I got to leave now before the sun comes up," I whispered, reaching for my boots, which were caked with dried mud. I'd put them on in the lean-to so I wouldn't track it all over the house.

"Bill, *no!*" she cried in a hoarse whisper. "You can't leave! It's too dangerous for you!" she frantically began untangling herself from the quilts, like she was making ready to physically stop me from going.

"Edith, listen to me," I told her, putting my boots down and swiftly crossing the room to the bed, plucking her wrapper from the back of the rocking chair as I went. "Calm down and hear me out." I put the wrapper around her shoulders, and she clutched it closed at her throat.

I got a match out of the tin and lit the lamp, turning it way down so it gave off no more light than the flame of a single candle. Then I turned to her, sitting down on the edge of the bed and taking her free hand.

"Honey, I got to get ahold of a wagon and team before we can leave here together, and I need a little more time to go by before I do. They've got deputies all over the Territories looking for me, and they'll be watching this place. If they don't see me come, maybe they'll figure I'm holed up somewhere else and count on folks in the area to watch out for me and tell them if I'm spotted. But I ain't aiming to let anyone who'll tell the law see me, so long as I can help it, and it won't be long before we can go."

"Why can't we just go now, Bill?" she asked me in a small voice, clearly trying not to let on how upset she was.

I pulled her into my lap, quilts and all, and nestled her head against my chest, my hand on her hair. "Edith, you know as well as I do we can't take Jay and our things without a wagon and team," I reasoned. "Once we leave here I won't ever be able to come back, so we'll only get one chance at this." I laid my cheek against the top of her head, trying to get my fill of the feel of her in my arms, since I'd have to go a few days without it. "You've always said you trusted me. Well, you got to keep on trusting me for a bit. Luck's always been on my side, " I told her, repeating the words Dan had told me. "I figure it'll keep on that way." I smiled at her when she pulled back to look at me.

"If that's what you think is best, I'll trust you," she finally said, her voice still small. Then she brightened. "Why don't we take Pa's wagon? He'll let us—"

"No, Edith," I interrupted firmly, shaking my head. "Your Pa's been more than generous to me these last few years, and Lord knows I've done nothing but put him and your Ma out and make trouble for them, what with all the lawdogs sniffing around here, and them having to put you and Jay up. I ain't aiming to take advantage of his kindness any longer. He needs his wagon and team for tending to his crops and his work in town."

Edith was looking at me in surprise. "They haven't minded," she told me softly. "I didn't know it bothered you so much, Bill."

I set my jaw and lowered my eyes from hers a minute. "It always bothers a man when he can't take care of his own family proper without leanin' on someone else—or, at least, it *should.*" I collected myself and let her go, then stood up and went for my boots.

She got out of bed and slipped herself into her wrapper, pushing her hair back over her shoulders. "Will you see Jay?" she asked me, sounding resigned.

"I don't want to wake him," I told her, my tone reluctant. I'd seen him last night, before Edith and I had turned in, and he'd been so excited to see me it had taken a good long while for him to go back to sleep. I knew if he were to wake up now he'd get upset that I was going—and I couldn't stay any longer. Already it was getting closer to dawn than I'd wanted.

Edith handed me the money she had left from the stack I'd given her in Burden, but I only took a little bit and handed the rest back. If, God forbid, something did happen to me, I wanted to leave her with something to survive on for a time. "I'll be going now, honey," I told her, reaching for my hat.

She came over to me and put her arms around me, returning the kiss I gave her, hard. "When will you be back?" she asked me in a whisper.

"A couple of days," I told her, putting my hat on my head. "That's a promise."

FORTY-SEVEN

"**BOTH OF THESE** geldings are in good shape and drive well," the livery owner at Lawson said to me very early one morning a couple of weeks later. He was holding the halters of two strong-looking bays as we stood at the fence of the small corral in back of the livery. "I'm willing to sell them at a good price. I got them and the wagon from a man selling out and taking his family back East by way of the railroad; he didn't have need of 'em anymore."

I nodded quickly and glanced over at him, trying to act natural. It was my first time in town since I'd come back to the Mud Creek hideout, but no one had looked at me funny, even though I was expecting at any moment to be recognized. Like Ingalls, Lawson had always been friendly toward men like me, and I was counting on that to continue until I'd done what I'd come to do.

"You mind if I take a look?" I asked, raising my

eyebrows at him from under my hat's brim.

"Sure, son, go right ahead," he said agreeably, tying their lead-lines to the top rail of the fence. I ducked through the rails and ran my hands over the horses, over their backs and down their legs, feeling for any sign of lameness. I lifted up their feet, one by one, and checked their hooves over carefully. They stood placidly while I did it, swishing their tails gently. Satisfied, I straightened up and nodded to him. "Think they'll do just fine," I said, and he smiled.

"I'll help you hitch 'em up, then, and I'll throw in the harness for free, seeing as how you're buying the wagon and the team, too."

"Much obliged," I told him. Then I helped him get the harness on; it was used but in good shape. Together we backed them into place and when we were done I paid him what I owed him, eager to be on my way.

I'd been to the farm a few nights since that first one, and now it was getting near to the middle of August and time, I figured, to go. Dan and Dick and I hadn't seen hide nor hair of anyone with a tin star on in the area, and I felt like now was as good a time as any to be heading out. We'd been watching the papers, when we could get them, and I'd seen an article from awhile back about how Dan and I robbed a place near Okeene, which wasn't true, but I took it as a sign that maybe, against all odds, they were looking for us someplace besides where we were. I decided to seize the opportunity.

I drove through town and kept a wary eye out all the while, sitting hunched over a bit on the wagon seat to hide my height and making sure my hat was pulled down nice and low. It was gray and foggy out, that morning, and there weren't too many folks out in the weather at that early hour. As I got to the end of town I came upon the Noble family's blacksmith shop and saw one of the Noble brothers bent over the anvil, forging a horseshoe out of a red-hot piece of iron. Sparks flew out to either side of him with each stoke of his hammer. As I went past I saw the young man straighten up; as he did he happened to glance my way. His eyes met mine for an instant and the hair rose up on the back of my neck. I forced myself not to whip the team into a faster gait and turned my face toward the road in front of me, not wanting to stare back at him. Once I'd gotten aways past I glanced casually back—and saw him working again, apparently paying me no more mind. I let out a breath and slapped the reins over the horses' backs, putting them into a trot and heading for the farm.

"Papa, why do you have to go?" Jay demanded, climbing up into my lap that night after supper was over. He looked up at me with a pout and reached up to tug at my beard.

I gently pulled his hands away and held them in mine for a minute, bouncing him on my knees to make him laugh—and to turn his mind off waiting for me to answer the question he'd just asked. It worked; he shrieked with laughter and held tight to my hands, making no more mention of my upcoming departure. Edith passed behind my chair with our empty plates; she smiled at Jay but sobered a little when her eyes met mine. I was not going to stay the night this time, and she knew it. I'd brought the wagon and team, but I felt like I'd taken a chance buying it in town and I wanted to be back at the hideout where I felt safest. On top of all my usual worries, too, was the memory of the way Charlie Noble had looked at me this morning as I'd passed him working. All day I'd waited on pins and needles, my hand never far from my gun, expecting some lawdog he'd tipped off to come out of nowhere and slap shackles on me, even though I knew I was probably making mountains out of molehills again.

After a bit Jay threw his arms around my middle and hugged me as I sat there in the chair, and then he climbed down off my knees and ran off to play with the jumping-jack and tin soldiers Edith's Pa had brought him from town. I took the chance to quietly slip outside, Edith at my heels, and take Black Devil out of the barn. It was good to have a horse I could count on under me once again, and I was damned glad Edith's Pa had stayed true to his word and kept him there for me all that time.

"I'll be back in two days, Edith, and we'll load up the wagon, like we talked about," I said to her, low, then kissed her quickly and swung up into the saddle, trotting away in the direction of Mud Creek.

The sky was clear; the fog from the morning had lifted and it was warm out. The stars twinkled overhead. As I approached the Eagle Creek bridge the only sounds were the *clops* of Devil's hooves on the road, his soft breaths, and the ever-present songs of cicadas and crickets. Frogs added their voices to the chorus as I got closer to the creek.

I rode onto the bridge, like I always did, Devil's hooves thudding against the planks. When I got to the middle of it I pulled back on the reins, easing him to a stop with a murmured "whoa."

My spine prickled like something was crawling up it; the hair on the back of my neck raised. My heart seemed to thud loudly in my chest as I stared out into the brush on the far bank. Devil mouthed the bit and dipped his head impatiently, but I held him back, straining to see through the thin darkness. Something was out there, waiting for me. My hand went for my gun.

There was a sudden scrambling in the under-brush, and something darted out of it, moving at a low trot close to the ground. The moonlight shone off a coat of thick red fur and reflected in a pair of narrowed amber eyes.

I let my breath out; it was just a fox. I let go of my gun and put my heels to Devil's sides, putting him into a trot again. As he left the bridge I kicked him into a canter—but before I did I glanced behind me and thought I saw the crouched shape of a man, half-hidden by the same shrubs that had concealed the fox. Then I figured my mind must've been play-ing tricks on me, because when I looked again, it was gone. All the same, I kicked Devil into a gallop, suddenly feeling like I couldn't get out of there fast enough.

FORTY-EIGHT

I WAS TACKING Devil up two nights later on the twenty-fourth, getting ready to head to the farm when Dick West came up to me, leaning his elbow on one of the two massive boulders that rose up higher than a man's head out of the ground; they sheltered the little hollow we hobbled the horses in every night.

"You're aiming to leave soon, ain't you, Bill?" he asked, watching me. "I mean, for good."

I nodded, buckling the breastcollar across Devil's wide chest. "Tomorrow," I confirmed. "Figure now's as good a chance as ever."

"You going to stay at the farm tonight, then?"

"No, I don't feel right about it for some reason. I'm going to help Edith load up our wagon, spend a bit of time with them, and then I'll come back here. Edith's going to leave before dawn and meet up with me just south of here, and we'll head for the border."

I reached underneath Devil and brought the cinch up under his front legs.

Dick nodded slowly. "Well, I figure Dan and I will head out soon, too. Seems we all might have worn out our welcome here. Wasn't sure if you'd heard."

I glanced up at him warily as I drew the latigo tight. "Heard what?"

He lifted his chin up and scratched at the stubble creeping down his neck with his ragged fingernails. "I went into town today; heard some word there might be a posse out. There's talk that Heck Thomas is in the area, looking for you."

I set my jaw and reached for the bridle. "Well, he ain't going to find me," I said stoutly.

"If anyone can give him the slip, it's you," Dick agreed. He paused. "All the same, though, watch your back."

I threw him a quick, confident grin. "I always do," I said, tapping a finger against my gun as it rested in my holster. I threw the reins, first one, then the other, over Devil's neck, then reached for my rifle.

Dick shifted his weight from one boot to the other. "Bill, you ever forget why we started holding up trains, all those years ago?"

I slid the rifle into the scabbard on my saddle, giving him a puzzled glance. "No. Why?"

He shrugged his shoulders, idly scuffing the heel of one boot in the dirt, rolling the rowel of his spur back and forth in it. "Just seems like sometimes I think back to when I was working cows with you, and I try to remember how I came to spend my time pulling train jobs with you and the others instead, and it's gotten all blurry-like. Hell, it was fun, and I needed the money, I know, but I wonder sometimes why I just didn't stick it out on one of them ranches."

"Because there wasn't nothing to stick *with*, Dick," I reminded him, my voice hard. "No more big drives, just putting the damned cattle in railroad cars to be shipped off like they was a load of coal or some such, instead of animals needing to roam ranges. All them rich ranchers that fenced everything off and lowered our wages. The God-damned railroad taking whatever the hell it wanted, no matter the price folks would have to pay. *That's* why *I* started. The money didn't hurt none, either."

"If you still feel that way then why're you stopping?" he asked me, and I realized for the first time that he didn't want me to quit—that he was hoping I might change my mind.

"For the same reason I gave to Will, and to Creek and Charley when they asked: because I got a wife and son now, and they're more important to me than making the railroads and the banks pay any more than we've taken them for already. We had a hell of a long run, Dick, three more years than the Daltons did. We pulled a hell of a lot more jobs than them, and took bigger hauls to boot. Nobody's going to forget us anytime soon. But I'm too old for all of it now. I want to get out of these God-damned Territories and live the rest of my life in peace, someplace where I won't wonder all the time if my boy's going to forget me 'cause I been away too long, and I won't have to look over my shoulder every damned minute to make sure some lawdog ain't trailing me."

He took in my words a minute, then looked up at me with one corner of his mouth turned up in an almost wistful half-smile. "So the Wild Bunch is really gone, then?"

I clenched my jaw and swallowed hard, thinking of our friends who hadn't made it. "Gone for good, so far as I'm concerned. I'm letting it go, Dick; seems like maybe you and Dan should, too, while you're still sucking air." I took Devil by the reins and led him out of the little sheltered place, Dick standing aside to let us pass.

"I'll give it some thought, Bill," he said, throwing me a careless grin. He stuck his hand out to shake mine.

"What the hell's that for?" I asked him, raising

one eyebrow, a smile on my face. "I'll be back here before dawn."

"I know you will, Bill," he said. "But just in case I don't see you..."

I shook his hand, feeling a smile come up over my face. Then I put my foot into the stirrup and swung up into the saddle, pointing Devil's head toward the farm—and Edith and Jay, and the wagon that would take us to our new life.

EPILOGUE

"DID YOU SAY you've got Bill Doolin? *The* Bill Doolin?" The undertaker's face, which normally bore a morose expression befitting his profession, was wide-eyed with surprise as he stood in his doorway early that August morning, a lamp in his hand, still dressed in his somber black suit.

"You know of any other Bill Doolins, Rhoades?" Deputy Rufus Canon asked with a wry smile. "We got him in the wagon out there and we need to bring him in, quick, before all the damned reporters from the paper start swarming around, wanting the story out of us."

"It's after two in the morning," Rhoades pointed out, but Canon shook his head.

"That don't seem to matter none where news like this is concerned. Get a board ready for him. He's gonna get blood all over the place. Heck got him with a scattergun." He turned and headed back to the wagon tied outside Roades' undertaking rooms on Oklahoma Avenue in Guthrie.

The lawmen brought Doolin in and laid him out unceremoniously in the embalming room, and though it was not the undertaker's practice to gawk at any corpse brought into his establishment, he had to admit to himself that he was curious about this outlaw who had become so famous, and eluded so many, for so long. Doolin was taller than the average man and rail-thin, and even with a bushy beard covering most of it, Rhoades could see that his face was fine-featured and almost dashing—not rough-looking, like one would expect an outlaw to be. His eyes were open, shockingly blue against the death's pallor of his face. Rhoades reached out and respectfully closed them.

"What're you doing, Rhoades?" Canon asked sharply. "Heck doesn't want anyone doing anything to that corpse until Doc Smith gets here. We got to be especially careful to do everything nice and legal, with this one."

"For God's sake, Rufus, I only closed his eyes," the undertaker replied defensively. "The man deserves *some* manner of dignity. Show a little bit of sensitivity."

"Sensitivity's *your* job," Canon replied, hooking his thumbs on his gun belt. "Not mine, when it comes to men like him. You think he showed any *sensitivity* when he held up all those trains and banks like he done?" He jerked his chin toward Doolin's body.

Rhoades let out a quiet sigh, declining to answer, and retreated toward the door that led to his living quarters. "Let me know when you are ready for me, and when Doctor Smith is finished with his examination."

Canon nodded. Sometimes he wondered what undertakers like Rhoades thought, each time he or the lawmen he worked with brought in the shot-up corpse of some train-robber they'd been tracking relentlessly—but he never wondered too hard, always dismissing the thought. Rhoades was just there to do a job, same as him. He called after the undertaker as Heck Thomas strode back into the room to join him. "We'll photograph him in a bit, like all the others," he called.

Rhoades nodded in assent and left the room, leaving only Heck Thomas, Rufus Canon, and what remained of Bill Doolin there.

Canon shifted his weight from one boot to the other and looked at Thomas; the older man was gazing down at the outlaw's body, his eyes moving slowly over it as if he were trying to memorize what he saw. "Do you realize, Rufus, that he's the last?"

Thomas suddenly said in a distant tone, never taking his eyes off of Doolin's remains.

Canon's brow furrowed. "We still got two more of his organization, Clifton and West, to take down, at the very least. You know that as well as I do."

Thomas shook his head. "That's not what I meant. He was the last one of his caliber. The last leader of all the desperadoes this country's been plagued with for all these years."

Canon shrugged and rubbed at a crick in his neck, then turned as he heard the sound of Doc Smith knocking at the front door. "I'm sure they'll be others, Heck, so long as so much of this country ain't civilized or settled up good." He went to let the doctor in.

Heck Thomas shook his head, crossing his arms over his chest and standing to one side as the doctor came up to the table, briskly rolling up his shirt-sleeves. "Not quite like him, Rufus. You and I won't see another of Bill Doolin's like in our lifetime. I'll wager on that."

AFTERWORD

Bill Doolin's body, like those of his fellow Wild Bunch members, was dressed, photographed and put on display in Guthrie, where it was viewed by hundreds of people. He was buried in the 'Boot Hill' section of the cemetery there and a large tombstone marks his grave. Edith Doolin eventually remarried, and her son took his stepfather's last name. Jay Doolin Meek died in 1980, living to the ripe old age of 86.

After Bill's death, the few remaining members of the Wild Bunch were picked off by the law; every single member of the gang died a violent death. Dick West was the last active member of the gang to die, killed by Bill Tilghman and Heck Thomas during a shoot-out in 1898. Roy Daugherty, alias "Arkansas Tom Jones," was destined to be the longest-lived member of them all, eventually returning to his life of crime after being paroled from the prison sentence he'd been given for his part in the Battle of Ingalls. He died in 1924 after engaging law enforcement in a gunfight, and his death was ruled a justifiable homicide.

Bill Dunn was killed by Deputy Marshal Frank Canton, who was himself a former outlaw, in November of 1896—only three months after he'd helped Heck Thomas track down and kill Bill Doolin. Rose Dunn married Charles Noble, the young black-smith in the posse that took Bill down, and lived until 1955. She adamantly denied any knowledge of her brothers' plans to murder Bitter Creek Newcomb and Charley Pierce for the rest of her life.

AUTHOR'S NOTE

As is the case with both of my previous novels, almost all of the characters in *The Last Desperado* were real people and most of the events are true. As with most legendary western figures of their day, many of the tales told about Bill Doolin and his Wild Bunch have been exaggerated, misconstrued or fictionalized over the hundred-plus years since they actually took place. There are many speculations and various versions of key events, such as the infamous "Battle of Ingalls" in September of 1893, or what may or may not have led Bill Doolin to sever ties with Bob Dalton and the Dalton Gang just prior to their ill-fated raid on two banks in Coffeyville, Kansas, in October of 1892. There are also many conflicting accounts of which gang members participated in which robberies, who used which alias, who killed so-and-so...the list goes on. I found that many historians can't even agree on which foot Bill was shot in after the gang's robbery of the Santa Fe Train at Cimarron, Kansas in 1893 (I went with the more popular choice of the left; an old injury to his left foot was mentioned by his wife in an interview printed in the Guthrie, Oklahoma newspaper in 1896—though she did not, of course, attribute it to a gunshot wound). Even the date of Bill's death is shrouded in a bit of mystery, listed alternately as August 24th or August 25th, 1896. According to accounts, Thomas and his posse began their vigil on the evening of the 24th but Bill was killed between twelve o'clock and one o'clock in the morning, which would make his true date of death the 25th, as engraved on his tombstone.

I put a great deal of time into researching this novel, but as is often the case with historical fiction, it became necessary to add things, leave out others or make minor changes for the sake of the story's flow. One thing I found to be utterly consistent all throughout my research was that Bill Doolin lived an incredibly fascinating life—and packed quite a large amount of activity into his last five years on earth. Pretty much all accounts agree that while Bill was definitely a robber and a criminal who was capable of violence when he felt the occasion called for it, he was also a downright likeable man whose easy-going, fair nature and razor-sharp wit won him popularity and respect among his peers, and his place as leader of his gang—even the articles and interviews with him printed in the Guthrie newspaper in 1896 acknowledge as much. Despite his reputation his God-fearing, moral in-laws seemed to overlook his infamy, covering for him and providing him with shelter after he married their daughter—facts which speak volumes about his likeability and overall character. By all accounts he was, like some other "bad men" of his day, something of a paradox. Before his scuffle with the law in Coffeyville during the summer of 1891 set him on the outlaw trail, Bill was counted as a trustworthy, quiet, capable cowboy who rose the ranks of his fellow cowhands to become the foreman of several ranches. He was also a loving husband to his wife Edith, a preacher's daughter whom he married in 1893; his devotion to her and their young son Jay is what facilitated his eventual end. He was a smart, methodical and extremely cunning man whose prolific career in crime would eventually bring him the title of "King of the Oklahoma Outlaws," and I've always thought it a well-deserved title, for though there were a few that would come after him before the "Wild West" was a thing of the past, none of them quite lived up to his exploits, or his fame.

- Rebecca Rockwell, October 2013

9 781478 725442